TERI WOODS

DEADLY REIGNS

II

THE SECOND OF A TRILOGY

TERI WOODS

For information on how individual consumers can place orders, please write to Teri Woods Publishing, P.O. Box 20069, New York, NY 10001-0005.

For orders other than individual consumers, Teri Woods Publishing grants a discount on the purchase of twenty or more copies of a single title order for special markets or premium use.

For orders purchased through the P.O. Box, Teri Woods Publishing offers a 25% discount off the sale price for orders being shipped to prisons, including, but not limited to, federal, state, and county.

Published by Teri Woods Publishing

TERI WOODS

DEADLY REIGNS

II

THE SECOND OF A TRILOGY

TERI WOODS

Note:
Sale of this book without a front cover may be unauthorized. If this book is purchased without a cover it may be reported to the publisher as "unsold or destroyed." Neither the author nor the publisher may receive payment for the sale of this book.

This novel is a work of fiction. Any resemblance to real people, living or dead, actual events, establishments, organizations, and/or locales are intended to give it a sense of reality and authenticity. Other names, characters, places and incidents are either products of the author's imagination or are used fictitiously, as are those fictionalized events and incidents that involve real persons and did not occur or are set in the future.

Published by:
TERI WOODS PUBLISHING
P.O. Box 20069
New York, NY 10001-0005
www.teriwoodspublishing.com

Library of Congress Catalog Card No:2006902432
ISBN: 0-9773234-1-2
Copyright: To Be Supplied

DEADLY REIGNS CREDITS
Revised by Teri Woods
Edited by Teri Woods
Text formation by Teri Woods
Cover concept by Lucas Riggins

TERI WOODS

DEADLY REIGNS

II

THE SECOND OF A TRILOGY

TERI WOODS

Chapter One

Grace Moore knew that she was going to die. Grace sat up in bed and counted the hulking shadows as they darted past her moonlit window, all heading toward some unknown gathering place in her backyard. Five of them she counted, but she knew that there undoubtedly were more. Over the past two years, all of the previous attempts on her life had involved no less than ten hit men. One particularly violent and all too close encounter, had involved more than twenty. The Reigns family was creative and persistent, if nothing else. And now, they were here again.

It had been two years since she and Damian had fallen in love, two years since they had created the son that he so desperately wanted, two years since she had been shot by his brother, Dante, and two years since she had sent the only man she had ever truly loved, to prison. Two years of running and of hiding, of visiting her son in secret locations around the country. Two years of attempts on her life, of changing identities, and of waking up to nights like this. Two years of hell.

If there was any good to come out of the last two years, it was that she had two years of experience under her belt. Two years of deadly practice, of planning, and of rehearsal. For the last two years she had been stockpiling weapons; and installing security systems, cameras, monitors, and various other detection and alert devices. Two years of exercise and drill practice. Two years of checking

1

and rechecking. She knew exactly what to do, where to go, and how to react, and she could do it all in her sleep. She had planned her reaction so thoroughly, so methodically, that she had practically transformed it into a science. The past two years of deadly dress rehearsals, had lead her up to this day. Two years of practice, to either kill or to die.

Grace pressed the alert button on her nightstand drawer, sending the emergency signal to the local FBI field office, to the local police department, to the local sheriff's department, and to a special monitoring office in Quantico, Virginia. The signal that she transmitted meant that an agent was in immediate need of assistance, and the local law enforcement officers were instructed to respond accordingly. They would burn rubber, ignore all traffic signs and lights, drop whatever they were doing at that moment, and rush to her assistance. It was a tried-and-true system that she was forced to use on several occasions over the last two years. It was a system that she believed in, a system that she knew that she had to believe in, in order to keep her sanity. *Help will come, they will come,* she told herself. But for now, she was alone and on her own. For now, she had to find a way to survive.

Grace got out of bed, rushed to her closet, and slid open the doors as quietly as possible. It was inside this closet where her lifeline was kept. It was inside this closet where her ability to sleep at night was stored. It was inside this ordinary-looking closet, where she stored her arsenal.

The first thing that Grace reached for was her utility belt. It contained her Glock 45, and fifteen full clips of ammunition. It was what she called her getaway belt. She could drop her other weapons, pull out her Glock, climb through a window, scale a fence, ford a creek, or do whatever else that she needed to do, in order to escape. If necessary, she could simply take cover and hold off her attackers until help arrived.

Grace buckled the utility belt around her waist, and then removed her bulletproof vest from the closet. She had come to depend on her vest, and had a great appreciation for the technology behind it. Were it not for her trusty vest, she would be lying six feet underground right now. Dante had shot her, and one year later, she had been shot by another drug lord, while operating undercover in New York. She prayed silently that her vest's winning streak would continue tonight. She knew that she would need it.

Grace slung the bulletproof vest over her body, and fastened it snugly. She then reached back into her closet and pulled from it an M-16 A3 assault rifle, with an M203 grenade launcher attached to the bottom. The grenade launcher would be her equalizer. It would make the unfair fight, a lot fairer, unless of course, they were carrying them too.

Grace pulled her black utility bag from the closet, and slung it over her shoulder. It was inside this bag, where she carried the grenades for the launcher, some extra clips of ammunition for the M-16, her Desert Eagle .50 magnum pistol, her night vision goggles, and a few extra goodies that she had borrowed from the Bureau arsenal. She would need all of the tricks in her bag tonight.

Grace slipped her petite feet into her tennis shoes, placed her night vision goggles over her head, and then flipped the power switch that was in her closet. The entire neighborhood turned pitch-black. She had spiked the entire grid, creating a blackout that covered quite a few blocks. It would give her the darkness she needed to fight and escape. The night vision goggles would give her the advantage she needed to operate, to maneuver, to survive. The Reigns family wasn't the only ones who could use high-tech devices to gain an advantage. The FBI was pretty good about it too; especially when it came to protecting one of their own.

The neighborhood blackout coincided with the breaching of her back wall. This time they were not going for stealth and surprise, this time, they weren't going for shock and awe. The explosion that blew a hole through the rear of her home also blew out all of her windows, and those of her

3

neighbors. It also slammed her back into a wall, and created a fireball that could be seen a mile away. They were definitely here.

Grace slowly rose from the floor, dusted off the glass and plaster and debris from her black warm-ups, pulled her night vision goggles down over her eyes, and lifted her M-16. It was time to rock and roll.

The first one through her bedroom door was a large burly African-American man in a tight black suit, holding a Mossberg pump shotgun. The shotgun looked new, as did the suit. *Shame, shame, he'll never get to use his new shotgun*, Grace told herself, *but he can use the suit again. They can bury him in it.*

Grace lifted her assault weapon, and pummeled two shots into his forehead. Her attacker fell back into the arms of a second man, exposing him, and the man behind him as well. Grace was known as a marksman at the FBI shooting ranges, and after tonight, her attackers would know why. She quickly shifted her weapon from the falling attacker to the one just behind him. She squeezed her trigger until the weapon popped, and her attacker's head did the same. His blood and brain fragments flew into the eyes of the third attacker, blinding him momentarily. The exploding head of his partner would be the last thing that he would ever see. Grace sent a 5.56-millimeter round straight through his mouth and out the back of his head.

Things appeared to be going well, she told herself. Three down, and probably seven more to go, and help was on the way. The window just to her right suddenly exploded in a hail of gunfire. The windows had long ago been replaced with see-through armor, and they could withstand multiple direct hits from small-caliber assault type weapons, but they couldn't hold up against a sustained barrage. The patter of automatic rifle fire tapped against the bulletproof glass, sending long spider-like cracks throughout its surface. The glass was definitely going to give.

Grace flung her body away from the cracking glass,

just in time. A stream of bullets tore through the room, ripping through sheetrock, mattress foam, and wood. Since volley after volley raked the wall above her head, she crouched down low behind the footboard of her bed. She had to return fire before her assailants became confident enough to peer into the room and take aim. For the moment, they were firing blindly, but if they realized they had her pinned down, she knew that she would be in trouble. She also knew that she was still vulnerable to her rear. They would try to come through the bedroom door again, and soon seize control of the situation.

Fire, she told herself. *Lift your weapon and fire*. It was what she had been trained to do. She had to be the one on the offensive.

Grace lifted her weapon into the air, and fired toward the window. Her shots must have rang true, because shortly afterward, she heard a voice cry out in pain. The son-of-bitch must have been trying to peek through the window.

The firing at the window slowed to a few short bursts and then ceased all together. They must be trying to outflank her, and to try the bedroom door again.

The first hand-grenade rolled through the window, bounced off of her wooden bedpost, and flew to the right. It rolled gently beneath her dresser drawer, as if it were nothing more than a cup falling off her window ledge. The second hand-grenade landed on her thick down-filled comforter, and rested on her bed as if taking a gentle nap. The third hand-grenade landed just beside her, and spun around like a child's toy. She knew she was in trouble. She knew that she had to get the fuck out of the room, and she had to do it now.

Grace lifted her M-16, aimed it toward her bedroom door, and squeezed the trigger on the grenade launcher. The grenade flew out of the barrel and slammed into some unknown object down the hall, exploding with a force that she had yet to experience before. The explosion ripped through her home, sending a fireball back toward her bedroom, a fireball that was welcomed with the love that one reserves for cherished family members. For it was a fireball that told her that all was clear in the hallway, and that anyone who had been waiting to ambush her, was dead. It was a fireball that gave her permission to run.

Grace rose from the floor, fired toward her window, and raced through the wrecked, blackened, smoldering ruins of her home, until she reached what was left of her living room. A series of explosions wiped her bedroom from existence. The deafening sound and powerful force from the explosions flung her and her entire living room set against a nearby wall, splintering the furniture, and knocking her into a semiconscious state. Semiconsciousness meant death. Death meant no one left to protect her son from the monsters who were trying to get him. She willed herself to get up.

The sound of wood being kicked out of the way fully restored Grace's consciousness. Her assailants were making their way through the wreckage and coming to get her. She knew she had to find cover, but where? All of her furniture was in splinters. Grace peered around what remained of her living room, and decided to take cover in the only place left that provided even a resemblance of protection; an old tattered and overturned limestone whiskey bar in the far left corner of the room. Grace stumbled forward and made it behind the bar just as the first suit peered around the corner. She quickly pulled her Glock from its holster and put a bullet through his eye.

"She's behind the bar!" A husky male voice called out.

Grace hunkered down. She could hear sirens now, and they were growing louder by the moment.

Bullets raked the bar just behind her, and a few whizzed by over her head. The bar was good for a few shots, but soon the bullets would wear it down, and she would be a sitting duck. Her only hope would be to get off one more good shot with her grenade launcher, and hope that she killed enough of them to cause them to abort their mission. She lifted her M-16.

Grace pulled a grenade from her utility bag, and loaded it into the breach of the grenade launcher. She locked and loaded the grenade, readied her rifle, and rose quickly to fire it. Someone grabbed the barrel of her weapon as she stood.

"Uh-un, bitch!" Angela told her. "Enough of this shit!"

Grace was shocked. How had she allowed one of them to close in on her? How had this woman made her way through the rifle fire of her own people and got in close enough to do this? How could she have allowed them to pin her down, while one of their own quietly closed in?

"Let go of the rifle, bitch!" Angela commanded. She backhanded Grace across her cheek, as they struggled for the rifle.

Grace saw the others moving in to join the struggle, and quickly realized that she had to do something. Anything! She pulled the trigger on the grenade launcher, sending the grenade crashing and exploding into the living room wall behind them. The blast created a fireball and shock wave that the confined space of the living room could not contain. It blew the roof off of her home.

Angela, having her back to the blast, cried out the loudest as the blast propelled her through the air, and into another wall. Most of the other attackers were blown into the air as well, with many of them dying before their bodies hit the ground. Grace was blown back into the wall next to Angela, and again, she nearly lost consciousness. Her ringing ears and blurry eyes could barely make out the petite feminine figure making its way through the smoke and haze. The clicking heels, seductive walk, and Chanel perfume meant that it could only be one person; the person who had tormented her life over the last two years. It had to be Princess.

Princess Reigns strode calmly through the still burning wreckage of Grace's home, quietly surveying the damage. Her death black Ferragamo jacket, skirt, shoes, and hat were all as clean and neat as the moment she had put them on. She had come dressed to kill tonight, and as always, she would not leave disappointed. She walked to where Grace was laying helpless on the ground.

"Hurry up and get our people out of here," she ordered what was left of her men. "Put Angela in my car, and have the doctor meet us at the airport."

"Yes, ma'am," said one of the hulking, suited men standing just behind her. "And, ma'am we've searched the entire house."

"Gary, I like you, but don't ever be the bearer of bad news, sweetie," Princess told him.

Gary nodded and moved away from his boss.

"Who was in charge of this fiasco?" Princess asked. "Whose job was it to track down this FBI cunt and watch her?"

"Larry," a voice from behind replied.

"Bring him to me," Princess ordered.

A young, dark-suited, African-American gentleman with short wavy hair, and a neatly trimmed beard stepped forward.

"Yes, ma'am?" Larry asked.

"Larry, where's the kid?" Princess asked.

"Ma'am?"

"My nephew, Larry," Princess added. "Where is he? He was supposed to be here! This is why we're here, this is why eight of my men are dead, and this is why Angela is lying in the backseat of my car wounded! Now, where is he?"

"I... I don't know what happened," Larry stuttered. "I could have sworn..."

Princess Reigns pulled her 45-caliber Beretta pistol from her purse, pointed it at Larry's forehead, and squeezed the trigger.

Larry's body crumpled to the ground, landing on top of Grace.

"Excuses are like assholes, Larry," Princess told the body. "Everybody's got one." She turned to the rest of her

8

men. "Listen up, people! What we have here, is another fuckup, another costly operation and no kid. I will not tolerate fuckups, or excuses! You fail me, and you die! Is that understood?"

Gary placed his arm around Princess's waist and began guiding her toward the back door.

"Ma'am, we've got to get you out of here. The police are right around the corner."

"And the worst part about your fuckups is that I have to leave this bitch alive again, so that she can lead us to him! Does anyone have any idea of how bad I want to kill this FBI bitch? Do any of you?"

Angrily, Princess turned, lifted her weapon, and fired at Grace's head. The bullet struck Grace in the side of her neck, causing her head to jerk, and the rest of her body to fall over.

"Take that, bitch," Princess told Grace. "When you get out of the hospital, go and see your son. That way we can track you, I can take him, and then I can finally kill you. Oh, I can't wait for that day. I'm going to cum like I've never cum before! Every time I squeeze the trigger, my pussy is going to gush like Old Faithful! Whoooeee!"

Chapter Two

The governor was in attendance, as was the mayor, and most of the Texas legislature. Both Texas senators and the majority of Texas' delegation to the U.S House of Representatives were also in attendance. It was a black-tie affair, and the singular most important economic event in Texas history. The luminaries were all gathered to witness and celebrate the founding of Bio One.

Bio One was the culmination of a dream by Damian Reigns. It had been his passion, his baby, his obsession as far back as he could remember. It had been the driving force behind every business decision he had ever made. All of his investments, and his energy, had been sunk into its creation. And now his dream was being celebrated by an entire state.

Bio One was the largest biotechnological, pharmaceutical, medical supply, and medical research corporation in the nation. It was created as a result of mergers of numerous small research companies, medical equipment companies, and pharmaceutical companies, into one medical leviathan. What it did not manufacture itself, it imported from Asia. Imaging equipment from Korea, alcohol wipes from China, and monitoring equipment from Japan. The massive medical supply side of the company was partnered with the equally expansive research side, and an overpowering marketing arm that had made it a household name even before the company's official launch. The television commercials advising consumers to look for the

Bio One label inside their doctors' offices and hospitals, had been saturating the marketplace for sometime. The television and radio slogans, "If your doctor, pharmacist or hospital isn't using Bio One, they're not using the best," had been rammed into everyone's brain. The commercials had urged the consumers to not only look for the labels, but to ask the medical providers if they were using Bio One equipment. The medical and pharmaceutical communities had been sufficiently frightened to run out and purchase buildings worth of equipment. So much so, that Bio One had a back-order of several billion dollars in medical and pharmaceutical equipment. And several billions of dollars in back-orders, translated into tens of billions of dollars a year in sales, and several billions of dollars in taxable revenue. Texas had a reason to smile.

Bio One's unofficial headquarters was situated on an idyllic campus, which was nestled on fifty acres of prime hill country property. It was a massive wooded campus, filled with highly paid executives, who spent all of their hefty salaries on cars, homes, and other consumer goods in the local community. This thrilled the local business community. The official headquarters was a massive eighty-story, baby blue, glass building in downtown San Antonio. The Bio One construction spree also included a brand-new, world-class medical research center and hospital, just east of the downtown headquarter. The downtown medical complex was a separate entity from the one-hundred-fifty-acre southeast biotechnological and pharmaceutical research complex. There were a total of five Bio One complexes in all, and they were filled to the brim with enough doctors, scientists, and high-dollar executives, to make San Antonio the medical research and pharmaceutical capital of the world. Bio One was the pride of the city, the flagship of the state, the envy of the nation, and it was all owned, by none other than Damian Reigns.

"Great party, Damian!" Senator Marshall pronounced, while slapping Damian across his back. "This building's

11

fantastic!"

"Glad you like it," Damian replied. "And of course, we have you to thank for spearheading the generous tax incentives that the state granted us."

"But, did it have to be so big?" Stacia Hess asked seductively, while wrapping her arm around Damian's waist. "Eighty stories of hardened steel and glass, with that long antenna protruding from the top?"

Stacia peered up toward the massive chandelier that hung down from the glass roof of the ten-story ballroom where the celebration was being held. Italian travertine marble graced the floor; and massive marble statues, Etruscan vases, and Florentine columns were spaced throughout the room; while priceless works of art and equally priceless Persian tapestries graced the walls. A two-hundred piece orchestra provided the entertainment, while massive glass fountains were filled with champagne, and an army of white-jacketed sommeliers made sure that all glasses remained full.

"Excuse me, Senator," Cherin King interrupted. "I have to steal my client away from you for a moment."

Cherin was Damian's lead attorney. She was a brilliant and hawkish defense attorney, with an Ivy League education, and an iron will. She instilled fear and respect into everyone she dealt with, and her sole occupation after graduating from Harvard Law, had been to protect Damian from all enemies, both personal and professional. She was fiercely loyal, and was rewarded for her loyalty to her sole client, by being made a millionaire the day she signed on. That had been six years ago, and today, her net worth was $6,000,000. Her salary was $1,800,000 a year; plus a home; a new car of her choosing every two years; use of any of the Reigns family vacation homes, and corporate jets; an apartment in Washington D.C.; a penthouse in Manhattan; and access to a defense fund that exceeded most medium-size cities budgets. Her job was to preside over a legal team that included two full-time defense attorneys, two full-time

12

corporate attorneys, a tax attorney, a family law attorney, two paralegals, six secretaries, and three private investigators. Together, their job was to keep Damian a free man. They checked and rechecked the work of Damian's numerous corporate attorneys; went over his accounts and the work of his accountants; kept the FBI, IRS, DEA, Treasury Department, and Customs Agency at bay. She was well-known, and even feared, within the law enforcement community. Tonight, however, Cherin was fulfilling another role. Tonight she was the MC of this historic event.

Cherin escorted Damian through the crowd, and up to an elaborately decorated stage of the room. The impeccably dressed Damian stood just to her side.

"May I have your attention please," Cherin said.

A hush slowly came over the ballroom, as the gathered patrons grew silent with hungry anticipation. The evening had reached its climax, and the raison d'etre for this gala affair was about to be announced.

"As you all know," Cherin continued. "We're gathered here this evening to celebrate the founding of a new American institution. We're here to celebrate the founding of Bio One."

Applause thundered throughout the room.

"For sometime now, this has been the singular dream of one man, a man who took his dream, shared it with others, and then brought that dream into fruition." Cherin turned toward Damian. "In our society, such men are rightfully awarded with the title, 'visionary'. And so tonight, we're here not only to celebrate the founding of a new national institution, but the visionary who blessed us with it. Ladies and gentlemen, I present to you, Mr. Damian Reigns."

There was rapturous applause as Damian stepped to the microphone and bowed slightly.

"I want to thank you," Damian told the gathering.

The applause echoed throughout the hall, preventing Damian from speaking.

"I want to thank you all for coming," Damian

continued over the applause. "I want you all to know, that none of this would have been possible without the Man upstairs. Many times I lost focus, and I know that it was only through His Grace, that I was able to keep going. I want to thank Cherin King, whose work on this project was invaluable. Without her, I think we would still be in the planning stages. I want to thank my mother and my father, without whom, I don't know where I'd be. The lessons that they taught me about life, about faith, about courage, and about charity, were the values that propelled me forward on this project. And most of all, I want to thank my brother, Dante, without whom, I'd be lost. Dante's my rock, my soul, my strength."

Cherin handed Damian a large pair of scissors.

"There are just so many others, who I would like to thank," Damian continued hurriedly. "Joel, the project manager; Nicky, the construction manager; Gloria Amaretta, Vick Bernstein, Terrence Schumacher."

Cherin clasped Damian's arm, and turned him toward the massive red ribbon that they had placed in front of the entrance doors just behind them. The crowd laughed hysterically.

Damian lifted the scissors that he held in his hands, and cut the ribbon. The black-tie crowd clapped enthusiastically.

Cherin turned back to the microphone. "Ladies and gentlemen, Bio One!"

Damian lifted his champagne glass into the air to the roaring applause, and then slowly made his way from the stage.

"Good job, son!" the governor told him, slapping him across his back.

Damian shook hands with the governor, and then spotted his brother in the corner. He immediately made his way toward him.

"Were you going to thank the guys who cleared the building sites?" Dante asked with a smile. "How about the waitress who served them dinner, the transportation officials who approved the roads or the deer who happily gave up the land for the Hill Country Campus?"

Damian smiled and clasped his brother's extended hand. "I would have, if I had enough time."

Dante shook his head and laughed. "Always the polite one."

"Remember, the flight would never leave the ground without the ground crews," Damian playfully admonished his brother. "It's not just the pilots who deserve recognition."

Dante pulled his brother closed and embraced him tightly. "You did it. You pulled it off. You built your dream."

Damian shook his head. "No, we did it. All of us."

Dante leaned back and clasped his brother's shoulders. "I'm proud of you, Damian. Congratulations."

Damian nodded solemnly. "Thanks. Hey, you seen Dad?"

"Last time I saw him, he and Mom were beaming like two lighthouses over by the cocktail tables," Dante answered. Dante shifted his gaze toward his watch. "I've got to get going in a minute. I got an early flight to catch."

"The meeting, I completely forgot about it."

"Relax, bro," Dante told him. "You know I got your back. I've taken care of everything."

Damian shifted his gaze to the ground.

"I've just been so consumed by this project."

"Hey, relax," Dante ordered. "I've got everything covered. It's all under control. You stay here, and you enjoy your night. This is your night!"

"Thanks, Dante. I don't know where I'd be without you."

"Dead," Dante replied with a smile.

Damian returned his brother's smile. "Hey, make sure everything goes over smoothly. This is our last meeting. Princess is in charge of that business now; make that clear to them. There's no telling what's going on in El Jeffe's head right now. Just make it clear that we're completely out, and

15

that we want peace with him. And make peace overtures toward the remainder of the Commission. If the opportunity presents itself, make peace and end all of the hostilities with whomever you can."

"Gotcha."

"Dante, the last time you said that, we ended up at war with the entire Commission."

"That wasn't my fault, Damian."

Damian eyed his brother suspiciously, and then shook his head and exhaled. "Yeah, right. In any event, make sure that this meeting goes smoothly."

Dante shrugged his shoulders. "Yeah, this should be a cakewalk. I'll walk in, thank everyone, tell them how much a pleasure it's been to know them, and then leave."

"Exactly," Damian lifted his champagne flute and sipped from it. "And, Dante."

"Yeah?"

"No bodies this time."

Dante shook his head incredulously. "Damian, I didn't kill anyone last time!"

"Your word, Dante," Damian added. "Give me your word. No bodies."

Dante smiled and placed his hand over his heart.

"You have my word. I won't kill a soul."

"Thankyou."

Chapter Three

The meeting was held in Las Vegas, Nevada, in a place that very few knew existed. The casino was considered a landmark. Many had come to call the megalithic structure the eighth wonder of the world. Although many tens of millions had traipsed through its cavernous halls, few had been this deep below the massive casino complex. No, this ultraluxurious, secret, underground portion of the building was reserved only for the few who knew about its existence. And those few were the heads of the Commission.

The fact that the Commission had even been able to build a casino in Las Vegas was in and of itself a minor miracle. The Old Ones had long ago locked down the town, and declared it strictly off-limits to any newcomers. You had to be Sicilian, and you had to be family, old family at that. Only, someone had forgotten to tell the Russians.

The Russian mafia, the ex-Speztnaz or Russian Special Forces hit Las Vegas like a category six hurricane. They hit hard, and landed with a fury that swept away much of the old guard, and the old ways of thinking.

The Old Ones were left defenseless. They had not the skill, the manpower, nor even the will to combat such a violent, ruthless, and crafty enemy. It was if Mother Russia herself had declared war on them, and sent her finest soldiers to bring death and destruction to their doorsteps. It took less than a year for them to surrender and make room for the Russians. It was during this capitulation, that the

Commission had been able to step in, seize their piece of the lucrative Las Vegas entertainment pie, and establish themselves.

Not wanting another war, the Old Ones simply moved over a little more, and let the Commission eat from the trough.

The Commission's opportunistic power grab left the Old Ones pissed, and they had yet to forget it. To the Old Ones, the Commission was nothing more than a bunch of drug-peddling upstarts, niggers, Mexicans, rednecks, Colombians, and a wide assortment of international trash that needed to be dealt with. The Old Ones' war with the Russians was over, and it had taught them an invaluable lesson. They had reduced their strength too much over the preceding decades, and relied too much on political power. But now, they were ready. They had spent the last few years getting strong, building up their manpower, organizing, tightening their chain of command, and generally rebuilding their families until they now resembled the powerful families of old. The Old Ones were now feared again.

Today's meeting of the Commission concerned the powerful Old Ones, and the Commission's impending expansion into several eastern states. The Commission members in the east were all for it, as it gave them more strength, and a more powerful voice. The western members were generally against it, as an eastern expansion would definitely cause war with the Old Ones. And a war with the Old Ones, whose strength in Las Vegas was only surpassed by their strength in New York, was something that the western branch of the Commission wished to avoid. Life in the west was good, profits were up, and the peace was holding. Why ruin a good thing?

Don Kiki De La Luna leaned forward and called the meeting to order.

"Gentlemen, we all know why we're here," Don Kiki De La Luna started. "So, I suggest that we just get right down to business."

"Which business is that?" Barry Groomes of Arkansas posed. "The business with the conniving Reigns family or with the stupid East Coast idiots trying to take us to war!"

Dante leaned forward and smiled. "Barry, we've been in the room for just sixty seconds, and you've managed to insult me. You're losing your touch. It usually takes about thirty seconds."

The Commission members around the table snickered and laughed.

"Gentlemen, please!" Kikki De La Luna interrupted. Kikki was El Jeffe's personal representative at the Commission, and as such, he was chairing the meeting today. Being that Dante had killed El Jeffe's last emissary to the Commission, was a fact lost on no one today.

"I vote no to expansion!" Adolfus Brandt of Colorado shouted.

"Expansion into those territories will cause war," Frediano Ambrogiano of Las Vegas added. "I tell you, the old Dons have all made it clear. We expand, and we're at war!"

"Gentlemen, excuse me," Dante interjected. "I know that you have a lot of matters to discuss, and I don't want to hold you up. So, if you'll allow me to speak, I promise you that I'll be very brief."

Ceasario Chavez of Arizona snickered. "A promise from Dante Reigns."

The Commission members gathered around the table laughed.

"Nevertheless, what I wish to say is that, the Reigns family is turning over all of its distribution operations to my sister Princess Reigns, who's now the head of her own independent entity. Damian and I are officially out, after this meeting."

Adolfus huffed. "What a big surprise."

"Only El Jeffe can approve of such a transfer," Paco Menendez interjected. "And he hasn't given any such approval."

"Your seat on the Commission is not some sort of hereditary position that's subject to dynastic transfer," Don De La Luna told Dante. "We're not European royalty."

The Commission members seated around the conference table laughed.

"We're out," Dante repeated.

Barry slammed his fist on the table and rose. "You can't just walk in here and make declarations, Dante! You leave; you go to war with the rest of this Commission!"

"Very well then, we'll go to war," Dante said calmly.

Several Commission members swallowed hard. A war with the Reigns family was not something that they took lightly, even if the rest of the Commission was united.

"You go to war with the Reigns family, we take all of New Mexico in two months," Dante told them. "Then Nevada, then Colorado, then Arizona, and then everything else. And what we don't take, the Old Ones will."

Don De La Luna lifted his hands to restore calm. "Perhaps we're getting ahead of ourselves." Don De La Luna shifted his head toward Dante. "I'll bring up the Reigns family's transfer to El Jeffe, and we'll deal with this matter accordingly."

Dante nodded.

The matter at hand gentlemen, is expansion, and an impending war with the Old Ones."

"Yeah, and once we handle those greaseball fuckers, we'll deal with those black traitor sons of bitches in Texas!" Barry declared.

Dante smiled. "Don't we already control half of your state, Barry?"

Barry rose from the table again. "You son of a bitch! I'm going to enjoy killing you, Dante!"

"Bold words from the trailer park," Dante said calmly.

"Fuck you!"

Don de La Luna lifted his hands in a calming motion. "Gentlemen, please!"

Paco peered around the table. "Where do we stand on eastern expansion?"

"I vote no." Adolfus announced.

"Hell no!" Barry declared.

Marion 'Big Hustler' Rooks of California nodded. "I say yes."

"Marion, your vote wouldn't happen to have anything to do with the fact that a certain record label owner is backed by the New York Old Ones, would it?" Adolphus posed. "Your petty bicoastal feud should have nothing to do with this Commission! This is serious business! Not shaking your ass on television, parading in front of the cameras, and making newspaper headlines."

"Hey, what I do on my own time is none of your fucking business!" Marion banged his fist on the table. "As long as I keep the California well-heads open and flowing smoothly."

"You're a fucking embarrassment to us all!" Barry shouted. "You get more press than fucking Madonna!"

"Your exposure is putting this Commission at risk!" Frediano added. "The LAPD investigation into your petty little music company could bring us all down."

"Or jeopardize our West Coast distribution methods!" Barry told them.

Don De La Luna lifted his hands to silence the Commission members. "Marion, they're right. Your exposure's bad for the Commission. You must end it."

"I have commitments; I have artists; I can't just shut down the whole operation!" Marion protested.

"Either that or you're off this Commission," Paco told him. "And once we take away your seat on this Commission, your body will never be found."

"Disappear for a little while. Let your company go down the drain. And slowly, become a has-been, and then a nobody," Dante suggested.

"Disappear?" Marion leaned forward. "Where the fuck would I go?"

Don De La Luna smirked. "Prison."

"We'll take care of everything," Paco told him. "And after this, no more bullshit. You become a shadow, just like the rest of us. Everyone in this business who craved the limelight, has ended up very dead and very missing. Don't become one of them, Marion."

"Back to the subject at hand, gentlemen," Don De La Luna told them.

"I vote no to expansion," Frediano told them.

Barry laughed. "Of course you do, Freddo. We all know where you stand."

"And what's that supposed to mean?" Frediano asked.

"It means, we all know who you're in bed with, Fat Boy," Ceasario told him. "Just like we all know that the Old Ones will know exactly what was said and by who, at this meeting."

The Commission members around the table laughed.

Frediano pointed his finger at Ceasario. "Listen up, you fucking wetback son of a bitch! I've been doing this shit since long before your momma shitted you out!"

"You made your bones a long time ago Freddo; is that what you want to say?" Marion interjected. "We all know how bad you want to ride with your fellow greaseballs."

"Where do your loyalties lay, Senor Ambrogino?" Paco inquired.

"I'm a member of this Commission, damn it!" Frediano protested. "I've always been loyal!"

"Yes, but to whom?" Aldophus asked with a smile.

"It's no secret that you're always hanging out with the Vegas Old Ones," Barry told him. "Everybody knows that you want to roll with them."

"I'm loyal to this Commission," Frediano declared. "Unlike many of us around here, I plan to remain loyal."

Dante exhaled. "The Reigns family votes yes to expansion."

Adolphus huffed. "Yes, commit us to war, and then leave the Commission. You and your brother will be relaxing on the beach, while our men are dying. You shouldn't even have a vote."

"I'm now here in the stead of my sister and her organization," Dante told them. "Her men will fight just like your men, and die if necessary."

"What do we gain by expansion, Dante?" Barry asked. "Tell us why you believe war's worth it."

"Because they're going to go to war with us anyway," Dante explained. "They're ready, and growing stronger each day. Why not strike first, and choose the time and place?"

"Are we strong enough, Senor Reigns?" Paco asked.

"Nearly," Dante nodded. "My sister's organization has been growing stronger each day."

Adolphus lifted an eyebrow. "Oh, really?"

"Yes, really," Dante replied. "We saw this coming a long time ago. Optimism is one thing; stupidity is another. No one wants a war, but in this business."

"And these recruits of yours, Senor Reigns?" Don De La Luna leaned forward. "Are they here in Nevada or will they have to be flown in?"

"No," Dante told them as he rose. He began a slow pace around the conference table. "We thought it wise to place them in a more strategic location."

"We're listening," Paco told him.

"Gentlemen, what I'm about to say, must not leave this room," Dante told them.

"Then maybe Freddo should cover his ears," Barry said with a laugh.

Several Commission members laughed.

"Gentlemen, we're building armies on the East Coast," Dante told him. "We've positioned troops inside the heart of the Old Ones' territories."

"Bullshit!" Barry shouted.

"My cousin Joshua has built up a sizable force in Philadelphia. My cousin Brandon has built up an even larger force in Maryland. We sent Nicanor Moreno Mata to New Jersey, Philip St. Augustine to Delaware, and our longtime associate, Renato Celestino to New York. And just so you know how serious we are about building up an East Coast force, we've sent my wife Angela out there to coordinate the entire operation."

Paco whistled. "Sounds like the old Reigns family is back."

Dante shook his head. "No, Princess and her new family are in charge."

"And those soldiers who you have on the East Coast, what happens when the war's over?" Adolpus asked. "What happens if you win?"

"You know what happens, Adolpus," Dante told him.

"That's unacceptable," Adolphus shouted.

"That's the way it goes," Dante told him. "The Reigns family is taking most of the risks, shouldering most of the burden, and committing most of the resources. It is only natural that we be able to reward our people."

"No!" Don De La Luna shouted. "Then, this would no longer be a Commission. It would merely be a Reigns family reunion."

"We take those states, we're keeping them," Dante announced. "Brandon will get Maryland, Joshua will get Philly, Renato will get New York, St. Augustine will get Delaware, and Nicanor will get Jersey."

"Senor Reigns, in case you forgot, I'm the personal representative of El Jeffe to this Commission," Don De La Luna told him. "You cannot waltz in here and give your sister your seat, nor can you create additional seats on the Commission, and just give them out to whomever you like."

"Princess will keep those territories, if the Reigns family takes them," Dante declared.

"Princess," Don De La Luna leaned forward. "Princess can keep nothing, because she doesn't sit at this table! The only way that she'll ever sit at this table, is if she's representing Damian. Otherwise, that bitch sister of yours will sit at this table, only over my dead body!"

"I'll be sure and let my sister know how you feel, Don De La Luna," Dante told him.

"I don't fear your sister, Dante," Don De La Luna told him. "Nor do I fear anyone else in your organization. As a matter-of-fact, you communicate to Damian, that if he tries to leave the Commission, he's subject to the same penalties as everyone else. He leaves, you all die!"

"Well then, gentlemen, it appears that we have nothing else to talk about," Dante told them.

"We'll crush you first, and worry about the Old Ones later!" Don De La Luna shouted. Spittle flew from the corners of his mouth as he spoke.

Dante waved his hand, and a suited man standing next to the door opened it. Dante walked to the door and then turned back toward the members seated around the conference table.

"One last thought, before you gentlemen get all war happy," Dante told them. "Damian has ordered Princess to sit at this table. It's my job to turn his orders into actions. My sister will sit at this table, if I have to kill each and every one of you. If any of you wish to support this decision, then I suggest that you do so by remaining neutral. Anyone who has a problem with my sister taking over our distribution operations, I suggest that you go home and spend some quality time with your families, and then write out a will."

Dante turned toward Paco. "Do you really want to see the old Reigns family back in action? If so, then you've just gotten your wish."

Dante turned, and stormed out of the conference room.

Who in the hell do those mother fuckers think they are, Don De La Luna wondered, as he peered out of the dark-tinted limousine windows on the way to the airport. Dante Reigns was a mayate, a black fuck, and nothing more. *Who does he think he is to tell the great Don Kiki De La Luna what to do? Assign seats on the Commission! How dare him! And to*

25

vote yes, so that the Commission can go to war over states that he and his brother plan on controlling after it's all over. He and his brother were dead men walking, and they were fools if they didn't know that yet! *El Jeffe will have their heads on a stick!*

Don De La Luna's limousine caravan pulled into a private hanger at the Las Vegas International Airport, where his Gulfstream GV was sitting fueled and ready, waiting to fly him straight to Colombia for a meeting with the Boss. The thought of flying home brought a smile to his face. The Don reclined in his seat and thought of the thick homemade flour bread, wrapped around delectable chunks of prime Argentine beef that he would eat once he arrived back at his estate. Yes, he would meet with El Jeffe, down a couple of carne guisadas, and then go horseback riding. The sunset would be particularly beautiful tonight, as it always was whenever he returned home from a trip abroad. Colombia, for all of its problems, its violence, its politics, and its poverty, there was something beautiful, even mystical about it. It was home, with its lush green mountains, river-etched valleys, and beautiful powdered beaches. The sand on those beaches always seemed to be just the right temperature. Warm enough to feel marvelous to the toes, but not hot enough to burn the bottom of ones feet, ahhh, Colombia, beautiful Colombia.

The Don's security guard opened the door, climbed out of the limousine, and reached back inside to help the large-framed Don out of the car. The Don pulled and bounced and struggled and finally managed to work his body out of the backseat of the limousine. The turbines on the jet were just starting to spool up, and the maintenance and fuel people were just wrapping up. The trip back to Colombia would be a quick one. Their flight plan had them cruising at speeds above eight hundred kilometers per hour. He had brought along a couple of prostitutes from the city, so that he could entertain himself for a couple of hours, with a pair of young, healthy, nubile, and willing playmates. Indeed, time would surely fly.

The good Don headed for the steps leading up to the cabin, only to find his path blocked by one of the coverall-clad maintenance workers.

"Hey, move your ass out of my way!" The Don huffed.

The maintenance worker turned and faced the Don. He held in his hand an Uzi submachine gun. The other maintenance workers quickly produced weapons, some pulling them from their toolboxes, while others pulled them from their baggy coveralls. The Don and his men were quickly surrounded.

"What's the meaning of this?" The Don shouted. "I am the personal representative of El Jeffe! You'll move out of my way or you'll pay the consequences!"

"We all know who you are, Fat Boy," a voice called out.

"Dante!" The Don bellowed. "I should have known!"

Dante strolled from around the black limousine and slowly approached the Don.

"Dante, you'll remove your men from this hangar immediately!" The Don ordered. "And you'll allow this jet to take off without delay. I assure you, Senor Reigns, that your actions will be reported to El Jeffe. The Boss will see this as a personal affront!"

"Kiki, this plane will take off," Dante told him. "And it'll fly to Colombia, and someone will get off and deliver a message to El Jeffe. But the bad news is, it won't be you."

"Senor Reigns, as I made it clear to you in the hotel, I don't fear you!" The Don barked.

"And you shouldn't, my dear Don," Dante said with a smile. "As I promised my brother, I wouldn't kill a soul during this trip. Now, that's the good news. The bad news is, my dear Don, my sister made no such promises."

Princess Reigns walked seductively from around the Gulfstream G V, with her Manolo Blahnik heels clicking on the concrete floor of the hangar. Her Black Coco Chanel hat was tilted just to the side, and it matched her death black

Chanel skirt and jacket. As always, she was literally dressed to kill.

"You had something that you wanted to say to my sister?" Dante asked with a smile.

The Don eyes grew wide at the sight of Princess Reigns, and he began to swallow hard. "I am the personal representative of El Jeffe."

Princess stopped just in front of the Don, then leaned to the side and hugged her brother. "Dante here said that you had something that you wanted to tell me. Something about your dead body being my welcome mat to the Commission?"

Sweat began to pour from The Don's forehead. "I am the personal representative of El Jeffe."

Princess lifted her hand to The Don face and pinched his fat cheek. "Of course you are, sweetie. And I'm sure El Jeffe's going to miss you."

The Don face became flush. "You can't"

"Of course she can, Kiki," Dante told him. "Remember, we're at war."

"Senor," The Don swallowed hard. "Sometimes things are said out of haste. You know in the heat of the moment. I had to reestablish control of the meeting. Senor..."

Dante shook his head in disgust. "Don, if it were up to me, I would have my men lift you and your men into the blades of this jet's turbofans. But, since it's not up to me..."

"It's up to me," Princess interjected. "I'm only going to take you to one of our clean houses here in Vegas, and have some fun. I haven't tortured anyone to death in weeks, and I need to cum."

"But, before we go," Dante added. He turned toward the jet engine, where one of the Don's men was kicking and screaming as he was being hoisted up.

"Senor, please!" The Don pleaded.

Dante's men shoved the Don's bodyguard into the rapidly spinning turbofan blades, causing a loud pop, followed by a crashing noise and a flame shooting forward from the engine. An almost continuous stream of blood shot out of the back of the now damaged turbofan engine. The Don covered his face and began crying heavily. Princess turned toward her men. "Take the rest of the Don's men out to the desert, and make sure that they are never found, all except for Paco." Princess turned toward Paco. "Tell El Jeffe that my brothers are out. I control the Reigns family's operations now. We can go to war and disrupt the entire chain or he can accept my brother's departure, allow me back into the Commission, and continue to make a fortune. The choice is his."

Paco bowed his head slightly. "One thing, senorita."

"What's that?" Princess asked.

"My transportation home," Paco told her. He peered up at the blood-covered fuselage of the Don's private jet. "My jet appears to be out of commission at the moment."

"Our jets are parked just behind this one," Dante told him. "One of ours will fly you home, so that you can deliver our message."

"And the reason for killing Kiki?" Paco inquired. "Your message could be delivered with just as much clarity with him alive."

Dante shook his head. "No, Paco. You know El Jeffe just as well as I. The only thing that man understands is violence. You tell him that the Reigns family is strong again. We've recruited a lot of men, and all of the areas that we had pulled out of, we took back. Princess will give him exactly what he wants, a stronger, more centralized main distribution chain."

"And killing those men serves what purpose?" Paco asked.

"They won't have an opportunity to kill us," Dante told him. "Get on the plane and go home, Paco."

"Thank you," Paco told Princess. "Thank you for my life."

"We've always liked you, Paco" Dante told him. "You've always dealt with everyone straight up. Hopefully, El

29

Jeffe will promote you, and make you his official representative to the Commission."

Dante extended his hand, and Paco shook it.

"Good luck, Senor Reigns," Paco told him. "If we could all be so fortunate enough to leave this life behind."

"Good luck to you, Paco." Dante turned toward the rest of his men. "Let's clear this scene. No fingerprints, no forensic evidence whatsoever. Gentlemen, we're out of here in five minutes!"

Chapter Four

The crystal clear water looked as though it were a shimmering blue diamond from the top of the forty-foot diving board. It was a view that Stacia had come to treasure. On a sunny day, she could drop a coin in the water, and have absolutely no trouble finding it. It was a game that she loved to play in Damian's backyard water paradise.

Damian's lakefront mega mansion was truly a water lover's paradise. Not only did his backyard water park contain an Olympic-size diving pool, but it also had a kiddy wading pool, a forty by sixty-foot fun pool with basketball goals, rock slides, a swim up bar, and a volleyball net that stretched across the center of the pool, as well as three separate twenty-person capacity Jacuzzis. The crown jewel of the entire water complex was a sixty-foot by eighty-foot pool that blended seamlessly with the lake that sat nestled just to the rear of the property. As evening approached, the lake radiated a brilliant black orange reflection from its surface. It was a hidden paradise.

Stacia rose from the pool, and flung her long silky chestnut-colored tresses over her caramel-colored shoulders. Damian's mouth fell open at the sight of her skimpily clad body.

Stacia Hess, known in all circles as a fashion diva, had outdone herself today. She wore a red, white, and blue, star-spangled Perry Ellis, two-piece string bikini, which had been cleverly torn in just the right places. Her bikini revealed all, covering just enough to keep her from getting arrested for indecent exposure, while at the same time leaving little to anyone's imagination. Her tight, muscular body, large and perky breasts, chiseled abs, and firm, but bodacious buttocks, were out there for all to see. Stacia had a body that could stop traffic. She could make grown men cry, and straight women lust. It was a package that had been coupled with brains, culture, sophistication, class, and an Ivy League education. Stacia had a law degree from Harvard, and business suits that fit her body in such a way, that judges lost their concentration when she strolled into their courtrooms. She was the woman who men dreamed of having, but her heart had long ago been captured by one man, and one man alone. Stacia was married to another, but her heart belonged to Damian.

"If you were in the Olympics, you would have garnered a perfect score for that one," Damian told her.

Stacia leaned forward and kissed Damian on his cheek. "Diving's not my best skill."

"And what would your best skill be, Ms. Stacia?" Damian inquired with a mischievous smile.

Stacia returned his devilish smile with one of her own. She seated herself on a chaise lounge near the pool, and reclined seductively. Her wet, toned, and taunt body glistened.

"Why don't you come over here and allow me to show you, Mr. Damian," Stacia told him, extending her arms. "Let me show you my true gold medal-winning talent."

Damian threw his head back in laughter. "Sounds tempting and it's definitely an offer that I want to take you up on. But, right now, I want to show you something."

"Yes, my thoughts exactly," Stacia replied seductively. "Why don't you come over here and show it to me."

Again, Damian laughed. "No, what I have to show you right now is out front."

"Out front?" Stacia rose from the recliner. Her

curiosity was piqued. "Okay, Mr. Mysterious, I'll play along."

Damian clasped Stacia's hand, and pulled her along. He led her through the massive double doors into the massive kitchen, and then through the family room and over the marble floors into the foyer. He paused at the twelve-foot, solid mahogany double doors that graced the entrance to his fifty-five thousand square foot home.

"Close your eyes," Damian whispered.

Stacia exhaled. "Okay."

Damian threw open the doors to his home, clasped Stacia's hand, and led her outside to the stone-paved circular drive.

"Okay, you can open them now," Damian told her softly.

Stacia opened her eyes, and gasped. Before her sat a brand new Fiorno red Ferrari F430 Spider.

"Oh my God!" Stacia covered her mouth in astonishment. "It's just like the one in the magazine! Damian, it's gorgeous! You have to let me drive it! You know how much I love this car!"

Stacia climbed into the convertible, seating herself behind the steering wheel. She honked the horn and quickly turned toward Damian and held out her hand. "Okay, where are the keys?"

Damian pointed. "In the ignition."

"Can I drive it?" Stacia asked giddily.

"I don't see why not," Damian told her. "It's yours."

Stacia froze. "Damian, you didn't."

"Stacia, you talked about this car for four days."

"Yeah, but that didn't mean you had to go out and buy me one!" Stacia climbed out of the car. "We talked about this already, Damian. I don't want you to keep buying me expensive gifts."

"How am I going to explain this to my husband?"

"You don't have to explain anything to that jerk," Damian told her.

Stacia turned back toward Damian. "Yeah, and then

when our marriage falls apart what are you going to do, Damian?" A half smile crept across her face. "Are you going to marry me?"

Damian lifted an eyebrow, and tilted his head slightly.

Stacia laughed and turned away. "I didn't think so."

"I didn't say anything," Damian told her.

"You didn't have to," Stacia replied. "Marriage isn't for us. Not with each other, anyway. It would ruin everything that we have, everything that we are."

"And what is that, Stacia?" Damian inquired.

"Perfection." Stacia turned and faced him. "Right now, this is a wonderful dream life that we share. And the moment we bring it back down to reality with a wedding ring, that's the exact moment that this picture-perfect glass world that we've created, will shatter. The moment you go from being my soul mate, my beautiful black knight, my Prince Charming, to being my husband, is the moment I'll die. I'll have nothing to live for, no soul mate to talk to, to share my dreams, my aspirations, my desires, my secrets, my problems, my everything."

Damian pulled Stacia close and wrapped his arms around her. He knew exactly what she meant. What they shared was special. It was something magical. They had been together since childhood, and they would always be together, no matter who else came into their lives. They were more than just lovers or friends or even husband and wife. They were a part of each other, and they would always be a part of each other. They were one soul, shared by two bodies. And for them, that was much more than enough.

In the San Antonio Federal Bureau of Investigation Field Office, Agent Bob Ritchie exclaimed ecstatically. "I think we got him!" He lifted his bespectacled head from the video microscope and turned toward Nathan. "We can definitely place Dante at the hospital, on that specific date."

Agent Ritchie was a forensic electronic media examiner, and a member of the Bureau's vaunted Science and Technology Department. The equipment that he was currently using, took grainy low-grade video, cleaned it up, and expanded the image inside of a microscope-like device, enabling the agents to see objects and images on the peripheral edges of the video. The FBI had forensic equipment that made CSI look like they were still in the Stone Age.

"I don't know" Agent Alex Roush shook his head and exhaled. "I still think it's kind of shaky."

"Can we take it to the judge?" Agent Philip Grey asked.

Agent Ritchie removed his glasses and wiped the perspiration from around his eyes. "I think we can take it to the bank."

Agent Jason Peters turned toward Agent Roush. "Al, you want to take another look?"

"I would feel better if I had some backup on this one."

Agent Roush maneuvered around the others, and peered down into the video microscope.

"Al," Agent Peters called out calmly. "Take your time; this is very important."

Agent Roush lifted his hand, silencing the other agents. "I'm willing to go so far as to say that there's a high probability, that this could be Dante Reigns."

"Could be or is?" Agent Michael Rogers asked impatiently.

Agent Roush stepped away from the forensic video microscope and exhaled. "If we were talking percentages, I'd say better than fifty."

"What?" Agent Grey prodded. "Sixty? Seventy?"

Agent Roush winced, "Better than fifty."

Special Agent in Charge, Nathan Hess, rose from his seat in the corner of the room. "Gentlemen, this is probably the singular most important moment in the history of this field office. We've been given an opportunity to bring to justice, one of the lowest life forms ever brought into existence. This is no man; this is a monster. A monster who's killed a lot of innocent people. He's killed our brother agents, members of his own organization, friends, family, and only God knows who else. To remove this monster from society, is to bring to justice the singular most important, most maniacal, most devious killer, in our nation's history. Make no doubts about the importance of your findings, nor what they would mean to the families of his victims."

Agent Roush exhaled. "Nathan, I'll give you seventy percent. But, I reserve the right to add an addendum to the report."

Hess smiled, patted Agent Roush on his shoulder, and turned to Agent Rogers. "Mike, draft an arrest warrant for one Dante Reigns, and get it over to Judge Prago to sign."

"Prago is old school, Nathan," Agent Peters interjected. "Are you sure that we have enough evidence?"

"Besides, murder is a state charge," Agent Grey added. "Prago isn't going to want to get involved in that."

"Dante Reigns murdered several of my agents, while they were in the process of investigating the Reigns criminal organization," Nathan pointed out. "That makes it federal!"

"Nathan," Agent Roush interjected. "What Phil and Jay are saying, is that in this particular instance, the victim was not an FBI agent."

"I know what they're saying, Alex," Hess stated forcefully. "I don't need a translator. And in case all of you have forgotten, the good doctor here was a military doctor, assigned to Lackland Air Force Base."

Hess pulled a cigar from his pocket and placed it between his teeth. "And that my dear Watson, makes this case federal. Call Prago, and tell that son of a bitch that I need an arrest warrant, and I need it now!"

Chapter Five

The Reigns family picnics were legendary affairs. Reigns family members traveled from distant cities, distant states, and occasionally from distant continents, to enjoy these momentous events. Aunt Marjorie's potato salad, Aunt Beverly's 'sock-it-to-me' cakes, Uncle Todd's honey-glazed mesquite-flavored barbecue, all conspired to make the annual affair, a must attend event. The food, however, was overshadowed by one particular event, the annual Reigns family's tackle football game; family members, young and old participated.

The family football game pitted sister against sister, brother against brother, and cousin against cousin. Fathers played against sons, mothers tackled daughters, and nieces and nephews were flung to the ground with the ferocity of a Super Bowl game. Grandmothers cheered their children and grandchildren, while great-grandmothers routed for everyone, and all had a rousing good time.

The gathering this year was at Damian's working cattle ranch in West Texas. Small private chartered planes whisked family members from the larger airports in El Paso and San Angelo, to the ranch's small but modern, airstrip. The ranch proper, sat above a massive underground aquifer, and as such, was one of the few West Texas ranches that remained green all-year around. The fact that three large rivers flowed through the property, did not hurt either.

Damian's 65,000 acres, 30,000 head of cattle, and acres of brand-new facilities filled to the brim with brand new state-of-the-art equipment, made his operation the envy of ranchers throughout the country. The Reigns Ranch, also known as the Double R Ranch, was a first-class operation, through and through.

The main house was 30,000 square feet, and contained 20 bedrooms, 23 bathrooms, 6 living areas, a massive main dining hall, and an equally massive home theater. The seamed metal-roofed structure had been constructed to stand the test of time. It was a post and beam affair, made out of a beautiful white limestone known as Sisterdale Cream, named after the area from which it had been quarried. Inside, massive intertwined antlers had been transformed into beautiful chandeliers, while antiqued, rough-hewn boards salvaged and restored from old Texas barns, covered the floor. The main house was a grand Texas style mansion, decorated in a relaxed elegance.

The ranch was a sportsman and outdoor lover's paradise. Bucks, deer, elk, wild turkeys, hogs, quail, pheasant, and a variety of other game, called the ranch home. They fed near one of the three well-stocked spring-fed lakes or sometimes near one of over a dozen spring-fed creeks located on the property. On the ranch, Damian had constructed regulation-size basketball courts, tennis courts, a clay-shooting field, a football field, and a golf course. It was the football field, however, which held everyone's attention today.

"Go long!" Damian shouted, waving his hands through the air.

Darius Reigns performed a quick shimmy, and then a shake, and then sprinted hurriedly down the field. Damian lobbed the ball through the air, sending it down the field and into the hands of its sprinting recipient.

"Yes!" Darius shouted as he clutched the football and headed into the end zone.

Damian and the rest of his teammates raised their

arms and cheered. They ran down the field to the end zone, where they quickly assembled for their celebratory dance.

"Just kick the ball off, will you!" Dante shouted. He turned toward his brother Dajon. "I'll take this one. I'm going to try to run it all the way back on their asses."

"C'mon, kick the ball off, cowards!" Dajon shouted and clapped his hands. He, like Dante, was eager to score and catch up.

Damian and his team lined up just outside the end zone, and waited impatiently as Zach Reigns kicked the football. The football soared through the air, over the head of Dante and his waiting teammates, and into the hands of a stranger rounding the corner of the house. The stranger was Nathan Hess, and he was surrounded by a large group of G-men.

"Nathan!" Damian shouted furiously. "What in the hell is the meaning of this?"

"Leave this property, immediately!" Dante shouted.

Nathan approached the group of Reigns family members gathering just before him. He stopped just in front of Dante.

"Dante Reigns, it is my distinct pleasure," Nathan Hess smiled, "to announce that you're under arrest, you son of a bitch!"

"Yeah right!" Dante huffed. "Under arrest for what?"

"For the murder of one Dr. Julian Huffington," Nathan informed him. "Now, turn around, and place your hands behind your head."

Davidian and Emory Reigns, Dante's parents, made their way through the crowd of relatives, and approached Nathan.

"Nathaniel Ezekiel Hess, what's the meaning of this?" Emory demanded.

"Em, your son's under arrest," Nathan informed her.

"My boy's under arrest?" Davidian bellowed. "For what?"

Nathan shook his head. "Dee, Em, I've been trying to

tell you about your sons for the last eight years. For some reason, you refused to listen. I know that you've heard the gossip, the rumors, and the stories, just like everyone else has. But, for some reason, you refused to listen. Your son's under arrest for murder."

Emory whimpered as tears began to stream down her face.

"Nathan, my boys are innocent!" Davidian shouted. "Damn it, Nathan, why didn't you call me and talk to me first!"

"Dee, I and the entire world, have been trying to talk to you about your children," Nathan responded. "How could the two of you have been so blind?"

"Blind?" Davidian shouted. "Blind to what? Blind to their success, blind to their education, blind to what?"

"Your children have created a drug empire that stretches across half the country!" Nathan shouted. "They have murdered, maimed, bribed, coerced, and cajoled their way to the top of a drug Commission so notorious, so bloody, and so ruthless, that it defies description!"

"Bullshit!" Davidian shouted. "I know what this is about, Nathan! This is about a father getting revenge for his daughter! This is about nothing more than Damian and Stacia!"

Nathan threw his head back in laughter. "Dee, you cannot possibly be that stupid."

"Let it go, Nathan!" Davidian shouted. "Stacia has moved on; why haven't you?"

"Dee, this is about a daughter all right," Nathan shouted. "But not about mine. It's about your daughter, Princess, and about the number of bodies that she has left scattered all throughout the country. It's about a son, Dante. A son so murderous, so ruthless, so damn cold and calculating, that he makes Satan blush! And a son, Damian, who had the entire world at his feet. A son who could have done so much good, a son who could have been great, who could have been a senator, a governor or anything that he wanted to be. A son who used his brilliance to bring death and destruction to his own people. Your children, Dee, whose activities and personalities and lives you're ultimately responsible for. The blood on their hands is also on yours. You raised these coldhearted murderous bastards."

"Nathaniel Ezekiel Hess!" Emory shouted. "That's quite enough!"

"Nathan!" Davidian shouted. "Nathan." Davidian clutched his chest. "Nathan."

"Dad!" Damian shouted.

Davidian clutched at his chest and fell to the ground.

"Davidian!" Emory dropped to her knees and cradled her husband.

"Paramedics, get the paramedics here quick,!" Nathan shouted.

A group of uniformed FBI men dressed in black combat gear removed their helmets, dropped to their knees, and begin to work on Davidian. One pressed on Dravidian's chest, while the other breathed into his mouth.

Nathan lifted his handheld communicator. "Eagle One, this is Command; get that bird on the ground right now. We need an emergency transport to the hospital."

Princess pushed her way through the crowd, knelt down by her father, and stared up at Nathan. "This is your fault."

"I was just doing my job," Nathan told her.

"If he dies," Princess told him. "The gloves come off."

The number of limousines that lined the cemetery was reminiscent of Mann's Chinese Theater during Oscar night. There were hundreds of them; Maybach limousines, Mercedes limousines, BMW limousines, Lincoln Town Car limousines, Rolls Royce limousines, and dozens upon dozens of long, black Cadillac limousines. A phalanx of black-suited patrons lined up just in front of the Reigns family, to pay their respects to Davidian, and to pass along their condolences to Emory and to the rest of the Reigns family. It

41

was a procession that stretched for several hundred yards throughout the massive Catholic cemetery.

The casket of Davidian Reigns had been constructed of titanium, surrounded by intricately carved imported African ebony. Tufts of imported hand-woven Persian silk lined the interior, and highly polished chrome accents and inlays tastefully decorated the exterior of the coffin. It was clear to everyone in attendance, that the family had spent tens of thousands of dollars, just on the box alone.

Roses draped the coffin, and covered the table upon which it sat, giving the illusion that the coffin sat upon a massive bed of flowers. The cemetery itself was Catholic through and through, but it was also very private. The Reigns family had been devout Catholics for as far back as anyone could remember, and this was the family's very own private cemetery. It sat on several acres, within the confines of the Reigns family's large South Central Texas hill country ranch, and held a commanding hilltop view of several beautiful hills, valleys, and creeks. It was without a doubt, a beautiful place to spend one's eternal resting days.

Emory sat between her four sons, with Dante sitting on the end next to two U.S. Marshals. Princess sat on the other side of her mother, holding her hand and comforting her. Even beneath her massive black Chanel hat and black Chanel sunglasses, one could sense her seething, fiery anger.

Davidian had been more than the patriarch of a large, clan; he had been the wisdom, the light, and the love of an entire generation of nieces and nephews. He was the uncle with the kind words of encouragement. He was the uncle who made them laugh. He was the uncle who told them about the importance of education. He was the uncle with the sunshine smile, who always had shiny quarters when the ice-cream truck rounded the corner. He was a marvelous father to his children and a magical daddy to his little princess who loved her father more than life itself, and that was an understatement. She was his only daughter, and was treated as such growing up. He didn't buy her My Little Ponies while growing up; instead, his only baby girl was given real ponies on her birthdays. Not content to shower his precious little princess with Barbie Corvettes on Christmas, he bought her a real corvette on her sixteenth birthday, as well as an estate in Beverly Hills on her twenty-second birthday. He gave her everything her heart desired, and more importantly, he gave her life. He brought her into this world, and he protected her from the monsters that roamed within it. And now, when he needed her protection the most, she couldn't give it. She couldn't protect him from the Nathans of this world. Her daddy was her beloved and precious father. She could not bring him back. But she would do the next best thing. Death would come to those responsible. Death would rain down on those FBI agents who intruded into their lives and took her daddy away. Death would come to Nathan as swift and as furious as a category five hurricane. It would swoop down on him, and wipe away not only his existence, but all that stood in the way. She wanted his home, gone; his wife, gone; his family, gone; his cars, gone and all that he held sacred and dear, gone. He would pay for her father's death, one hundred times over. And Damian, if he tried to stop her, he would pay to. No one, not Dante, not Damian, not the Commission, not the angels in heaven, could stop the hell that was going to be delivered to Special Agent in Charge, Nathaniel Hess. He was, to borrow a well-worn cliché, a dead man walking.

"Princess, I just wanted to stop and give my condolences to you and to your family," Don Frediano Ambrogino of Las Vegas told her. "Your father was a good man."

Princess crossed her legs and leaned back. "Don Ambrogino, my family and I accept your condolences. We'll remember all those who stood by our side during our time of tragedy and grief."

Don Ambrogino nodded, and continued down the line.

"Senora Reigns, I want to know if there's anything that

I can do for you or your family?" Don Graziella Biaggio of New York inquired.

Princess nodded slightly. "Don Biaggio, you've done more than enough," Princess responded icily. "Your deeds and actions will certainly be remembered."

Her words brought a chill to all nearby, and caused the hairs on the Don's forearms to stand at attention.

Don Biaggio leaned forward. "The Dons would like to meet with you and your brothers, as soon as it can be arranged. We would like to pay tribute to your brother, and express our condolences in a more private setting."

"No meetings," Princess informed the Don. "Tell the Dons that their sympathy is noted, and that their presence here today is more than an adequate tribute to my family. We, the Reigns family, are going to have our own private meeting after the services. Therefore, Damian has asked that the Dons forgive him for not being able to meet with them. He understands that they have made considerable sacrifices to be here today, and that they have traveled great distances, but he asks that they forgive him during this most tragic and tumultuous time."

Don Biaggio nodded. "I'll convey your brother's wishes, senora."

"Thank you, Don Biaggio." Princess nodded politely.

"Senora, one last thing," Don Biaggio whispered. "The Dons are concerned about rumors that have been circulating. You know, a war with the FBI could potentially expose all of our operations."

Princess smiled. "Don Biaggio, let me assure you that there'll be no war with the FBI. The Reigns family knows that things can get out of hand if such a war were to occur."

Don Biaggio bowed slightly. "Thank you, senora."

The meeting was held at the family mansion just outside the city. The home, which previously belonged to the now deceased Davidian Reigns, was a twenty-five-thousand-square-foot plantation style mansion, nestled on a hilltop.

The spread was not only a working dairy farm, but an actual modern day sugar plantation, a vineyard, and a horse-breeding farm all rolled into one. It was on the majestic home's second-floor veranda where the meeting was being held.

"Before you say anything, just be seated and hear me out," Damian told Princess.

Princess seated herself on a wicker rocking chair just opposite her brother. She lifted a pitcher of lemonade from a table, and poured herself a glass.

"I know what you're thinking, sis," Damian continued. "I know what you want. You want blood to flow."

"The Commission is nervous, as are the other families around the country," Angela added. "They don't want this thing to spiral out of control. They don't want their operations exposed."

"I got the same message today from Biaggio," Princess added.

Damian nodded. "I know. Their message is loud and clear."

"El Jeffe is pissed," Anjouinette added. Anjouinette Tibbideaux was in charge of Louisiana. She inherited her husband's seat on the Commission after Dante killed him. "The Vegas families are even more pissed. The Commission's pissed. And we're all two seconds away from going to war with the New York families."

"Damian, why don't we wait?" Emil suggested. Emil was a member of the Commission and the powerful head of the entire state of Georgia. "We can hit whomever we need to hit anytime we choose. Let this thing with the Commission settle down first. Let this thing with Vegas pass, and let things settle down with El Jeffe. Let's see what moves New York makes, and let's get Dante out of jail first and foremost. There are too many things going on at once, too many variables. We don't need to get into a pissing match with the FBI right now."

"That's easy for you to say, Emil; he wasn't your

45

uncle," Brandon Reigns told him.

"I loved Davidian like a father," Emil countered.

Damian rose, walked to the balcony, and peered off into the distance. Slowly, his hand rose to his forehead, where he began to massage his temples.

"I say, we hit them all, we hit them hard, and we hit them now!" Joshua Reigns said forcefully.

"Damian, is this your decision or is this my decision?" Princess asked. "This decision is clear."

Damian lifted his hand, silencing them all. He turned and faced them.

"For right now, things remain as is," he ordered. "Meaning, we won't make the transition or separation until after things calm down."

"And Nathan?" Princess inquired.

Damian turned, and again peered off into the distance. "With every fiber of my being, I want that son of a bitch dead. Every part of me that is a son and every part of me that's human and every part of me that can feel wants Nathan Hess dead."

"Then give the order, bro," Princess urged him. "Give the order, and my men will have it done by midnight. Give the order, and Nathan won't live to see tomorrow."

"And the Commission?" Anjouinette asked.

"Think this one over carefully, Damian," Emil warned him.

"Damian, in your heart, you know what you have to do," Joshua told him.

"And that's my dilemma," Damian whispered. "If I used my heart, Nathan would already be dead. But, I owe it to the people who work for me, to use my head. I owe it to their wives and their children, to make decisions without passion or prejudice. I owe it to my people, to make sure that they have the best chance possible to go home to their families at night."

"And what do you owe to your father?" Princess asked.

"To be the best that I can be, to be man enough to

46

make the right decision no matter what the consequences."

"Damian," Princess said softly. "Nathan's going to die."

"Will the Bureau come after us?" Damian asked.

"In all likelihood," Emil answered. "My advice is, we can't afford to do it right now, later, definitely. But, now no way."

"My soldiers were flown in from Florida two days ago," Princess told him. "They're waiting for the order. Everything's been arranged."

"So, if I don't give the order and sanction this hit, then you'll hit him anyway, using soldiers from Florida who are loyal to only you?" Damian asked.

Princess nodded. "I'm sorry, Damian."

"Try to make it look like an accident," Damian said softly.

"I wanted it very public," Princess replied. "I want to send a very loud and clear message."

"You have my consent," Damian told her.

Princess nodded. She lifted her cell phone from her purse; speed dialed a preprogrammed number, and placed the phone to her ear.

"The baby's in the crib," Princess said softly, and then hung up.

Darius Reigns burst through the door, and out onto the veranda.

"I want in!" Darius demanded.

"Darius, we're having a meeting here," Damian told his younger brother.

"I know, and I want in!" Darius repeated.

"In what?" Damian asked. "Do you even know what you're talking about?"

"Damian, I'm not stupid!" Darius shouted. "Mom and Dad may have been blind to what you do, but I'm not! I know who you are, and I know what you do!"

"Darius, now's not the time and place for this conversation," Damian told him.

"Now's the perfect time!" Darius demanded. "You're

going to go after the people who killed Dad. I want to be a part of it!"

"Darius, you're only sixteen. You have to finish high school, you have to finish college, and then you have to go to graduate school" Princess told him.

"And then, you can go to work for the family at Bio One," Damian added. "None of us have science degrees, or medical degrees. We need you to get your degree in nanotechnology or biotechnology or medicine or something equivalent. Then you can help run Bio One and watch over the family's interest."

"I want to help now!" Darius demanded. "I'm ready. I want to help get the men that killed Dad."

Princess rose, clasped her brother's neck, and pulled him close.

"Darius, your time will come. Don't rush it; trust me; stay young for as long as you can."

Darius pulled away from his sister, and stormed inside.

Emil rose and shrugged his shoulders. "Damian, I sure as hell hope that you're right about this one."

"If I'm not, then we'll know soon enough," Damian replied.

Anjouinette rose. "Yes, I suppose they can bury us all in the same cemetery," then she stormed off the veranda.

Chapter Six

Nathan climbed out of his burgundy Jaguar XJ, peered over the car's low rooftop, and waved at his next door neighbors. A good assortment of business owners, corporate executives, and professional athletes, actors, and singers called the highly secured community home. They were attracted to the twenty-four hour monitored security cameras, the two separate guarded entry gates that one needed to pass through to gain entry into the community, as well as the armed mobile units that patrolled the neighborhood twenty-four hours a day, seven days a week. To say that the community was secure, was an understatement.

Nathan could afford to live in the community by virtue of his wife, who happened to be one of the top renowned cardiovascular surgeons and basically a living legend. She was the first African-American woman doctor to separate multiple conjoined twins. Her specialty was prenatal and neonatal heart abnormalities, and she was damn good at it. She was also well paid for it. And as such, could afford to live in a fifteen thousand square-foot mansion.

Dr. Cynthia Hess, affectionately known to most as simply Cissy, waved to her husband. "Sweetie, could you be a dear and get the mail for me?"

Nathan nodded and silently grumbled. He was the director of the San Antonio field office, and the newly appointed executive assistant director for criminal investigations, once his senate confirmation was complete. What in the hell made her think that he was some god damned mail boy. He couldn't perform a triple bypass, nor could he install a balloon stint inside an aortic valve, but in the next couple of months he was going to be the third highest-ranking law enforcement officer in the most powerful nation on the planet. Surely that accounted for something. Surely, he rated higher than a god damned mail boy.

"Get the mail," he grumbled beneath his breath. My hands are just too precious to open and close such a primitive contraption, blah, blah, blah."

Nathan stormed to the curb where his oversize metal mailbox stood, and pulled down the door. He knew that he was in trouble the moment he felt the tug of the thick black wire.

There are many things that go through a man's head in the last few seconds before he leaves this world, and all of them passed through his mind with some semblance of clarity. Nathan saw the smiling faces of his beloved daughter, and his wife of more than thirty years. He knew that they'd be okay, since they were strong, wealthy, and educated. He knew that they'd mourn him for quite some time, but eventually, that they would go on with their lives. Nathan's thoughts also fleetingly turned to Damian, the man who he knew was responsible for his death on this day. The Reigns family, how did they get in? Surely, they couldn't blame him for Davidian's death, which occurred when he came to the Reigns family's annual picnic and arrested Dante for the murder of Dr. Julian Huffington. That was the day when Nathan told Davidian that he was responsible for raising cold-blooded killers.

Nathan's thoughts flashed through his mind, and the white flash from the explosion lit the air around him. The last thing he remembered was his ears locking and shutting down because of the loudness of the explosion. And then, came darkness.

The meeting was being held in Las Vegas, deep within the labyrinth-like bowels of the city's latest and most excessive, over-the-top megalithic structure. The building was called The Coliseum, and it was Las Vegas' latest attempt to outdo the rest of the casino world. It would be the superpower of casinos, and when complete, would have more money flowing through it, than most countries' gross national products.

The Coliseum would stand over one hundred stories tall. Its exterior would be fashioned to look like a massive version of the actual coliseum in Rome, with gigantic statues, and equally enormous colonnades, all carved from Italian marble.

The Coliseum was being built to cater to an entirely different clientele than most Vegas casinos were used to. This casino was not being constructed with family vacationers in mind, nor was it being built for the rich; this casino would be the exclusive playground for the world's elite. It would be the playground for Middle Eastern sheiks, European royalty, Asian mega-tycoons, and American captains of industry. Some members of that exclusive club were gathered several stories below ground inside of the structure, at that very moment.

"Welcome! Welcome!" Don Salvatore Tiziano of Las Vegas greeted the dark-suited men gathered around the three hundred year-old mahogany hand-carved table. "Gentlemen, please make yourselves at home, and if there's anything that I can do to make your stay here more comfortable, please don't hesitate to ask. Your wish is my command."

Don Marcellino Pancrazio lifted his glass of Chateau Haut-Brion and raised it to the air. "Don Tiziano, your hospitality's legendary."

"Gentlemen, I'm sure that you all know Don Pancrazio of New York," Don Tiziano pronounced. "Please, allow me to introduce the rest of our compatriots. I'll introduce our New York brethren first. At the end of the table to the far right, is

51

Don Tito Bonafacio, of the Bonafacio family. To Don Bonafacio's right, is Don Gianpaulo Cipriano of the Cipriano family, and just to his left, is Don Graziella Biaggio of the Biaggio family. Seated next to Don Biaggio is of course the good and kind-hearted Don Nicostrato Cinzia of the Cinzia family. On the opposite side of the table we have our Las Vegas brethren, beginning with Don Anastasio Crencenzo of the Crencenzo family. Next we have Don Nestor Melchiorre of the Melchiorre family, and then we have Don Patrizio Giovanneta of the Giovanneta family. Last but certainly not least, we have Don Umberto Constantino of the Constantino family. And of course many of you already know me; I'm Salvatore Tiziano."

Don Anastasio Crencenzo leaned forward and cleared his throat. "Gentlemen, I wish to thank you all for coming. The matters that we are to discuss today are of great consequence to us all. As you are all well aware, we're the last of the old guard. We represent the original families, the first families that came over from the old country and organized themselves so that hardworking Sicilians could protect themselves and prosper in this new land."

"The Las Vegas families are under siege," Don Melchiorre declared. "Those new bastards, those Colombians, the filthy Mexicans, and their nigger allies, are making inroads into our territory. Not to mention, those commie Russian son of bitches."

"Why, Nestor, I was under the impression that the Russians were capitalist now," Don Bonifacio declared.

The Dons gathered around the table broke into laughter.

Don Cinzia leaned forward and interlaced his fingers. "Excuse me, my dear friends. I certainly sympathize with your dilemma; however I'm confused. I don't understand why these issues are of concern to those of us from New York."

"Why, the answer to that question is quite simple, Don Cinzia," Don Giovanneta told him. The Don waved his hand around the room. "Your interest in this new casino."

"Is our interest in the casino not safe?" Don Biaggio inquired. "We were under the impression that our investment in this establishment was guaranteed."

Don Salvatore Tiziano waved his hands in an effort to calm the New York Dons. "Gentlemen, your investment in this casino is quite safe. What Patricio was saying, is that for the first time in a very long time, the New York and Las Vegas families are once again united in business and friendship. This casino is going to make all of our families rich beyond our wildest dreams. However, there are issues at hand, which could potentially cause our smooth road, to suddenly become a very difficult one to travel down."

"And what issues are those?" Don Cipriano inquired.

"This new upstart Commission," Don Constantino answered.

"They're a bunch of niggers and Mexicans, and Colombians, and God knows what else, who deal drugs all over the place," Don Giovanneta added. "They use violence, regardless of the consequences."

"Gentlemen, again, I sympathize," Don Cinzia told them. "But I don't understand how it affects our business relationship."

"This Commission," Don Tiziano explained, "is organized by states. Each member is the head of a state. Collectively, they answer to a Colombian whose identity is supposed to be a great mystery. Our people say his name is Cedras. Ponce Guadelupe Jaria Cedras, to be precise. He's better protected than the president of the United States. He has his own private little army, plus the entire Colombian army and their national intelligence service is on his payroll."

"Gentlemen, this Commission is moving into our territory," Don Melchiorre explained. "They're trying to muscle into the Vegas commodities market, and even trying to challenge our casinos."

"What do you mean, challenge our casinos?" Don Bonafacio inquired.

"They've opened up several rival casinos on their

53

own," Don Tiziano answered.

"Opened up their own casinos?" Don Biaggio repeated. "How? It was my understanding that no one could fart in Vegas, without your permission. Gentlemen, you control the Gaming Commission; you control the politicians and the police. How did this happen?"

"They slipped in when we were at war with the Russians," Don Constantino answered. We couldn't fight two wars at the same time."

"And now?" Don Pancrazio inquired. "Why not use your political power to squeeze them out?"

"Because they managed to dig in fast and deep," Don Crencenzo answered. "They have some political protection, but we don't know where or how deep. We do know that this Commission is spread throughout the country, and so we believe that they're bringing pressure to bear from the national level."

"And therein lies our problem," Don Tiziano added. "Gentlemen, war with this Commission is inevitable. However, we're not strong enough to go to war with this organization at the present time. This is the reason we called this meeting. We lose this war; we lose Las Vegas. We lose Las Vegas, and more likely than not, we'll lose this casino."

"We'll also lose our way of life," Don Constantino added. "We're the last, gentlemen. Let us not underestimate the importance of Las Vegas, and the Las Vegas families. New York cannot survive long without the money that it receives from its Vegas investments."

"This so-called Commission is also expanding east, if I may remind you," Don Giovanneta warned. "They're also seeking to expand into New Jersey, Philadelphia, Maryland, Delaware, and even New York."

"Unity of action is required," Don Crencenzo told them.

Don Bonafacio leaned forward. "Gentlemen, of course we'll assist you. What can we do to help?"

"We need the muscle and political power of our New

York brethren," Don Tiziano answered.

"What do you know about these cockroaches?" Don Pancrazio asked.

"We know a lot," Don Constantino informed them. "We have someone on the inside."

"Someone on the inside?" Don Biaggio repeated with a raised eyebrow. "Interesting, how valuable is he?"

Don Giovannetta huffed. "How valuable? He's a member of their Commission."

The Las Vegas members around the table laughed.

"A member of their Commission?" Don Cipriano asked incredulously. "How?"

"That is what happens with mongrels get in bed with one another," Don Crencenzo told them. "They all try to fuck each other."

The Dons again joined in laughter.

"This informant who we have, he's supposedly the head of the Las Vegas part of their Commission," Don Tiziano informed them. "He's Sicilian, and he desperately wants to be part of the old family. He informs us of everything that they say and do."

"So, why don't we give him his own tiny little family, and let him use his soldiers to help us fight against his old comrades?" Don Cipriano inquired.

"Because, Paulo, nobody likes a snitch," Don Cinzia told him.

The Dons again broke into laughter.

"So, Don Tiziano, has this traitor told you how to squash these little upstart bugs?" Don Biaggio asked.

"They're having internal problems with one of their members," Don Tiziano informed them. "Damian Reigns, he's trying to leave their organization."

Don Pancrazio lifted an eyebrow. "So?"

"Well, it seems that the Reigns family controls seventy percent of the states in this Commission," Don Constantino answered. "It appears that this Commission has gone to war with this family before and apparently lost."

"The Reigns family devastated the rest of the Commission," Don Tiziano informed them. "To give a more honest assessment of the situation, the Reigns family is not going to leave the Commission; it's trying to turn over its seat on the Commission to another family member. Apparently, they want to turn over all of their illegal operations to the sister."

"The sister?" Don Bonafacio lifted an eyebrow.

"You know her; we all know her," Don Giovanneta told them. "Princess Reigns."

Don Pancrazio rose from his seat. "That Reigns family, the ones who went to war with us in D.C.?"

"No, Don," Don Constantino smiled. "The Reigns family who obliterated your men in D.C. and then took all of Maryland from you in less than two days. The very same Princess Reigns who killed Don Mafalda's brother on the streets of Baltimore."

"They're again at war with their Commission," Don Tiziano informed them. "Their Commission is weak, they're divided, and the Reigns family is financially vulnerable right now. Damian has invested all of his family's money in his little biotech company, and divested his money from all of their other previous enterprises. He's put all of his little eggs into one easily crushable basket."

"Now's the time for us to strike them, run them out of Las Vegas, run them out of the East, and teach these upstarts a lesson that they won't soon forget," Don Constantino added.

Don Pancrazio nodded. "We're with you."

"A familia!" Don Biaggio lifted his glass into the air.

"A familia!" The other Dons roared as they joined in his toast.

Chapter Seven

The restaurant was called Dante's Inferno. It was a five-star affair, with an informal bar and grill in the back. Dante's Inferno was also the in place to dine, if one was conducting business rooms filled with Ceruti, Armani, and Brioni clad patrons.

The restaurant was located in the brand-new haute couture shopping center, on the city's far north side. The Shops, as it was known to its rich and famous clientele, was the area's premier shopping destination. The shopping center was anchored by none other than Neiman Marcus and Saks Fifth Avenue, with several other high-end department stores, expensive boutiques, and galleries, as well as numerous equally expensive eateries in between. The shopping center, like the restaurant, catered solely to the citie's elite.

Damian sat in his usual seat, located on the second floor overlooking the city's distant skyline. This was his second favorite seat in the establishment; his first being the table with views of Six Flags Fiesta Texas, and its world famous roller coaster, The Rattler. It was the child inside that made him smile every time he saw the roller coaster slowly clicking along the top of the tracks, before finally swooping down into its terrifying nosedive. He loved to close his eyes and imagine that he was in the front car, without anyplace to go, without a care in the world, aaah to be young again.

"Tell me what you're thinking." Illyassa whispered. She reached across the table and caressed Damian's cheek.

"Nothing." Damian shook his head, and shifted his gaze toward his date. She was more than beautiful.

Illyassa Malaika had graced more magazine covers by the time she had turned seventeen, than most supermodels could ever dream of being on throughout their entire careers. Born in Addis Ababa, Ethiopia, to parents of royal lineage, she was blessed with reddish-brown skin. Skin that resembled the soft earthen clays of her ancestral village near the city of Hemet, which itself was near the Red Sea, where she played and swam as a child. Illyassa's most striking feature, and the one that gained for her an international following, were her blue-green eyes. They were pale powder gems that resembled seashells from the beaches on the Gulf of Aden, where she vacationed with her parents as a girl. Her eyes were mystifying, striking, and captivating. They made men and women stop in their tracks and gasp.

"You seem distracted," Illyassa told him.

"Sorry," Damian smiled sheepishly. "I guess my age is showing. Here I'm with the most beautiful woman in the world, and I'm staring off into space."

"Damian, you know I hate it when you call me that," she told him.

"You hate the truth?" Damian teased. "Time magazine called you a modern day Helen of Troy."

Illyassa laughed. "I know that writer. He's had chocolate fantasies since I was sixteen, the pervert."

Damian laughed. "Hey, just don't start a war, huh?"

"Ever thought that we would see this day?" Illyassa asked.

"What day is that?"

"The day when an African-American man is one of the wealthiest men in the world," she told him. "While an African woman is hailed as the most beautiful woman in the world."

Damian smiled. "I knew that one day I would be one of

the wealthiest men in the world.

"I see that you're as modest as ever."

Damian laughed.

"I think that it's your confidence that makes you so attractive, Mr. Reigns," Illyassa told him.

"And I think that it's your entire being, down to the very essence of your soul, which makes you so attractive, Ms. Malaika," Damian replied.

Illyassa blushed.

"I can't believe that someone who's so used to crowds and attention and compliments, could be made to blush so easily," Damian mused.

"You seem to have that affect on me," Illyassa replied. "She lifted her glass of Petrus and sipped. "You seem to have that affect on all women."

"Oh, no," Damian waved her off. "Don't try to make me out to be some kind of playboy."

"Playboy?" Illyassa laughed. "No, no, no, not you Mr. Damian."

"And you, the beautiful Illyassa?" Damian leaned forward and whispered. "The woman who could have any man on earth. What would you want with an ordinary guy like me?"

Illyassa laughed. "Damian Reigns, ordinary? Where did this humility come from?"

Damian joined in her laughter. "I mean, you're beautiful; you're intelligent; you're classy; you have everything."

"And yet, still not enough to snag you," she interrupted.

"Snag me?" Damian smiled and tilted his head to the side. "C'mon, Illyassa, you and I both know that you're not ready to settle down."

"And why do you say that?"

"Because, you're at the top of your game!" Damian said excitedly. "You're the world's top model; why would you give that up?"

"Give what up?" Illyassa turned her palms skyward. "I've been modeling since I was a baby. I've won every award there was to win, garnered every accolade, graced the covers of every magazine, walked all the top runways for all the top designers; I have all the money I could ever want; I don't crave the fame; I mean, what's left? I could honestly say that I could walk away, and walk away fulfilled, if the right proposition came along."

"I wasn't aware of that," Damian said softly. "I thought you were happy."

"I'm happy," Illyassa told him. "Who wouldn't be happy? I'm very successful at my career and I've been blessed to be able to do what I love doing. I'm just saying, I could walk away from it all, and still be happy."

"So, here I am inside my brother's restaurant, seated in front of a woman whom I love very much," Damian whispered. "A woman who has just informed me that she would be happy to walk away from an awesome career and give me her hand in matrimony."

"How does that make you feel, Damian?" Illyassa said softly. "I don't want to be one of those sad whiny women who wonder what they're doing or where their relationship's going. If we were to never move forward, and our relationship remained as is, I'd still be happy, Damian."

"And that's what makes you different from ninety-nine percent of the women I've dated," Damian told her. "Your confidence and your self-assurance, that's why I love you, Illyassa."

The steak knife slammed into the table just in front of Damian, causing him to leap from the table.

"You son of a bitch!" Stacia Hess screamed hysterically. "You murdering, lying, back-stabbing son of a bitch!"

Damian's bodyguards rose from a nearby table, and rushed to where Stacia was standing, and tried to subdue her.

"You tried to kill my father!" Stacia screamed. "You

60

tried to kill my father!"

Damian fastened the buttons on his jacket and peered around nervously. "Stacia, what the hell are you talking about?"

"You know what I'm talking about, Damian!" Stacia screamed. "You planted a bomb in my parents' mailbox! You tried to kill my father!"

"Stacia, obviously you're not in a proper mental state right now," Damian told her. He rose from the table, clasped her arm, and turned her toward the exit. "Why don't you go home, and let me call you later."

"Call me!" Stacia jerked her arm away from him. "Get your fucking hands off of me, you goddamned murderer!"

"Stacia, please!" Damian pleaded.

"You know what, Damian?" Stacia told him, while crying heavily. "I thought that if I were on your team, that I could protect my family. I thought that if I helped you, and was a part of your family, that I could protect my father, protect my husband, protect my children, but I see that loyalty only flows one way with you! You care only about Damian, and only about what others can do for you! You care nothing about me, or about anyone else for that matter! You're a user, a coldhearted, blood-stained user! You use people to kill for you; you use your brother; you use your sister; you use your cousins; you use everyone you come into contact with. You're a murderer, and you're the worst kind of murderer. You kill for money. You would kill the whole world, just to make a fucking dollar. You're going down, Damian! You're going down!"

Damian nodded toward his bodyguards. "Get her out of here."

"If I have to go to prison for the rest of my life, you're going down, you son of a bitch!" Stacia screamed, as she was being carried away.

Princess strolled to the massive wall of clerestory windows and peered out over the seemingly endless, still crystal lake. She loved Damian's lakefront home, and envied him for being able to wake up each morning to such a view. The evening sun radiated off of the glass-like waters, reflecting brilliant hues of orange, yellow, purple, blue, and black. The water's surface reminded her of a brilliant black highly polished granite countertop. Nero's gold, she believed it was called. The exquisite colors veined the surface of the water, giving the appearance of an exotic African rainbow lying at rest. The view was truly breathtaking.

Princess lifted her glass of Black Pepper Shiraz and savored the spicy cherry flavor of the silkily smooth imported spirit.

"Okay, so let's hear it," Damian told her, as he breezed into the room.

"What do you want to hear?" Princess inquired.

"Did we mess up by hitting Nathan? Did we mess up by losing Stacia as an ally? Did we cross the line with the FBI? And most importantly, how do we minimize the damage that we caused?"

Princess sipped from her glass of wine, and then slowly turned to face her brother. "If you want me to say that it was a mistake to kill the man responsible for daddy's death, I'm sorry. I can't say that."

"First of all, he's not dead," Damian told her. "Nathan survived the blast. He's in intensive care, under heavy guard, at a military hospital. He's in a coma, and he's barely alive, but he's alive nonetheless."

Princess clinched her teeth, and began to seethe.

"You can forget about trying to get to him again any time soon," Damian told her. "He's being guarded better than the Pope."

"Whichever of our men rigged that bomb," Princess shook her head, "he's dead. The price of failure for this one is nothing short of death."

"Princess, will you stop it!" Damian snapped. "Death, on top of death, brings nothing but death! You've created nothing but of cycle a doom for us, and for everyone around us! For once, can you see past the killing! For once, can you just strategize with me? For just one time, can the answer be something besides murder or punishment or retribution!"

"It's what I know how to do, Damian!" Princess shot back. "It's the way I lead, it's the way I control things, it's the way I know how to get things done!"

"It's not the only way to get things done!" Damian shouted. "I should have listened to Emil. He said for us to wait, that there were too man things going on all at once, with the Commission, with Vegas, with El Jeffe, with New York, with Dante still in jail. And now it looks as if we're going to have to wait to kill that son of a bitch anyway! All we did was tip our hand, and lose one of the best sources of information in history. We had the daughter of the special agent in charge of this field office, on our side. If he survives, Nathan's about to become the third most powerful man in the Bureau in a couple of months, and we would have had access to his computer, his files, his diaries, everything! And now, we've fucked it up!"

"Damian, you're acting like this is my fault!"

"I just want it cleaned up!" Damian shouted. "We're too overextended. We're about to be at war with the Commission; we're probably at war with El Jeffe; the Old Ones are pissed at us because of our membership on the Commission, and because of the Commission's expansion into their territories; and now, last but not least, we've just pissed off the FBI!"

"Damian, tell me what you want, and then consider it done," Princess told him. "You want me to silence Stacia; I'll do it. The bitch won't live to hear the Star Spangled Banner on her television tonight. She'll be dead before The Tonight Show's over."

Damian shook his head. "I don't know if that's the answer. Besides, you'd have to kill her husband, and if her children wake up, then what? No, I don't know if more FBI blood on our hands is the answer."

"Damian! You're not going to let this bitch live, are

63

you?" Princess asked incredulously. "After what she said? After the threats she made? She knows too much! She could bring down every single member of this family!"

"I know what she knows!" Damian snapped.

"Damian, you haven't fallen for Stacia again, have you?" Princess asked. "Because if you have, I'll handle this shit myself!"

"I know what we have to do!" Damian snapped. He walked to the massive wall of windows, and peered out into the lake. "We know just as much about Stacia, as she knows about us. We know what information she's given us, and I'm sure that the FBI would love to know how we know some of the things that we know."

"So you want to hang her out to dry before she hangs us?"

"It'll discredit her, when she does start singing. It'll appear as though she's singing to save her own neck."

"And?" Princess lifted an eyebrow. "Stool pigeons usually sing just to save their own necks. There's nothing discrediting about that, unless of course it's in court. And if they get us inside a courtroom, then we're already dead."

"I know," Damian exhaled. "Stacia's smart. She was just upset. She'll think things through, and she'll come to her senses. She's in too deep, and she's given us too much; she's facing the same sentence as the rest of us."

"So, do we sell her out or kill her?" Princess inquired.

"Neither, for right now," Damian answered. "Get a message to her. Let her know that she's in just as deep as the rest of us. She stands to lose not only her freedom, and possibly her life, but her husband and children as well. We'll use a tactic from the Cold War."

"And that is?" Princess smiled.

"Mutually assured destruction," Damian laughed. "She uses her nukes, we use ours, and we can all meet up again in hell."

Princess laughed and exhaled. "Any news about Dante?"

Damian shook his head. "Our lawyers say that they're working on it."

"Perhaps I should talk to the lawyers," Princess suggested.

"And why's that?"

"Perhaps I can find some ways to motivate them," Princess said coldly.

Damian laughed. "You're one evil bitch, my dear sister."

"Damian, I'm not a bitch," Princess pouted. "I'm just misunderstood."

Damian laughed. "I'm glad to have you on my side."

Princess handed her brother her drink, and smiled as he sipped from her glass. Not long ago, if she had handed her brother a drink, it would have been filled to the brim with cyanide.

"Any news about Grace and the baby?" Damian inquired.

"She's disappeared again," Princess told him. She reached out and gently caressed the side of Damian's face. "Don't worry; we'll find them. You'll have Little Damian by your side in no time. I'll find your son, and I'll bring him home to you. You have my word."

Damian nodded. "Thank you."

"One last piece of business," Princess informed him.

"What's that?" Damian asked.

"Brandon called," Princess said softly. "We've been hit." Brandon Reigns is their cousin; he controls the state of Maryland.

"What?"

"Someone hit us hard in New Jersey," Princess told him. "I've ordered Kevin to head up there. I think our cousin can let us know what's going on. He's going to pull some of our men from Maryland and D.C. for support."

"I don't like the sound of this," Damian told her. He turned away and shook his head. "Too many things happening at once, too many hits from too many directions.

65

It's like it's being coordinated by some unseen hand, but being made to look random."

"I've never been one to believe in chance," Princess told him.

"Me neither," Damian agreed. "Recall Nicanor. He's our must trusted field. Have him stand too, and start gathering our men. Get big, but do it quietly. Whomever our unseen enemy or enemies are, we don't want to alert them."

"Consider it done," Princess told him. "Also, I'll send Angela to the east." Dante can always count on his wife to do a good job."

Damian nodded. "Yes, and have our boys in Virginia and the Carolinas start recruiting in secret. Something tells me that we're going to need to get a lot of soldiers up north in a hurry. Damn! I thought I was finished with this shit! Can you believe it? The Reigns family is about to fight another major war."

"Last time you fought, you had Dante by your side," Princess told him. "This time, you'll have me."

The problem with you and Dante is that you both think too much. Dante is good, and he's ruthless, but he's not merciless. With me by your side, this'll be the last war. They'll never again what to challenge the Reigns family. I promise you that."

"And how can you be so sure of that?"

"Because, dead men can't make war." Princess spun on her heels and headed for the door. "I'm going to bury them all.

Chapter Eight

Dajon Reigns was an extremely successful attorney in his own right. It was through his own diligence, hard work, and determination to succeed, that he had risen so far, so fast. He was an alumnus of Harvard University and Harvard Law, as well as a former law clerk for the Honorable Gideon Reigns, senior judge, U.S. Eleventh Court of Appeals. The fact that Judge Reigns was his uncle, meant less to prospective employers, than the fact that he graduated first in his class at Harvard Law. Dajon had been born and bred for success.

Dajon had decided long ago that Dante was evil, and he knew that eventually, he and his brother would have little in common. He had a higher opinion of Damian, while Princess, his only sister, brought feelings of mixed emotions. He loved his older sister more than he loved his brothers, but his relationship with her was bittersweet at best. He was proud of her for graduating from college near the top of her class, but disappointment descended like a thick New Hampshire fog after she took over their family's businesses, and immersed the family into the miasmic activities of the criminal underworld. Nevertheless, he had fond memories of Princess, and counted those memories among the treasure trove of the many blessings that had been bestowed upon him. He remembered fondly the horseback rides, the trips to the movies, the trips to the parks, and the trips down the river in the old rickety canoe that they kept next to the equally rickety old dock on their grandparent's farm. He remembered being by his sister's side, growing, learning, and experiencing. *How could a girl so wonderful, turn out to be such an evil woman.*

Dajon's relationship with his younger brother Darius, was typical of siblings born so far apart. He gave him money and advice, and allowed his younger brother to come over on the weekends and relax. There was love, and there was hope, the promise of a sibling whose life he could influence. He was determined not to allow Darius to fall into the life that his other siblings chose for themselves. It was a mission that he considered to be nearly divine, to allow one less monster to walk this earth.

Dajon's relationship with Damian was similar to his relationship with his sister. He looked up to Damian, the brother who could do anything, the brother who always won, the brother who always came in first. Football, basketball, softball, no matter what, Damian's team was going to win. When he was younger, Damian was like a god to him. Damian could do anything, and he made everyone around him believe that anything was possible. If there ever was an African-American golden boy, Damian was it. Damian, the one who had everything going for him, the one who could have done anything with his life, who could have written his own ticket, chose a life of destruction instead. Dajon wondered if anyone else on the planet knew what it felt like, to have their hero, suddenly turn and join the dark side.

"You seem distracted," Daissala Reigns told him, while caressing his face. "What's the matter?"

Dajon shook his head. "Nothing." He took her hand, lifted it to his lips, and kissed it gently.

"I'm here if you want to talk," she told him softly.

Dajon nodded; he knew that nothing more needed to

be said. He knew that she would be there for him, like she always was, like she always would be. He counted his wife among the greatest of blessings that God had bestowed upon him.

Dr. Daissala Malaika Reigns was the sister to international supermodel, Illyassa Malaika, and daughter to Chief Immanuel Hillel Malaika, who was Minister of Intelligence, and Minister of the Secret State Security Service for the Federal Democratic Republic of Ethiopia, and a member of the Council of Ministers. Daissala was also a graduate of Oxford University, a prominent professor of ancient civilizations at one of the most prestigious small liberal arts colleges in the nation, and a direct descendent of one of the most prominent royal houses in the history of the world, the royal house of Abyssinia.

While not as strikingly beautiful as her famous sister, Daissala had a much more regal beauty about her. Her intelligence gave her beauty a dignity and an elegance that made it appear as though she were born to rule. Had she lived in another time, and another place, in all probability, she would have ruled. She had the Wisdom of Solomon inside of her, and the beauty of Sheba on the outside.

"Your mother called this morning," Daissala told him. "She said that she wants the children this weekend."

Dajon shrugged. "Fine by me."

"We get to go to Grandma's house?" D.J. inquired loudly from the backseat.

"Yes, sweetheart," Daissala responded in her distinctly British accent. "You and your sister will have your grandmother to yourselves for the entire weekend."

"Grandma lets me stay up late and eat ice cream," D.J. confessed.

"Does she?" Dajon inquired with a raised eyebrow. "Well, we'll have to see about that."

"Sweetheart, watch this car in front of us; it's slowing down considerably," Daisalla told him.

The black Chevrolet Suburban with dark-tinted

windows in front of Dajon's burgundy Bentley Flying Spur crawled to a stop. Dajon pounded on his car's horn.

"Can you pick up the pace, buddy?" Dajon shouted. "We're on the highway for Pete's sake!"

Dajon wasn't part of his brother's world. But a quick glance in his rearview mirror confirmed his suspicions. His family was in danger. It was a hit.

"Sweetie, get down!" Dajon shouted.

Dajon slammed on his breaks, causing the vehicles along side him to pass him up in order to create a gap large enough for his Flying Spur to squeeze through. He sliced through the gap and slammed his foot against the accelerator. It took only seconds for the big 552-horsepower W-12 to propel the sleek sedan to triple-digit speeds.

"Dajon, what's going on?" Daisalla asked nervously.

"The black trucks; they were trying to box us in!"

Daisalla peered over her shoulder at the trucks. "Are you sure?"

"I don't know!" Dajon shouted. "But it didn't look right."

"Dajon, why us?" Daisalla cried out. "We have nothing to do with your family!"

"I know sweetie; I know," Dajon said reassuringly. "Hopefully, it's just me being overly suspicious."

"No, Dajon!" Daisalla told him. "You're right. They're chasing us!"

"Oh, God! Oh my God!" Dajon maneuvered his Bentley around traffic, trying to escape their pursuers. "Just stay down!"

The Bentley raced up the highway, swerving around cars, until it found itself in a position where it could no longer maneuver. Traffic had become deadlocked.

"Call the police, honey!" Dajon shouted. "Use your cell phone and call the police."

Daisalla fumbled through her Louis Vuitton handbag, clumsily searching for her phone. "They're coming!" she screamed. "The men in the trucks are coming!"

"Fuck this shit!" Dajon shouted. He slammed his foot on the gas peddle, and turned his steering wheel to the side. The Bentley slammed into the car creeping along next to them, causing that car to stop, thus creating a narrow seam. Again, Dajon took what was given. He raced through the gap, slamming into the front of another car in the next lane, shearing off that car's front end. This opened up a narrow path to the guardrail, and just beyond that, to a steep grassy slope leading down to the access road. Dajon took it.

The smashed up Bentley barreled through the steel guardrail, dove nose first down the steep escarpment, bouncing, and shearing off additional pieces of its badly damaged front end.

"Hold on tight!" Dajon shouted.

The Bentley barreled down the slope and slammed into the undercarriage of an eighteen-wheeler that was stopped at a nearby intersection. The sound of exploding air bags pierced the cabin, only to be followed by the sound of steel rain penetrating the rooftop of the car. The last sound Dajon remembered, was the distinctive pinging sound of multiple objects striking his vehicle. The sound reminded him of the noise one hears when traveling over a gravel road, or even more so, of the sound one hears when their tires are slinging clumps of mud against the wheel wells, after having traveled over a deep muddy road. The pitter-patter of the bullets striking the top of his car, helped him slip off into a subconscious state.

Damian wiped the sweat from his forehead, and lifted his cell phone from a nearby weight bench. "Hello?"

"Damian, it's Princess; Dajon got hit."

"Hit?" Damian rose from the weight bench upon which he had been seated. "What do you mean, hit?"

"Someone ran him off the highway, and gunned him down," Princess told him. "D.J. and Daisalla were with him."

"Oh, my God!" Damian fell back down onto the bench. "Are they alright?"

"D.J.'s in a coma," Princess said softly. "He's probably not going to make it through the night."

"No! No! Noooo!" Damian let out an ear-piercing scream.

"Damian, calm down."

"And Ladybug?"

"Our niece wasn't with them." Princess told him. "They were on their way to pick her up from a friend's house."

"Oh my God, Damian gasped.

"Damian," Princess whispered. "Daisalla's dead."

Damian threw his phone against the wall and fell to the floor, where he curled into a ball, and cried like child.

Dajon awoke to find himself lying inside an intensive care unit with his head and body broken and bandaged, surrounded by doctors and nurses, and family and friends.

"D.J.?" Dajon whispered in low, hoarse tone. "Where's D.J.?"

Emory Reigns patted her son's hand. "Just get some rest, sweetie. The doctors are taking care of D.J."

Dajon shook his head. "D.J.," he whispered.

"Sweetheart, D.J.'s fine," Emory reassured her son. "You need to rest, take care of yourself, and get better. D.J.'s going to need you to be strong."

Dajon raised himself up.

Emory placed her hand on his chest. "No, no, no, lie down, baby. You can't sit up right now."

Dajon shook his head. "No, my family. Where's my family? Daisalla? Where's Daisalla?"

Tears flowed down Emory's cheeks.

Princess clasped her brother's hand. "Daisalla didn't make it."

Dajon fell back into the bed, and his mouth fell open. Although silence permeated the room, it was obvious to all who were present that he was screaming.

Dajon gasped for air. "Noooooooooo!"

Emory rose quickly from her chair next to her son's bedside, and embraced him tightly.

"Noooooooo!" Dajon shouted. "Noooooo! Why me, God? Why me? Why do this to my family; why us? No, don't take Daisalla; take me instead. Take me!"

A dark-suited man stuck his head through the hospital door, and nodded at Princess. She returned his nod, and then turned toward her mother.

"Are you okay?" Princess asked.

Emory nodded. "Everything's going to be okay. We just have to turn to the Lord, and put all of our faith in him, and trust in his plan for us."

Princess nodded, rose, and slowly exited the room.

The hospital corridor was lined with hulking dark-suited bodyguards, who stood like stoic centurions guarding their emperor's palace. Princess didn't recognize them, they were hired hands brought from out of town. This meant that Damian was either in his trust no one mode or that he had beefed up the San Antonio contingent of his army, she thought to herself. On second thought, considering what had just taken place, it was probably a combination of both.

Princess rounded the hospital corridor, just behind her two hulking escorts. Soon, they rounded another corner, where she walked through the double doors that were being held open for her, and entered the small hospital chapel. She could see her brother on his knees in front of the altar, praying. The chapel was teeming with bodyguards.

Princess genuflected, made the sign of the cross, kissed her fingers, and then seated herself in the rear of the chapel. She watched as another bodyguard approached her brother, whispered into his ear, and then backed away. Everyone knew their places, and everyone was doing their duties that evening with a proficiency and silent professionalism that was frightening. The coming storm could be felt.

Damian rose from the floor, and turned toward his

sister. He was quickly flanked by four bodyguards, who walked lock in step with their master. His praetorian guards were taking no chances. If anyone even looked suspicious tonight, the women in their family would be dusting off their black dresses.

Damian approached his sister, who slid over so that he could join her, which he did.

"What do we know?" Damian asked.

"Nothing," Princess told him softly. "We have absolutely nothing."

"I can't believe that four SUVs filled with hit men, could sneak into this town, and we didn't know about it," Damian said angrily. "This isn't some backwater town a thousand miles away that we took over from someone else; this is our headquarters; this is where we live. And these assassins were allowed to come into our home? They were allowed to just walk into where we live, and not just kill our soldiers, but actually kill Reigns family members?"

"Damian, calm down," Princess told him.

"No, I will not calm down," he said forcefully. "This is a monumental failure in intelligence."

"Dante isn't here right now," Princess retorted. "You know that he usually keeps everyone sharp on those types of things."

"Karl is my chief of intelligence," Damian told her. "Kill him. Kill him right now; kill him tonight. I don't want Karl to live to see Letterman. I want him dead, and if anyone gets in the way, I want them dead too!"

"I'll take care of it personally," Princess told him.

"How's Dajon?" Damian asked. "Does he know about Daisalla yet?"

Princess nodded. "He'll make it through; he's tough. Mom's in there with him right now."

"Does Dante know?" Damian asked.

"I imagine that Angela's gotten in touch with him by now. Angela tells him everything," Princess said. "I'll get a message to the prison chaplain to have him call home. I'm

74

sure the Feds know what just took place. They may have told him already."

"Do we have any people inside?" Damian asked.

"A couple of guys," Princess answered. "But none in isolation, that's where they're keeping him."

"Any guards on the payroll?" Damian asked. "If not, get some. And get some men inside to watch Dante's back. Hire some guys already on the inside, and send some more guys inside also."

Princess nodded.

"So, no idea who could have done this?" Damian asked again. "Commission? Feds? Local cops? El Jeffe? The Old Ones? Everyone knows that Dajon isn't part of our business; so who would try to take him out, and why? I mean, it's obvious that they were sending a message, but what message would that send? Why hit him, and not you or even me, for that matter? Why not hit Angela or Kevin or Nicanora? After all, Nicanora's our most trusted field commander. And Kevin's our cousin and why now? What triggered this attack now? No one has ever bothered Dajon before, because he didn't matter, so what's changed?"

"Could it be a message letting us know that the gloves are off?" Princess asked.

"They could have done that in any number of ways; why hit someone who isn't involved in the business?" Damian asked rhetorically. "Why waste the initiative, the element of surprise, a well-planned operation, on someone who doesn't give orders? I mean, it's not a secret that Dajon despises the family business."

"Who has the muscle, and the spine to pull off an attack like this?" Princess posed.

"Okay, by process of elimination," Damian suggested. Feds would have hit me or Dante, not Dajon, same with the local cops. El Jeffe wants me to remain on the Commission. It could be a message from him. But it would make more sense for him to take you out, than to send a message like that. Besides, from what I know, El Jeffe doesn't send messages. He just goes for the kill."

"The remainder of the Commission?" Princess asked.

Damian shook his head. "Not the muscle, nor the balls."

"Then that leaves us with the one group, and those sons of bitches love to send messages," Princess told him.

Damian exhaled. "Looks that way." Damian turned and stared at the large wooden crucifix mounted on the wall behind the altar. "We don't have the muscle to take on the Old Ones. Not alone, not without the rest of the Commission. Put some ears in the streets, and see if any other members have been hit or sent messages."

Princess nodded.

"And start recruiting," Damian ordered. Get big, and get big fast. If those son of bitches want a war, we'll give them one."

Princess rose from the pew. Damian clasped her arms.

"Make no mistake about what I'm ordering. I want blood to flow. They hit us; I want you to hit them back. I want them to understand my message, and I want them to understand it loud and clear. We want to move our operations away from illegitimate enterprises, to legal ones. We swim around acting peaceful, and so they thought that we were Flipper. Show them that we're Jaws. Show those garlic-loving, olive oil-sipping motherfuckers that we're the most feared predator in this fucking ocean. I want blood to flow like a fucking river. I want so much blood to run, that we can pull out the floats and have a god-damned river parade. I was wrong about what I said about killing, the other day. Sometimes, peace can only be found on the other side of war. We'll walk through a pile of their corpses to obtain that peace. That's my word; that's my order." Damian rose, lifted his hand, and slapped his sister across her cheek. "And that's so you'll remember it."

Chapter Nine

The Towers at Twin Sisters were said to be the most luxurious towers in the South, even more luxurious than the dozens of half-billion dollar beachfront buildings scattered up and down the Florida coastline. The Towers, as they were known to insiders, were more decadent than most of their Swiss counterparts, and could have easily blended in with their sister units scattered amid the majestic Alps.

The Towers were two Texas-size, one-hundred story glass sculptures, whose amenities and services would shame every luxury apartment and resort from Bali to Zurich. The Towers overlooked the Texas Hill country, and provided its residences with breathtaking views of two massive oak-covered peaks known as the Twin Sisters. The sun set between the hilltops, blessing all those fortunate enough to be within visual range, with a sight that was at once both mystical, and magical. It was a sight that was reminiscent of the ancient sun, coming to rest between the two great pyramids. A view that was awe-inspiring, halting, and almost religious.

The Towers themselves were designed by none other than the internationally renowned architect I.M. Pei. They were a futuristic design, a striking combination of glass and steel, of mirror and chrome, of crystal and marble. The

Towers were part of a larger hill country community, a community that included not only a Jack Nicklaus signature designed golf course, but also a world-renowned country club, the Clubs at Cordillera.

The Clubs at Cordillera encompassed not only a legendary golf club, but a rod and gun club, an elite social club, and a swim and tennis club. It also boasted of a concierge service, an on call masseuse, a world class pro shop, three highly rated restaurants, several upscale clothiers, and dozens upon dozens of other amenities that the rich and famous had become accustomed to. However, the community's most important feature was its security.

The nine-thousand-acre community was totally gated, with every square inch of the community covered by a monitored security camera. Infrared beams crisscrossed the uninhabited areas of the community, along with buried pressure sensors, and hidden trip wires, to alert security of any unwanted penetration. Armed security guards patrolled the community in trucks, while some patrolled on horseback, and others in golf carts and four-wheel all-terrain vehicles. These patrols were supplemented by armed foot patrols. To say that this community was impenetrable would be an understatement. There had never been a successful security breach and the community brochures stated that such a breach was impossible. The brochures also stated that if such a breach were to occur, its own private community response team of ex-Navy Seals, ex-Army Green Berets, ex-FBI Hostage Rescue teams, ex-Army Delta forces, and ex-SWAT team members, would contain it in a matter of moments.

The residents paid highly for this elite security and peace of mind, as their community association dues were higher than most people's mortgages. It was because of this tight community security that Karl, Damian's head of security, made the neighborhood his home. He chose to reside in the most secured area, of this highly secured community. He lived high above most of the other residences, a place where additional security checks, palm scanners, elevator cameras, and voice analyzers were used. He lived in an area where the residents were known as untouchables, and where security was said to be tighter than the White House. He lived on the ninetieth floor.

Princess sat down on the corner of the bed and shook Karl's shoulder gently until he woke. Karl rolled over in his bed to find Princess smiling at him, and several dark-suited men standing around his bedroom.

"What?" Karl stuttered and rubbed his sleepy eyes. "How? How did you get in here?"

"How, Karl, you'll find, is a much less important question, than why?" Princess told him.

Karl shook his head. "Is there an emergency, or something?"

"No, we're just here to talk about intelligence," Princess told him.

"What's happening now?" Karl asked. He sat up in his bed.

"Well, for one, my sister-in-law is dead, and my nephew's in the hospital dying," Princess told him.

Karl nodded. "Yeah, I heard about the hit on Dajon. I'm sorry about your sister in law and about D.J. I promise, we'll find out who's responsible for this, and we'll get the bastards."

"We already know who's responsible, Karl," Princess told him.

"You do?" Karl asked. "Who?"

"You," Princess told him coldly. "You're responsible."

"Me?"

"You're the family's head of security," Princess reminded him. "So, ultimately, it's your fault."

"Me?" Karl exclaimed. "Princess, you guys can't put this one on me. I've done nothing but a stand-up job for this family ever since I took over."

"Then stand up," Princess told him.

"My glasses," Karl rolled over, sliding his hand back

beneath his pillow. "Let me just get my glasses."

Princess smiled.

Karl rolled back over quickly, throwing the pillow off, and revealing a Glock semiautomatic handgun. One of Princess's bodyguards knocked the weapon away, while another struck Karl in the back of his head with his own weapon.

"Ahhhh!" Karl clutched the back of his head and fell back onto the bed.

"C'mon, Karl?" Princess smiled. "The old pistol under the pillow trick? I thought that went out of vogue with those old Western movies."

"Princess, I swear." Karl stuttered.

"You swear what?" she interrupted. "That you didn't just try to kill me? Or that you'll do better next time? Or that if I just give you one little chance, you'll make it all up to me? Which one, Karl?"

Princess threw her head back in laughter.

"My family," he whispered. "Please, I have a family."

"I know, Karl," Princess replied. "I know all about your family. For instance, I know that your wife and kids aren't here at the moment, which is good. Good thing you two had that argument, and she ran to her mother's house for the weekend."

Karl lowered his head. He couldn't believe how Princess knew everything, even personal details about his life.

"You know what, Karl?" Princess told him, while patting him on his shoulder. "You can look at it this way. That bitch is going to feel miserable for the rest of her life for this. In the back of her head, she's always going to wonder if things would have been different if she were home. If she could have somehow miraculously saved you. It's the ultimate payback on your part, Karl. You have a chance to make her crazy for the rest of her life."

"I want my family to get the benefits promised to me when I went to work for you," Karl told her. "I want my family taken care of. I served you loyally."

Princess nodded. "I know, Karl. You did. You just fucked up this one time. And really, under any other circumstances, you would have just been given a slap on the wrist. But Damian, he's pissed. You should have seen him, Karl. He was like the old Damian, back during the first war. He was ruthless, and calculating, and angry. I love him when he's like that. His anger brings clarity to his thoughts, and it gives us all a sense of purpose. He's going to rain fire down on everyone responsible for what happened to Dajon's family. It's going to be a good war, Karl; sorry you're going to miss it."

Karl turned and lifted his glass of water from his nightstand, and raised it in a toast. "To the old days."

Princess nodded. "To the old days."

"Karl, let me assure you, your children will be taken care of, their tuition will be paid all their way through college, and your mortgage will be paid off, as will all of your other bills. Your wife and children will want for nothing."

Karl nodded and smiled. "Everything I've worked for my whole life will be accomplished with one single bullet." Karl lowered his head and laughed. "Funny, you go through life working hard, trying to take care of your family, worried about health insurance, college tuition, braces, and all of the other bullshit that life throws at you, then suddenly, just like that, with the stroke of a bullet, everything's taken care of. Must be nice to play God, huh?"

"My, my, my, we're getting philosophical in our sunset minutes, aren't we?" Princess told him.

"You people, with all of your god-damned money, you think your money's going to make everything okay," Karl said angrily. "You think that just because you have money, you have the right to kill people. Is your money going to teach my kid how to ride a bike? Huh? Is your money going to teach my son how to throw a football or be there to scare away the purple monster under my daughter's bed?"

"You failed your children, not us," Princess replied.

81

"We paid you a lot of money, money that you used to give them a good life. You took the money, but you forgot about your job. Doing your job the right way, is what was supposed to keep you in their lives. You failed my nephew, my brother, and my sister-in-law, and so you failed your children as well. I have to bury a sister-in-law, and more likely than not, I have to bury my ten-year-old nephew. My brother has to bury his life partner, and he has to bury his child. My niece has to bury her mommy, and she has to bury her brother. Have you ever had to explain heaven and God to an eight-year-old?" Princess stepped in closer and stood nose to nose with Karl. "Don't you ever, try to get self-righteous with me, you son of a bitch! My blood is dead because you fucked up. So now, you have to pay for that fuckup, Karl."

"Don't pay off the mortgage on this place," Karl told her. "Get my family out of this, this fucking neighborhood. The security's a joke!"

"No, actually, the security here's quite good," Princess told him.

Karl lifted his arms into the air and smiled. "Oh yeah, then where the hell is it?"

"It's dead, Karl," Princess said softly. "The security's dead, all of them. From the fat old man at the front gate, to the young college kids sitting in the office watching the monitors; they're all dead."

Karl's mouth fell open.

"We're ninety stories up," Princess told her men. She turned toward Karl. "We're going to have a little race. We're going to see who can get to the first floor first. If you beat me, I'll let you go."

Princess's hulking bodyguards grabbed Karl and lifted him into the air.

"No! Princess, don't do this!" Karl shouted while struggling.

Princess turned, strutted out of Karl's apartment, and headed for the elevator. She could hear Karl's shouts as her men carried him out onto the balcony, and then pitched him over the railing. In the elevator, Princess turned toward one of her henchmen.

"Damn, he beat me."

The Clubs at Great Sharks Bay were near the top among the elite pantheon of golf clubs. International players and procircuit illuminati were dying to play the course, but were forced to wait for tee times behind the great captains of industry. One had to own, a major international corporation to avoid having to wait. And even those owners of lesser corporations had to get in line behind the major movers and shakers. The chair of General Motors could bump the chair of Tyco, and the chair of AOL Time Warner, could easily bump the chair of Atlantic Bell. The pecking order was solid, and the hierarchy set; breaches of etiquette were dealt with swiftly.

The club itself was nestled amid a massive grove of two-hundred year old pecan trees, and set on a bluff overlooking a heavily shark-infested inlet bordering the Atlantic Ocean. It was rumored that the pecan trees were planted by none other than Thomas Jefferson himself, and that the clubhouse had once served as lodging for none other than the great lieutenant general Charles Cornwallis during the Revolutionary War. The history that ran through the grounds of the club was legendary.

Don Teodosio Pancrazio inhaled deeply, taking in the sweet smell of pines, pecans, and lemons from a nearby grove. The air was perfect today. It was what he loved to call golf weather. He could see for miles in all directions, and the signature hole looked as though it were designed by the gods.

The sixteenth hole was nestled into a green that was cut between two rock waterfalls, on a peninsula that jutted out into the shark infested inlet. On a clear day such as this, one could see fins protruding through the waters, searching for unsuspecting seagulls and for the schools of fish that made the area a prime fishing ground. The danger of the waters just beyond the peninsula gave the hole a majestic feel, as though one were tempting the gods by playing it. The Don loved the idea that death was just a fifty-foot drop from the escarpment. It made him feel invigorated.

The clubs was private, and extremely restricted. Members only were allowed through the manned wrought iron gates, and security was considered to be airtight. It was for these reasons that the good Don felt little need for an extensive security detail, and brought with him only one bodyguard, who also doubled as his caddy. Who needed a trail of lackeys following them around, and getting in the way of such a pristine course, and heavenly golf experience? Even he, a major investor in the club, had to call at least twenty-four hours in advance, just to get tee time. No, such moments were not to be spoiled by suited buffoons wearing microphones and earpieces. Moments like these were to be treasured.

Don Pancrazio climbed out of his golf cart, and slowly made his way down the greens to his favorite hole, the sixteenth. It was a hole that was meant to be walked, meant to be savored, not driven through on some little plastic cart. Anyone who did so, did not understand the beauty of the hole, and obviously lacked a passion for the game. Such a person should be banished from clubs such as Great Shark, and be sent to play on local municipal courses, the Don thought to himself. If God golfed, this surely had to be his favored course.

The Don removed the sun cap he wore on his head, and wiped the sweat from his brow. The weather was beautiful, but slightly humid for this time of the year. It had less to do with the slight humidity, than with the sixty-five years of wear and tear on his body, he thought to himself. He would have to take it easy on himself for the rest of the week. No heart attack would come and steal him away like a thief in the night.

The Don approached the sixteenth hole, and extended his arm toward his bodyguard.

Deadly Reigns II, Teri Woods Publishing

"Fabrizio, putter."

Fabrizio, the Don's bodyguard and favorite nephew, quickly produced the correct club, and placed it his hand. And then, Fabrizio fell dead.

The Don had heard the whiz of the bullet fly through the air, but first had dismissed it as being nothing more than the buzz of a large insect. How could anyone possibly sneak a weapon in past security? None of it made sense, and the only thing that brought a grim reality to this truth, was the rapidly expanding stain spreading across Fabrizio's back. Slowly, the Don fell to his knees and pulled his bodyguard's head into his lap.

"Fabrizio," The Don called to his helpers, but there was no one around whom the Don could summon for help. "My dear Fabrizio!"

From behind the waterfalls that flanked the hole, came Princess, and several of her men. The Don shook his head and then lowered it. Princess approached.

"Don Pancrazio, it's a wonderful day for golf; is it not?" Princess asked with a smile.

"You." The Don spat at her feet. "I know you. I know who you are! You've drawn Pancrazio blood! You'll know suffering worse than a thousand deaths!"

"Don, I've done nothing that you and your cronies haven't done," Princess replied. "You drew first blood."

"What? What are you talking about?" The Don asked. "This is madness! You've murdered my sister's son! You've gone mad!"

"You murdered my sister-in-law, and you murdered my brother's son!" Princess told him.

"Murdered?" The Don rose. "I've murdered no one! I've ordered the murder of no one!"

"Don Pancrazio, it's obvious that it was the Old Ones who ordered the death of my innocent brother and his family," Princess told him. "Who else."

The Don interrupted. "What reason would we have to kill a nobody? We're businessmen, not murderers! We make business decisions based on reason, not on emotions! Kill you, yes! Kill your brothers, yes! Kill someone who makes absolutely no decisions whatsoever, never!"

"Don Pancrazio, the Old Ones have a problem with my family; what is it?" Princess asked.

"You ask now, after this?" The Don waved his hand over his nephew's body. "Our problem with your family is this!"

"You've wanted war with the Reigns family for several months now, long before this," Princess told him.

"We didn't assassinate your family!" Don Pancrazio told her.

"Don Pancrazio, I took the red-eye here so that I could kill you," Princess replied. "I'm very tired, very sleepy, and my mind's not in a fully functioning mode. I want to find out what exactly you know."

The Don spat on the ground. "I will never sell out my family. I'm no stool pigeon."

Princess pointed toward the distant sky. "That helicopter over there is ours. What I propose, is that we tie your arms to it, have it hover just over this inlet full of great white sharks, and lower you into the water so that the sharks can eat your old wrinkled ass, bit by greasy bit. Perhaps after they've eaten the lower half of your body, you'll be ready to talk."

The Don reached into his pocket, removed his pocket knife, and unfolded the blade. "I'll never give you one goddamned thing! May my brothers leave your corpse rotting in that miserable Texas desert from which you come!"

The Don took his pocket knife and sliced his wrist deeply. Blood shot over Princess and her men, causing them to wince. The Don then took the blade of the knife, and jabbed it into his neck. He was dead when he hit the ground.

Princess wiped the Don's blood off her face and then turned to her men. "That gentlemen, is old school. They don't make 'em like that anymore. You should all take a lesson from the good Don. Rather than face torture, and the possibility of giving up some information, the Don took his own life, and what he knew, to the grave." Princess clapped her hands. "Bravo, Don Pancrazio, bravo!"

One of Princesses's men stepped forward. "What should we do with the bodies?"

"Get them out of the grass, place them in the golf cart, and then call and alert the club staff," Princess told them.

"How about we just dump the bastard off the cliff and feed the sharks?" one of her men suggested.

"No, the Don was a soldier to the end," Princess told them. "He should be allowed to receive a soldier's burial. Treat his body with respect, gentlemen. He's among the last of a dying breed. A fucking Mafioso who kept his mouth shut."

Chapter Ten

Damian walked to the corner of the office and peered out the window into the city. He hated meetings, and he hated legal meetings even more so. Today, he had two of them scheduled. The first meeting, the one in which he was currently engaged, was with his chief legal adviser and sometimes lover, Cherin King, and also included his chief criminal attorney, the highly esteemed barrister, Adrian Andrews. After this meeting, he was scheduled to meet with his chief business attorney, Thomas Voight, and The United States Senator from Texas, Cameron Dusty Marshall.

"Damian, are you okay?" Cherin asked.

Damian turned away from the window, and refocused his attention to the task at hand. "Yes, I'm fine. Let's continue."

"Damian, they're not playing ball on this one," Adrian told him. "I think the feds are calling the shots on this one."

"Adrian, murder's a state charge, not a federal one," Damian replied. "Is there any way to bypass them, and use our contacts at the state level to handle this?"

Adrian shook his head. "Don't think so. The feds' hands are on this one real heavy. They want a Reigns conviction, anyway that they can get it. Whether in federal court, state court, hell, they'll take a conviction in The People's Court if they could get it. Damian, they've been given an opportunity, and they're pressing this to the fullest."

"So what are you saying, Adrian?" Damian exhaled. "Are you saying that this thing's actually going to go to trial?"

Adrian shook his head. "That's too early to call. All I'm saying is, the feds have their hands all over your brother's case, and they're pulling out all the stops for a conviction. They're giving the state everything it needs to win, and they're making sure that everything's played by the book procedurally."

"So, we have to let this thing play out?" Damian asked.

"No, we still have more motions to file," Adrian told him. "They have to turn over a couple of the hospital tapes that they say places your brother at the hospital at the time of the doctor's murder. They'll have to turn over everything they got at the evidentiary hearing, and we'll have a shot at a dismissal if the evidence isn't up to snuff. If the feds are leaning on the judge, it'll be tough to get it. Maybe that's where we can get our people to turn up the heat on the judge. He'll have the case before him, and enough of a reason to dismiss. He may ruin his chances of ever becoming a federal judge, but then again, he may not want to become a federal judge. There're just too many variables at play here."

"Adrian, I need Dante out of prison, and I need him out yesterday," Damian announced. "Do whatever you have to do to make that happen, but just make sure that it happens."

"Is their any way we can get another bail hearing?" Cherin asked.

"The motion's already been filed. We'll see if we can get him released into someone's custody. It's a murder charge, so I don't think we'll have much success. We're going to try everything possible."

Damian turned away from them, and massaged his temples. "I need him out. Too much is happening too fast, and from too many directions. I need my brother."

Adrian rose from his seat at the conference table. "Damian, we'll get him out. We'll do everything in our power to make it happen."

"No, I want you to do everything in my power, to get him out. Use whatever contacts you need; use whatever money and resources you need; you have carte blanche. Just return my brother to me."

Adrian nodded, gathered his briefcase, and headed for the door to the conference room. He stopped and turned back toward Damian. "You want me to send the others in?"

"Yes, please. And Adrian, thank you for everything. I know that you and your team are working diligently to secure my brother's release."

Adrian nodded, and walked out.

"Damian, are you okay?" Cherin asked.

"Just these headaches; they're back again." Damian exhaled, and turned toward her. "I'm so stressed out. This morning, I wanted a cup of coffee so bad, I thought of buying the Starbucks franchise."

"Damian, just relax. Take care of things, one at a time. Don't try to deal with too many things at once."

"And what if things are coming at you in droves?" Damian asked. "I can't just wave my hand and ask everyone to politely take turns."

"I'm going to send my masseuse over to your house tonight," Cherin told him. "I want you to relax and take it easy. And I'm canceling all of your appointments for tomorrow. You're no good to anyone like this."

Damian smiled at her, and then waved his hand toward Thomas Voight, his chief business attorney, who was just entering the room.

"Tommy, how was your flight?" Damian asked. He embraced Thomas tightly, and then clasped his hand and shook it firmly. "Hope that everything went well."

Thomas pulled one of the massive leather conference chairs from beneath the equally massive mahogany conference table, and seated himself.

"Damian, I wish I had some good news for you, buddy. Unfortunately, I don't."

Damian took the seat next to Thomas. "What were you able to find out?"

Thomas pulled off his small Armani-framed glasses from his face and shook his head.

"Not good, my friend. You're the victim of a well-organized, well-orchestrated, high-level conspiracy. And this conspiracy, involves some very, very powerful people."

Damian turned his head toward the table and lowered it.

"Who?"

"At least four senators," Thomas answered. "Inuit out of New Mexico, Benedetta from New Jersey, Peche from New York, and Amato out of Nevada."

"Inuit? What's New Mexico have to do with this? The others I can understand, but Inuit?"

"Two things," Thomas explained, shifting in his seat and clearing his throat. "One, he's still pissed about someone killing Chacho Hernandez. I suppose Chacho was greasing his palms. And two, and this one is probably the most important reason, is that all of the casinos are in collusion with one another."

Damian leaned back in his chair and exhaled forcibly.

"Damian, my people are tracking down the ownership of several different casinos, ranging from New Jersey to New Mexico, and from Nevada to Mississippi. These things have shell corporations on top of shell corporations. They go offshore, with ownership in the Caribbean and Europe, and come back onshore, and then go offshore again. They all have false walls, to make it appear as though one has finally ascertained the enterprise's final ownership, but once we get through those walls, a line of shell companies turn up again. This is going to be interesting to see, and everything's too early to be definitive, but I can tell you this. Just by examining the way these casinos' shell companies are set up, it tells me that they either all using the same money launderers and tax attorneys or that their ownership has more in common than appears on the surface."

Damian rose from his seat and again walked to the window and peered out over the city. "Do you realize what you're saying, Tommy?"

Thomas nodded solemnly.

Damian exhaled. "One group of people may control every casino in this country, with the exception of the ones that the Commission controls. This same group of people control at least four U.S. senators, and enough government officials to block the Justice Departments approval of Bio One's last three acquisitions, as well as to block the Food and Drug Administration's approval of our request to bring our drugs to market."

Damian turned toward Thomas. "If we don't get approval for those last acquisitions, my company is through. If we don't get FDA approval to sell our pharmaceuticals, then Bio One is finished. I've sold off all of my family's assets, and placed every penny that we own, into Bio One. If Bio One fails, then my family is bankrupt. If my family goes bankrupt, we all die. Our enemies will wipe us off the face of this earth so fast, that we won't have time for our lives to even flash before our eyes. Tommy, the survival of my family, hangs in the balance."

Cherin fell back into one of the conference chairs. "We're all dead," she whispered.

"Strings are being pulled from somewhere," Damian said softly. "Someone's trying to destroy my family."

"Or take Bio One away," Thomas suggested. "Damian, I told you that we would be too exposed. I warned you that you were risking everything, by placing all of your assets into one company."

"Tommy, it was a good risk, as long as everyone played by the rules. We were out of the illegal stuff! No one had any reason to go after us. Hell, who has the power to control the Justice Department, the FDA, and that many senators? Who and for what reason? Bio One is not publicly held!" Damian shouted, banging his hand on the table. "They couldn't perform a hostile takeover if they wanted to!"

"Damian, calm down," Cherin told him.

"I will not calm down!" Damian shouted. "We must complete those mergers! Without those pharmaceutical companies, Bio One cannot exist! My family cannot exist!"

"Damian, we're working on it!" Cherin told him forcefully. "Thomas is on it. He has a very capable team of lawyers, and they're all working on it."

"Call in all our favors," Damian ordered. "Do whatever it takes to get this merger out of committee, through antitrust approval at Justice, and then get those pharmaceuticals approved by the FDA. That's your team's only assignment right now."

"You want us to stop our dig on the ownership of the casinos?" Thomas asked.

"No. In fact, get more lawyers on it. Hire more attorneys, and more investigators. You can use my people to help with the footwork. I'll have all our states alerted, and they'll give you whatever you need in manpower and resources. Track them down as fast as you can. I'll have my sister track down the benefactors of our honorable senators."

"Can we somehow influence these senators and their colleagues to switch sides?" Cherin posed.

Thomas shook his head. "I'm not sure. Usually, they're so far in with the first guy, that they're scared to change loyalties for fear that the guy they betrayed, will burn them too."

"Buy some more senators," Damian commanded. "Buy more influence at Justice, at Commerce, and everywhere that we need to. Hell, you can even buy the damn college interns if you think it'll help."

Thomas nodded and gathered his materials. "Damian, don't worry; we'll get through this."

"Why does everyone keep telling me that?" Damian asked in frustration.

"You have to start thinking about diversifying,"

Thomas told him.

Damian clapped his hands and rubbed them together. "Thanks, guys. I'm through with meetings for now. I have a guest waiting for me in my private study. Cherin, I'll be in touch. Tommy, keep me posted."

Damian turned, walked to a giant set of double doors nestled in the far right corner of his conference room, and barreled through them. Illyassa stood inside his study, peering out of the window.

"We were supposed to have lunch at the Astoria today," Illyassa told him softly. She wiped the tear escaping down her cheek, and then recrossed her arms. "I woke up this morning, and I lifted the telephone to call her."

Damian rushed to where Illyassa was standing, and wrapped his arms around her.

"We were supposed to grow old together, Damian," she told him with her voice breaking. "We were supposed to grow old and watch our children and grandchildren grow tall. It wasn't supposed to be like this, Damian. It was supposed to end like this."

Illyassa broke down into tears. Damian turned her around until she faced him, and then embraced her tightly.

"It's going to be okay," Damian said softly.

"I can't go on without her," Illyassa replied. "I don't know how to go on. She was more than my sister; she was more than my best friend; she was a part of my soul, my essence. I can't breathe without my sister, Damian."

"I wish there were words that I could say; I wish that I could somehow bring her back; I wish so many things right now," Damian whispered. "I just wish that I could take away your pain."

Illyassa nodded. "I know; I know you do. How's your brother holding up? He truly loved her. His pain, it must be without end."

"He's doing bad," Damian told her. "He's doing really bad. His life has been taken away from him."

Again, Illyassa nodded. Illyassa pulled away from

94

Damian, and wiped away her tears. "How's D.J.?"

Damian shook his head. "Not good. His condition hasn't improved. The doctors are preparing everyone for the worst."

Illyassa shook her head and began to cry again.

Damian pulled her close. "C'mon, it'll be okay."

Illyassa pulled away from him again. "No, I'm being selfish. How are you holding up, Damian?"

"Illyassa, you're not being selfish," Damian said softly. "You have a right to grieve; you just lost your sister. It's okay to let it out."

Illyassa shook her head. "I've cried for days. It's time for me to stop, and for me to be strong. Daissala was strong, and she'd want me to be strong."

"You are strong," Damian told her.

Illyassa walked behind Damian's giant wood desk, pulled out his leather chair, and pointed to it. "Sit down, Damian."

Damian walked to the overstuffed chair and sat down. Illyassa stood just behind him and began to massage his shoulders.

"Hmmmm, that feels good," Damian said.

"You're tense," she told him.

"I'm beyond tense," Damian replied. "I'm like a knotted and twisted piece of metal."

"You've been through a lot recently," she said softly. "First your father, then Dante's arrest, then with what happened to Daissala and D.J."

"And my company," Damian added.

"What's the matter with the company?"

"Someone with a lot of power and a lot of connections has gotten a group of senators to oppose the merger, and stall it in committee."

"No!" Illyassa exclaimed. "What about your people?"

"We're working on them," Damian answered. "But they're running scared. It's like they sense blood, and it's made some of them bold enough to even try to cut ties or rearrange the terms of our agreements."

"They no longer fear you," Illyassa told him.

"Seems like it. They know that Dante's locked up, and that my money's tied up. They may all just sit on the sidelines until they see if we can survive."

"Survive?"

Damian nodded. "Yes, survive. Whoever's pulling the strings has really long arms. The Justice Department's antitrust division is sitting on its approval of our last three mergers, and the FDA is sitting on the approval of our last three applications to bring some of our products to market. We spent all our cash on those mergers, and even borrowed some money on the last one. Without the approval, Bio One's basically out of the pharmaceutical industry. And we were counting on the pharmaceutical side of the company to bring in some badly needed immediate cash flow. We don't get those approvals, we can't service the loan. We lose Bio One, we've lost everything. We lose everything; we're a target for everyone we have ever had issues with. We're all dead."

"Then let me help you," she told him. "I'll speak to my father after the funeral, and we'll help you."

Damian shook his head. "I'm afraid that the help I need, your father can't give."

"Don't underestimate my father," Illyassa cautioned. "My father has great political connections in this country. Remember, my father's the minister of secret police, and he sits on the High Council in my country. Someday, he'll be president. He's personal friends with your president. He can help you, Damian."

"The people we're dealing with, are people who've been paid very well," Damian told her. "They care little about international politics, and even less about the horn of Africa. They care only about money and their reelection, Illyassa."

"You understand very little about politics, Damian Reigns," she told him with a smile.

"Well, can your father talk to our creditors?" Damian asked sarcastically. "How's his pull with the banks?"

"My father's wealthy, Damian, extremely wealthy." Illyassa shrugged her shoulders. "If it's money you need, then that's easy."

Damian smiled at her, clasped her hands, and pulled her around the chair and into his lap. "You really want to help me, don't you?"

"Of course," she answered.

Damian kissed her hands. "That's sweet of you, and I thank you."

"You smile and kiss me like I'm some naive little girl who has just offered you her piggy bank."

"No, sweetheart," Damian told her, kissing her hands again. "I didn't mean it like that. I know that you really want to help me, and I love you for it. I really do."

Illyassa caressed the side of Damian's face. "And I love you."

"I'll avenge your sister," he whispered. "If it takes me the rest of my life, and if it costs me my own life, I'll punish those who made you suffer."

Illyassa shook her head, sending her silky ponytail flying over her shoulder. "Oh, Damian, you truly don't understand my father. The men who killed my sister, will face a death a thousand times worse than you could ever imagine. They're already walking dead men. You really do underestimate my family. And you underestimate Ethiopia. Ethiopia is a powerful nation, Damian."

Illyassa rose, and walked to the window, where again, she peered out over the city. "They truly, don't know what they've done. They've harmed a Malkia. The sons of Abyssinia will scatter their bones to the four corners of the earth."

Chapter Eleven

"Chow time!" the prison guard shouted into the open dormitory.

Dante rolled off his bunk and slipped into his tennis shoes. He was hungry today, and the menu called for fried chicken, one of his favorites. He was being housed in a high-security federal correctional institute, Three Rivers, instead of the local county jail. The feds had offered the housing arrangement, and even agreed to provide a group of U.S. Marshals to transport him whenever he needed to appear in court. The feds felt that he would be more secure that way, and they also felt it would give the state less of a chance to mess things up. He would remain under their watchful eye until he was convicted and sent off to a maximum security state facility to serve out his time. They were playing this one tight, and Dante knew it.

The trip to the mess hall was a quick one, as was the trip to just about anywhere within the four-hundred acre walled and barbed wired confines of the prison. He could reach the clinic, the library, the gym, the jogging track, the chapel, and the weight room all within a few minutes. It was one of the benefits of being locked up.

"Hey, my man, D!" Prentice called out to Dante as they approached the mess hall line. "Tell me again, what does it feel like to have all that paper!"

Dante laughed. "Prentice, in here, the most any of us

can spend, is a hundred-seventy-five dollars a month. So I feel just like everyone else."

"Why don't you just have your brother send a helicopter to pick you up from the football field when you're at rec?" Prentice asked.

"Because then, I'd be a fugitive, and I'd have to leave the country."

"Fuck it; go live in Europe!" Prentice told him. "I hear they got finer hoes over there anyway."

"Well, there's such a thing as an extradition treaty, Prentice," Dante informed him. "The other countries would just arrest me, and send me back."

"Man, with all that money, you could buy your own island, make your own country, and tell these crackers to kiss your black ass!"

Dante threw his head back in laughter. "I wish that it was all that simple."

His dorm mates thought him a quiet oddity, a billionaire black man, with a graduate degree from Princeton, in a federal prison, on a state murder charge. He was truly the legendary Dante Reigns, the hammer for the most powerful, most mysterious, most notorious, drug family in creation, and he was here, among them. Few understood his choice of books and magazines. Why read, Fortune, and Forbes, when Murder Dog, XXL, and Don Diva were readily available? Why read The Wealth of Nations, The Iliad, and War and Peace, when True to the Game, Eastside, and Dutch could be found on any given shelf, in dozens of lockers? Many of the other prisoners had asked him to sign something, anything like papers, pictures, books, greeting cards and especially the newspaper articles about him and his family. Friends and friendships came slowly, as most were afraid to approach him. Prentice, was not one of those.

Prentice had been born in Shreveport, Louisiana, in an area known as The Bottom. He had dropped out of the legendary Booker T. Washington High School in the tenth grade, and solidified his ties to the notorious Bottom Boy

Gang, a ruthless gang of murdering drug dealers and local assassins. That affiliation, and a major drug deal gone bad, had earned nineteen year-old Prentice a twenty-year sentence under the federal minimum mandatory sentencing laws. That was eight years and three prisons ago, and now he was in Texas, hoping to eventually work his way to the federal correctional institute, Texarkana, located near the Texas, Arkansas, and Louisiana borders. Texarkana was less than an hour away from Shreveport, and he was hoping its proximity to his hometown would garner him a visit from his ex-girlfriend. She had gone on with her life, but they would forever have a bond through their daughter, a daughter who he had not seen in over eight years.

"You want my cake, Dante?" Prentice asked.

Dante shook his head. "No, but I'll take your chicken."

"Nigga please," Prentice told him. "You know how we colored folks are about our chicken."

Dante laughed and pulled two serving trays from the pile in which they were kept. He handed one to Prentice, and rubbed the other against his clothing in an effort to dry it off completely. He could tell by the water in the corner of his tray that it had just come from the kitchen. The tray was also warm to the touch, and it was a warmth that felt good against his stomach.

Dante lifted his tray onto the serving line, and began to examine the food beneath the heat lamps.

"Hey, Mayate, let's have some of your chicken!"

Dante turned in the direction from which the voice had come. It was Loco, a heavily tattooed and pierced member of the resident Hispanic prison gang, Los Paesanos, along with three of his cohorts.

"Your daddy's a mayate," Dante told him.

Prentice laughed.

"Oh, that's funny, motherfucker." Loco asked. "How about this? Is this funny?"

Loco reached beneath his khaki shirt and pulled from it a nine-inch butcher knife. His fellow gang members each

100

produced weapons of their own.

"You been a bad boy, Dante," Loco told him. "Somebody with a lot of money wants you dead."

"The only thing about killing for money, Loco, is that you have to actually kill the person in order to collect the money," Dante told him.

"What do you think I'm doing here, fuck face?" Loco smiled. "I got bills in the free world."

"Don't worry; your insurance will pay them off when you're dead," Dante smiled.

"You forgot something," Loco told him.

"What's that?" Dante asked.

"I'm the one holding the knife, you stupid fuck!" Loco told him, as he swung the blade at Dante.

Dante leaped back, allowing the blade to swing past him. He then clasped his serving tray in both hands, and swung hard at Loco's head. The hard plastic tray crashed into Loco's nose, sending him flying back into a group of lunch tables. Blood gushed from his nose and mouth like soda from a shaken can. Loco's cohort, Paco, swung his makeshift shank at Dante, who lifted his tray and parried the rusted blade. Prentice grabbed Loco's other companion by his neck, lifted him into the air, and threw him into the third member of their entourage. Dante swung his tray at Paco's throat, striking his larynx. Paco immediately fell to the ground, grabbing at his throat and gasping for air.

Loco rose from the ground, found his knife, and again charged at Dante. Dante waited for Loco to come within striking distance, and then spin kicked him, sending him flying back once again. Gordo, one of Loco's companions, rose from the ground, and rushed at Prentice with his knife. Prentice took two steps back, readied himself, and then plied powerful punches into his assailant. Gordo dropped to the ground.

Chewy, the fourth member of Paco's entourage, ran up behind Prentice while he was occupied with Gordo, and managed to stick his blade into Prentice's side.

"Dante!" Prentice cried out while clasping his side. "The motherfucker got me!"

Dante turned and rushed to his friend's side.

"Everyone on the ground!" The prison guards shouted.

The assassination attempt had quickly spiraled into a full-blown prison race riot. Blacks and Hispanics were battling throughout the cafeteria, while the prison's sirens had began blaring.

"Riot Team, report to the cafeteria!" blared over the loud peakers.

"Dante, look out!" Prentice shouted.

Dante turned, only to find Loco rushing toward him. Dante lifted his tray and deflected Loco's first strike, and then stepped to the side to avoid Loco's second. He was taken by surprise when he felt someone leap onto his back.

Loco's smile told Dante what he needed to know. The person on his back was going to hold him, while Loco turned him into a kabob. The knife Loco held was brand-new, stainless steel, and straight from the free world. It had a nine-inch blade, and a five-inch handle, giving him one hell of a reach. He needed to do something, and do something fast.

Dante tried to flip his assailant off his back, but couldn't, as his attacker was holding on for dear life. Dante peered around the room, located his bloody tray, and quickly dropped to his knees. The rapidity of his descent caused the assailant on his back to fly forward. Dante grabbed his tray and lifted it above his head just in time to block Loco's oncoming blade. The blade sliced through the tray, but fortunately, at an angle. Loco yanked the blade from the tray, and swung again. Dante rolled away from the knife, causing Loco to miss. He quickly rolled over onto one knee, clasped the tray with both of his hands, and swung as hard as he could at Loco's knees. The tray connected, and a loud crack rang out from behind Loco's khakis. Loco screamed, fell to the ground, and dropped his knife. Another assailant ran at Dante, who was still kneeling. Again, Dante swung his tray

102

at his attacker's knees, and again, the result was the same. Another attacker fell to the ground in bone-crushing pain.

Dante rose, and stumbled over to where Prentice was lying on the ground holding his side. Dante dropped to his knees next to his friend.

"Why didn't you stay your big dumb ass out of the way?" Dante asked.

"Because I wasn't gonna let them motherfuckers jump you," Prentice replied.

"You don't owe me anything," Dante told him.

"You still don't understand," Prentice told him. "We're all brothers, Dante. We all have to stick together."

Exhausted, Dante leaned back against the serving bar and watched as the prison guards slowly regained control of the cafeteria. An attempt had been made on his life. Fortunately for him it was by an imbecile who was more bark than bite. But, the next time, it could be a prison guard or a group of guards. Next time, he may not be so lucky.

"Dante, promise me something," Prentice told him. "Promise me, that if anything happens to me, you'll look after my little girl."

"Why would I promise you that?" Dante told him. "I hardly know you."

"Because you're not an asshole like everyone thinks," Prentice told him with a wide grin.

Dante turned away from Prentice and peered off into the distance. He had to get word to Damian, and more importantly, he had to get out of there. He had been attacked. Dajon had been attacked. Damian and Princess or even their mother, may be next. Someone had reach, and someone had the balls to use that reach. It sounded like either the Commission or El Jeffe. It could even be the Old Ones, but they would have attacked the Commission first. It would make no sense for them to attack the Reigns family, the family who was trying to leave the organization. No, this had to be either the Commission or El Jeffe. Either way, he had to get a message to his family, and he had to get it to them quickly.

Emil rushed into the room and handed Princess a slip of paper containing a message from her brother.

"Emil," Princess was surprised. "What are you doing here? I thought you had flown back to Georgia. What's this?"

"It's a message from Dante," Emil told her. "It came through about half an hour ago. There was an attempt on his life."

Princess unfolded the message and read quickly. She turned to Emil. "Who do we have inside?"

"Last I heard, Mina was still working on it."

"Damn!" Princess crumpled the paper in her hand. "We need to get him some backup in there! What about the guards? Have we bought any of them yet?"

"Don't know yet. I'll have someone place a call to Mina and see where we're at on this."

"Damn!" Princess turned and folded her arms.

Emil walked to where Princess was standing, and placed his arms on her shoulders.

"Everything's going to be okay," Emil told her. "Dante's strong, he's a warrior, and he can handle himself."

Princess turned, and found herself face-to-face with Emil, a fellow member of the Commission, the head of the entire state of Georgia and more importantly, a young, single, wealthy, educated, and powerful African-American man. He was independently powerful, strong, gifted, a natural born leader, a man's man. He was everything her ex-husband had not been; he was everything that she did not currently have in her life at that moment; he was everything that she needed tonight.

Somehow, someway, Princess found herself floating closer to Emil, closer to his body, closer to his lips. She closed her eyes, and drifted forward until their lips met, timidly at first, and then slowly, assuredly, their pecks built into a deep, passionate, engulfing kiss.

One of the bodyguards stepped into the room and cleared his throat. "Excuse me, ma'am."

Princess quickly pushed Emil away. "Yes, what is it?"

Emil straightened his tie, and smoothed out the crisp white sleeves of his shirt.

"The daily briefing package has arrived," the bodyguard informed her. He handed her a black attaché.

Princess lifted the attaché and placed it on a nearby table, where she carefully entered her code. She had only two chances to get the code right or else the briefcase would incinerate its contents. It was another one of Dante's acquisitions from the government.

Princess opened the attaché case and pulled out some manila envelopes. From the first envelope she pulled the edited summary from Damian's earlier meeting with his attorneys. The family had developed this system so that they could communicate with one another without fear of the government intercepting their telephone calls and two, it would allow every member of the family to know exactly what was going on and to have a total picture of the entire operation, in case the others became incapacitated. The briefcases were a very well-kept secret within the family, and their existence and transport routes were known only to an elite and trusted few. This few included only the executive level members of the family, and the briefcase's armed couriers.

Princess scanned through the folders, and then turned to Emil.

"FDA approval for Bio One's being held up, antitrust approval is being held up at Justice and approval is stalled in Congress."

Emil shook his head. "Dante got hit, Dajon got hit, and the government is playing games, too many coincidences. Somebody's pulling some strings and calling some shots."

"Who could influence Congress, Justice, and Agriculture, and also reach out and put hits on Dante in

prison, and have the balls to hit my innocent brother?"
Princess turned and dropped the briefing pages on the floor.

"Oh my God!"

"What?" Emil asked.

Princess raced for the door. "I've got to get to Damian! I'll explain it to you later!"

Princess raced to her Bentley Continental GT, pressed her key fob, and threw open the door to climb inside. She heard a familiar click and had just enough time to smile at the irony of it all. It was a click she had heard many times before. It was a click that she had arranged dozens of times in her lifetime. It was the click of the trigger that would set off the car bomb that had been planted beneath her brand-new two-hundred thousand dollar car.

Emil was standing at the door as the beautiful Obsidian Black Bentley suddenly turned into a red-orange fireball. The explosion sent him flying back into the living room and onto the ground. He found Princess lying beneath the charred, armored driver's side door, some fifty yards from where she once stood. Her body was crumpled, her face black, and her breathing shallow. Emil dropped to his knees and gathered her up into his arms.

"Help!" Emil shouted, while holding Princess's crumpled blackened body in his arms. "Get some help!" he shouted to the guards.

Emil wiped the hair and blood from Princess's face. "I can't lose you now, Princess, not now. Don't you die on me! You live; you be stubborn and live, baby. Be the stubborn bitch that everybody says you are; live, baby, live."

Chapter Twelve

The funeral was held at Temple Shin Beth, the largest synagogue in the South. The structure rose six stories into the air in a majestic mixture of glass and stone. The temple's wealthy patrons included the crème de la crème of South Texas society. They were the bankers, corporate executives, and business owners who made the economy tick. They were Daissala.

Daissala Hillel Malaika Reigns was a devout Hebrew, whose family's Jewish heritage dated back to the days of Makeda and Solomon. They were the old blood, and hailed from one of the oldest families in what was considered the oldest nation on the planet. Her family's status, as well as her father's political connections, brought out the who's who in the Jewish world community. If one was Ethiopian, American, Israeli, and Jewish, with power, money, or fame, one was in attendance today.

Because Daissala's husband was a Gentile, courtesy was given to Catholic priests during the service, allowing them to perform a brief ceremony. The fabulously devout Catholic Reigns family was in attendance today, and as was the ritual when burying one of their own, they showed up in droves. They numbered well over five hundred today, not including the children. And this number included only those with the Reigns surname. The married family members, along with various cousins and all of their offspring, drove

107

that number well past the one thousand mark. Needless to say, Daissala's funeral was standing room only.

Her father spent $150,000 to send her away in style. This number was actually achieved, because of the tasteful restraint of her husband, who resisted the demands of her father, who persistently tried to keep adding additional costs to the funeral. There was a small choir. Her father, however, wanted a massive Ethiopian Hebrew choir to be flown in from her native country. Dajon also limited the flowers to $25,000 worth of white roses; her father thought that his daughter should be lifted to heaven on a bed of roses. Dajon wanted dignity, not excess. Daissala was nothing, if not the epitome of dignity. She would want a very beautiful, and elegant, but dignified service.

Her casket was white diamond, with chrome fixtures and trim, along with a beautiful white silk interior. White roses surrounded the coffin, and made it appear as though it were suspended on a bed of roses. Dajon had his wife dressed in an elegant white gown, with beautiful Mikimoto pearls embroidered into the collar. Similar pearls graced her hair, which was fixed into a tight, silky French roll. A gorgeous black diamond and black pearl pendant shaped as a dove, was affixed to her breast. It was the black dove that symbolized her status as a female member of African royalty.

The president of Ethiopia was in attendance, as was the prime minister, and the vast majority of the members of the Ruling Council. The prime minister of Israel was in attendance, as were several members of his cabinet, as most of them were friends with Daisalla's father. The prime ministers of several European and Middle Eastern nations were also in attendance, not to mention those of a handful of Asia Pacific nations. Immanuel Hillel Malaika was believed to be the future president of his country, and as such, had powerful friends across the globe. His tragedy was their tragedy, even if deep down they really did not give a shit. Future presidents had that kind of effect on people.

"Minister Malaika wishes to speak with you after the

service," a tall, well-groomed Ethiopian man whispered into Damian's ear.

"Please inform the minister that he's invited to my home after the service," Damian told the messenger. "We can discuss his concerns over tea, in a much more comfortable environment."

The messenger touched his earpiece and spoke in rapid Amharic. He paused for several seconds, before leaning over and whispering into Damian's ear once again. "His Excellency said that he'll meet with you here, right after the service."

Damian peered off into the distance, and nodded solemnly.

It was the first time that Damian had ever been frisked, and it was the first time that his bodyguards had ever been outnumbered, outgunned, and completely overmatched. His sizable detail had been relegated to rear security, and was responsible for protecting the flank of a fleet of armored limousines that could withstand anything short of a direct hit from an M1A1 Abrams Main Battle Tank. The minister's security detail was in charge now, and they menacingly and proficiently warded off any unwanted strays or forays toward their charges.

Minister Malaika took Damian's arm and guided him along a small road leading deep into the cemetery. The two of them walked slowly just ahead of their fleet of armored limousines and armed to the teeth bodyguards. Five of the minister's bodyguards walked fifty yards ahead of them, ready to ward off or take down anything in their paths. Several more men walked along either side of them, with their arms folded and guns at the ready. Minister Malaika may have been the future president of his nation, but for the moment, he was even more powerful. For the moment, he was the minister of secret state security services, an organization feared by many.

"Excellency, I'm deeply sorry for the loss of your

daughter," Damian told him.

"No parent should have to bury their child," Minister Malaika replied. Damian nodded, and lowered his head.

"My daughter joined your family, and she became a part of your house," the minister stated. "My condolences go out to your house as well."

Damian nodded. "It's hard to imagine what my brother's feeling at this moment. Daisalla was his life. You think that you're going to spend your entire life with someone, you plan on it, you look forward to it, and then something as tragic as this happens."

Minister Malaika nodded. "Now is when one must turn to God, trust in him, believe in him. One must believe in his plan for us, and each of us must fulfill our own destiny."

Damian bowed his head slightly. "Words of wisdom, your Excellency."

"Young man, I believe in Yahweh, and I believe in his plan for us." Minister Malaika said. "But I believe that the men who did this, were operating outside of God's plan, outside of God's will."

Damian tried to hide his shock and disbelief. "Can one operate in the shadows of God?"

"Men can be minions of Lucifer," the minister replied. "The devil's henchmen are accountable only to the devil himself, such men do not know God."

Damian nodded.

"It's up to the men of God, to cleanse the earth of the scourge who killed my daughter, so that we can once again enjoy his bountiful garden," the minister said with a smile. "Good men such as ourselves must come together and do what is just, and right, and holy. We must also come together and protect ourselves, and protect our daughters. A tragedy such as this must not be allowed to happen again."

"I shall do all that I can, your Excellency." Damian bowed his head slightly. "Everything that I am, everything that I have, and all that I command, is at your service, your Excellency."

"That's good to know," the minister nodded. "I know that you're a good man, Damian. Your father would be very proud of you. You are a man of honor and of loyalty. Loyalty is a quality that's valued in the world, Damian. A young man who understands loyalty, can go far."

"With the right mentor, your Excellency." Damian said, with a lifted eyebrow.

"With the right patron," Minister Malaika nodded. "We're family, Damian. We shall always remain family. And we must do what's necessary for our family."

Damian was tired of the minister's setup. He wanted to be through with the word dance and decided to be direct.

"What can I do for you, your Excellency?" Damian asked.

Minister Malaika halted, and then turned and faced Damian. "Who are the men who would perpetrate such a heinous act against my daughter?"

"I don't know yet, but soon I'll give you all the information you need." Damian informed him.

"I come to you because you have resources in America that I don't have. You perhaps, will be more efficient in discovering the true culprits behind this act. My contacts in America are of a political nature. They would have difficulties operating within the spheres necessary to obtain such information."

You son of a bitch, Damian thought to himself. *He just called me a low-life son of bitch to my face, and thinks that I'm too stupid to understand.*

"I'm willing to help you with whatever it is you need to complete your quest," Minister Malaika continued. "Let my people know what it is that you need, and your request will be fulfilled promptly."

"I'll do my best, your Excellency," Damian nodded. "You can trust that we'll find the perpetrators of this heinous act."

"As soon as you do, please convey the information to my staff," Minister Malaika told him. "Together, you and I will bring these godless men to justice."

Vengeance is mine, sayeth the Lord, Damian thought to himself. He turned and extended his hand toward the minister. "I'll do all that I can, your Excellency."

Minister Malaika patted Damian on his shoulder. "I knew that I could count on you."

Damian walked to the wall of clerestory windows that were spread across room. He peered out over his backyard into the massive spring-fed lake. His mind replayed the day's events and conversations slowly, hoping to catch something that he may have missed initially. His sister-in-law's funeral was particularly troublesome today, particularly, the conversation with her father afterward. The minister was adamant about being able to personally bring to justice the men who murdered his daughter. The idea of having agents from the Ethiopian Secret State Security Service running around the country popping Mafioso was extremely troublesome. Particularly if those agents were linked back to the minister, and then the minister's connection to the Reigns family through his daughter was discovered. The Reigns family could be at war with the entire nation. Foreign agents running around this country assassinating people, was not just troublesome; it was down-right scary. The potential for things to take a catastrophic turn, were too great. He would have to find a way to placate the minister and buy time.

Damian rubbed his chin, walked to the bar, and prepared himself a Rum and Coke. Not normally a drinker, he felt he needed to calm himself, to slip off into another world. He first had to get things under control. His family was under siege. His brother had been attacked, his sister-in-law killed. His company was being threatened, approval for his last mergers were being withheld, approval to bring those companies drugs to the market was being withheld, an attempt had been made on Dante's life, and Princess was in the hospital in critical condition. He was at war with the

Commission, at war with El Jeffe, and perhaps at war with the Old Ones. He had struck a high-ranking FBI agent at his home, and his investors were getting anxious. He needed to be able to meet his fiscal obligations for the next fiscal quarter, or his company was finished. He and his family would be broke. He and his family would be like a wounded lion, trapped amid a field of hyenas; lunch for all who wanted a bite. His mother, nieces and nephews, uncles, aunts, brothers, sister, cousins, and everyone who ever worked for him and their families, would all be dead in a matter of weeks. He had to make peace with whomever this powerful hand was, who was destroying his family. He had to find out who it was. But then again, there was the minister.

If he made a truce with the men who killed the minister's daughter, and the minister found out about it, then the minister would become his enemy. And from the things that he read about the minister, he couldn't afford to have him as an enemy. Instead of foreign agents roaming the country taking out Mafioso, there would be foreign agents in South Texas, taking out his family. The minister's ruthlessness was legendary. He crushed everyone in his path to rise to his position and he deals with all challenges to the state's authority with a ruthlessness and swiftness that made it appear as though the hand of God had swung an axe down from heaven. No, he needed to keep the minister on his side or neutral, at best. However, he also needed to keep the minister and his minions out of the way while he saved his family. Damian's thoughts were interrupted.

"Get down! FBI, everyone on the ground now! FBI! Search warrant!"

Damian turned and watched as the agents raced throughout his home.

"Hands!" The masked FBI agent called out to Damian. "Let me see your hands!"

Damian lifted his hands into the air. "What the hell is the meaning of this?"

Two of the masked, black uniformed agents raced to

where Damian was standing, and handcuffed him. And then the suits walked in.

Damian recognized most of them from previous raids, and some of them he knew really well. Nathan was absent for obvious reasons, but his protégé, Stacia's husband, was there.

"What the hell is the meaning of this?" Damian asked again.

"Mr. Reigns, good evening," Agent Philip Grey greeted him. "We're here to execute a search warrant, looking for evidence of explosive materials that were possibly used in the attempted assassination of a federal agent."

Damian exhaled. "Look, I didn't blow Nathan up. And guys, give me some credit, I'm not going to have any explosive materials in my home!"

"Of course not," Agent Jason Peters concurred. "But give us some credit. You know that we're not just going to fucking curl up and roll away with our tails between our legs."

"So, this is just another one of your harassment searches?" Damian asked.

Agent Grey nodded. "Well yes, and no. Yes, it's basically just a harassment search, but, we know you did it. So this is just a courtesy call, to let you know that the gloves are off, and that we're going to be digging so far up your ass, you'll think that we're the Federal Bureau of Proctology."

"Message received," Damian told them coldly. "Now, get the fuck out of my house."

Agent Peters seated himself on Damian's couch, crossed his leg, and began to eat an apple from Damian's coffee table. "We'll leave when we're good and god-damned ready to."

"Gentlemen, can you please remove these cuffs, so that I may examine your search warrant, and place a telephone call to my lawyers?" Damian asked.

"What, you want to call your lawyer?" Agent Peters asked. "Wow, that's a surprise; you usually telephone that bitch when we execute a search warrant on one of your properties."

"I did ask to call my attorney, Agent Peters," Damian said loudly.

Agent Peters shook his head. "I didn't hear any such request. What about you, Phil?"

Agent Grey shook his head. "Didn't hear a thing."

"Oh, so you guys are playing dirty now?" Damian asked. "What, have you been hanging out with the ATF lately?"

Agent Dan Pendleton laughed, "Cute."

"You made it this way, Damian, not us," Agent Peters told him. "You took the gloves off, when you went after Nathan. It was just business before, but now it's personal. Nathan meant a lot, to a whole bunch of really important people. Every FBI agent in the country wants to work on this case."

Agent Pendleton nodded. "You're fucked now, buddy."

"Speaking of fucking," Agent Michael Rogers said, while approaching Damian. "Does having billions of dollars, and being a big-time sleazy ass drug dealer, give you the right to sleep with another man's wife?"

Damian peered into Agent Rogers's eyes, and realized that the agent knew that he had been sleeping with his wife since they were kids. "Hey, get this man away from me!" Damian shouted.

"A man's wife!" Agent Rogers's shouted. "You dared to touch another man's wife!"

"Get a hold of your agent!" Damian shouted to Agent Peters.

Agent Rogers pulled his Sig Sauer semiautomatic handgun from its holster. "How long have you been fucking Stacia?"

"Get him!" Damian shouted.

Several agents rushed to grab Agent Rogers.

"Mike, wait!" Agent Peters shouted. "Think about what you're doing!"

"Mike, he's not worth it!" Agent Grey shouted as he lunged for the weapon.

Agent Rogers quickly lifted his weapon and fired several shots toward Damian. The agents all surrounded and grabbed their fellow agent, lowered him to the ground, and forcibly removed his weapon. The other FBI agents inside the residence quickly ran into the room with their weapons drawn.

Agent Frank Hawk shouted from the doorway. "Get a paramedic!"

Agent Grey waved his hand. "No we're okay; everyone's okay."

"I wasn't talking about you guys!" Agent Hawk shouted. He rushed to where Damian was lying on the ground. "Mr. Reigns, can you hear me?"

Damian nodded.

"He's been hit twice!" Agent Hawk shouted. "Get a paramedic!"

Agent Grey rushed to where Damian was lying on the floor. "Where are you hit?"

Damian's breathing became labored. The agents ripped open Damian's shirt, to find three bullet wounds. One bullet had struck him in the chest, while another had struck him in his stomach. The third and final bullet had gone through the side of his neck. Blood poured rapidly from all three wounds, and formed a pool beneath him.

Damian peered up at the agents and smiled. Of all the things that he thought would end his life, a jealous husband wasn't one of them. He had been sleeping with Stacia since they were in middle school. He had known Stacia since they were babies in their mothers' arms. They caught frogs together, made mud pies with her tea and bake set, shared their first kiss, first dates, and had lost their innocence to one another. She had been his and he had been hers long before there was even the thought that a Michael Rogers existed. And now, now he was lying on the ground in his living room, staring up at his ceiling, with blood pouring out

116

of his body in only God knew how many locations. His love for Stacia, a woman who now detested the very ground that he walked on, had brought him to this point in his life. He needed a lot of answers, but one thing was certain. Princess was on her death-bed, Dante would not survive prison, and Darius was too young and still in high school, eventhough he wanted to avenge his father's death. If Dante died, his family was doomed. This was his last thought as he closed his eyes and drifted away.

Chapter Thirteen

Dajon crept gently into the hospital room, not
wanting to disturb the sleeping patient. Dajon marveled at
the angelic smile, and allowed himself a smile, as he had not
seen such a peaceful and serene look in ages. He wondered if
there existed some secret pact or chant or spell or talisman
that could rewind time to the simpler days of his youth. He
would give anything to have those days back again. He would
give anything to just have the previous four weeks back
again. There were so many things that he would have done
differently.

Dajon lowered his head into his hands, and leaned his
elbows against the railing of the hospital bed. His actions
caused the sleeping patient to begin stirring. Dajon smiled at
the sight of open eyes.

Damian peered around the hospital room, wondering
where he was, and how he had come to be there.

"You're in the hospital," Dajon told his brother.
"Stacia's husband shot you."

Damian turned away. Tears begin pouring from his
eyes. *I'm alive.* His thoughts turned to God, and to the
second chance that he had been blessed with. He knew that
second chances weren't granted often. In fact, he himself had
granted very few of them to others. He marveled at the irony
of it all.

His life had changed, he was certain of that, but how
much it had changed, was a question that he couldn't

answer at that moment. He knew that he still had a job to
do. His family needed him; his life and their lives, depended
on him. He knew that he was supposed to hand over the
reigns to the family's illegitimate enterprises to Princess, but
could he even do that now? He knew that his sister wouldn't
be willing to walk away from that side of the family business,
and join him on the legitimate side. She was a brilliant and
efficient manager, with a creativity that surpassed most. She
would have been someone's corporate star in another life. So
would he, for that matter. In fact, he once had been. But that
had been long ago; so many years, and so much blood had
passed. So much had happened. How could he have been
given a second chance, and Daisalla not? He was a monster;
she was an angel. Why?

"Damian, it's good to see you awake."

"How long have I been asleep?" Damian asked. His
voice was hoarse, and his throat was sore. "Water, I need
some water."

"You've been asleep for five days," Dajon told him. He
lifted the water pitcher on the tray next to Damian's bed, and
poured his brother a glass of water. He raised the automatic
bed, placed the cup to his brother's lips, and allowed him to
sip from it. "We were really worried about you."

"Princess?" Damian asked.

Dajon shook his head. "Still no change."

"D.J.?" Damian asked. "How's D.J.?"

Dajon smiled. "Better, much better. He's awake, and
smiling, and asking questions. We haven't told him about his
mother yet. I think it's best if we allow him to recover more
before we tell him."

Damian nodded. "Dante?"

"Okay," Dajon told him. "We're still working on trying
to get him out."

Damian frowned. "Who's we?"

Dajon shrugged. "Well, basically me."

Damian shook his head. "Call Angela; tell Dante's wife
to get down here immediately."

Dajon shook his head. "She called. If she leaves the East Coast, we lose everything from Pennsylvania to D.C. Maybe even Virginia."

Damian shook his head. "Dajon, you can't run this. You don't know anything about this business."

"Damian, in case you don't realize it, I'm it!" Dajon snapped. "I'm all you've got. Princess is lying in a hospital bed very similar to this one, Dante's in prison, you're here, and Darius is too young. Nicanor is up to his ass in a war to hold onto our territory, and you know he's our most trusted field commander, and so is Angela. There's no one else!"

"Who's been briefing you?" Damian asked.

"Emil's been helping out," Dajon answered. "But he's going to have to fly back to Georgia to take care of dissension in his own house."

"Dajon, you've never been involved in this," Damian told him. "This is a whole different world."

"I'm a grown man, Damian. I can handle it. I have to handle it!" Dajon said forcefully. "Is it true about the company?"

"Is what true?" Damian asked.

"Bio One's being threatened?"

Damian nodded.

"Is it true about what will happen if Bio One fails?" Dajon asked.

Damian nodded. "No money means that we don't have the resources to pay our soldiers. No soldiers, we're all dead. Our life depends on us having a bunch of soldiers to fight our enemies. We have a lot of enemies. Some of them act like friends right now, but that's only because we're strong. Once they sense weakness, they join with our enemies, and come after us with a vengeance."

"So our lives are in my hands?" Dajon asked.

Damian turned away from his brother. The thought that their lives were in Dajon's hands, was frightening. It wasn't that Dajon was a coward; it was that he was inexperienced, and unhardened. The Commission would eat him alive. His own under bosses would eat him alive. Dajon was a good, honorable and decent man. In the business they were involved in, one had to be cold, ruthless, conniving, and suspicious almost to the point of paranoia.

"Damian, I know that you don't think I'm capable of doing this," Dajon told his brother. "I know that I've always stayed away from the business, and even despised you for being a part of it. But a few weeks ago, my life changed. Everything that I was, everything that made me good, was taken from me. I understand why you do it now. I truly understand. It's about protecting our family from the monsters that roam this earth. I have to protect you, and Princess, and Dante, and Darius, and Mom. But even more importantly, I have two children whom I love more than life itself, who need my protection. Don't let my children die because you don't believe in me. You believed in me when we were children; believe in me again. I'm your brother; I'm still that same old boring, reliable, trustworthy Dajon, who I've always been. I'll consult with you daily, I'll make sure that you're up to speed on everything, and I'll carry out your orders to the letter. Please, let me help."

Damian turned back toward his brother, and lifted his hand into the air. Dajon clasped his brother's hand, and shook it.

"I believe in you, Dajon," Damian told him. "I always have. I just didn't want you to become a part of this mess. You were always my light at the end of the tunnel. I looked at you, and at the life you had, and I knew that one day, I too would be able to get out of this life, and have those things. Dajon, you were everything that I wanted to become. I never stopped believing in you, because you were everything that I wanted to be."

The door to the hospital room slid open, and Anjouinette Tibbideaux, the Commission member in charge of Louisiana, stepped inside. The Reigns family had supported her move to take over her husband's seat, and

121

had sent troops to Louisiana to squash all rebellions from her late husband's under bosses, who had resisted her takeover. They had given Anjouinette money, lawyers, politicians, advisers, and an open invitation to draw upon their resources. They had made it clear, a war against Anjouinette, was a war against the Reigns family. She had been left alone, and was able to consolidate her power. She was now grooming her son, a recent Xavier graduate, to take over. He was her closest adviser, and the hammer for her family; a very good and feared hammer.

"I came as soon as I heard, monsieur," Anjouinette said, in her thick French accent. She rushed to Damian's bed. "Tell me who to kill, and they will be dead by the week's end, if not sooner."

Dajon blinked twice at the sight of Anjouinette. She was half Cherokee Indian and half French Creole, with gray eyes, and long black silky hair that flowed past her thighs. She had been graced with her mother's high cheekbones, and a reddish bronze complexion that would have Crayola scrambling to discover a new color in order to define it. She was beyond beautiful.

Dajon had never looked at another woman since his Daissalla came into his life, and was certain that he would never marry again. And yet, he wanted to move closer and examine the beautiful creature standing just before him. He was a widow, a new widow at that. He still cried nightly over the death of his soul mate, so the thick lump inside of his throat, the goose bumps creeping up his arms, and the deer in the headlights stare that was now affixed to his face, confused him.

"Anjouinette, your friendship, your compassion, and your concern at this time of great need, brings me so much comfort," Damian told her.

"Dispense with the formalities and all the bullshit, Damian," Anjouinette told him. "What do you need? Command me and it's done."

Damian smiled. Although officially in charge of her

own organization, it was no secret that Anjouinette was really just an under boss, although an under boss with an entire state under her control. She was powerful, and reliable, and brought immeasurable strength to his organization. She was also one of his most capable field commanders, and a trusted and competent adviser.

"I need you, Anjouinette," Damian said feebly. "This is my brother, Dajon."

Anjouinette turned, clasped Dajon's hand, and shook it. "Enchante', monsieur."

The touch of her hand caused Dajon's throat to turn dry. He swallowed hard. "No, the pleasure is all mine."

"Anjouinette, a lot has happened," Damian told her. "Princess is in critical condition, Dante's in prison, my family's in grave danger, and from now on, Dajon will be running things for me."

Anjouinette nodded.

"Dajon will brief you," Damian told her. "But he's not familiar with the nature of our business. He'll need your assistance and counsel. Will you please help me?"

Anjouinette nodded. "First, we make sure that you, Princess, and Dante are safe. Next, we must contact all of the under bosses and let them know that Dajon's in charge now. Then, we must strike those who struck at us. Do we know who struck Princess and Dante?"

Damian shook his head. "We have a pretty good idea."

"Have we sent anyone inside to help protect Dante?" Anjouinette asked.

"We're trying to get people inside," Damian announced. "The soldiers who we sent inside, are still making their way through the slow federal prisoner transportation system. No telling how long it'll take them to get to Three Rivers Federal Prison. We're trying to get some guards on the payroll."

"We'll speed that process up," Anjouinette said. "Do you want us to kill that FBI agent who shot you?"

"He's in custody," Dajon announced. "It would be

impossible to get to him."

Anjouinette smiled. "He's green." She turned toward Dajon. "Anyone can be gotten too. And if they're incarcerated, then it makes it even easier. They can't run."

Damian shook his head. "No, leave him be. That had nothing to do with business. That was a personal issue. It was Stacia's husband."

Anjouinette laughed. "Oh, that idiot. He's not even worth killing. You've been sleeping with Stacia for how long? And he just recently discovered it?"

Damian laughed.

The door to Damian's room slid open once more, and this time, Emil, the powerful head of the state of Georgia, walked into the room.

"Damian, you're awake!" Emil said. "Good to see you back with us. So, how do you feel?"

"He's been shot, you idiot," Anjouinette said. "How do you think he feels?"

Emil laughed. He leaned forward and embraced Anjouinette tightly.

"Hello, beautiful."

Anjouinette smiled. "Hello, handsome."

Emil stuck out his hand and clasped Dajon's hand tightly. "How's it going, Dajon?"

Dajon nodded.

"I believe I know who hit Princess," Emil announced. "I had my people drop everything, and made it a priority to find out. The explosives were traced to a quarry-blasting company out of Las Vegas. The mining company's owned by a couple of fronts, and the bottom company's owned by none other than one Nestor Melchiorre."

"Nestor!" Anjouinette pounded her tiny fist into the palm of her other hand. "That slimy, greasy, weasel of a man."

Damian shook his head. "It just doesn't make sense. We're trying to leave the Commission. If we leave the Commission, that means we also divest from the

Commission's casino interest in Vegas. Why would they attack us?" Damian began sweating profusely."

"Damian, are you okay?" Dajon asked.

Damian shook his head.

"We hit Nestor as soon as possible," Anjouinette told them.

"How? Look at Damian," Emil waved his hand toward the hospital bed. "He's not up for this."

"Dajon's in charge now," Anjouinette told Emil.

"Dajon!" Emil said surprised. "Dajon's not part of this side of the family. He doesn't know the first thing about this business!"

Damian swallowed hard and nodded. "Dajon's in charge."

"Damian! Are you sure you know what you're saying?" Emil asked forcefully. "Dajon can't run this family! He's greener than a bell pepper!"

Damian lifted his finger and pointed toward Emil. "You help him. I need you, Emil. Be loyal to me."

Emil turned and huffed. "Damian, he's inexperienced; he's not ruthless enough!"

Damian smiled. "Help me."

Dajon pressed the intercom. "Can we get a nurse in here?"

"On the way," the voice on the other side of the intercom shouted.

Emil turned toward Dajon. "Do you understand what you're getting yourself into?"

Dajon nodded.

Emil warned him. "You walk out this door, and you give one command to any one of those men out there, and you're in for life. You're marked as a leader of the Reigns family and you can never go back. There's no turning back, Dajon; do you understand that? Your life will change; the lives of your children will change. No more going to school without an army of bodyguards spread throughout the campus, no more running out to the store for ice cream, no more spontaneous trips to the park, no more just being a regular family. You lose everything; you lose all of your freedom; you lose, period. If I could go back and change the hands of time, I would have run away from this life so fast, you would have thought I was Michael Green."

"I understand what I'm losing. I also understand what's at stake if I don't. A Reigns has to run this family; you have your own family to run, and so does Anjouinette. There's no one left; I'm it. If I don't do this, then my family's dead."

Emil exhaled, lowered his head, and nodded. "Get word to your under bosses. When you walk out into that hallway, and you walk up to that first bodyguard and give him an order, make sure that you give that order with firmness and confidence. No hesitation in your voice. Be sure about everything that you say. Your men look to you for leadership, and they get their confidence from you. Remember, their lives, and the lives of their families, depend on you knowing what the hell you're doing."

"Remember, you're a Reigns," Anjouinette told him. "Initially, they will follow you for that reason alone. Afterward, once they have had a chance to check you out, they'll form their own decision about you. Stay away from them, never ask one of your men for advice, and always be confident and firm."

"Run all your decisions by Anjouinette first," Emil told him.

"You'll have to give the final orders to strike back," Anjouinette told him.

"Do you understand what strike back means?" Emil asked. "We're in the business of drugs, money, and murder, Dajon. Make no mistakes about what we do. It's a dirty business, and in order to survive, you have to be ruthless. Can you give those kinds of orders?"

Dajon looked down and nodded.

The door swung open and the nurse rushed to Damian's bed. She turned toward Dajon and the others. "He doesn't look good. You're going to have to leave now."

Anjouinette brushed the lint off of Dajon's shirt, and then straightened his collar. "Suits from now on."

Dajon nodded.

"Ready?" Emil asked.

Dajon exhaled and nodded.

Emil opened the door and he, Dajon and Anjouinette strode into the hallway. Dajon stopped at one of the men standing in the hallway.

"Increase the number of guards on my brother and my sister. Call all of the under bosses, and have them report to me. I'll be staying at Damian's."

"Yes, sir," the suited man standing just outside of the door told him.

Dajon continued down the hall, followed by Anjouinette and Emil. The bodyguards on either side of the hall stared at one another for several seconds, before quickly falling into place behind them. Several of them rushed ahead and opened the doors for Dajon. The Reigns family had just gained a new leader.

Chapter Fourteen

Shopping was a passion that burned brightly in Don
Nestor Melchiorre's heart. He loved the hunt; to find a new
fabric or pattern to add to his already significant wardrobe,
was akin to discovering a Renoir beneath an old unwanted
painting that Grandma had left in her will. It was delight
beyond ecstasy.

The Don was also a donna. He loved to be fawned
over, to be pampered; he loved when salespersons and tailors
hovered around him and catered to his every whim. It was
his heart's greatest joy to be the center of attention. It was
when the fat Don was in his element.

"Mr. Melchiorre, here's the caramel-almond espresso
you requested," an attendant informed him, while passing
him a cup made of the finest antique china.

The Royal Imperial Clothiers and Fitters Club catered
to the extremely rich. Even being famous was not enough to
gain one shopping time at the RIC. The RIC had been formed
in the twelfth century by a group of English, Dutch, French,
and Italian imperial clothiers, valets, tailors, importers, and
shop owners, who were responsible for procuring,
manufacturing, importing, tailoring, and fitting fabrics and
garments for their respective monarchs. The Club functioned
as a clothier's guild, allowing these craftsmen to share trade
secrets, new sewing techniques, new fabrics from the Orient,

and the pricing of those fabrics, as well as sharing in the shipping cost, cargo insurance, and other expenses. The club's clients were European, and later, Middle Eastern royalty. Few outside of these circles even knew of its existence. The club now had fifty locations in forty countries, and its secret list of clientele included only the movers and shakers of the international order. Heads of state shopped at the RIC; actors and musicians did not.

"Bring me that Kiton jacket!" the Don bellowed.

The fat Don rose from the soft-silk covered stool upon which he had been seated, and lifted his arms so that one of his five attendants could easily remove the Ermenegildo Zegna slacks he had tried on.

"I'll take the Zegna suit," the Don informed the attendant. "Have Joseph take an inch off the leg."

The attendant obediently bowed and shuffled out of the Don's way. The Don made his way across the rich silk carpeting of the private dressing area, to a private gentleman's fitting room that had been fashioned from the finest Brazilian Cherry wood. The Don sipped from his cup of espresso, placed the cup on a small Cherry coffee table, and then seated himself on the matching wood-and-silk-covered bench. The attendant would be in shortly to help him.

Suddenly, screams and shouts and pleas of the people outside the Don's private fitting could be heard.

The door to the Don's private fitting room flew open, and standing before the Don, holding a still smoking pistol with a large silencer on the tip, was Anjouinette Tibbideaux.

"Anjouinette!" The Don shouted furiously. "What's the meaning of this? The Don glanced around Anjouinette, and could see bodies and pools of blood lying on the ground in the room behind her. At this moment he knew that his bodyguards were dead.

"Nestor," Anjouinette smiled. "We meet again."

"What are you doing?" the Don sneered. "Do you have any idea what you've just done? Do you realize who I am? Do you understand what my associates will do to you?"

129

"Nothing that you haven't already been doing," Anjouinette replied. "You've been a bad boy Nestor. You've been very, very bad."

"What are you talking about?" The Don asked.

"You've been playing with explosives, Nestor," Anjouinette told him.

"I own a quarry and a construction firm; of course I play with explosives!" the Don sneered.

"Princess Reigns car's a quarry now?" Anjouinette asked.

The Don's expression shifted from anger, to one of realization, and then back to anger. "So, you're here on behalf of your masters. I always took you for a lackey."

"And I always took you for being a homosexual, Nestor," Anjouinette smiled.

"How much are they paying you?" The Don inquired. "I'll double it."

"They're paying me nothing, Nestor. But, what they've given me, is more than you could ever offer. Dante freed me from the monster who shared my bed, when he killed my husband. He allowed me to keep everything, and he spared the lives of me and my children. He allowed me to be able to put my children through college. He became a father to my children, and was there for me and them, whenever I called. You could never pay me enough, Nestor."

"Ah, so you're the whore of the Reigns family?" The Don sneered. "Tell me, whore, which brother is better, Damian or Dante?"

Anjouinette laughed. "You can't get me angry, Nestor. Dead men can't upset me. I came here for one purpose and one purpose only, to kill you. Now, if you want to make it easy on yourself, you can. Tell me, why are you and your associates waging war on the Reigns family?"

"You may as well pull the trigger, you black bitch," The Don told her. "You'll get nothing out of me."

"Okay," Anjouinette shrugged her shoulders, and

lifted her weapon. She squeezed the trigger on her 40-caliber Smith and Wesson semiautomatic four times, sending two rounds into Don's chest, one into his stomach, and one into the middle of his forehead. The Don died with his eyes open.

This was the worst part of her current assignment, Grace thought to herself. Having to be the good, reliable, bubbly neighbor, was taxing her acting abilities and her patience to the fullest. Today, she had to pick up her neighbor's child from school, and then keep him until they arrived home from whatever it was that they had to do. Under any other circumstances she would have told them to go to hell, and then had child protective services investigate them. But this time, things were different. This time, the child-abandoning misfits were her targets. They were suspected meth amphetamine manufacturers and dealers; a husband and wife team, who used the kids as cover when they transported their wares. It was even believed that the wife had once used her son's entire soccer team as a cover, and conducted a multimillion-dollar deal in the parking lot of the neighboring playground. It was Grace's job to get close to them, and then to bring them down.

She couldn't believe that she had allowed herself to be suckered into this baby-sitting gig. She knew that she was supposed to gain her neighbor's trust; but she didn't think that part of the deal was that she would have to pick up their snot-nosed brat from school. She had met the kid a couple of times; a nose-picking, booger-flinging monster, with blue eyes, blond hair, and beige freckles. She hoped that she could resist the urge to pull out her Sig Sauer pistol and use the kid for target practice.

Franklin Delanor Roosevelt Primary School was a monument to suburban excess and sprawl. It housed two thousand yelling, screaming, and shouting wealthy elementary school brats. A quick expansion project and several dozen trailers, expanded the schools capacity to just over three thousand, and the parking lot reflected that enrollment number. After school traffic, was worst than the Los Angeles 405 Freeway during rush hour traffic. To say that the six pick-up lanes were congested, was like saying the Grand Canyon was deep. It was a vast understatement.

"Tyler, over here!" Grace waved her hand motioning for Tyler to come to her.

Tyler bounded to Grace's Range Rover, and climbed inside. He strapped himself into the rear booster seat, and immediately began fumbling with the remote that controlled the SUV's rear DVD entertainment system.

Grace exhaled, and pulled away from the school, heading in the direction of her home. "So, how was your day, Tyler?"

"I had a bad day," Tyler answered. "The teacher gave me a bad star on the wall."

"Why?" Grace asked.

"She said that I wouldn't stop talking."

"Sounds about right," Grace said with a smile.

Grace made a right turn onto a local avenue, and quickly realized that she had picked up a tail.

Black Lincoln town cars were fairly uncommon in these parts of the country, particularly black town cars carrying four men in dark suits. Unless of course they were part of a funeral procession. Being that there were no hearses around, Grace quickly ruled out that possibility. She made a quick right turn to see if they would follow. They did.

Grace sped up slightly, not wanting to alert Tyler, nor alert those town cars that she knew that she was being tailed. Her increased speed brought an increase in their speed. She was now certain that it was a hit.

Grace hit the gas on her Range Rover, sending the needle on her tachometer spinning. The town car sped up, and the windows came down and their guns appeared.

"Tyler, get down, baby!" Grace shouted.

Tyler unbuckled his booster seat, and climbed down onto the floor.

The occupants in the Lincoln opened fire.

"God damn it!" Grace shouted. "This isn't Little Damian, you idiots!"

Grace made a sharp right turn in her Range Rover, sending it sliding on two wheels for several moments, before finally regaining control. The Lincoln was barely able to make the same turn, but made it nonetheless. They were still behind her.

"You've got the wrong kid!" Grace shouted. "You've got the wrong god damned kid!"

Grace made a sharp left turn, sliding her vehicle off the main street. She had to think; she had to get help, while at the same time, she had to keep her cover. She knew exactly where she was headed; she just hoped that someone would be outside to help her.

The Lincoln made the same left turn, although at a considerably slower pace. Navigating the big town car was considerably more difficult than slinging around the significantly more rigid Range Rover. The last turn bought Grace some additional time, time that she did not need, but that she certainly would accept. She was nearing her destination. A quick turn into the parking lot, and she would be there. She made the turn.

The occupants of the Lincoln town car swerved into the parking lot following the Range Rover, only to find that they were in the middle of the parking lot of one of the local police department's substations. Grace had set them up.

Grace threw her vehicle into park, and leaped out of the Range Rover just in front of the police substation. She pulled out her semiautomatic and readied herself.

"FBI! Agent needs assistance!" Grace shouted to a couple of uniformed officers walking into the building. She opened fire on the occupants of the towncar, striking the driver in his chest.

The occupants of the town car quickly poured out, and began returning fire. Grace shifted her aim, and quickly downed the suit hiding behind the rear passenger door. The two police officers to her rear, made quick work out of the other two occupants of the Lincoln. Grace turned, flashed her badge, and then quickly headed for the entrance to the substation.

"Secure the child in the backseat of my vehicle," Grace shouted. She raced into the substation, searching for a telephone. She had to get word to her fellow agents, and she had to get an agent over to her son's boarding school. The men who she had just downed were white, whereas the Reigns family's soldiers were primarily African-American. Whoever it was, wasn't after the kid, because they had opened fire and placed the kid's life in danger. Whoever it was, had tried to kill her and the kid, which meant that it definitely was not Damian's people. She was now in danger, and so was her child. She had to get to her child, and then she had to get away fast. She would go underground again, this time deeper than anyone ever thought possible. She would do whatever it took to protect her child; whatever it took. She was not going to lose her child to some god damned mob war, even if it meant killing Mafia dons.

Whatever it takes, Grace, she told herself as she quickly dialed numbers. *Whatever it takes.*

Chapter Fifteen

Too much blood had been shed in the last few weeks. The number of hits, car bombs, counterhits, and retaliatory strikes had quickly spiraled out of control. The Reigns family had been holding its own on the East Coast, thanks in no small part to the generalship of Angela Reigns, Dante's wife, and Nicanor Moreno Mata, one of the Reigns family's most reliable and trusted field commanders. They had whipped the East Coast branches of the Reigns family into shape, and recruited, trained, and led an all-out war effort against several of the largest New York families. The Reigns family had taken a few hits. Damian was in the hospital, Princess was in critical condition, Dante was in prison, Daissalla was dead, Davidian was dead, and little D.J. was still in the hospital. But all in all, they had given as well as they had got. Don Pancrazio was dead. Don Melchiorre was also dead, shot in the private fitting room of an exclusive men's clothing store. In the process of getting to those two, they had also killed scores of bodyguards, a few nephews, a couple of sons, and several innocent bystanders. If a score was to be tallied, the Reigns family was ahead. No one had yet to score a knockout.

The stalemate was the reason for the meeting today. Stalemates meant that blood was being shed for no reason. No one was winning, and in all likelihood, no one was going to win in the near future. The situation was not unlike the Western Front during World War I, bloodshed and sacrifice just to trade a piece of worthless real estate back and forth. The cost in lives wasn't worth it.

Today's meeting was being held in Vegas, at the Mandalay Bay Resort and Casino, which was supposedly neutral. Its real owners were the Russians, who had a vested interest in securing a peaceful solution, as all of the bombs and bloodshed was having a negative affect on them as well. The Russians had learned the art of subtlety since roaring onto the scene with a hail of bullets and explosives, and they now preferred anonymity and quiet to the sound of Claymore antipersonnel mines going off inside subzero refrigerators in the middle of the night.

Everyone was represented today; the entire western branch of the Commission was on hand, as well as a couple of the southern members. They were joined by the heads of the Las Vegas families and a few of the East Coast families as well. This was going to be a no holds barred everything out in the air meeting. Formality was being foregone, in order to get to the heart of the matter, and walk away with concrete solutions at the end of the day. The Russians were chairing the meeting.

"I want to thank all of you for being here today," Vladimir Pugachev said. "Some of you came great distances to be here, which speaks volumes of your commitment to peace. Let us hope that it's that spirit that permeates today's meeting. As agreed, we will forego the formalities, and get straight to business. Each of you will have a turn to say his peace. Now, who wishes to go first?"

"Why's my family being attacked?" Dajon asked.

Emil cringed. Dajon had just shown his inexperience, and he also let everyone know that he was being attacked, and that those attacks were bothering the Reigns family. He couldn't assist Dajon at this meeting, because he was here representing his own family, as head of the state of Georgia and to do so would be a great embarrassment to the Reigns family.

Don Marcellino Pancrazio of New York leaned forward. "You ask why you're being attacked. You kill my brother and my sister's son, and you ask why you're being attacked?"

"You hit my family, killed my wife, and injured my innocent son!" Dajon shouted.

"The Pancrazio family did nothing of the sort!" Don Pancrazio fired back. "And to accuse us of such an act is an insult to our honor! We do not attack innocent women and children!"

"Why is your Commission building more casinos in Las Vegas?" Don Patrizio Giovanneta asked. "Las Vegas belongs to us! We do not go out and sell drugs in Texas, Arizona, New Mexico or Florida, so why are you coming here, and interfering with our livelihood?"

"Who said Las Vegas belongs to you and you only?" Barry Groomes of Arkansas asked.

"Las Vegas has always belonged to us," Don Salvatore Tiziano told them. "We built Las Vegas. We owned and controlled Las Vegas before any of you were born!"

"You made room for the Russians," Aldophus Brandt of Colorado told them. "Why not scoot over just a little bit more."

The Russian hosts looked down in embarrassment.

"We made an arrangement that you wouldn't understand," Don Anastasio Crencenzo of Las Vegas told them. "But that's another matter, which is of no concern to you. Why is your Commission muscling in on our territory?"

"Our Commission owns three measly hotels here, and is building a fourth," Juan Zapata of Arizona told them. "We're of no threat to you."

"Vegas is big enough to let everyone eat from the trough," Julian Jones of Mississippi announced. "What's the problem?"

"You're muscling in on our casinos, as well as in our other activities," Don Tito Bonafacio of New York told them. "Your Commission has been engaged in warlike activities with us for the last year."

"You're trying to expand your Commission into the East Coast," Don Gianpaulo Cipriano of New York told them. "These territories have always been ours. Your Commission is going to create seats for New York, New Jersey, Philadelphia, Massachusetts, and Delaware. And that's only because we have already conceded Maryland."

"Expansion's a natural occurrence," Steve Hawk of Kansas told them.

"What's the Commission's problem with my family?" Dajon asked.

"Your family's trying to leave the Commission, and you control the majority of our reliable distribution points," Chacho Hernandez of New Mexico told him. "You control eighty percent of my state, and I want it back."

"You control sixty percent of my territory," Julian announced. "The Reigns family's aggressiveness is legendary."

"Your family's very expansionistic," Juan told him. "That and we don't want Princess to sit on this Commission again. She's too aggressive, too overbearing, and she loves war too much."

"We want Damian to remain on the Commission," Jamie Forrest of Tennessee told Dajon. "He understands business."

"And if we withdrew from those territories?" Dajon proposed. "And turned over our seat on the Commission to someone else in our family besides Princess?"

"Then peace would be possible," Jamie Forrest told him.

"Peace within your Commission," Marcellino Pancrazio told them. "But that does not change the fact that my brother's dead. And what of the Reigns family's expansion into the East Coast? What about that?" asked Don Pancrazio.

"To my understanding, it's the Commission that's expanding into those territories, not the Reigns family,"

Dajon told them.

"What, are you stupid?" Don Frediano Ambrogino of Nevada asked incredulously. "Those are troops from your family up there doing battle, and they're being led by generals from your family, and being bankrolled by your family. It's the Reigns family that's trying to install their own people into those territories, and then grant them a seat on our Commission."

"As if we already didn't have enough of your family's flunkies on the Commission," Marion 'Big Hustler' Rook of California told Dajon.

The men seated around the conference table laughed heartily.

"Isn't that right?" Marion asked.

Again, the conference's attendees broke into laughter.

"Watch your mouth, fat boy!" James Speech of Virginia shouted to Marion.

"Or what?" Marion asked. "You're going to run to Texas and ask Damian if you can go to war? Oh, I forgot, you can't do that. He's in the hospital because he was sharpening his pencil inside of some cop's old lady. You'll have to ask his weak little brother, the corporate attorney over here."

Emil cringed.

"Big words, from a big fat mouth," Anjouinette told him. I'll enjoy making you eat them."

"I'd rather eat you, Anjouinette," Marion smiled.

"The Reigns family can no longer just seat people at this table at its fancy," Don Ambrogino told Dajon.

"I thought we came to discuss peace, not insult one another," Dajon told them.

"You want peace? Withdraw from all of our territories, or else suffer the consequences, Senor," Chacho told him.

"The Reigns family must halt its East Coast expansion," Don Graziella Biaggio of New York told Dajon. "Or else it must face the wrath of those it offends."

"Don Graziella, those are not the words of peace,"

Emil told him. "Must I remind you that an attack on one member of our Commission, is considered an attack on all?"

"My organization won't go to war over the independent ambitions of the Reigns family," Don Ambrogino announced. "Their continuous expansionistic and ultra-aggressive policies will not drag me into their private little wars!"

"Hell, I'm not gaining anything from Damian sticking his cousin in Pennsylvania, and then giving him a seat on the Commission," Marion told them. "Screw that shit!"

"When this Commission met to discuss the issue of East Coast expansion, approval was granted by majority vote," Dajon told them. "The Reigns family bankrolled much of the operation, and the Reigns family provided the majority of the troops. We also provided the operational experience and leadership necessary to carry out the expansions. Therefore, isn't it only natural, since we did perform the bulk of the work, to be able to have a say in who's seated as our representative in those territories?"

"You wish to turn our Commission into your own private little family club!" Barry shouted. "That's unacceptable!"

"So you're okay with expansion; you just want to pick the new members who we seat?" Dajon asked. "Okay, so who will we seat? Who do we know in those territories who we can safely bring into our organization? Yes, my cousin Brandon wants to be seated as the representative from Maryland, but that's because he already controls all of Maryland. He fought for that territory, and successfully won it, and unified it. It's his. The same goes for my cousin Joshua and the state of Pennsylvania. He earned that territory with his own sweat, blood, and sacrifice."

"And the troops they used to take over those territories?" Chacho asked. "Were they not Reigns family soldiers imported from Texas?"

Dajon nodded. "They were."

"So, if I sent five hundred guys to Alaska, could I have the pipeline?" Barry asked in his deep Arkansas drawl.

The men seated around the table laughed.

"You sent those troops on behalf of the Commission, not on behalf of the Reigns family," Adolphus told Dajon. "Now, you want to change the rules. You sent them men, so now you get to keep the territory?"

"We took the risk; we took the territory; we should reap the benefits," Dajon told them. "But in essence, we'll all reap the benefits of the expansion. More territory, means more consumers, which means that collectively, we place larger orders, and receive bigger discounts. We have a larger manpower base during conflicts."

"And we have more Reigns control over this organization," Juan interrupted.

"Gentlemen, it's our desire that your Commission doesn't expand into our territories, period," Don Nicostrato Cinzia of New York told them. "This debate about who sits in those seats on your Commission would be superfluous, if you didn't create the seats to begin with. Expansion means war. The equation's simple."

"How about, we cease all hostilities, and everyone keeps their men in place?" Dajon suggested.

"Territories can't be divided along that nature," Don Bonafacio told him. "Besides, even if we halted today, you would still have men in our territories, you would still control part of our territories, and nothing would have been resolved. No, your people must withdraw."

"I can't make that decision alone," Dajon informed the East Coast families. "The decision to expand was a joint decision by our Commission. Several of those members are not in attendance today. We must again vote."

"Dajon, it's simple," Don Ambrogino told him. "Withdraw your troops from the East Coast, and the expansion can't continue."

"Again, it's a Commission decision, not a Reigns family decision," Dajon reiterated.

The New York and Las Vegas attendees exchanged glances.

141

"We'll give you two weeks to make a decision," Don Cipriano announced. "After that, if you haven't made a decision to withdraw, then the war continues until the last man has drawn his final breath."

"Gentlemen, it's simple," Don Crencenzo told them. "Sell your Las Vegas holdings, withdraw your people from the East Coast, and we shall have peace. Do not, and we'll have war."

"Gentlemen, we shall reconvene at a later date to conclude our peace agreements," Vladmir informed the attendees. "We all know what must be done to end the war, and to bring peace and stability once again. Let us all do what's necessary to make peace happen. Gentlemen, this conference is adjourned."

Dajon waited in a private anteroom just down the hall from where the conference had been held. Ajouinette, Emil, and Malcolm 'Baby Doc' Mueller of Alabama stormed into the room.

"What in the hell were you thinking?" Anjouinette demanded. "You can't give those territories back. Those territories were taken for a reason. Those are buffer areas, centers of gravity, population centers. They were taken for a reason. They were taken to keep your enemies weak, to prevent them from growing strong and being able to threaten you!"

"You showed the Old Ones that their activities against your family were having an effect!" Emil shouted.

"You were insulted, Dajon, and yet you said nothing!" Anjouinette said. "You showed weakness, and the weaker you appeared, the bolder they became!"

"You weren't ready for this," Emil told him. "You don't know the history, the nuances, the reasoning beyond so many of your family's previous decisions. You're too green."

"Now, you must strike back, and you must strike hard," Anjouinette told him. "You must send a message."

"They walked away licking their chops over your

territory, and ecstatic over how weak you appeared," Emil told him.

"Did you hear Frediano?" Malcolm asked. "He's in bed with them one hundred percent, no doubt about it."

"No surprise," Anjouinette announced. "Frediano has always wanted to be a 'made man'. I think he fantasizes about being a Genovese or something."

"He probably has posters of John Gotti all over his bedroom." Emil told them. "I wouldn't be surprised if he whacked off to them at night."

They all shared a quick laugh.

"You're going to have to kill Marion for his insult," Anjouinette told him. "Frediano also and you're going to have to send a message or you're going to be in for an even bigger war. They're going to unify, and they're going to come after your territory. You're going to have to show them that you're not weak, and that you still command the most powerful family in the history of this country."

Dajon nodded.

"My jet's waiting at the airport," Anjouinette told him. "You can fly home with me."

"My family jet's also at the airport," Dajon told her.

Anjouinette waved her hand, dismissing the issue. "Your plane can follow mines."

Anjouinette placed her arms inside Dajon's, and led him out of the room and down the hall. "Come, we'll discuss ways to kill Fediano. I'm from Louisiana, and I have a particular method in mind.

Chapter Sixteen

Don Ambrogino hated those middle of the night trips to the bathroom. He wished that some designer or architect or plumbing company would invent some fashionable porcelain hole that one could mount into the floor right next the bed. If his wife would let him get away with it, he would have had a urinal installed in the space where his nightstand sat.

He entered his luxurious, marble-filled master bathroom. His sleep-filled eyes were half closed, and his aged bones made each step to his toilet a painful adventure.

The Don loosened the hole on his pajamas, and proceeded to relieve himself. The procedure lasted longer than usual, as tonight's dinner party saw the consumption of several bottles of Pessac-Leognan. He suspected that tonight's excesses were partly the reason for his pounding head, unsure feet, and extreme fatigue. He also believed that it was the reason why he smelled the faint scent of alcohol. It wasn't.

The chemically laced rag flew over The Don's nose and mouth with enough speed and adroitness to muffle his voice long before he could even think to shout. He struggled and breathed deeply, causing the chemical to take affect more rapidly than normal. The Don was out within seconds.

Anjouinette snapped her fingers, and one of her men

leaned forward and waved smelling salt beneath the Don's nose. The Don slowly regained consciousness.

"What the hell?" The Don asked groggily. "Where in the hell am I?"

"You're in New Braunsfels, Texas, at a place called the Snake Farm," Anjouinette told him. "It's like a small animal farm slash petting zoo, where tourists can walk through and examine reptiles in their cages. Some of the snakes are humongous, some are small, some are poisonous, and some aren't dangerous at all. But the section we're in tonight, is the section that contains the alligators."

"What's the meaning of this?" The Don asked. He tried to move, only to realize that his hands were tied behind his back, and his legs were bound. "What are you doing?"

"We're going to feed you to the alligators," Anjouinette told him. "See, your legs are attached to a small crane, Frediano. When I give the word, the crane operator's going to lift you into the air, swing you over the alligator pit, and lower you down into it."

The Don began struggling with his bindings. "What about the peace treaty?"

"That treaty was between the Commission and the Old Ones, not between Commission members," Anjouinette told him.

"We were supposed to be settling our differences!" the Don shouted.

"Freddy, after tonight, I promise you, we'll never have another disagreement again," Anjouinette told him.

The bodyguards gathered around the alligator pit broke into laughter.

"Why are you doing this?" The Don asked. "What have I done to deserve this?"

"You offended the Reigns family in public, you humiliated the head of the family, and then you have the nerve to ask why," Anjouinette told him.

"This has nothing to do with you!" The Don shouted. "This is between me and the Reigns family!"

Anjouinette lifted her hand, and the crane operator went to work. He threw the levers forward that would lift the Don into the air, and then pushed forward another lever turning the crane, and positioning him over the center of the gator pit.

"Stop! Wait!" The Don shouted. "We can make an arrangement! Listen to me!"

"What is it, Freddy?" Anjouinette asked impatiently.

"The Reigns family is weak right now," The Don explained. "Damian is wounded; Princess is wounded; Dante is out of the picture; they're vulnerable. The only thing holding them together is the loyalty of their under bosses and close associates, such as yourself! We can unite, and deal them a death blow. You can have all of Texas, if you like."

"Don you can't give, what you do not own," Anjouinette told him.

"They killed your husband!" The Don shouted. "Now's the time to seek your revenge!"

"Don, yes, it's true that the Reigns family killed my husband, but now I sit on the Commission and control the entire state of Louisiana. That was my husband's seat. And you're sadly mistaken, the Reigns family is far from being imperiled," Anjouinette told him. "A Reigns still sits at the head of the family, and they're as strong as ever."

"I talked to some of their under bosses!" the Don shouted. "They're willing to defect! Join us, and I promise you all of Texas! You can control the majority of the Commission's entrance points!"

"Which under bosses agreed to defect?" Anjouinette asked.

"Cut me down and join us!" the Don shouted.

Anjouinette nodded toward the crane operator. The crane whirred alive, and slowly Ambrogino was lowered into the pit. The alligators just below had been aroused by all of the nocturnal activity around them. They had gathered at the center of the pit, and were watching as their midnight

146

snack was being lowered down to them. Several of the gators sat frozen in place, with their mouths wide-open.

The Don screamed with the ferocity of a wounded hyena, when the first gator clamped down upon his bound arms. The second gator bite snapped his left arm in two, like a dry string of spaghetti. The Don cried out once again, and Anjouinette had the crane operator pull him up.

"You can make this easy, or you can make this excruciatingly painful, Frediano," Anjouinette told him. "The choice is yours. Now, which under bosses agreed to betray the Reigns family?"

"Please." The Don pleaded. "Please, don't do this. We can make a deal!"

Anjouinette nodded toward her crane operator, who again lowered the Don into the alligator pit. This time, the gators were worked up in a frenzy. The Don lost his hand as soon as he came within reach of the pit. His right arm was shattered seconds later.

"I'll tell you!" the Don shouted in excruciating pain. "I'll tell you what you want to know!"

Anjouinette lifted her hand, and the crane operator raised the Don into the air.

"I'm listening," Anjouinette shouted.

"It was Justin and Allen; they agreed to betray your family!" the Don shouted. "They wanted to cut a deal!"

"And the Old Ones?" Anjouinette asked. "What was their deal with you?"

"What deal?" Don Ambrogino asked. "I don't know what you're talking about."

Anjouinette pointed to the pit. "See that two-hundred-fifty pound gator right in the middle, the one with the silvery tint to his skin. I call him Caligula. He eats with a decadence that was rivaled only by his namesake."

"Okay, okay," Don shouted. "I get to be made. I get to buy into a couple of casinos, and I get to be a full member of their organization."

"And what did they get in exchange?" Ajouinette

asked.

"Information, they mainly wanted information," The Don shouted. "I also bring over my entire army, and I become the enforcer and protector after all is said and done."

"You betrayed the entire Commission, Frediano," Anjouinette told him.

"Your Commission is nothing but a motley connection of niggers, Mexicans, and rednecks," the Don shouted. "I'm Sicilian, a descendant of a very old and proud Sicilian family. That's why I did what I did."

Anjouinette made the sign of the cross. "Go with God, Freddy."

Anjouinette turned toward the crane operator, and nodded. The operator released the cable that the Don was tied to, dropping the Don into the pit of alligators. His shouts stopped three minutes after he landed, and the only sound that remained, was the snarling, chomping, and biting of the feeding alligators.

"You want us to get rid of the body, ma'am?" one of her men asked.

Anjouinette shook her head. "No, let the workers find his remains in the morning. The reason we flew him here to Texas was to make it public and messy, and to send a very clear message about the resolve and strength of the Reigns family. I think this message will be received loud and clear. The Reigns family is still strong, and very much capable and willing to use its muscle. Just clear our guys out, and don't leave any trace of our involvement."

Don Salvatore Tiziano stormed into the conference room like a category five hurricane. His fury was matched only by that of those already inside of the room, awaiting his arrival.

"They've gone too far now!" Don Tiziano told the others. "They must be taught a lesson!"

Don Patrizio Giovanneta nodded solemnly. "We're in agreement; they must be punished. They came to Las Vegas, kidnapped a Sicilian from his bathroom, while his wife was asleep in the bedroom, flew him out of town, and fed him to a bunch of god damned alligators! And they did it without even so much as a hello!"

"This kind of disrespect cannot be tolerated!" Don Anastasio Crencenzo added. "If they can just waltz into our territory, and do anything they want, without asking for permission, then what's next?"

"Next it'll be the Chinese, then the Colombians or the Cubans," Don Giovanneta announced. "Even the fucking Haitians or the Jamaicans!"

"Those uppity niggers must be taught a lesson," Don Tiziano said forcefully. "They must be put back in their place!"

Don Umberto Constantino leaned forward and cleared his throat. "I'm just as upset as the next man," he told them. "They should have respected us enough to ask for permission. But there's another issue at hand here. Don Ambrogino was a member of their Commission. He wasn't a member of our organization. He was subject to their rules and he operated within their circles. Do we go to war over someone who wasn't really one of us?"

"Don Ambrogino was Sicilian!" Don Tiziano shouted. "He was from the old country. His family's town is next to my ancestor's town. He was of the truest blood and his death at the hands of those monkeys should be avenged."

Don Constantino leaned forward calmly. "He died at the hands of alligators, not monkeys. There's a saying, Salvatore. You lie down with dogs; you come up with fleas. Don Ambrogino, God rest his soul, chose to lie down with these dogs. Can we truly be upset because some of them went for his throat?"

"We cannot allow a bunch of niggers to run roughshod over us!" Don Tiziano shouted. "Regardless of Don Ambrogino's affiliations, he was Sicilian! And he was living right here in Vegas among us! Are we to allow anyone to come into our homes and take whoever they wish? What happened to the old school code? Our organizations were originally founded to protect our people from just this sort of thing! Are we forgetting where we came from? Have we forgotten the reason for our very existence? They must be hit, and they must be hit immediately!"

Don Constantino clapped his hands slowly and methodically.

"Very impassioned speech, Sal, but that doesn't change the fact that Frediano chose to belong to that group. It does not change the fact that he wasn't really one of us. Are we to ask our men to sacrifice their lives, for a Sicilian who betrayed his own people, to run with dogs? Frediano, God rest his soul, was nothing more than a puppet to that monkey in Colombia. He was a drug dealer! A peddler of smack and coke and God knows what else. Are we to ask our men to sacrifice their lives for such an individual?"

"We also cannot ignore the fact that they came into our territory and conducted an operation without asking for permission," Don Giovanneta told them.

"They killed Freddy in a very brutal and public manner," Don Crencenzo told them. "It was their intention to send a message. Frediano insulted their family at our conference, and they want everyone to know that they have the muscle and the willpower to act."

"Such messages are usually given by those who are insecure about themselves and their positions," Don Giovanneta announced. "It's a sign of the young Reigns' weakness and inexperience."

"They've sent a message," Don Tiziano told them. "We must send a message back."

"Are we all in agreement then?" Don Crencenzo asked. "We'll retaliate for the death of Don Ambrogino?"

Nods swept around the table.

"Has anyone been in contact with our compatriots in New York?" Don Constantino asked.

"New York's fully aware of what has transpired," Don Tiziano announced.

"How is it to be done?" Don Constantino asked.

"Damian's to be dismissed from the hospital on Monday," Don Crencenzo announced. "I think that it's within our best interest, if he doesn't resume his position at the head of their family."

Don Giovanneta laughed. "You mean you wish to keep the weak brother in charge, while we divide up their territory?"

The others gathered around the table joined in the laughter.

"Gentlemen, we have a unique opportunity here," Don Crenzenzo told them. "We have an opportunity to take over all of the territory that the Reigns family controls, and to make a profit from the lucrative narcotics business, by controlling the main entrance points in Texas, New Mexico, and Florida. We bring this upstart Commission to its knees, charge those filthy Colombians and Mexicans a healthy tariff to use our entrance points, and we make a fortune. And we do it, without actually selling one gram of narcotics."

"Beautiful!" Don Constantino lifted his glass of wine into the air.

The men seated around the table lifted their glasses into the air as well.

"To the death of the Reigns family and to the beginning of a new fortune!" Don Tiziano shouted.

"To Dajon!" Don Crencenzo toasted. "To being such a fool and an idiot!"

The Dons around the table laughed hardily, and drank in celebration of their new plan.

Chapter Seventeen

The Town and Country Bowl was one of the most popular high school football games in South Central Texas. Two of the area's wealthiest public schools were playing today. Halftime saw the waving of platinum credit cards and Louis Vuitton purses in the air, exotic cars, and a general display of enough material wealth, to make Donald Trump blush. Each year, thirty thousand people turned out to watch these two communities battle it out and showcase their wealth. It was these thirty thousand fans that had caused the massive traffic jam that Vincenzo and his caravan was now trapped in.

Damian rose and made the sign of the cross. The ceremony had been particularly meaningful today, as Father O'Connell had spoke of change and redemption, and of becoming a new man through the acceptance of Jesus Christ as savior. Because of the events of the last few weeks, he had begun to read the Bible again, and this time, each book brought a new discovery, a new meaning and a new revelation. Although he had read the Bible more than two dozen times throughout his life, he was amazed that somehow, someway, he always found something new. Since the attempt on his life, he had managed to find many new things. It seemed as though God was speaking to him

152

directly.

"C'mon, will ya!" Vincenzo shouted, as he honked his horn. He was late, and he had a package to deliver. It was a delivery that had to be timed perfectly.

"Damian, good to see you here," Father O'Connell told him with a big wide grin. He clasped Damian's hand and shook it firmly. "So, how do you feel, son?"

Damian shook his head. "Not too good, Father. Some days are better than others, but for the most part, I feel lousy."

"The Lord heals, Damian," Father O'Connell told him. "He heals your physical wounds, as well as your spiritual ones. And sometimes, it takes the healing of the soul, before we can begin the healing of the body."

"You were talking directly to me today, weren't you, Father?" Damian asked.

Father O'Connell shook his head. "I was speaking the Lord's words, son. If they meant something to you, then it was he who was talking to you. Now, it's up to you to respond."

"I waited patiently for the Lord to help me," Damian whispered. "And he turned to me and heard my cry. He lifted me out of the pit of despair, out of the mud and the mire. He set my feet on solid ground and steadied me as I walked along. He has given me a new song to sing, a hymn of praise to our God."

"Many will see what he has done and be astounded," Father O'Connell continued. "They'll put their trust in the Lord, Psalm forty."

"That's one of my favorites," Damian told him.

"The Lord hears his people when they call to him for help," Father O'Connell told him. "He rescues them from all their troubles. The righteous face many troubles, but the Lord rescues them from each and every one, Psalm thirty-four."

"Thank you for everything that you've done for me, Father," Damian told him. "When I was lying in that hospital bed, just opening my eyes and seeing you sitting there, meant so much to me."

"Damian, I've known you since you were born," Father O'Connell smiled his gentle all-knowing smile. "I watched you grow strong and tall. I watched you go off to college, and then to graduate school, and then take that job with Price Waterhouse Coopers. Our entire parish was so proud of you."

"Father."

Father O'Connell lifted his hand, stopping Damian from speaking. "Sometimes, even the best of our flock strays. The straying is not the important part; it's returning to the fold that is. God understands. It's the reason why Jesus died for us. And because he died for us, we have all been given a new beginning. Come back into the fold, son."

Emory Reigns clasped her son's hand, peered into his eyes, and nodded solemnly. "Sometimes God allows things to happen to his children, in order to remind them of what they should be doing with their lives."

Damian steadied himself with his cane and smiled. "Father, you can expect to see me around here, a lot more."

"I'd like that very much, Damian," Father O'Connell told him with a smile.

Vincenzo turned the corner, and could finally see the cathedral. He had finally made his way past that morass of traffic pouring out from the city's famed Alamo Dome, and was now approaching his delivery point. The other armored trucks following just behind him, followed their own predetermined routes. They each had their own missions to complete. Vincenzo waved his arms toward his fellow drivers, bidding them farewell, and wishing each of them luck on their assignments. Even though they were now within eyesight of their targets, so many things could go wrong. The armored trucks, had been stolen earlier in the day from the Brinks armored truck depot, and he was certain that they had been reported missing by now. The police officer outside the cathedral directing traffic, made him extremely nervous.

Damian's bodyguards clasped his forearm, and that of his mother who accompanied him that day, and began to assist them out of the cathedral. The cathedral had been packed. The bodyguards slowly, and politely, made a small path toward the door for Damian and his mother. Vincenzo kissed the photo of his daughters that he had pasted on the dashboard of the stolen armored truck. He had been diagnosed with full-blown AIDS, and like so many others, he carried not one cent of medical or life insurance. He was dying, and he was going to die soon.

He had been approached by a nurse who suggested that he call her cousin, who was interested in helping people with no insurance, who were dying and who had families to take care of. He listened to the proposal, which involved recruiting two other terminally ill patients from the clinic. They were to steal armored trucks and blow up a church where one of the parishioners was none other than Damian Reigns. He was offered two million dollars for this assignment. At first, he walked away from it and thought he would finish his life in a quiet hospice for the homeless. Vince now found himself in Texas, barreling down a crowded street toward a two-hundred-year-old cathedral. It was for his family, he kept repeating to himself; it was for his little girls. He had a plan. A plan that would take good care of them, after he was gone. It was all that he had ever wanted, to be able to take care of his little girls. He just hoped that he wasn't too late, because of that stupid football game.

The sun was shining brightly today. Because of the glint from the cars passing by, as well as from the windows from the nearby building, the bodyguards almost missed the armored trucks coming from both ends of the street. And then suddenly, the trucks accelerated rapidly.

"It's a hit!" Damian's bodyguard shouted into his earpiece.

The men surrounding Damian scooped him into the air, raced to the limousine, and dumped him inside. His mother was quickly tossed into the vehicle on top of him.

"Go! Go! Go!" a bodyguard shouted, while banging on the roof of the limousine.

The limousine driver hit the gas, and sped down the street, just before reaching the first armored car.

The armored cars were unaware that their target had just sped off in a black, armored, Hummer limousine. They raced for the cathedral. Their mission was to deliver their cargo of C-4 high explosives. The armor was to protect the drivers and the cargo from the small arms fire that was now plinking off the sides and windshields of the trucks.

The first armored truck bounced up the cathedral's massive stairs, slammed through the double front entry doors, barreled inside of the building, and exploded just inside.

The second armored truck plowed through the manicured lawn of the cathedral, and slammed into the right side of the building, while the third armored truck did the same on the left side of the building. The massive blasts from the nearly simultaneous explosions turned the cathedral into a massive fireball with burning bricks flying through the air and dealing death and destruction to all who were unfortunate enough to be within range. The blast was felt throughout the city.

"Momma, are you okay?" Damian gasped.

Emory nodded. Tears poured from her wrinkled and weary eyes. "The church! They blew up the church!" Emory lowered her head into the palms of her hands, and wept uncontrollably.

They had just tried to kill him and in doing so, they almost killed his mother. Not an army on this planet would be able to stop Dante once he was out of prison. There would be no peace agreements, no plea bargains, no-cease fires, no nothing. Dante would kill everything moving, until he was the last man standing.

Dajon paced back and forth, pausing only to bite his fingernails, and to peer out at the lake. Damian's living room was too big for his taste; Damian's home was too big for his taste; Damian's shoes were too big to fill. His brother had been hit, his wounds reopened, and he was now back in the hospital under heavy sedation, and under even heavier guard.

"What kind of monsters am I dealing with?" Dajon wondered aloud. They had blown up a church, killed over two hundred of its parishioners, and wounded over three hundred more. The death toll was expected to climb dramatically. Nothing was sacred to these people, not church, not God, not family, nothing. Father O'Connell had been gravely wounded, as had Father Greely and Father Dominguez. City Council-member Mary Allen Tanner was dead, as was State Representative Helen Hawk. There were doctors, lawyers, civic, and business leaders, who were all gone. Dead.

They killed his precious Daisalla; they almost killed his son D.J. They tried to kill his sister, had attempted to kill both of his brothers, tried to kill him. They were ruining his family's company, threatening his family wealth, and grinding his family down with a war that was clearly a stalemate. His under bosses were on the verge of defecting, his mother was a nervous wreck, and his father was dead. They were too powerful. Whoever it was, was just too powerful. The cost was too high.

Anjouinette strode into the room and walked to where Dajon was standing.

"It was the Old Ones," she told him. "They're retaliating for Don Ambrogino. Apparently, he was a lot closer to them than anyone knew."

157

Anjouinette exhaled and shook her head. "These Sicilians and their glorified sense of honor and family are a bit extreme. I cannot believe that they're willing to go to war over a member of our Commission. It just doesn't make sense. Why risk it, over someone who was not part of their organization? There must be more to it, something that we're not seeing."

"There's always something more, some hidden agenda, some unknown motivation, some ridiculous reason for more murder." Dajon shook his head.

"Dajon."

"You're right; I don't understand," Dajon interrupted. "That was what you were going to say, weren't you? That I don't understand the way things are; that I don't understand the reasoning, the history, behind all of this madness. Well you're right, and to tell you the truth, I don't want to understand it! I don't think anyone really understands it! I think everyone just rolls with the punches, and tries to outdo the next madman. The more bodies you pile up, the more you get it; is that how this works? Well I don't want to get it! I don't! I can't do this anymore! I can't! I retaliate, then they retaliate, then I retaliate some more, and then they retaliate some more, and pretty soon, we've all blown each other to hell! This is bullshit! This is not business; this is bullshit!"

Anjouinette lifted her hand and slapped Dajon across his face. "Look here, Dajon! You'd better get it together, and get it together quickly. We told you in the beginning, that this was not the Boy Scouts that you were joining. We told you in the beginning that these were special times; that these were difficult circumstances under. Your family's under siege, and they need you! They need for you to step up and be strong. They need for you to be half the man that your brother is. That's all they need for you to be, just half."

Anjouinette shoved Dajon back onto a nearby sofa. "Are you going to turn tail and run at the first sign of danger? Are you going to curl up in a corner and quit at the first setback? If you are, tell me now, and I'll just shoot you myself! I'll shoot you, I'll take over the Reigns family, and I'll do what you're not man enough to do. I'll save your family. Your mother, your daughter, your nieces, your nephews, your cousins, your entire family, needs you right now. They need for you to be the head of their family. Are you going to do it or do you want me to do it?"

Dajon sniffled.

"And let this be the last time that I find you crying like a sniveling bitch!" Anjouinette told him.

Emil kissed Princess's hand and gently caressed her face. Her eyes opened, and she smiled.

"Security has cleared the corridors for us," Emil told her. "Are you ready to go for your daily walk?"

Princess nodded, and pressed the remote control that was attached to her hospital bed, causing the bed to lift her up. With great effort, she threw the covers off her legs, and allowed Emil to assist her in climbing out of the bed.

"So, what's the latest news?" she asked.

Emil shook his head. "Not good. They made an attempt on your brother's life. They used armored trucks, and terminally ill drivers as smart bombs, and they leveled the church."

Princess closed her eyes and shook her head. "I told him not to go there. It was too soon. He should have stayed at home, under heavy guard, where he could recuperate."

"I told him the same thing," Emil admitted. "But for some reason, he felt that he had to go. Damian doesn't seem to be the same since the shooting. He's into spirituality a lot more."

"Probably just a phase," Princess told him. "You know how it is. His shooting was a life-altering experience for him. It'll probably take some time, but he'll be back."

Emil nodded. "I hope you're right.."

Princess grabbed her walker.

"And our little deception, is it still in place."

"As far as anyone knows, you're still in a coma," Emil

told her.

"Good," she nodded. "I can't wait to show up on those sons of bitches' doorsteps, and personally shove sticks of dynamite up their asses."

Chapter Eighteen

Emory kissed her son's forehead, waking him from his peaceful rest. Damian opened his weary eyes all tired and worn-out from the events of the last month. He had been through hell, came back, and walked through hell a second time. Rest was what he craved; a long, deep, relaxing sleep was what he desperately needed. His body felt as though someone had laid an anvil on top of him; he could hardly move, and his head felt as though he had been heavily drugged. He would give anything to rewind the hands of time, if even just back to the previous thirty days.

"How do you feel, baby?" Emory asked her son.

"I don't know," Damian whispered. "I don't know if the medicine has me feeling this way or if it's just my body telling me that it's time."

"Time for what?"

"Time to give up," Damian told her. Tears slowly begin to stream from his eyes. "I'm so tired, Momma. I'm just so tired."

"Then rest, baby." Emory caressed her son's forehead. "Give it all up to the Lord, and let him take care of it. Whatever your burdens are, Damian, give them to the Lord. If you're that tired and if you truly in fact have run your race, then the Lord will call you home."

Emory leaned back in her chair and closed her eyes. "But those who wait on the Lord shall find new strength.

They shall fly on wings like eagles. They shall run and not grow weary. They will walk and not faint."

"What book is that, Momma?" Damian asked. "I can't remember."

"It's in Isaiah, baby, chapter forty, verse thirty-one."

Damian shook his head and looked away. "So many people are counting on me."

Emory sat up again, smiled at her son, and patted his arm.

"Then Jesus said, come to me, all of you who are weary and carry heavy burdens, and I'll give you rest. Take my yoke upon you. Let me teach you, because I'm humble and gentle, and you'll find rest for your souls. For my yoke fits perfectly, and the burden I give you is light."

"How did you do it for all of these years, Mom?" Damian asked. "How did you stay true; how did you keep your faith?"

"By having faith, sweetie, you have to simply have faith," Emory told him. "If man only had faith the size of a mustard seed, he would be able to move mountains. Damian, the Lord understands that you're not perfect; he doesn't expect you to be. Just be the best person that you know how to be. In your heart, you know goodness. Not just right from wrong, but goodness. Don't just obey God's commandments, but go out there, and help his children. Baby, you've been blessed. You have an obligation to God, to share that bounty. Use whatever gifts, whatever talents, whatever resources that you have, to do good things in this world."

Damian peered into his mother's eyes. "Momma, I've done so much bad, so much bad."

"I taught you to believe in a loving God, in a forgiving God. You can change your life."

"And what if I lose everything?" Damian asked. Tears again poured from his eyes. The medication had wreaked havoc on his emotional stability. "What if I lose the company, my family, you?"

162

Emory shook her head and smiled. "Sweetie, you came into this world with nothing. When you leave this world, you'll take nothing with you. Only a person who's empty on the inside would fear losing everything on the outside. Lose it all, and then start over from the beginning. I didn't raise my children to be quitters, Damian. If we lose the company, we'll come back even stronger in a few years. And as far as losing me, you can never lose me, Damian. I'm your mother, and I always will be. I'll always be a part of you, and you'll always be a part of me; you're my child."

"It takes money to start over, Mom," Damian told her."

"Damian, I sent you to Harvard for a reason," Emory snapped. "I sent you there, not to become brilliant, but because you were brilliant. As long as you have your mind, you have the potential to accomplish anything. Damian, your father left me very well off. Whatever you need to start over again, you'll have it."

Damian smiled and turned away. "Momma, we're talking tens of millions of dollars."

"No, Damian, we're not," Emory countered. "You can take $1,000,000 head to Wall Street, and turn that money into a fortune. I've seen you do it before. Besides, if you need more, you'll have it. I have about $32,000,000 in cash saved up, about $36,000,000 in stocks, about $6,000,000 in certificates of deposit at our bank, about four million in Treasury bonds, and another $6,000,000 to $10,000,000 scattered in various other investments."

"Mom!" Damian began choking. "Where did it come from? How did you and Dad keep that a secret from us?"

"Damian, your father owned one of the largest construction companies in the state, before he retired and left it to you. Your father, he was no fool. He invested very well, and he made sure that regardless of how you children ran the businesses that we gave you, that he and I would be comfortable in our old age." Emory smiled, and patted her son's arm. "Not that we didn't trust you children, but life taught us to always have a backup."

163

"Does Princess know about this other money?" Damian asked.

"No, we told no one," Emory answered. "Why should we have told any of you? It is our money. Besides, in the event that you weren't successful with the businesses that we turned over to you, we didn't want you running back to us asking for money. Damian, we gave you the education to succeed, and started you off with businesses to help you succeed. Now, if you ran those into the ground, that's your fault, not ours. But, it turns out that you kids didn't; you were very successful. Your father and I have always been so proud of you."

Damian turned away and smiled. Even if Bio One failed, he would have the capital to start over, to meet his payroll, to protect his family. He could do it. Now, his main concern was staying alive, recuperating, and then coming out swinging. He would protect his family, he would leave the Commission, and then he would get his life together. He was going to be the man that his mother would be proud of. He was going to the man that Nathan wanted him to be. His thoughts turned to Stacia. He owed her more than words could say. He owed her for years of loyalty, for years of unconditional love. He owed her for years of friendship, and for years of companionship. She stood by him, watched and waited as he looked past her, and fell into the beds of other women. Why he could not marry her, was a reason so trivial, so childish, as to not be worthy of mention. She had given her love to another when they were sixteen, and then to another at the age of eighteen. His jealousy and ego had prevented him from making a wife out of his soul mate. She was now married to another, and he had squandered a rare gift given to precious few. He would do right things by her, and eventually even by Nathan, a man who despised him for everything that he had become. A man who only wanted him to become what his community wanted him to be. Yes, he would become that man. But first, he needed to resolve the current issues of the day. He needed to be finished with the

Commission, with El Jeffe, with the Old Ones, with that entire group of dregs. He would need the Lord to forgive this one last discretion, this one last romp. He needed to be evil for one last time, so that he could once again be good. His thoughts turned to Princess. His sister's secret recovery would be his ace in the hole. He would surprise his enemies with her sudden emergence. They thought his family was weakened, lying on its deathbed. They thought the Reigns family was growing weaker, when in fact it was growing stronger.

Emory, leaned over her son's bed, and kissed him on his cheek.

"Get some rest son," Emory whispered. "Get some rest." She pulled the thin knit hospital blanket over his shoulders, and tucked him in.

Kiawah Island, South Carolina, was a ten-thousand-acre island that catered only to the very rich. The island community built seven premium golf courses, designed by the likes of such stellar designers as Pete Dye, Tom Fazio, and Tom Watson. The courses surrounded a massive Southern Style plantation, which had been converted into a luxurious private resort hotel. The Reigns family owned a summer residence on the island that they used when schedules permitted.

Their mansion boasted no less than thirty-two massive two-story Doric columns. The columns supported the white-washed mahogany wraparound porch, as well as the mansion's wraparound second-floor veranda. Although there had been some recent construction, the house looked as though it had been plucked from along the banks of the Mississippi River, and transported through time. It exuded a Southern charm and elegance of a long bygone era.

The meeting with the under bosses was being held in the mahogany-paneled conference room in the mansion's basement. All of the family's under bosses were present, many of them eager to see if Dajon, the family's new head leader, was as weak and inexperienced as he was rumored to be, many of them eager to find the opportunity to pull away and start their own families.

Dajon paced around the room impatiently, trying not to be nervous; he knew what he had to do. He could feel Anjouinette's eyes following him around the room. They were piercing, yet in some strange way, steadying.

What was it about this woman that brought out so many emotions? He cursed her strength, her willpower, and her assertiveness, while at the same time she gave him spine; she provided him with confidence and strength to carry on through some of his darkest moments. He didn't mind showing his weakness around her; he didn't mind showing his uncertainty, his inexperience. He hadn't felt this comfortable with a woman since Daisalla.

Daisalla was the wind beneath his wings, much like Anjouinette was these days. Daisalla gave him the confidence to do things that he had never done before. She gave him strength and even inspiration? That was too strong a word, especially for a woman who wasn't his wife. No, he couldn't use that word, not now, not yet. His beloved Daissalla had been gone only a short time and he was certain that he would love no one else ever in life. *Love? Where did that word come from?* he asked himself. Why had such a word popped into his head? Was he falling in love with Anjouinette? Was that possible? He loved Daissalla, and nothing would ever change that, not distance, not time, not death, not anything. So how could he possibly be falling for another woman? Say her name, he told himself you can say her name. *Anjouinette.* How could he be falling for Anjouinette? Could a man love two women at the same time? What did he love about Anjouinette? He simply loved strong black women. But how could he have found love again so soon? *Does it mean I didn't really love Daissalla?* No, that thought was ridiculous. He loved her with all his heart. The entire universe couldn't contain the love that he felt for her. But was he betraying her by having these other feelings? *Daissalla, talk to me. Tell me what's going on; tell me what you feel.*

"It appears as though we're all here, Mr. Reigns," Andrew Titan told him. "I really hate to sound impatient, but as you're probably aware, I run the District of Columbia operations for the family. We are knee-deep in a war with the Old Ones, and my presence is required at home."

Dajon nodded. "Yes, I'm aware of that, Andrew. In fact, I'm aware that we all have pressing concerns elsewhere, so I won't hold us up for long. I just have some pressing concerns that need to be addressed."

Dajon paused, cleared his throat, and then resumed his pacing. "As you all probably know by now, I'm in charge of the family, until my brother recuperates from his wounds."

"Or, until Princess recuperates?" Brian Vance asked.

"No, until Damian recuperates," Dajon told them. "My sister's still in a coma, and if by some miracle she was able to recover and resume operational status, she would assume a position as my deputy. A position currently occupied by our family friend, Anjouinette Tibbideaux. Now, as most of you already know, I've never been involved in the activities of my family's various enterprises, until very recently. The activities of the previous weeks have thrust me into a position in which I am unfamiliar and inexperienced. I have learned much and have grown quickly into my current position. It's because of my inexperience, that my leadership of this family has been questioned, challenged, and undermined not only by members of the Commission, but by my own under bosses as well. We're here today to clear up any misunderstandings about the leadership of this family."

"Who in this room wants out of this family?" Brandon Reigns, head of the state of Maryland, asked.

Ajouinette lifted her hand, silencing Brandon. She nodded toward Dajon, indicating that he could continue.

"Thank you, Brandon, but I'll take things from here," Dajon told his cousin. "Gentlemen, it has recently come to our attention, that some of you want to defect. Some of you in this room want to take your armies and your territories and venture out on your own or align yourselves with others, in anticipation of the Reigns family's demise. Gentlemen, I can assure you that the news of this family's demise has been greatly exaggerated. We're here, and we shall remain open for business."

Dajon nodded toward his bodyguards, who were standing against the walls. Several of the bodyguards quickly made their way to the conference table, where they stood just behind under bosses Justin Tanner and Allan Lemen.

"Gentlemen, we're at war with several enemies, and our resources have been stretched to the max," Dajon continued. "But it's at times like these, when we need to come together as a family and overcome our difficulties, rather than seek individual opportunities for material gratification."

Allan peered over his shoulders at the hulking men standing just behind him. "What are you saying, Dajon?"

"I'm saying, don't try to cut a stupid ass deal like you did, asshole," Dajon told him.

The bodyguards standing behind Justin and Allan grabbed them, and wrestled them to the ground. Two large hollowed out leather punching bags were produced, and the bodyguards proceeded to stuff the two under bosses in the bags, and then to zip the bags up, locking the men inside. One of the bodyguards handed Dajon a thick tire iron.

The two leather punching bags with the still struggling under bosses stuffed inside of them, were hung on two massive hooks inside the conference room. Dajon walked around the bags, cradling his tire iron.

"Disloyalty is the worst offense one can perpetrate," Dajon told them. "It was disloyalty to Caesar that began the decline of the Roman Empire. It was disloyalty to Christ that resulted in the crucifixion. It was the African's disloyalty to one another that allowed the slave traders to be so successful at garnering captives from inland. No more selling each other out!"

Dajon took his tire iron, and struck the punching bag

as hard as he could. A loud crack could be heard throughout the stunned room. Dajon swung his tire iron again, and then again, then again, until the kicking inside the bag ceased, and blood oozed from the seams of the bag. A couple of the under bosses seated around the conference table began to vomit.

"Does everyone here get what I'm saying?" Dajon shouted. "Are there any questions about who's in charge of this family?"

Silence permeated the room.

"Does anyone want to end up like either one of these son of bitches?" Dajon shouted. "Does anyone wish to leave this family or cut a deal for themselves?"

Again, silence reigned supreme.

"Good because I don't have time for this shit!" Dajon removed a pistol from one of his bodyguard's waist, walked to the punching bag, and fired several shots into it. "Dump those motherfuckers into the ocean!"

Dajon turned, and headed for the stairs leading out of the basement. "This meeting is adjourned!"

Ajouinette beamed with the pride of a mother who had just watched her son score his first touchdown. She followed Dajon up the stairs into a private room just off the living area; closing the door behind her, she then walked into the adjoining restroom. Dajon was hunched over the commode vomiting.

"I've never killed anyone before," he told her between his lurches.

Anjouinette patted his back. "I know. The first time's always difficult. You'll get used to it."

Dajon shook his head. "I don't want to get used to it!"

Anjouinette smiled. "You did well in there. Now, they'll be no more talk of defection."

"How did you feel when you first, you know."

"It felt good," Anjouinette told him. "The first person I went after, was my husband's brother, and then my father, who gave me to my husband because of a gambling debt."

169

Dajon rose and peered into Anjouinette's eyes. "You're father gave you away to pay his gambling debt?"

Anjouinette smiled. "My father was a lousy dice player. I gave him a chance to change his luck before I shot him though. The unlucky bastard crapped out on the second roll."

Dajon turned back toward the commode, and began vomiting again.

Chapter Nineteen

Stacia crept into the hospital room. The sight of Damian lying in the hospital bed with intravenous tubes protruding from his arms, made her cry. She had never seen him so helpless, so defenseless. The darkness around his eyes made him look as though he had went a couple of rounds with Roy Jones Jr, while the dried white substance at the corners of his mouth made him look as though he had eaten a package of white powdered doughnuts. She wanted her Damian back, the old Damian, the Damian who was sure, and confident, and so full of life. She wanted desperately to gather him up and carry him away from that place, that place of sickness and death.

Damian felt someone's presence and opened his eyes. He thought that he was dreaming at first.

"Stacia?"

With tears still flowing from her eyes, Stacia nodded. "Yes, it's me, Damian."

"What...what are you doing here?"

"I couldn't stay away from you, Damian," she told him. "No matter how hard I tried, I couldn't stay away from you."

Damian smiled, extended his hand, and waited for her to take it.

"I'm sorry, Damian," Stacia told him, clasping his hand. "I allowed my emotions to get the best of me. I know that this is the business that we've chosen, and I know that my father's line of work places him within direct contravention of what you do. He's made it his life to bring you down. I was a fool to think that you two would never clash, and that the clash wouldn't be violent. Deep down I guess I was dreaming that neither of you would ever be hurt."

"Stacia, I'm sorry," Damian told her. "I'm sorry for everything. I'm sorry that you wound up in the middle of all of this; I'm sorry for not being the man I should have been. We should have been so much more, Stacia. I should have made it all legal, all legitimate in the eyes of the church."

"Oh, Damian, we don't need anyone's approval. The love that we share is legitimate, because it's pure. I don't need a piece of paper to be your wife, and you don't need a piece of paper to be my husband, and we don't need titles or labels for what we feel for one another. I know what we have. You can run around with all your little hoochie mammas, but at the end of the day, your heart belongs to me. It always has, and it always will."

"I need you, Stacia," Damian whispered to her. "I need you like a fish needs water, like the earth needs the sun; you're my air."

Stacia nodded. "I know exactly how you feel, baby." She allowed herself to laugh. "That's a shame."

"What?"

"We're both fucking hooked."

"Like a junkie needs his fix?"

"Hit me with some sugar," Stacia told him. She leaned forward, and kissed Damian on his cheek.

"How's your father doing?" Damian asked.

"Better. He's up, walking, talking, and getting feistier by the day. The Bureau sped up his promotion. He leaves for Washington, as soon as he's able."

Damian shook his head. "Stacia, everything your father said to me, everything that he's tried to tell me all these years, he was right."

"Excuse me?"

"Your father, he used to be like a father to me, when

we were growing up," Damian explained. "He was as proud of me as my own father, when I graduated from college, and then grad school. And I never realized it until recently, but when I took over my family's businesses, including the ones started by Princess, I broke his heart. I broke your father's heart."

Stacia nodded solemnly, and again her tears slowly made their way down her bronze cheeks.

"He expected so much more from me; instead, I became the monster that he had pledged to protect society from. I was the son he always wanted, and like all fathers, I was supposed to live out his dreams for me. Sons disappoint their fathers, but not in the way I disappointed him. I told myself, Stacia, that I'm going to make it right."

Stacia waved her hand. "Damian, don't worry about that."

"No," he replied. "I'm going to make it right. I'm going to make it right by changing my life, by finally leaving the Commission, by ending all the wars, and by living my life the right way. And, I intend to make an honest woman out of his little girl."

Stacia laughed. "Yeah, I'd like to see you ask him for my hand in marriage. He'd definitely kill you, Damian Reigns. Besides, I believe you've forgotten one little detail."

"And that is?"

"I'm already married."

"Get rid of that bozo."

"Ah, what if I don't want to marry you?" Stacia asked. Damian laughed.

"What if I just want to continue screwing your brains out, and living in sin?" Stacia asked with a smile.

"I'll have you kidnapped, and flown to my island in the Pacific," Damian told her. "You forgot about that? I'm Damian Reigns, you know?"

Stacia laughed. "Seriously Damian, we really have to get down to business. Your shit is all fucked up."

Damian nodded. "I know. How's Dajon doing?"

"Not bad, not bad at all," she told him. "He's got the under bosses back in check, he's given those motherfuckers in Vegas pause, and Angela's actually fucking winning in New Jersey. She's winning in mob territory. Dante's wife is something fierce!"

"Well, that doesn't sound like all bad news," Damian told her.

"Actually, baby, that was the good news," Stacia patted Damian's forearm. "Now, for the real shit, the thorn in your side is one senator Sandra Fitzhugh."

"Senator Sandra Fitzhugh?" Damian repeated, puzzled. "Why?"

"She's the one who sicced the FBI on you really hard a couple of years ago, resulting in Operation Sunshine, and one really pretty confused little FBI agent becoming pregnant."

Damian nodded. He remembered Stacia telling him something about the senator a few years ago, but couldn't recall all of the details. "So, tell me why the good senator from California has a hard-on for the Reigns family?"

"You killed her godson and she still hasn't forgotten about it," Stacia explained. "She's been working to destroy you ever since. She's the main reason why your drug approvals are stalled over at the Food and Drug Administration. She's most likely why Justice hasn't given you antitrust approval for the last couple of acquisitions that you made. She knows you're extended, and she's trying to hold off those approvals until after your first loan payments are due. She's trying to bankrupt your company."

"Any way around her?" Damian asked.

Stacia shook her head. "She's powerful, Damian. Those approvals aren't coming until she gives the nod. You're going to have to make those payments, without those new drugs, and without actual control of those new acquisitions."

"Which means that the acquisitions will be null and void if we can't gain antitrust approval. Damn! Can we get her out of the way?"

"She's virtually made herself untouchable," Stacia told him.

"Anyone can be gotten to, Stacia!"

"Extremely difficult in this case, Damian," Stacia told him. "Don't do it, not yet anyway."

"How come she's so well protected?" Damian asked.

"California's right next to Nevada," Stacia smiled.

"Those sons of bitches!" Damian shouted. "She's being protected by the mob!"

"Our friends in Vegas own a couple of very large security companies, and they provide the senator with a pretty large contingent of around-the-clock security."

"Stacia, I'm going to lose my company!"

"Are you ready for the really shitty news?"

Damian shook his head and looked down. "There's more?"

"The state has informed federal law enforcement authorities, that they don't have enough evidence to uphold the charges against your brother," Stacia told him.

Damian paused for several seconds, while his mind digested the information. "Stacia, this is good news! Then they have to let him go."

"No, listen, the Bureau's being pressured from above and they in turn are pressuring the state. The Federal Bureau of Prisons has been ordered to lose your brother's paperwork. He's now being treated as a federal prisoner, as if he had gone to trial and been convicted on a federal offense, right. So, now their next trick is that after they relocate the paperwork, they'll mix it up and detain your brother under the bogus charges of illegal immigration."

"Those sons of bitches!" Damian pounded his fist into the palm of his other hand. "Where are our people? I've paid tens of millions of dollars in bribes and campaign contributions, to dozens of politicians."

"Damian, after what happened to you and then to Princess and Dante being in prison, the word on the street is that your family's days are numbered. No one wants to back a losing horse."

"And if I walk out of this hospital?"

Stacia gave Damian a half nod, half shrug. "Things may get better. But they don't fear you, not while you're alone. Besides, Angela's busy, Nicanor's busy, Princess is on her deathbed, and Dante's in jail. Everyone is betting that at the rate you're going you will lose the East Coast; it's that simple."

"Then how do I go about getting Dante out?"

"There's only one solution and one solution only. You need to increase your political leverage."

"And how exactly do I do that?"

"The Senate belongs to Sandra Fitzhugh, and everything below that, she can influence," Stacia explained. "But the one thing that she can't influence is international politics. Only the president can exert downward pressure on her and only another president can exert any kind of pressure on our president."

"Or only a potential president."

Stacia smiled and nodded.

"I can contact Minister Malaika," Damian suggested.

Stacia shook her head. "Why would he cash in a political chip for you? His daughter's gone, and as far as he's concerned, so is his interest in the well-being of this family."

"Then what are you getting at, Stacia?"

"He has another daughter, remember" Stacia told him. "A daughter who loves you dearly. A daughter who could get the minister to have a vested interest in this family."

"So, you think I should have Illyassa talk to her father?" Damian asked.

"She would, but even her talking to her father, would not give him a vested interest in this family."

"Little D.J. and Cheyenne?" Damian asked. "Use his grandchildren.?"

Stacia shook her head. "He'd be willing to assist you if Illyassa wasn't asking on behalf of her boyfriend, but on behalf of her husband."

"Your want me to marry Illyassa?" Damian asked.

"What choice do you have? Political marriages have been around almost since the beginning of time, Damian. They're nothing new. Illyassa's a beautiful woman, and her father's a very powerful man. It's the perfect match, and it'll help you solve your dilemmas."

"I can't just up and ask her to marry me out of the blue!" Damian protested. "What would I say? Illyassa, will you marry me, and by the way, see if your father can speak to the president of the United States about my brother, a suspected cop killer, and get him released for me!"

Stacia shook her head. "Damian, she'll take you any way she can get you. All you have to do is give her a reason to help you, without directly asking her too. You tell her you want to marry her, but you can't because..."

Damian smiled. "Because I have so many things going on. I have my sister's health, my company's financial health, and my brother rotting away in a prison. If I could only solve some of those problems, why, we could be married before Christmas!"

Stacia laughed and pointed her index finger at Damian. "Bingo! Now, you got it. Anyway, if you can fool an FBI bitch for several months, then you definitely should be able to fool America's top model, don't you think?"

Damian got serious for a moment.

"Stacia, that FBI bitch, as you call her, is the mother of my son, so I'd really prefer if you wouldn't call her that. Now getting back to Illyassa, you think she would get her father to help me?"

"Okay I'm sorry Damian, I didn't mean to show disrespect to FBI Agent Grace Moore. Now, for Illyassa, I'm a woman and a daddy's little girl just like she is. Trust me, the first person we run to when things need fixing, is our big, powerful, want to fix it all daddies."

"And you believe the minister has this kind of juice?"

Stacia lifted her thin attaché from the ground, and removed from it a folder stamped Top Secret.

"A gift from some friends of mine in the intelligence community."

Stacia opened the folder, took the seat next to Damian's bed, and crossed her legs as she thumbed through it. "I'll give you the quick version of it. The United States is pulling out of Saudi Arabia, and needs another major installation in the area. The French are anxious for the United States to leave their base in Djibouti, and the United States wants to keep a massive installation in the region, if just to use it for pre-positioning their heavy equipment, which would take too long to get back into the area, because it would have to go by sea. Somalia is politically untouchable, too many Black Hawk Down memories. A base in Iraq is now out of the question and besides Kuwait, no other nation will allow them in. The short of it all, is that they're negotiating a secret deal with the Ethiopians, for a pre-positioning base on the Red Sea. The United States gets to keep heavy units right across the sea from their precious Saudi oil fields, however, since they're no longer on Saudi soil, they can claim to be completely out of the Holy Land."

Damian nodded. "I'm following you, but I don't understand what this has to do with Dante."

"Okay, here's the deal. The United States gets their military base, the Ethiopians get billions of dollars a year pumped into their economy, in addition to a generous aid package, and access to U.S. training and equipment. The minister was crucial in setting this deal up. One phone call to the U.S. State Department or to the Department of Defense and he can get Dante thrown into the deal."

"Throw Dante into the deal?" Damian asked incredulously. "This is something way beyond us, way beyond our level, Stacia."

"That's right, that's why you need Illyassa. She's used to deals done on this level."

"And what makes you think that they'd be willing to throw my brother into this deal?"

"Damian, there's been so much money thrown around

178

on this thing already, Dante means nothing to anyone. The minister's bribe on this was something on the order of fifty million dollars and that was just his take alone. The United States sat down at the negotiating table, opened up its big fat checkbook, and greased every hand that it had to, in order to get this deal done. Trust me, Dante is like a drop of water in a great big ocean. He means nothing to these people. No one at that level even knows who he is. Look, get Illyassa to beg her daddy for his help, and Dante will be out of that place. One phone call to the State Department from the minister is all it will take."

"Stacia, how long have you been working on this?" Damian asked.

"Since the day Dante went to prison," Stacia replied.

"What do I have to do to make this outrageous plan of yours work?" Damian asked with a smile.

"Illyassa's still in town," Stacia told him. "Call her and ask the girl to marry you."

"I can't believe you want me to marry Illyassa. But speaking of marriage how's that husband of yours? That was really something when he shot me during that FBI raid. The feds are looking for explosives they thought I used in the attempted assassination of your father, and Michael's pissed because he just figures out that I'm sleeping with his wife."

"Suspended," Stacia told him. "The Bureau placed him on suspension with pay, pending the investigation. And he's been ordered to undergo psychological evaluation and counseling."

"And your marriage?"

"Well, I told him that he's a fool and that nothing was going on between us. He'll eventually come around. The man loves me, and love makes people stupid. Look at me, I'm telling the man I love to go and marry an international supermodel."

Damian laughed. "And you think this will work?"

"If she begs and pleads for Daddy's help, then yes. The deal's not the problem; Dante's not even considered small potatoes on this level; he's more like a gnat. Hell, on a deal like this, the United States would throw in Charles Manson. They want that base across from all of that sweet Arabian crude, and they'll do anything to get it. One phone call; that's all it'll take. Just do it, be Damian Reigns."

Stacia stuffed the envelope back inside her attaché. "Get some rest, sweetie; you look tired."

"Okay, I will."

Stacia paused, and stared into Damian's eyes. "Don't you dare, Damian Reigns. You and I are way beyond that bullshit!"

Damian laughed.

"Dajon's out in the waiting room; do you want me to send him in?" Stacia asked.

"Yeah, get him in here. We got to make plans for Dante's return."

Stacia winked at him. "You're damned right you do. Damian, I just realized something else."

"What's that?"

"Without me, you ain't shit!"

Damian threw his head back in laughter. Stacia was still Stacia. He felt better just seeing her, and now, after talking to her, he felt ready to take on the world again.

Stacia gathered her attaché, leaned into the hospital bed, and kissed Damian on his forehead. "Get better, you. Either that or I'm going to sneak into this hospital bed with you one of these nights."

"I'd love that."

"I'll bet your freaky ass would," Stacia told him. "What do you think the nurses would say?"

"They'd probably want to join in."

Stacia licked her lips. "Well, there was this one out there who was kind of fine."

Again, Damian laughed.

Stacia returned Damian's look; she knew what his eyes were saying .And then she said it out loud.

"I love you too."

Damian smiled and watched with a little bit of sadness, as she turned and left his room.

Chapter Twenty

Dajon strolled into Damian's hospital room, followed closely behind by Tommy Voight, Damian's business attorney.

"Hey, bro." Dajon leaned into the hospital bed and hugged his brother as best he could. "You're looking better."

Damian smiled and shook his head. "It's because of Stacia."

"How'd you two manage to make up?" Dajon asked.

Damian shrugged.

Dajon frowned. "Don't think it's a setup, do you?"

Damian smiled, and punched his brother's shoulder. "Look at you, being all suspicious and stuff. You're starting to sound like Dante!"

Dajon cracked a smile. "This business will do it to you."

Tommy clasped Damian's hand and shook it firmly. "Well, it's good to see you up and alert, Damian. If there's anything that I can do to assist you, don't hesitate to call."

"There's something you can do, Tommy," Damian told him.

"Name it," Tommy replied.

"Find out about those casinos," Damian told him.

"Done." Tommy seated himself in the chair next to Damian's bed, and removed a folder from his briefcase.

"You're not going to believe this one, Damian."

"More bad news." Damian smiled. "You people really don't understand the concept of recovery. Part of it, is to bring good news, so that the patient can improve."

Tommy shrugged. "Sorry. I don't do the hugs and kisses and sunshine bit; I only report the truth."

"And the truth is?" Damian asked. He began a soft drum roll against the metal railing of his hospital bed.

"They're all fucking connected," Tommy told him. "Every fucking casino in this country is interconnected, even the ones supposedly owned by the tribes. And their ownership can all be traced back to the American Gaming Corporation."

"What?" Damian laughed. "Wasn't that the company formed by the old Vegas mobsters? I mean, like Ben Segal, Meyer Lansky, and those characters?"

"And it's still around," Tommy told him. "The front names have changed, but behind it all, the Old Ones control every fucking casino in this country."

"And that means, it's the Old Ones who've been pulling the strings behind this shit all along," Damian whispered.

"They're mad about our New York, New Jersey and Pennsylvania expansion," Dajon told him. "Also, I don't believe that they're alone. Damian, I think that some of the hits came from members on the Commission, and some from El Jeffe."

"That's what I think," Damian told him. "But I also believe that they're all connected somehow. I know the connection between El Jeffe and the Commission, and I know that the senators are in cahoots with the Old Ones, but what I'm missing is the connection between the Commission and the Old Ones."

"Don Ambrogino played both sides of the field," Dajon told them. "He was one of the linchpins."

"Yes, but not a strong enough key," Damian told him. "There is something else, some other link."

"Yes, but is it even important?" Tommy asked.

"Finding out what the link is, is less important than knowing that a link exist. We know that there're two groups and both are waging war on us. Let's just handle the two groups."

"The link may be important," Damian explained. "Because sometimes you can sever that link, split whatever coalition they've formed, make a truce with one group, while you destroy the other group."

"And then go back and destroy the second group, after you've finished with the first." Tommy nodded.

"Tommy, you did good digging up the link between the casinos," Damian told him. "What I need for you to do now is to find the link between the Old Ones and the Commission. Those bastards are up to something and I need to know what."

Tommy nodded. "I'm on it." He leaned over, gathered his briefcase, and headed for the door. "You take care of yourself."

Damian smiled and waved, and Dajon did the same.

"I'll call you later, Tommy," Dajon told the lawyer.

Tommy gave a halfhearted friendly salute and closed the door behind him.

"Stacia's come up with a plan to get Dante out," Damian told his brother. "I believe it's a long shot, even bordering on the outrageous. But, over the years, I've learned not to doubt her. Make preparations to get an armed caravan down to Three Rivers Federal Correctional Institute, just in case."

Dajon nodded.

Damian extended his hand. "Hand me the telephone. I have an important phone call to make."

Dajon handed his brother the oversize white hospital telephone.

"By the way, did I tell you that I was getting married?" Damian asked with a smile.

"Yeah, right," Dajon said.

Damian rapidly punched a set of numbers into the

telephone, and then placed the receiver to his ear. "Yes, Illyassa? This is Damian; I was wondering if we could get together tomorrow and have dinner at my house. You know, I'm getting out of this place tomorrow morning."

Dajon smiled, gave his brother the thumbs-up, and exited the hospital room.

Damian ran his hand across the leg of his Kiton trousers, taking in the quality of the fine wool fabric. He was ecstatic to be out of those blue rags the hospital had the nerve to call garments. And now, he was about to enjoy a feast; the main course was a succulent roasted chicken, with a sweet and tangy Carribean sauce consisting of coconut, pineapple, papaya, and cashews, quite a change from the hospital food he had gotten use to.

Damian removed the dish from the oven, stirred the rice around the chicken, and placed the dish on top of his stove. It was almost show time.

"Damian," Illyassa called out to him in a singsong voice. "Something smells delicious, sweetie."

Damian turned to find Illyassa making her way into his kitchen. He rushed to her, pulled her close, and kissed her passionately.

"Hmmm, one more kiss like that, and we'll be skipping dinner," Illyassa told him.

"Sounds good to me," Damian told her. "I can stick this stuff in the oven and then we can cuddle up and keep each other warm."

"Well I'm famished," Illyassa replied. "How about we eat this wonderful concoction of yours, and then have each other for dessert?"

Damian embraced her tightly.

"Even better."

Illyassa recoiled. "Hey, what's that down there? That better be something in your pocket. I know that it's been awhile, but you can't be that happy to see me."

Damian laughed. "You're going to ruin my surprise."

"Damian, you know how I hate surprises," she pouted. "Come on, out with it."

Damian exhaled. "Okay, but at least go in the living room and sit down."

Illyassa seated herself on the couch, and extended the palm of her hand. "Let's have it!"

Damian blushed. "You're ruining my after dinner surprise, Illyassa!"

"I don't get my gift; there'll be no after dinner surprise!" Illyassa told him with a smile.

Damian laughed. Slowly, he dropped down to one knee just in front of her, and removed the ring box from his pocket.

Illyassa gasped.

"Illyassa, I've had time to think, time to reevaluate my life, to examine what's really important. You're important to me and I never want to lose you. I want us to be together forever. You're my life, my love, my every thing. Illyassa, will you walk side by side with me on this magical journey that we call life? Will you do me the honor of becoming my lawfully wedded wife?"

Illyassa wiped the heavily flowing stream of tears from her eyes, and then leaned forward and hugged him. "Yes, Damian. Yes, I'll be your wife!"

Damian embraced her tightly. "The ring; we forgot about the ring."

Together they laughed.

Damian opened the Harry Winston box to reveal a flawless three-diamond ring, mounted on a sparkling platinum base. Each of the massive stones sat prominently at the top of the ring, with each of the side stones weighing more than three carats, while the center stone itself, weighed in at an impressive five carats. The brilliance from the diamonds was blinding.

"Oh my God!" Illyassa gasped.

"Here," Damian took her hand, and placed the ring on her finger. It fit perfectly.

Illyassa leaned forward once again and embraced him. "Oh, Damian, I'm so happy! I can't wait to tell my father!"

"I know that he'll be happy," Damian told her.

"We'll have to set a date!" Illyassa told him excitedly. "I want a winter wedding, Damian."

"That would mean we'd have to get things rolling pretty quickly," Damian told her.

"Why, is there a problem?" she asked.

Damian shook his head. "Not really. It's just that I have so much to do, and so many things on my mind. You know, with Princess being in the hospital. I'm really worried about Dante."

"What's the matter?" Illyassa caressed the side of Damian's face.

"Well, the state doesn't want to hold Dante anymore, but the feds are putting pressure on them to hold him," Damian explained. "And all my contacts at the federal level have run for cover."

"My father has contacts in your government, Damian," Illyassa told him. "I keep telling you this over and over. Let me speak to my father."

Damian exhaled and shifted his gaze to the ground. "Do you think that he would? I mean, I don't want to."

"Oh don't be silly, Damian," Illyassa interrupted. "My father will be glad to help us. I'll call him right now, and I'll have him speak to his contacts first thing tomorrow morning."

"And then we can plan our beautiful winter wedding," Damian told her.

"Yes!" Illyassa told him. "Oh, Damian, you've made me so happy!"

"And you've made me the happiest man in the world, Illyassa," he told her.

"I'm going to call my father right now, and give him the news."

She turned, and like a schoolgirl who had just been asked to the prom, raced off to the telephone in the kitchen to tell everyone.

"Damian removed his cell phone from his pocket, flipped it open, and quickly dialed a set of numbers from memory. He placed the phone up to his ear, and waited for his party to answer, and in a hushed voice said, "It's done. The canary's in the cage. Prepare to roll the canoes."

Damian took a seat on his massive leather sofa. He had just become engaged to a woman who he loved, but did not wish to be married to. He had sold his freedom for that of his brother's.

Dante, this is going to cost you, big time.

Damian had just made the ultimate sacrifice for his family. You better be worth it, you son of a gun, Damian told himself with a smile. Deep down, he knew that with Dante's release, meant that the balance of power had just shifted.

Chapter Twenty One

Dante breezed into Damian's mansion with the playfulness of a newly adopted kitten.

When Damian saw his brother, he scaled his silk-covered ottoman in one leap and crashed into his brother, and the two of them fell to the floor.

"Dante, it's so good to have you home!" Damian shouted, as the two of them rolled around on his living room floor.

Dante rose from off of the floor, and dusted off his clothing. "Hey, you better be careful, Bro. Watch those stitches."

"Ah, screw the stitches!" Damian said. "Man, how're you doing?"

"I really think we should get down to business."

Damian rose from the floor, and seated himself in his chaise lounge. "What do you know?"

"I know everything," Dante told him. "I read the briefing package that you sent with the guys when they picked me up from prison."

Damian nodded.

"I think you missed something," Dante told him.

"And what's that?" Damian asked.

"Angela's report to you, from three weeks ago," Dante

explained. "My wife came across some soldiers in Jersey who she tortured for information."

"I remember that report," Damian told him. "They didn't give her any information, because they weren't familiar with the area, and they weren't of any significant rank."

"Wrong," Dante told him. "They couldn't provide her with any information, because they weren't from the area. They were from Chicago."

"They were from Chicago," Damian repeated slowly, trying to find meaning in what Dante was trying to say.

"They were Sicilians, they were soldiers, and they were all from Chicago," Dante told him. "Damian, you're fighting the Vegas crew, the New York crew, and the Chicago crew. You've dug up links to the American Gaming Corporation, and these people have dozens of politicians in their pockets. They're able to stall things inside the Justice Department. Their reach is long and deep because they're old and established, and their power base stretches from coast to coast."

"Dante, you're not getting at what I think you're getting at?" Damian asked.

Dante nodded. "Yes, it's not just the damn Old Ones from New York and New Jersey, it's their Vegas spin-offs that we're fighting. They're all united again, Damian."

"Damn it!" Damian said forcefully. "Why didn't I see that? Dante, do you know what this means? Do you know what it means when those families are all united under one banner?"

Dante nodded. "It means, my dear brother that we're at war with La Costa Nostra."

"Jesus!" Damian exclaimed. "No wonder they were so powerful, no wonder they had so many soldiers, and so much political power. No wonder my political power ran for cover!"

"They're pissed about our expansion and about our casinos in Vegas," Dante explained. "This thing's being pushed by those sons of bitches in Vegas, Damian. That's the linchpin holding this thing together. We need to shift the alignment in Vegas, in order to get peace."

"Shift the alignment?" Damian asked. "Those Dons are impossible to get to now, especially after we hit Nestor and Frediano. Remember we dumped Frediano's body into a pit with alligators?"

"Anyone can be gotten to, Damian; you know that." Dante said with a smile.

"They're protected by the Vegas police, Dante!" Damian exclaimed. "Their bodyguards have a license to kill!"

"Then we get rid of their police protection, and then we pop their asses!"

"How?" Damian asked. "You can't kill an entire police force, Dante."

"I don't have to; I just have to kill its leaders," Dante replied. "They own the chief of police, and they own the deputy chief, and the next two successors. We own the fifth man in the line of succession."

"And so, you think that you're just going to walk into Vegas, and start popping police chiefs, and no one will be the wiser?"

"No, we don't have to kill them all, bro," Dante smiled. "We just have to kill enough of them to get our man into position."

Damian exhaled. "Okay, let's hear it."

"We own the mayor of Reno, and we also own the mayor of Carson City," Dante explained. "We have them fire those chiefs, who we also own, and we have them hire a couple of the deputy chiefs. We'll have to kill the chief, and probably the deputy chief, and that's it. We'll just promote the other two sons of bitches."

Damian laughed, and clapped his hands. "Bravo, bravo, my dear brother."

"As a matter-of-fact, it doesn't even have to get that bloody," Dante told him. "We can even arrange to have the deputy chief set up in a sting operation. Call Stacia and we can put the Bureau on him."

Damian nodded.

"Well, I'm off to Vegas to kill some police chiefs," Dante told his brother. "But first, I have to pay a visit to California. That fuck face Marion Rook has some explaining to do."

"Dante."

"No, it's okay; I'm not going to go overboard," Dante told him. "I'm just going to explain to him, the meaning of unity."

Marion 'Big Hustler' Rook, a former tackle for the Miami Dolphins, yawned and stretched his six-foot seven-inch, three-hundred twenty-five pound frame. It was getting late, and the number of patrons inside his nightclub, were starting to dwindle. Marion rose from the VIP table which he had been seated, and motioned to his two bodyguards. He needed only two of them with him most of the time, because his hulking frame, and reputation for ruthlessness, kept most people at bay.

The state of California was his, and he ruled it with an iron hand. He was rumored to dangle his associates from the twentieth floor of his downtown high-rise if they displeased him. He was rumored to have set a couple of people on fire, after making them walk barefoot on glass, and drink embalming fluid. It was rumored that he loved to tie people up with telephone cords, torture them with sharp objects, and then dump their bodies in the Mojave Desert. All of the rumors were true. He loved the fact that most people had heard of his deeds, and he also loved the fact that he was feared.

"Bring the limousines around to the front," Marion ordered. "It's time to blow this joint." He rose, and headed for the exit.

Marion gained his seat on the Commission because of his reputation for ruthlessness, and because of his reputation as an astute businessman. Marion had built up one of the most successful hip hop labels in history, and he had all of the major distributors clamoring to do business with him. He also built up a significant narcotics distribution network on his own, and thus, was a natural to assume the seat on the Commission as the head of the state of California. His only fault, in the eyes of his fellow Commission members, was that he was drawn to cameras and publicity, like a moth to a flame.

Marion walked out of his club and inhaled deeply, taking in the fresh southern California night air. The weather was mild this time of the year. He could feel the breeze against his face, as thoughts of speeding down the Pacific Coast Highway in his Maranello Yellow Ferrari F430, raced through his head.

Marion's long black super stretched Cadillac Escalade limousine pulled up in front of the club, and his bodyguard opened the door for him to climb inside. He contorted his huge body in order to get inside the stretched SUV. Once inside, he looked up to find that he had a guest.

"What the hell!" Marion gasped. "What are you doing here? How did you get out?"

Dante smiled. "Hello, old friend." He waved his pistol at the two men seated on either side of him. "Don't mind us, we're just out here visiting old friends, relaxing, stretching our legs, enjoying this beautiful California weather."

"Dante, I..."

Dante placed his finger over his lips. "Shhhhhh," he told Marion. "Relax. We're about to go for a dip in the pool. Join us."

One of the men seated next to Dante shifted his weapon toward Marion and fired. The tranquilizer dart struck the music mogul directly in the side of his neck. Marion was sound asleep within seconds.

Dante dashed a handful of water into Marion's face. Marion slowly regained consciousness.

"What the hell is going on?" Marion asked. He coughed and wiped the water off his face. His eyes slowly came into focus, and before him stood a smiling Dante, and several of Dante's men.

"I'm just hanging out," Dante replied. "Now, the question is, what the hell did you think you were doing?"

Marion rubbed his hands over his eyes. "What are you talking about?"

"I'm talking about the little powwow you guys had in Vegas," Dante explained. "The one where you insulted my family, ridiculed my brother, and failed to live up to your obligation with the Commission."

Marion thought the Commission had enough flunkies from the Reigns family as members, and in front of everyone, called Dajon, Dante's weak little brother.

"Obligation?" Marion asked incredulously. "What obligation?"

"The one that requires you to come to our family's assistance if we're attacked by outsiders," Dante told him. "You left my family out to dry, you son of a bitch! We needed you in Vegas; we've needed you since day one. Your state is right next door to those salami-eating sons of bitches, and you could've taken a lot of pressure off of us."

"Dante, your beef ain't my beef," Marion told him.

"It's supposed to be!" Dante shouted. "We're supposed to defend one another from outside aggression, but you threw us to the wind, and you did it in front of our enemies!"

"Obligations?" Marion laughed sarcastically. "Since when has the Reigns family ever honored anything, let alone a mutual defense pact? Obligation? Your family's trying to leave the Commission; what of your obligation to us? What of that?"

"The Commission's not under direct attack, but we are," Dante told him. "We're under attack not only by the Old Ones, but by you assholes as well."

Marion bit down on his lip.

"What?" Dante asked. "Did you think that we were stupid?"

Marion heard a massive splash just to his left, and

tried to rise. But he couldn't since his wrist and ankles were bound together. He shifted his head to see where the noise was coming from, and to his astonishment, he was lying beside a seemingly endless pool.

"Where in the hell am I?" he asked angrily. "Dante, I'm a member of the Commission. Now, since you're so into following the rules all of a sudden, my position as a Commission head means that you can't kill me without permission from the rest of the Commission."

"Old rules, Marion," Dante told him. "The rules have now changed. The new rules are that there are no rules."

Marion heard another massive splash. "Dante, where in the hell are we? What is this place?"

Dante smiled. He turned to his men. "Get fatso here inside his suit."

Dante's bodyguards lifted Marion's body, and placed it inside a nylon sack that had a zipper in front. Some of the men held Marion down, while the others began stuffing tuna and cod inside the bag with him.

"Dante, what the hell are you doing?" Marion shouted. He squirmed, and tried to resist. The smell of the fish made him puke.

"Marion, I have good news and I have bad news," Dante told him. "Which do you want first?"

Marion spat in Dante's direction. "Fuck you, you punk ass motherfucker!"

"Okay, well judging by the hostility in your voice, it sounds like you're in need of some good news, so I'll give you that first. Drum roll please."

One of Dante's men made the sound of a drum roll, while the rest of his entourage broke into laughter.

"The good news is we're still in your home state of California. We didn't take you out of the state," Dante told him. He leaned down and squeezed Marion's right cheek. "Isn't that just grand?"

"Fuck you, Dante!" Marion told him. "Just do whatever you have to do and get it over with! Fuck your sick games!"

Dante tilted his head to the side. "Aw, someone's not playing well with others, Marion. And to think, we came all the way from Texas, just to play with you."

The bodyguards finished stuffing the sack with fish, and then zipped the bag up to Marion's neck, so that only his head was exposed.

"Okay, Marion, now here's the bad news. You're still in your home state of California, but the bad news is, you're going to die in your home state of California."

"Just fucking do it, you pussy!" Marion shouted. "And don't have one of your men do it; I want you to do it yourself!"

Dante shook his finger. "Pulling out my Glock and putting fifteen shots through your skull would be too easy. I have something else in store for you, a little home state entertainment."

Dante lifted his arms. "Take a look around you, Marion; don't you recognize this place?" Dante asked. He turned toward his bodyguards. "Have Joe hit the lights."

The bodyguard spoke rapidly into his earpiece, and seconds later, the lights slowly flickered on.

"What the hell?" Marion asked. He turned toward his left and was able to better gauge the size and scope of the body of water that he was lying next to. It was immense.

"We're inside the killer whale holding tank at Sea World," Dante told him.

Marion realized what Dante had in store for him. He screamed at the top of his lungs.

Dante placed his finger over his lips. "Shhhhh. You're going to scare them away. They're really timid and docile creatures, unless of course, they happen to mistake this black bag that you're in for a penguin or a seal or a walrus or something. Then, you're in trouble. Then they start to bite."

"Dante you son of a bitch!" Marion screamed. "You better not do this!"

Dante knelt down and pointed at the water. "See that

really big aggressive one that keeps leaping out of the water? That's Raikou; she's a big female from the North Pacific. They caught her off the waters of northern Japan a few years ago, and they've been trying to train her ever since. Her name means lightning in English. It's said that she was the young matriarch of a pretty large family, and that she's never gotten over her separation from her children. She blames humans, and she's been known to try to sneak a taste every now and then. You know, a finger here, a hand there. Imagine, once she smells past the fish, and realizes that she has a real live human swimming in her tank. She's liable to go bananas."

Dante nodded toward Marion, and one of his men quickly placed a strip of duct tape over Marion's mouth. Another zipped the bag up the rest of the way, completely enclosing Marion's body inside the sack.

"The best thing that you can hope for, is that they mistake you for a toy, play with you for a little while, and then become bored and kick you out of their pool," Dante told him. "The worst thing that could happen is that they're really, really hungry, and that they smell the fish inside the bag, and they start taking some really big bites. Either way, Big Man, you're fucked. I brought you here, because for the longest time you've been the biggest fish inside this small pond that we call California. Now, you get to see what it feels like to be the small fry. Good-bye, Marion. I really hope that they're hungry tonight. I want to watch them tear your fat ass up, limb by limb."

Dante turned toward his men. "Roll his big, stupid ass in the pool."

Dante's men lifted the giant sack, and tossed it as far as they could, into the pool. Another one of his men hit the lights. In the darkness, the orcas weren't sure of the object that they were now circling, prodding, and testing. Kitana, the largest of the males, decided to take the new object for a test drive. He hit it at full speed with his nose, sending it spiraling out of the tank, and high into the air. Marion was dead before he hit the water again.

The other whales followed Kitana's lead, and began to swipe at the object with their tales, and sent it flying through the water. Kitana raced from the other side of the pool, leaped high out of the water, and landed on top of the sack, sending it crashing down into the depths of the water. Then, Raikou intervened.

Whether she smelled Marion inside the sack was unknown or whether it was the fish that piqued her wild instinct remains debatable, but what was certain, was the size of the bite that she took out of the bag. Marion's right side disappeared instantly. The fish spiraled out of the torn bag, mixing with the fresh blood inside the water, sending the orcas into a frenzy. They gobbled up the loose fish, and then made quick work of the bag. The park officials would arrive the next morning to find the badly eaten remains of an unidentified victim, and a group of orcas that had reverted back to their natural state as killer whales.

Chapter Twenty Two

Agent Richard Starkey was tired of the bullshit. He was tired of the hits, the retaliatory strikes, the car bombs and the pile of bodies that had been scooped up off the streets of his hometown just this year alone. He was third-generation Bureau and he had committed his life to making his nation safer. He had lived his entire life by a code of honor with the people who he had sworn to protect. It was a code of honor that revolved around the word trust.

The people trusted him to do his job, to use the authority entrusted to him by virtue of his office, to make their lives better, and to perform his duty with honor, and fidelity. To not only uphold the law, but to serve as a living, breathing example to his fellow citizenry. Something that all law enforcement officers were bound to do. They were upholding a way of life; they were upholding the Constitution of the United States. It was for all of those reasons, that he hated corruption more than anything else. People put their trust in someone, and then are taken advantage of, by criminals in high offices. Had it been up to him, those types of people, would all be serving extremely long prison sentences, in an underground maximum security federal prison in Colorado.

Agent Starkey pulled his black baklava over his face,

and then tugged at the straps holding up his thick black body armor. Next, it was time to load some extra magazines into his utility belt.

Agent Laura Archer tapped Agent Starkey on his shoulder, and then shoved his black Kevlar helmet into his gut. "Hey, don't forget your helmet, tough guy."

"Anybody seen my knee pads?" Agent Mohammed Aziz shouted.

The FBI agents were going in wearing full body armor, with all of their tactical gear. They wanted to make sure that they would overwhelm their suspect, and that everyone came back alive. Their suspect was certainly armed.

"Aziz!" Agent Jaime Vara shouted. He tossed his fellow agent his knee pads. "Keep up with your own shit!"

Agent Dave Wellborn pulled back the bolt on his silenced H&K MPK5. "Time to rock and roll, guys."

The FBI agents all pulled on their masks, placed their helmets on their heads, cocked their weapons, and readied themselves for their tactical assault. They were using two assault teams of twelve members each, and they were going in fast and furious. Team one would go in on the ground, while team two would assault from the air by helicopter. Their target was asleep right now. They had been watching him for the last two days, and had developed a quick profile on his activities. He liked to nap during the middle of the afternoon, and they would use this to their advantage.

Agent Starkey keyed the handset mounted on his shoulder. "Driver, put us at the front door!"

The large FBI vans sped down the quiet residential street and quickly pulled into the circular drive of their target's home. The agents flew from the van to the front door, and stood to the side while the designated agent pounded the door open with his hydraulic jack. The double doors flew open and the agents poured inside.

"FBI! FBI! Search warrant! Search warrant!"

Deputy Chief Carson Brock leaped from his bed, just as the first agent was racing into his bedroom.

"What the hell is the meaning of this!" Chief Brock shouted. "I'm the deputy chief of police of Las Vegas!"

"Hands!" the FBI agent shouted. "Let me see your hands!"

The chief saw that the black-clad agents meant business, and they had the end of their submachine guns pointed directly at him. Slowly, he raised his hands into the air.

"Get down on the ground!" the FBI agent shouted.

Chief Brock dropped to his knees and then laid down on his bedroom floor. Seconds later he was cuffed.

"Stand up!" The FBI agent ordered, while assisting the chief to his feet. Is anyone else in the house?"

The chief shook his head. What the hell are you people doing in my home!"

Agent Starkey strode into the chief's bedroom, and held up the search warrant so that the chief could read it.

"I can't believe this shit!" Chief Brock shouted. "You're looking for marijuana! I'm the fucking deputy chief of police, you imbeciles!"

"And that's what makes this even worse!" Agent Archer shouted back at the chief.

"I'll have your badges for this one!" Chief Brock shouted. "You damn feds think that you can just waltz all over everybody; well, you just fucked with the wrong swinging dick now!"

"Hey, there's a lady in the room; do you mind?" Agent Aziz told the chief.

"Fuck you! Fuck your FBI cunt! Fuck your god damned junkie ass dogs! Fuck your director! Fuck the judge who signed this bogus ass warrant! And know this; I'm going to fuck over every one of you sons of bitches when it's all over with!"

Agent Wellborn stuck his head inside the bedroom. "Rich, we found it," he told Agent Starkey. "It's in the garage."

"What?" Chief Brock shouted. "This is bullshit!"

Agent Starkey patted the chief on his shoulder. "Nice act, Chief. Looks like you're going to be going on a nice long vacation."

"Horseshit!" Chief Brock shouted. "If there's anything in my garage, you sons of bitches put it there!"

"Wow, that's original," Agent Vara sneered. "Haven't heard that one before."

"Bring the chief, no, excuse me," Agent Starkey said. "Bring Mr. Brock to the garage; would you please."

Agents Aziz, Vara, and Archer clasped the chief's arms, and followed the other agents into the garage. The FBI agents already inside the garage were un-boxing and weighing bricks of marijuana on a scale that they had placed in the middle of the garage floor.

Agent Archer nodded her head. "Looks like a good bust."

"God damned right it is!" Agent Frank Diaz gave a high five to Agent Gaston Phillipe.

"This is bullshit!" Chief Brock shouted. "You people are trying to set me up! This is nothing but a sneaky conniving setup! I want my attorney, and I want him here now!"

"Only guilty men ask for their attorneys this early in the game, Mr. Brock," Agent Starkey told him. "You're a disgrace to the uniform; you're a disgrace to the entire profession of law enforcement. It's bad apples like you, that corrode our society. You disgust me."

Agent Starkey turned to his men. "Get this animal out of my sight."

The agents dragged the chief out of the garage to a waiting patrol car.

"I'm innocent!" Chief Brock shouted. "This is nothing more than a god-damned setup! I'm going to burn your asses for this!"

It was Deputy Chief Phil Newton's day off, and somehow, he had gotten suckered into taking the grandkids to the movies. If it was one thing that he hated more than anything else, it was being stuck someplace he didn't want to be. He brought the kids anyway, to shut his wife's big mouth. He would do anything, just to keep her mouth quiet, even if it meant sacrificing one headache for another.

The movie was an hour into its plodding directionless plot, and he was into his third hot-dog, second soda, and second bag of popcorn. He hoped the sleep gods would be merciful today, and allow him to escape the excruciating pain of watching yet another slasher movie. This one was even worse than all of the others. The killer in this movie seemed to plod along everywhere, but somehow seemed to miraculously turn up either right in front of his running victims or right behind them. And for Pete's sake, how many ways could Hollywood find to kill someone? The machete across the throat had been done at least two hundred times or more. The machete sticking out of the side of the head was a classic.

Chief Newton knew that he had to get out of there. He felt as though he was about to stand up and shout at the dumb characters on the movie screen. He had gone for sodas, candy, chips, popcorn, hot-dogs, and everything else that he could think of just to stretch his legs and get out of that theater. Now, he had a legitimate reason to get up and leave. The two sodas that he drank were now putting pressure on the walls of his bladder. A trip to the restroom would probably get him fifteen good minutes away from the ridiculous meandering fiasco playing out on the screen. He rose from his seat and turned to his wife.

"Sweetie, I'm going to go to the restroom, I'll be right back."

Chief Newton made his way through the crowded aisles, and then up the center aisles and out the door.

The restroom was located down the hall, and it took him less than thirty seconds to get there. Chief Newton opened the door, stepped inside and headed for one of the empty urinals. There was only one other guy inside, and he was finishing up at the next urinal. But there was something about the guy that wasn't right.

Chief Newton had been a law enforcement officer for the better part of thirty years and over that time he had come to develop an innate sense for danger. He had come to call it his 'spidey sense'. He had relied on this extrasensory perception to keep him alive many times throughout his long career and it had yet to fail him. But what was it about the guy? He looked mildly familiar, and that was what bothered him. The guy was also wearing an expensive Italian suit at the movie theater, which was way out of the ordinary. The chief shifted slightly, so that he could feel the weapon in his ankle holster. It brought him a sense of comfort. Though not as much as he would have had, if he had his trusty old Sig Sauer by his side. His wife wouldn't let him wear his side-arm when they were out in public with the grandkids. He cursed her for that many times. He was the deputy chief of police for the city of Las Vegas, and he had needed to keep his side-arm with him at all times. He had admonished many an officer, for not doing the same. 'Be prepared', was his motto and now, he had been caught ill prepared. Thus, he decided to go with rule number two. Fake it, and be authoritative and aggressive. He turned toward the man at the next urinal.

"Excuse me, son," the chief said. "But don't I know you from somewhere?"

"Why, yes," Dante smiled. "I'm certain that you know me, Chief Newton."

Chief Newton became extremely nervous. He was tempted to reach for his weapon.

"How do you know my name?" the chief asked.

"Because my name's Dante Reigns and I came to Las Vegas to kill you." Dante turned toward the chief and rapidly lifted a silenced Beretta pistol from below his waist, and pointed it toward the chief's head.

"Whoa!" Chief Newton threw up his hands. "What the hell are you doing, son?"

"I'm not your fucking son, asshole," Dante told him.

"Look, just calm down; we can work this out," Chief Newton pleaded. "Why are you doing this? What have I done to you?"

"Chief, I'm not angry with you," Dante told him. "It's absolutely nothing personal; I just have to get you out of the way."

"Out of the way?" Chief Newton asked. "Out of the way of what?"

"Out of the way, so that our man can be the next chief of police," Dante told him with a smile. "Then, we can proceed to knock off those spaghetti-eating sons of bitches who you've been protecting."

The chief's eyes flew wide. "What are you talking about?"

"Chief, let's not play stupid," Dante told him. "You're going to die. Now, how you chose to die, is up to you. You can die alone or I can go to your home tonight and send you some company. You have some really cute grandkids, if I may say so."

"You son of a bitch!" the chief howled. "You leave my family out of this!"

"Do you have any information that could save their lives?" Dante asked. "Give me a reason to spare them."

The chief lowered his head. "What do you want to know?"

"How can I get to the chief of police?" Dante asked. "When is he off the radar?"

"Do you know who we work for?" Chief Newton asked. "Do you know who Chief Scarno works for? You kill him or even me for that matter, but especially him, they'll come after you with a fury that you have never seen."

"I kill Chief Scarno and their protection's gone," Dante told him. "They become the hunted."

"You kill me and Chief Scarno, then Chief Brock will take over," Chief Newton explained. "And Carson will have your heads on a platter before nightfall."

205

"Deputy Chief Brock will be too busy fighting for his anal virginity by midnight to even think about anything else," Dante told him. "Chief Brock's now in custody for possession with intent to distribute two and a half tons of marijuana."

"Bullshit!" Chief Newton exclaimed. "I've known Carson for thirty years, and the man's as clean as a whistle."

"Trust me; Carson Brock was arrested by the feds today for having a shit load of marijuana in his garage," Dante told him. "How do I know? Because I not only put the marijuana in his garage, but I personally had my contacts from the FBI go there and arrest him, and I watched the entire thing from four feet away, dressed like a funky ass federal pig!"

"Patrick Shaw takes over after Carson; what are you going to do about him?" Chief Newton asked.

"Deputy Shaw's taking a position as the chief of police for the city of Reno," Dante laughed. "He officially accepted the position a few hours ago."

"And that leaves Percy Pruitt," Chief Newton told him.

"Percy belongs to us," Dante told him.

Chief Newton whistled. "Percy, you old sly son of bitch." The chief laughed. "I got to admit, Percy could always pick a winner. You should see that lucky son of a gun when we go to the track."

"I agree," Dante told him. "I went fishing with him a couple of times. I could have sworn that he had a couple of four-leaf clovers wrapped around the lucky horseshoe that he had tacked on to his rabbit's foot."

Chief Newton laughed. "Question."

"Shoot."

"Why didn't you come at me with some of your billions, Mr. Reigns?" the chief asked.

"Because you already belonged to the Vegas boys," Dante answered. "And if you were willing to switch sides on them, then that means that you could potentially do the same to us when we really needed you."

"Don't jump on the first gravy train that comes along,

huh?" the chief asked.

"A lesson for the next life, Chief."

"I know I have no right to ask, but I've been married for a long time," Chief Newton told him. "The old hag gets on my nerves, but I love the old gal. And I know she loves me. I want her to be able to see my face, and I want her to be able to have an open casket service."

"I'll do that for you."

Chief Newton nodded. "Thank you."

Dante lowered his weapon to the chief's stomach.

"One last thing," Chief Newton told him. "I never liked that son of a bitch, Scarno, anyway. You can catch him at Madam Rosado's bordello. It's on the far east side of town. Know where it is?"

"Infinity works there."

"Infinity, boy that's one fine mamma. My favorite's Preference."

Dante nodded. "I know her. Well, Chief, I'd love to stay and chat about our mutual acquaintances, but my men have been holding the door down for too long already. We put a wet floor sign outside the door, and started mopping in front of it. Pretty soon, someone from the theatre's going to realize that my men aren't really employees and call the cops."

Chief Newton nodded. "Are you really going to kill them all? The Old Ones, I mean?"

"Chief, I'm going to kill as many of those motherfuckers as I can."

"You're going to shift the balance of power, you know?" the chief told him. "Is the Reigns family prepared to step in and take over this much territory? Remember, your enemies will get fat off of what you leave behind."

"We're going to take over as much territory as we can. It'll take awhile, but eventually we'll do it. Besides, even if we don't, we still have another trick up our sleeve."

"And what's that?" The deputy chief asked.

"We're not planning on leaving any enemies behind," Dante said with a big wide grin. "Now, are you ready?"

"I guess I'm as ready as I'll ever be," the chief told him. He clenched his stomach muscles and readied himself.

"If I gave you some money and told you to disappear, would you?" Dante asked.

The chief shook his head. "I'm too old a dog, to learn any new tricks. I'd stay, and I'd keep on doing what I'm doing. Thanks for the offer though."

Dante nodded. He aimed for the deputy chief's stomach, and squeezed the trigger on his Beretta several times. Chief Newton shouted and fell to the ground. The lead from the bullets felt as though someone had stuffed a handful of fiery red-hot coals inside his stomach.

Dante stood over the dying chief, and squeezed the trigger on his weapon several more times. The chief's body jumped, and then went limp. A pool of blood slowly poured from beneath his body, and spread across the restroom floor. Dante stared at the chief's body for several seconds to make sure that he wasn't breathing, and then turned and slowly exited the restroom.

Chapter Twenty Three

"Oh, fuck me baby; fuck me!" Chief of Police Bruno Scarno shouted at the top of his lungs. "That feels so good; give it all to me; give me that pussy, honey!"

Tonight he was doing Swetha, a rare dark-skinned beauty, with green eyes that sparkled like emeralds on St. Patrick's Day. Swetha Rahman was from Bangalore, India. She had worked her way through several prestigious Indian universities, and held a degree in biotechnology and nano-engineering. She came to America to complete her Ph.D.'s in nanotechnology and microbiology, but along the way met and fell in love with another Indian student who turned out to be nothing more than an abusive pimp. He sold her only to his friends at first, in an effort to pay his tuition and make ends meet. But, as the time went by, and as the money started rolling in, she found her list of clientele growing more extensive with each passing week. Her so-called boyfriend, Ghee, was killed in a drug deal turned sour, and she suddenly found herself keeping the money that she was earning. She had no idea that she was making so much.

Swetha's first purchase with her newfound wealth was a black Three Series BMW; two months later she followed that up with a brand-new black Corvette Z06. Today, she drove her Porsche to work. Her home went from a sleazy two-bedroom shack, to a posh three-bedroom condo with a view of downtown Las Vegas. Her clothing went from Wal-Mart to

Neiman Marcus, and her list of clientele became even more exclusive. That was, until she met the Madame.

Madame Rosado was a Puerto Rican and former Hollywood actress, who brought her limited fame and fortune to the desert and cashed in. In the old days, washed-up actresses had very few choices; they could stay in California and maintain the facade, go back to their hometowns and be the big fish in the small pond, become a Vegas showgirl or lower themselves to doing porn. None of these choices suited Rosado Marquez. She was too young and too beautiful to call it quits, and she had invested too much time and effort screwing her way into Hollywood, to allow herself to be used up and sent packing all the way back to the island. No, she had to come up with another way.

Madame Rosado's opportunity came when she met the legendary Madame Khan, from the famed Dude Ranch. Madame Khan took her in and showed her the ropes, told her to avoid the streets, the corners, and most of all, the pimps. Madame Khan put books in her hand, and educated her on art, culture, and etiquette. She read the classics; went to the opera; listened to classical music; and learned to play the piano, the harp, and the violin. Language lessons came later; French was first, Japanese was second, and finally Chinese. She learned French because it was the language of romance, of the old nobility, of education and class. She learned Japanese and Chinese because they were the languages of a large block of her clientele. But most of all, she learned the art of pleasure.

Madame Rosado's stay at the Dude Ranch came to an end when one of her regulars decided that she deserved her own establishment, one that was less structured and steeped in tradition, and more amicable to change, something more upscale, more modern, something with different sections, each with its own different theme. A meeting between her best clientele quickly produced the cash necessary for her to open her own establishment. Madame Rosado struck out on her own, taking with her some of her investor's favorite girls, and bringing over some new meat from the Ukraine. Her primarily Asian investors went crazy, and her clientele expanded beyond what she thought possible. Blonds from the Ukraine were brought in, and again her list of clientele exploded. She paid her investors back within a year.

Swetha had come over during the first expansion. She wanted something new, something different, something exotic, and the Madame's establishment offered her all of those things. It also offered her something she craved more than the other things. It offered her safety.

Swetha brought with her a considerable number of clients, which Madame Rosado loved; she also brought with her a rare and exotic beauty, which was lacking among her blond-haired, blue-eyed Ukrainian Barbie dolls. The girls from the Ukraine were the Asian men's fantasy, while Swetha was the American male's exotic fantasy. Her swarthy skin made them swoon like reeds in the wind.

Swetha had learned a lot from Madam Rosado, particularly about the art of lovemaking. Make love to the client's mind, and you'll have them for life. It was a practice that Swetha followed religiously; it was a practice that she had become one of the best at. Her clientele were fanatically devoted to her. Some would wait hours, just for her patronage. Tonight, Chief Scarno himself had to wait for a half an hour, while she readied herself.

"Say it, baby!" Chief Scarno shouted. "Say it to me!"

"You pig!" Swetha shouted. "You fucking big dick, pig! I'm going to take it from you! I'm going to make you cum!"

Swetha slapped Chief Scarno across his face, as she continued to straddle him and grind away. Chief Scarno himself was handcuffed to the bedpost, while his ankles were tied tightly to the post at the bottom of the bed. He loved to play bondage games with Swetha, he loved to be dominated, and he loved the feeling of sexual helplessness. As the chief of police he was always the one doing the dominating, and as a police officer for more than thirty years, he had always been the one doing the handcuffing. It was alone in the darkness with Swetha, where he could experience the feeling of captivity, of helplessness, of domination. It brought him to an ecstasy that he was only able to achieve with her.

"Bite me, baby!" Chief Scarno told her. "Bite me!"

Swetha leaned forward and bit him on his nipple. He screamed with a joyful passion that was almost inhuman.

"Give me what I what!" Swetha shouted. "Give it to me!"

"No, you're not going to make me cum!" Chief Scarno shouted.

"If she can't, I'll bet you I can," a voice called out from the shadows.

"What the fuck!" Chief Scarno shifted his gaze to the shadows. "Who the fuck is there? Get the fuck outta here; can't ya see we're fucking busy!"

Swetha climbed off of the chief, and backed away from the bed.

"Swe, where are you going, baby?" Chief Scarno asked.

The figure in the shadows slowly stepped forward. The chief's eyes flew wide.

"What the fuck are you doing here?" Chief Scarno shouted. "You're supposed to be."

"Dead?" Princess asked with a raised eyebrow. "Yeah, I'm supposed to be a lot of things, Bruno. I'm supposed to be a welfare queen, a loose jungle bunny, a hyper aggressive sexual species, the object of all your white boys' sexual fantasies. It depends on who you ask, Bruno, but dead, not quite. That's just wishful thinking on your part."

"Swe, run for help!" Chief Scarno shouted.

Swetha stepped back until she stood next to Princess. She turned toward Princess. "Help," she whispered.

Swetha and Princess shared a laugh, and then leaned over and shared a passionate French kiss.

"What the fuck?" Chief Scarno shouted.

"Oh, Bruno, she has a Ph.D. in microbiology and a Ph.D. in nanotechnology," Princess told him. "You didn't think that she would stay your fucking sex slave forever, did you?"

"What?"

Swetha nodded. "I'm finished," she smiled. "You big old dick, you."

Princess hugged her. "We're so proud of her. She's coming to work for us, at Bio One."

"That's all nice and good, but what the fuck does it have to do with me?" Chief Scarno shouted. He turned toward Swetha. "Bitch, come untie me, before I have the INS come and take your ass back to that cesspool you call a country!"

"Oh, Bruno, what a horrible thing to say!" Princess told him. "I thought that you would be a better loser than that."

"Loser?" Chief Scarno asked. "Loser? I don't fucking lose, you fucking lose! Bitch, I'm Bruno Scarno, chief of police of the city of Las Vegas! I got legal muscle, as well as illegal muscle. I got thousands of soldiers with a license to kill and thousands more that I'll give a pass to, so that they can crucify your black ass! You untie me, and I'll give you twelve hours to get the fuck out of town!"

Chief Scarno struggled to break free of his bonds. "I said untie me, god damn it!"

Princess walked to the bed. "What are these?" Princess leaned forward, and yanked a string of beads that were lying on the bed. Chief Scarno shouted and clinched his buttocks, as the beads streamed out of him.

"Whoa, you freaky motherfucker, you!" Princess laughed.

"You bitch!" Chief Scarno shouted. "I'm going to kill you! I'm going to cut off your tits, and feed them to the fucking buzzards! You fucked with the wrong guy, honey!"

"Bruno, right now there are three live people in this room," Princess told him. "When all is said and done, there will be two live people walking out of this room, and one dead one staying. Now, I'll give you three guesses as to who the dead one will be, but the first two guesses won't count."

"You can't kill a chief of police!" Chief Scarno shouted. "That's an automatic death penalty! The Old Ones, they're going to come after you like you've never been come after before!" Chief Scarno shouted.

"I kill you; then their police protection's gone," Princess told him. "They'll be sitting ducks. I'm back, Dante's out of prison, Damian's out of the hospital, and everyone who crossed us, is fucked."

Princess pulled out her H&K semiautomatic pistol, screwed on a large silencer, and pointed the weapon at Chief Scarno's privates.

"No! Don't do this!" Chief Scarno shouted. "You want the Old Ones; I'll help you get them. I'll pull their protection! Let's make a deal, you tell me what you want, and consider it done!"

"I want you dead, Bruno; can you do that for me?" Princess asked. She squeezed the trigger on her weapon and watched as Chief Scarno's penis exploded, leaving nothing but a blood-gushing hole. Bruno screamed out in pain.

"Oh shut up, Bruno, you know the rooms here are soundproof for privacy," Princess told him. "One last thing, Deputy Chief Newton wanted us to let you know that he told us where you'd be, and what time you'd be here. He said to tell you to go fuck yourself, you big fat son of a bitch!"

"Bye bye, Bruno!" Princess told him. She squeezed the trigger on her weapon several more times, peppering Chief Scarno's body with bullet holes.

Swetha wrapped her arms around Princess's waist, and hugged her tightly. Princess turned toward Swetha, and again the two shared a passionate kiss.

"I want to make love to you right here," Swetha whispered. "Here, in front of his body."

Princess unbuttoned her Caroline Herrera suit jacket, and Swetha's hand found its way to her breast.

Damian opened his front door to find a surprise guest

standing before him.

"Uncle Deacon!" Damian exclaimed. He leaned forward and embraced his uncle.

Deacon Reigns was the brother of Damian's father, Davidian. He was the spitting image of his late brother. His job as a U.S. Appeals Court Judge had been good to him.

"Unc, what are you doing here?" Damian asked. "Why didn't you let me know that you were coming? I could have prepared something special for you! Come in!"

Damian waved for his uncle to come into his home, and then led him into his living room.

"Have a seat, Unc," Damian told him. "Can I get you something to drink?"

Deacon waved him off. "No thank you, I won't be staying long."

"This is a surprise," Damian told him. "A pleasant one, but a surprise nonetheless. So, how long will you be in town?"

"I'm just checking on your mother, making sure her affairs are in order, things of that nature, you boys need to visit with her more often. You know, she and your father spent all of their waking moments together. She really misses him, and she's lonely without him," Deacon told him.

Damian nodded. "Will do, Unc. I've just been so busy lately."

Deacon nodded. "So I've heard. Lot's of trouble with the Commission and with the mob."

Damian's mouth fell open. He had no idea that his uncle knew about the activities of the Reigns family.

"Oh, come on now, Damian," Deacon told him. "I'm a federal circuit court judge, for Christ's sakes. You don't think I know about you, your brother, your sister, and the rest of you kids? The FBI came to my home yesterday, and filled me in on all your latest activities. Jesus, son, what in the hell are you doing?"

"What, what do you mean, Unc?" Damian stuttered.

"Damian, this war of yours, is leaving a pile of bodies

from New York to California, and the cost in human lives, in manpower, in resources, is unacceptable. It's time to call it quits, son. You want out of the Commission, then stop this thing and get out."

"Things aren't as simple as they appear to be," Damian told him.

"The attempt on your life almost killed your mother. Your continuous back and forth with Nathan, killed your father. Your war with the Commission and with the Mafia, took the life of your brother's wife, and almost took the lives of two of your brothers, your sister, and your nephew. When does it stop, son? Tell me, when does it stop?"

"Things are complicated," Damian told him. "The company's in trouble and things are hectic right now. Territories are chopped up and unorganized." Damian never spoke to his uncle about the Reigns family's activities, so this conversation made him very uncomfortable.

"Yeah, every time you whack someone, their territory fractures. The petty underlings go to war for control of the entire thing, and bodies start piling up. You created a mess in California, son. You've created the same kind of mess in many other places. Usually, when you whack someone you take over their territory, and bring everything under control. You guys are just hitting leaders and leaving a great big old mess behind you."

"Are you telling me that the FBI wants us to step in, consolidate those territories, and bring them under our dominion?" Damian asked incredulously. "Is that what you're telling me, Unc?"

"Damian, the Bureau knows that I'm your uncle, and they know that they're in a precarious situation. Local law enforcement in those territories is reeling, and the local politicians are clamoring for assistance. Everybody's head is in the guillotine."

Damian nodded.

"Now, as your uncle, what I'm telling you, is fuck the FBI," Deacon told him. "Son, I want you to get your life together. I want you to leave this bullshit alone, and I want you to be the man that your father and I always expected you to be. You're too brilliant for this bullshit. You have a company that can do great things. You have the ability to help mankind, through Bio One. You could find a cure for cancer, for AIDS, for sickle cell anemia, for diabetes. Use Bio One to leave your mark in this world. Do good things, Damian. Use the rest of your life to make up for all this bullshit. Think of how many deaths you're responsible for; think of how many deaths that you've ordered. That's the number you owe me; that's the number of people that you have to save to break even. Get it together, son."

Since he saw that his uncle knew so much, he felt he could really talk to him. "If I take California, I'll control ninety-five percent of the entrance points in this country," Damian said softly. "I control Texas, Florida, most of New Mexico, all of Louisiana, and some of Mississippi. The only thing missing is Arizona."

"Son, the FBI will use you like a piece of toilet paper," Deacon told him. "Trust me, I see cases all of the time where they've clearly fucked over people. They're ruthless, son. They only care about making themselves look good, and getting more funding, and more power for their agency. You have to make your own decision."

"And in exchange for me consolidating those areas and stopping the violence?" Damian asked.

"They agree to look the other way," Deacon told him. "Nothing more. They'll look the other way, and get the local police agencies to do the same, until you've consolidated your power. After that, it's back to business as usual."

"There're a block of senators from the gambling states who are controlled by La Costa Nostra; these senators are a thorn in my side. They handle those senators; I'll end the violence in California and those other leaderless territories."

Deacon nodded. "They'll go for that."

Damian rose, and hugged his uncle.

"Damian, get out of this business, as soon as you

217

can," Deacon whispered.

Damian nodded. "I will, unc. I promise."

Chapter Twenty Four

Grace adjusted the watchman's cap she wore over her head. The cap was more for disguise than comfort, although the temperature had become quite cool over the preceding week. Winter came so early in northern Minnesota.

She had relocated to a remote cabin on the far outskirts of northern St. Paul, after the most recent attempt on her life. She had fallen in love with the log cabin's old school cottage charm at first sight. The logs were thick enough to stop a high-caliber weapon, the sight lines were excellent, and the entire property was surrounded by a high fence.

Grace bought the property from an old couple who used it as a summer vacation home in their younger years, but who were now too old to chop wood and maintain the immense acreage. She added perimeter sensors, cameras, buried pressure pads, and numerous electronic trip wires throughout the property. The entire alarm system was wired into the local sheriff department's headquarters, as well as into the FBI's regional field office in Minneapolis. The wiring into the sheriff department's monitoring station insured that help would arrive within minutes. It helped her sleep at night.

Grace pulled a couple of cans of spaghetti off the store shelf, and placed them her shopping cart. She hated canned

219

spaghetti almost as much as she hated grocery shopping itself. But stocking up on canned goods for the coming winter months, was something that she knew that she had to do. Minnesota was known for extremely hostile winters, including being snowed in for days or even weeks at a time. She was glad that she brought her Jeep Wrangler four by four, because she hated the idea of having to pull her Range Rover out of the garage during the harshest days. The rocks, the sand, and the other road debris were hell on her paintjob.

Grace placed a dozen cans of chili with meat and beans into her shopping cart, and continued down the aisles. Her thoughts turned to bottled water, and then to canned vegetables, and finally, to the dark-suited men who blocked the aisles in front of her. It was a hit.

Grace pulled her 40-caliber Glock from her hip, dropped behind her shopping cart, and fired. She caught two of them with her first volley, and sent the other three scrambling. Grace knew that she was a sitting duck in the middle of the aisle. She rammed her body into the shelf behind her, sending it falling over, and onto one of the men trying to outflank her. Grace tumbled over, rose to her feet, and fired into her attacker's gut, sending him flying into the aisle from which she had just escaped.

Gunfire came from her left, striking several cans of beans just behind her head. Grace dropped to her knee and quickly returned fire. The attacker ducked back around the corner just in time.

Where's the other one and why hasn't he fired yet, she wondered? Grace lifted her weapon, and fired at the fluorescent lighting in the ceiling. Sparks flew everywhere, and the lights went out. Grace ran into the shelf to her rear, again sending it falling over and herself into another aisle. Then she found the second shooter.

Shooter number two punched his way through the shelves on the aisle two rows over and fired at her. The bullets whizzed past her ear and through her hair. Grace dropped to the ground and returned fire. The shooter to her left came around the corner and fired again. This time, his bullets struck high. Grace shifted her weapon and fired twice in his direction, sending him ducking back around the corner for cover. She rose, and rammed into the shelf to her rear, sending it falling over, and then she leaped into the next aisle. Grace ejected the magazine clip that was inside her weapon, and then quickly loaded a new one.

Shooter number two fired at her again, this time, grazing her side. Grace fell over and grabbed her side where the bullet struck. It was an intense burning sensation. Shooter number one came around the corner again, and fired at the place where he thought she was. Grace rolled over on the ground, and fired in his direction. Again he ducked. And then she heard his magazine hit the ground.

Get up, Grace. Get up and go get him, she told herself.

Grace willed herself to rise, and then willed her feet to move faster than they had ever moved before. She rounded the corner and came face-to-face with her assailant. He was just snapping his new clip into his weapon. Grace held her weapon to his forehead.

"Who are you?" she asked, while still breathing heavily. "Who do you work for? Who sent you?"

The assassin smiled, and quickly tried to knock her gun away. Grace put a bullet through his forehead. The second shooter appeared from around the shelves, and put a bullet into her shoulder. Grace fell to the ground and screamed. Her gun landed four feet away.

The second shooter closed the distance quickly, and stood over her with his weapon aimed at her head.

"Put the gun down now!" the elderly store owner shouted. He held in his trembling hands, an old 8-gauge shotgun. "I promise you, I'll shoot!"

The assassin reluctantly dropped his weapon, turned away from them, lifted his hands into the air, and then brought them down to the back of his head, where he interlaced his fingers.

221

Grace immediately began crawling along the floor toward her weapon. She saw the move coming, long before the store owner did.

The assassin quickly turned and dropped to one knee, and pulled another weapon from between his shoulder blades. He pumped six shots into the old man, and then shifted his weapon to where Grace once was. The can of beans struck him in the head like a ton of bricks. The shooter recovered, and tried to turn his weapon in the direction from which the can had been thrown, but to his surprise, he found the weapon being kicked out of his hand.

"You bitch!" he shouted, and rose quickly.

Grace shifted into a martial arts stance.

"Oh, I'm going to enjoy this!" The attacker told her. "I think after I whip your ass, I'll take you back to my room and have a little fun with you."

"Bring it on," Grace told him.

The attacker swung first, and Grace leaped back out of his reach. The maneuver caused the gash on her side to open up. She cried out in pain.

"That's right, sugar," he told her. "You're all banged up. Well, the pain from those bullet wounds is nothing compared to the pain you're gonna have between your legs!"

Grace punched him with her good arm, and then took his legs out from beneath him with a power sweep of her right leg. He fell to the ground and rolled over in an effort to get up quickly. Grace caught him in his ribs with a quick kick to his stomach. The attacker collapsed to the ground, and Grace lifted a can from the ground, and threw it at his head. The can struck her attacker in the back of his head. Grace ran and dove for her weapon, while her attacker rose. He ran for her.

Grace grabbed her weapon and rolled over on her back and faced her oncoming attacker. He stopped at her feet, and lifted his hands into the air.

"Who sent you?" Grace asked, while breathing heavily.

The attacker smiled. "C'mon, doll. You know I can't

tell you that."

"Why are you after me?" Grace asked.

"Hey, doll, I don't answer questions without my attorney," the attacker told her. "Now get up, run along, and call the cops."

"Who sent you?" Grace asked again.

"Hey, doll," the attacker told her forcefully. "I'm not going to tell you again; I'm not saying anything without my attorney present. Now read me my fucking rights, bitch."

"You want me to read you your rights?" Grace asked.

"You're a fucking FBI pig!" the attacker laughed.

"In the name of the Father, the Son, and the Holy Spirit," Grace began.

"Hey, hey, hey, what the fuck are you doing?" The attacker asked.

"You wanted me to read you your rights," Grace told him. "These are your last rites, you son of a bitch!"

"You're a fucking FBI agent!" the attacker shouted.

"I'm a mother who's willing to do anything to protect her child," Grace told him. "And the way I see it, you're one less son of a bitch who I have to worry about."

"No!" The attacker raised his hand and then leaped at Grace.

Grace squeezed the trigger on her weapon, and the bullets sent her attacker flying backward away from her. Slowly, Grace rose, and stumbled over to where he was lying on the ground.

"Adios, amigo," Grace told him. She fired several more shots into his body, and then stumbled out of the store.

Damian lifted his telephone and found a familiar old voice on the other side of the line.

"Damian?" the voice asked.

"Grace?"

"Yes, it's me."

"Grace, where are you?" Damian asked. "Are you okay? Is Little Damian okay?"

223

"Yes, we're okay for now," she told him.

"What do you mean, for now?" Damian asked.

"Damian, I've been hit three times in the last month."

"Grace, they weren't my people."

"I know, because they didn't try to capture us; they tried to kill us."

"What?"

Damian, they've found me in three different locations, in opposite parts of the country, and they found me quick. Whoever they are, they have someone inside the relocation department in the Bureau.

"Grace, calm down," Damian told her. "Things are hectic right now, but we're getting the situation under control. Trust me; things are going to get better."

"Damian, I'm wounded," Grace told him. "My side's bandaged, and my arm's in a sling."

"My God," Damian exhaled. "Grace, let me send a plane for you. Come, stay here where you'll be safe."

"Sorry," she told him. "I like living."

"Grace, you're in no danger. You come here, stay with me, and I promise you, once you heal, I'll let you walk out of here."

"I can't trust you, Damian."

"Grace, you can trust me."

"Damian, you told me that once before, and I trusted you, and you broke my heart. I can't trust you again, not like that."

"Grace, what do you want from me?" Damian asked. "Tell me how I can help you. I'll do anything, Grace, anything. I just need to know that you and my son are safe."

"Damian, there's something you can do for me," Grace told him. "While I don't trust you with my life, I do however trust you with your son's. I know that you'll keep him safe. I can't do it right now, not with my arm like this."

"Grace, I want both of you safe. Let me protect you both."

"No, Damian," she told him. "I'll be okay. I can protect

224

myself with one arm, but I can't grab Little Damian and run and shoot if I had too. You have to take care of him, just for a little while."

"Grace, of course. But please, let me help you too."

"No, Damian, like I said, I'll be okay," Grace told him. "After my arm heals, I'm going after them. I'm going after the people who are a threat to my child. I'm going to kill them all, and I'm going to make it safe for my baby to live a normal life again."

"Grace, no!" Damian told her. "Let us handle it! We're handling it right now. Don't go out there and get yourself killed!"

"Damian, I'm sending you a file; take a look at it; I'm sure that it'll be of assistance to you."

"Grace, let me protect you," Damian pleaded.

"Damian, I'm sending our child to you," Grace told him. She sniffled loudly, and began to cry. "You protect my baby with your life, Damian. Do you hear me? With your life! If anything happens to him, I'll spend the rest of my life hunting you down, you hear me. He dies; you die!"

"Grace, I'd give my life for my son," he told her. "I'd give my life to protect the mother of my son."

"Damian, don't go there," she whispered. "Just take care of our baby."

"I will; I promise. You just take care of yourself. And if you ever need me, if you ever need to run or get away, of if you need any kind of help, you call me. I can get men to you faster than the FBI can!"

"I will," Grace whispered. "Damian, one last thing."

"What's that?"

"Once this thing's over, I'm coming for my child," Grace told him. "I am coming to get my baby back."

"Once this thing's over, I'll give him back to you, Grace; I promise. I just want to spend some time with him, that's all."

"I already told you, Damian. If you want to be a part of his life, you're going to have to change your life around for real. No more Commission, no more drugs, nothing illegal."

"When this thing is over, I'll be completely legitimate, Grace."

"We're getting on a plane," Grace told him. "Send someone I recognize to come and get him."

"From where?"

"Dallas Fort Worth International Airport," Grace told him. "Get someone there in about two hours."

"Will do," Damian told her. "And, Grace."

"Yeah?"

"Thank you."

Damian lifted his telephone rapidly and dialed a number from memory.

"Hello?"

"Angela?"

"Speaking."

"Yeah, this is Damian; where are you?"

"In the air, headed in your direction."

"You have a layover at Dallas Forth Worth International Airport, don't you?"

"Unfortunately."

"Good, I need for you to retrieve a package for me. It's a very valuable package. I'm sending some soldiers there to provide security. They'll brief you once your flight arrives."

"Gotcha," Angela told him. "I'll take care of it."

"I know," Damian told her. "Thanks, Angela."

Damian then dialed another telephone number.

"Hello?"

"Princess?"

"Yeah."

"Hey, sis, this is Damian. Look, I'm sending you a hundred soldiers. I'm also sending Emil down to San Diego with a hundred soldiers. He can leave Georgia for a while. I need you in L.A. Take it, link up with Emil, and take all of southern California. Solidify, and then move north. I want the entire state."

"I'll give it to you by the summer," she told him.

"We'll have to postpone our Vegas moves. Dante said that the road's open, so we can come back and take that anytime."

"I'll handle it," Princess told him. "Send Dante to Vegas; we can take California and Nevada simultaneously."

"I don't know if we have the soldiers to do both," Damian told her.

"We do," Princess told him. "Pull soldiers from Louisiana and North Texas. I'll send out the order to the under bosses to recruit and get bigger."

"Good, get it done."

"It already is," Princess told him.

Chapter Twenty Five

Stacia strolled into the living room, followed by a familiar face. Damian's eyes lit up with excitement. "Dante!"

Damian raced to his brother and embraced him. "I hadn't expected to see you back so soon." He turned to Stacia and embraced her as well. "Good to see you, sweetie."

Stacia gave Damian a peck on his cheek. "I hope that you've been taking care of yourself."

Damian waved his hand. "I've been trying to. You know how it is; some days are better than others."

Stacia led Damian to a nearby sofa. "Sit down, Damian. You know that you shouldn't be standing so much, not this soon anyway."

Dante took a seat across from his brother, while Stacia seated herself next to Damian.

"Vegas is ours for the taking," Dante announced. "Our man's in the catbird's seat. He's already announced the changes that we wanted him to make. He's pulled his officers away from the casinos, the dons' houses, from the armored trucks that carry their money; he's restricted his off duty officers from serving as bodyguards and security consultants to individuals with questionable ties; he's doing it all. Their police protection is melting away faster than an ice cube in a deep fryer."

Stacia caressed the side of Damian's face. "You can take Vegas anytime you want."

"Manpower's the problem right now," Damian told

them. "We're still stretched too thin. And now, there's California."

Dante shook his head. "I picked up bits and pieces of it from Princess, but we didn't want to say too much; we weren't sure about the security of our phone system."

"We're taking California," Damian announced.

"Why are we going to waste our time doing that?" Dante asked. "At least for the time being, let's finish up some of our other operations, and then go back and take California."

"Well, California would be easier to take right now, because Marion's death left a power vacuum," Damian explained. "His under bosses are warring with one another for control of what he left behind, so they can be taken out piecemeal right now. Also, control of California would give us control of ninety-five percent of the narcotics flowing into this country. The only major piece that we would be missing is Arizona, which we will take later. The Commission, will literally, be at our mercy. We would basically act as a commodities board, and charge the rest of the country whatever way we wanted to."

"And because the FBI begged you to take it, in order to stop the violence consuming the state," Stacia added.

Damian knew that the surprised look on his face, had given him away.

"Oh, c'mon, Damian," Stacia told him seductively. "You know I'm wired into the Bureau through and through. No one farts over at Justice, without me knowing about it."

Damian and Dante laughed heartily.

"Good thing you're on our side," Dante told her.

Damian nodded. "We can take it, and the FBI will look the other way. They've also agreed to get rid of our congressional-size headaches."

"So, our last couple of mergers should clear antitrust now?" Dante asked.

Damian shook his head. "No. We still have a senator who isn't going to go away that easily."

Dante shook his head. "Not her again."

"Yes her," Damian told him. "Dante, we killed her godson; she was apparently very close to him. We're going to have to make her go away."

"Damn!" Dante exclaimed. "I hate doing politicians! Everything has to be so neat and pristine. For once, I'd like to do one of those sons of bitches, and not make it look like an accident. Make it nice and public, and extremely messy, and I'll bet you those assholes will stay out of our business then."

Damian shifted his head to one side. "Are you done?"

Dante adjusted his tie. "Yes, I'm done."

"Take care of the senator, Dante," Damian ordered. "And do it the right way."

Dante nodded and left.

"So when do we get to kill the Old Ones?" Stacia asked.

"As soon as we get enough manpower to do so," Damian told her. "Our political protection's coming back. I've gotten a couple of apologetic phone calls from some of our people. Amazing what Dante's freedom can do, everyone is singing a different song, now."

Stacia kissed Damian's neck. "After your wedding to Illyassa, you'll be untouchable politically."

Damian lifted an eyebrow. "You think?"

Stacia clenched Damian's earlobe between her teeth. "I know."

Dallas Fort Worth International Airport was a massive symphony of precision, professionalism, and improvisation. The daily coordination of hundreds of jumbo jets, and the transfer of over fifty-three million passengers annually, required a great deal of ingenuity on the part of the airport's enormous staff. It was into this mass of organized chaos that Angela found herself being thrown. She frenetically marched through the airport searching for the party with whom she was to rendezvous. She spotted them across the crowded concourse, and lifted her hand into the air.

"Grace!" Angela called out to them. "Grace, over here!"

Grace pulled her son close, and headed toward Angela and her entourage of foreboding dark-suited men. Grace remembered the night when Damian's people invaded her home in a hail of gunfire, looking for their son. She remembered struggling with Angela until she pulled the trigger, creating a blast that propelled Angela through the air and crashing into the wall. She was now entrusting her son to this woman. *Maybe this is a mistake. I can't trust her, what was I thinking.* Her heart told her to turn and run away. She could catch the next flight to anywhere, and then get lost. But her mind told her that her child would be safe with his father. She knew that this was the best thing for her child; she knew that this was the right thing to do.

Grace approached the waiting entourage, and slowly walked her eyes across them all. She didn't recognize any of the men. Angela was the only familiar face in the group.

"Hi," Grace gave a slight wave, and shifted her weight to one side.

"Hello," Angela told her. She extended her hand to Grace and the two shook hands firmly.

"What were the chances of Damian sending you here?" Grace asked nervously. "Kind of ironic, huh?"

"No," Angela answered flatly. "I was the closest senior-level personnel in the area."

Grace kicked at the ground just before her. "So, how are you"

"I'm fine," Angela told her. "I've healed up just fine."

"Sorry about that," Grace told her. "You know, me shooting you and everything."

"Apologies not necessary," Angela replied. "I would have done the same thing. In fact, I'm pretty sure that I'll have the opportunity to repay the favor in the near future."

Grace looked down and smiled. "Not if I see you first, sister."

Angela returned her smile, and then shifted her gaze toward Little Damian. "And who do we have here?"

"D, this is your Aunt Angela," Grace told her son. "She's going to take you to stay with your daddy for a little while."

Little Damian clung to his mother's blue jeans. Angela knelt down just in front of him.

"Don't be afraid, Aunt Angela's going to take really good care of you," Angela said softly. "We're going to ride on an airplane again, and we're going to eat ice cream, and we're going to have lots of fun. You like ice cream?"

Little Damian nodded.

Angela lifted her hand and snapped her fingers, and one of her men quickly placed a small stuffed animal in her hand.

"You like tigers?" Angela asked, holding the stuffed animal. "He needs a friend. You want to be his friend?"

Little Damian nodded.

Grace knelt in front of her child. "Remember the pictures that Mommy showed you?"

Little Damian nodded.

"Remember everything that Mommy told you about daddy?" Grace asked. "Daddy loves you with all of his heart, and he wants to see you and spend time with you. He's going to take you to the park, and he's going to take you to ride some of his horses, and he's going to let you swim in his swimming pool. You're going to have so much fun with daddy."

Little Damian nodded. "When are you coming back?" he asked.

"Mommy will be back in a couple of weeks," Grace told him softly. "Mommy's going to let the doctor take care of her broken arm, and then Mommy's going to come back and get you."

"Southwest Airlines Flight One Zero Eight for San Antonio is now boarding," the intercom blared.

"Are you ready to go and see daddy?" Angela asked.

Little Damian nodded. He released Grace's hand, and clasped Angela's.

Grace rose and faced Angela. "Tell Damian that I'm coming for my baby in a couple of weeks. Nothing and no one will keep me from my baby."

Angela nodded. Grace had shot her, and she surely had no hesitation about killing her. As a mother to a young child, she empathized with Grace. She would certainly do the same thing if the circumstances were reversed. In fact, she felt a slight admiration for Grace's courage and determination. She was a woman who had survived attempts on her life, many of which she herself had participated in. Grace had outfoxed them for more than two years.

"I'll take care of him, Grace," Angela told her.

Grace nodded. "I know that you will."

Grace reached inside her pants pockets, and pulled out a small memory stick. She tossed it to Angela.

"What's this?" Angela asked.

"It contains some data that I think Damian will find useful," Grace told her. "It's the Bureau's intelligence files on the war. It details who did what, who hit whom, who flew whom where and why, and transcripts from Mob meetings in Chicago, New York, and Las Vegas. It also contains everything that we know about those sons of bitches. If they have a routine that they follow when they shit, then we have it documented."

Angela tossed the file into the air, caught it, and tucked it away. "Thanks; I'm sure that it'll come in handy."

"Hey, good work in New Jersey," Grace told her.

"Thanks," Angela smiled. Again, they shook hands.

"Take care of my baby, Angela."

"With my life, Grace," Angela stared into Grace's eyes assuringly. "With my life."

Angela turned, and headed for the gate to board her plane. She held Little Damian's tiny hand, and walked slowly through the terminal with her bodyguards in tow. Grace stood, wiping away her tears, and watching as her baby went to live with the largest, most powerful, most violent criminal enterprise ever known to man. She knew what she would have to do to get her baby back. She would have to heal first, and then she would have to plan accordingly. Her task was extremely difficult at best, impossible at worst. She was going to take out the heads of the leading New York and Vegas families, and then she was going to take on the Reigns family if necessary. She had work to do, a rehabilitation program to carry out, and weapons and equipment to procure.

Grace turned, wiped her tears, and stormed to the gate that would take her back to her refuge.

Anjouinette climbed out of her whirlpool bathtub, wrapped in a towel, and hurried into her living room.

"Who is it, Ella?" she asked her housekeeper.

Dajon turned and faced her. "It's me, Anjouinette."

"Dajon," she said surprised. "What are you doing here? Is everything okay?"

Dajon nodded. "Yes, everything's okay."

"What are you doing here?" Anjouinette asked. "In Louisiana, I mean?"

Dajon shook his head and shifted his gaze toward the ground, embarrassed that he caught Anjouinette only wearing a towel. "I came to thank you for all that you did for me."

Anjouinette waved her hand through the air, dismissing him, while clutching the towel with her other hand. "Oh, Dajon, don't be silly; it was nothing. You did all the work yourself."

"Dajon shook his head. "No, Anjouinette, seriously, without you, I would have been completely lost; those people would have eaten me alive."

"No, they wouldn't have," Anjouinette told him. "You would have found your way."

Dajon laughed. "I don't think so. You saved me, and you saved my family."

"Dajon, don't be silly," Anjouinette told him. "It was you who saved your family. What you did, stepping in like that, was very brave."

"You gave me the strength to accomplish what I accomplished."

"You had the strength inside you all along, Dajon," Anjouinette said softly. "No one can give you strength, and no one can give you courage; those things come from inside."

Dajon again shifted his gaze to the floor. Anjouinette made him feel good about himself; she had given him confidence, and pride in what he had done. No other woman in his life besides his beautiful Daissala had done that. He didn't know what possessed him to come here, what mystical power willed his feet to board his family's jet and whisk him to Louisiana, but what he did know, was that this was where he wanted to be.

"Daissala." Dajon called out, and then he realized what name he had spoken. "Excuse me, Anjouinette."

"That's okay Dajon," she said softly.

Dajon remained silent; he rocked slightly forward as if trying to get the words that were stuck inside of him, to tumble out.

"What's the matter, Dajon?" Anjouinette asked softly.

"I don't know how to say what I want to say," he said softly. "I have so many things that I want to say to you, so many things that I need to tell you, but every time I get ready to say them, I lose my nerve."

Anjouinette peered into Dajon's eyes for several moments. She now knew what it was that he was trying to say.

Anjouinette folded her arms. "Oh, no," she said softly.

Dajon closed his eyes. "Don't say that, Anjouinette. Please, don't say that."

"Dajon, we've been working together every day, and during that time we grew very close. But, sweetheart, you just lost you wife. Don't confuse loneliness with love."

"I'm a grown man, Anjouinette; I know the difference between the two, and I know what my heart's feeling."

Anjouinette turned away from him, and peered out of her massive clerestory windows.

Dajon approached her, and placed his hands on her shoulders. "I loved Daissala with all of my heart; she was my everything. During the time we've been spending together, I began to feel things that I had never felt with another woman, besides Daissala. I thought that I was disrespecting her memory. I felt as though I was being unfaithful to her, then it hit me. Yesterday afternoon, it just hit me. What Daissala and I shared was special, magical almost, and it will never be re-created. I would never try to re-create it. But life goes on, and I realized that my heart can love again. I was always told that love comes, when you least expect it. And that your heart would let you know when it was true love, and when it was really ready to love."

Dajon turned Anjouinette around, and brought her face-to-face with him. "I'm ready to love again. You have a beauty, a flame, that I'm drawn to like a moth. I love you, and I realized yesterday, that I can't stay away from you."

"Dajon, I'm Anjouinette, and if you're looking for another Daissala, then you're making a mistake."

Dajon shook his head. "I've always lived my life as the brother who didn't make any mistakes. I was always the careful one, the good one, the responsible one. I graduated from college, married, bought a house, and had two children. I washed my cars on Saturday, mowed my lawn on Sundays, and attended Mass every Friday. I recycled paper and plastics, I attended every goddamned PTA meeting that they ever called. I was a scoutmaster, a peewee soccer coach, a Little League baseball coach, and I won freaking best yard of the month thirty times in the last five years! All my life, I've played it safe. That life died in a hail of bullets one sad Friday afternoon. But you, Anjouinette, you brought me back to life!"

Anjouinette stared at the ground. "I don't know, Dajon. Something tells me that in the end, I'm going to get hurt. It's the rebound relationships that don't last."

236

"I'm a very philosophical person," Dajon explained to her. "I searched for answers after my wife's death, but at first none came. And then I recalled some of the things that Father McConnell taught me while I was growing up. God has a plan for each and every one of us, and God doesn't make mistakes. Was it meant for Daisalla to be taken from me? Was it meant for you and me to meet? Was it meant for me to have the feelings that I have for you?"

"Time, Dajon," Anjouinette told him. "All I'm asking for is a little bit of time to digest all of this."

"Alright," Dajon told her. "I can wait."

Anjouinette leaned forward and kissed Dajon on his cheek. She then turned, and briskly headed into her bedroom to dress.

Chapter Twenty Six

Damian paced nervously back and forth in his living room. He was about to meet his son for the very first time, and with each aching moment, he was quickly becoming a nervous wreck.

He had spent the last three years trying to find his son, and now that the moment of truth had arrived, he had no idea what to say or do. Did they look alike? Did his son have dimples when he smiled? What were his interests? All of these questions were about to be answered in a few seconds. The limousine was already at his front door.

Angela opened the front door and led Little Damian into the house. She stopped at the living room entrance.

"Do you know who that is?" Angela asked, while pointing toward Damian.

Little Damian nodded.

"Who is that?" Angela asked.

"My daddy," Little Damian told her.

Damian dropped to his knees and threw open his arms. "Come here, little man."

Little Damian walked to where his father was kneeling, and leaned forward and hugged him. Damian burst into tears.

Angela, a person not known for being sentimental, wept. She had spearheaded the effort to locate Little Damian, and for more than two years had come up short. Now, she understood the true meaning of her hunt. Seeing Damian on the floor hugging his child and bawling like a baby, allowed her to see that it had all been worth it.

Damian lifted his son into the air and spun him around. "Daddy loves you so much!" Damian placed a big kiss on Little Damian's forehead. "Do you love Daddy?"

Little Damian nodded and smiled.

"Daddy loves you!" Damian exclaimed. "We're going to have so much fun together! Daddy's going to take you to Sea World, and to Fiesta Texas, and to ride horses, and to Splash Town."

Damian lifted his son into the air again, and spun him around. Little Damian's giggles echoed throughout the house.

"Are you hungry?" Damian asked.

Little Damian shook his head.

"He shouldn't be," Angela told him. "He ate two whole slices of pizza at the airport."

"Two slices of pizza!" Damian exclaimed. He tickled Little Damian's stomach. What are doing eating two slices of pizza? You're trying to be Daddy's little fullback, or something?"

"He's a big boy," Angela told him.

Damian shifted his gaze toward her. "How's Grace?"

Angela nodded. "She's okay."

"How'd she look?"

"She looked good," Angela told him. "Her arm was in a sling, but other than that, she looked okay to me."

"Mommy's fine," Little Damian told him. "She broke her arm at work."

"She did?" Damian asked.

Little Damian nodded. "She said that she wanted me to come and play with you, while the doctors made her arm better."

"Daddy wanted you to come and play with him so much," Damian told him. "I'm so glad that Mommy let you come and play with me. And I want you to know something; Mommy's arm's going to be all better real soon."

"How about some ice cream?" Angela asked.

Little Damian nodded enthusiastically.

"Good," Damian told him. "Hey, Rocky here's going to take you into the kitchen and fix you some ice cream, while Daddy talks with Auntie Angela. And as soon as Daddy finishes, I'm coming right into the kitchen and eat some ice cream with you."

Little Damian nodded, and then turned toward Angela. "Auntie, are you coming too?"

Angela nodded. "You bet I am."

Rocky, one of Damian's men, led Little Damian into the kitchen. Damian turned toward Angela.

"Why didn't she come?"

"Would you have come if you were her?" Angela asked. "I mean, we've been trying to kill her for the last three years."

"We've been trying to find my son for the last three years," Damian corrected her. "So tell me, what's the deal with the East Coast?"

"Maryland's ours, as I reported last month," Angela told him. "The situation is D.C. is under control. Virginia's ours, and we've officially taken New Jersey."

"What?"

"I give you the state of New Jersey, as my Christmas gift to you," Angela told him. "I killed the last of those pastrami-eating son of bitches personally. New Jersey's quiet, it's pacified, and it belongs to us."

"It's peaceful for now," Damian told her. "They aren't going to give up Jersey. We'd have to kill them all, before they give up Jersey, trust me."

"They'd give up Jersey, if they were about to lose Philadelphia, and, if things were going bad for them in New York," Angela explained.

Damian smiled like a kid on Christmas morning. "Are they about to lose Philly? Are things going that bad for them in New York?"

"Niccolo's taking it to their asses in New York," Angela informed him. Niccolo Costa Mendez, was also known as

Nicanor Morenci Mata, of the Honduran death squad. She leaned in, as if she were about to reveal a great secret. "Before I left, Niccolo called and reported that he had just taken all of Brooklyn."

Damian clapped his hands and leaped into the air. "Whoooo! Yes, baby! That's what I'm talking about!" He grabbed Angela, lifted her into the air and spun her around. "We took Brooklyn from those sons of bitches! We took Brooklyn!"

"Put me down!" Angela laughed.

Damian kissed her on her cheek repeatedly. "Yes, yes, yes! You're brilliant, brilliant, brilliant! I love you Angela! I love you; I love you; I love you!"

"Careful, Dante sees you, and he may get suspicious."

Damian turned around. Stacia was leaning against the kitchen wall with her arms crossed.

Angela exhaled. "Hello, Stacia."

Stacia tilted her head. "The feeling's mutual, Angela." Stacia certainly couldn't forget when Princess and Angela invaded her home and tried to kill her while they were looking for Damian's son.

"Bitch."

"Your mother."

"Okay, you two, enough of all that mushy sentimental stuff," Damian told them.

"Suddenly, I have a taste for some ice cream," Angela announced. "I'll be in the kitchen, Damian."

"The sister-in-law is here too, huh?" Stacia fumed. "Wow, we're getting mighty domesticated around here."

Little Damian ran into the living room with an ice-cream cone. "Daddy, Daddy, look! I made an ice-cream cone!"

Damian scooped his son up into his arms. "I see! That looks like it's pretty tasty! Can Daddy have some?"

Little Damian nodded, and held the cone up to Damian mouth. Using his lips, Damian pulled off a small bit of ice cream and swallowed it.

"That was the best ice cream that I ever tasted!" Damian exclaimed.

Stacia threw her head back, exhaled forcibly, and headed for the front door.

"What the hell's wrong with you?" Damian asked. "He turned to his son. "Go into the kitchen with Auntie Angela and make Daddy an ice-cream cone."

"Okay," Little Damian told him. He pulled away from his father, and bolted into the kitchen.

Damian turned toward Stacia.

"He can't help who his mother is," he told her. "He's my son."

Stacia shrugged.

"You have a problem with that?"

"No, Damian, I don't have a problem with that," Stacia snapped. "Congratulations, you finally got what you wanted."

"What the hell's wrong with you?" Damian asked forcefully.

"Nothing! Nothing's wrong, Damian," Stacia snapped. "All's fucking perfect with the world, isn't it? You have your family with you now, so all's well."

"Yes, yes it is!" Damian told her. "Is that what this is about? Are you jealous of a three-year-old child?"

"Jealous of a three-year-old child?" Stacia asked. "No! Yes! Kind of! Hell, I don't fucking know!"

"Stacia, what the hell's wrong with you?"

Stacia exhaled. "Damian, you're so fucking smart, that you're just plain stupid!"

"And what's that supposed to mean?" Damian clasped her arms, and pulled her close. "Stacia, of all people, I thought you'd be happy for me!"

"Happy for you? Happy for you?" Stacia pulled away from him. "Happy for you, Damian? I thought that I would be happy for you, but... I..."

"What?" Damian shook his head in confusion. "What?"

"Because I want the same thing for my children, the same feelings, the same joy."

242

"Are you having problems with Michael?"

Stacia turned away. "Oh, Damian, how could you be so stupid?"

"What in the hell are you talking about?"

"You spent millions of dollars in manpower and resources tracking down Little Damian, when you have four kids of your own right here!"

"What?" Damian again shook his head in confusion.

"Damian, Michael's impotent; he can't have kids!"

"Stacia, you and Michael have four kids together!"

"No, Damian, you and I have four kids together!" Stacia shouted, not caring that Angela was in the kitchen and heard everything. Angela was in shock, but said nothing. She just continued making an ice-cream cone with Little Damian. She didn't think it was her place to say anything, or at least not at the moment.

Damian reeled. "What?"

Stacia turned. "Michael can't have children, Damian. He never could. We tried everything. He wore looser underwear; he drank more water; he took vitamins; he tried yoga; we counted days; we monitored my period; I took fertility pills; we did everything. And finally, when it happened, the damn fool thought that it was because he switched to boxers from briefs." Stacia shook her head and smiled, as she peered off into the distance.

Damian shook his head. "Stacia, no."

She turned and faced him. "What do you mean, no?"

"Don't do this to me," he whispered.

"Don't do what to you?"

"How could you have done this to me?"

"I was married to an FBI agent, and my father was the special agent in charge of the San Antonio field office. What was I supposed to do? I was married, and you had no intention of marrying me. I didn't even know if I wanted to marry you."

"My father, he never got to know his grandchildren."

"Damian, he never got to know Little Damian either,"

Stacia told him.

"That's different," Damian countered. "He couldn't. But your kids, they were right here."

Damian shook his head. "How could you have done this to me?"

"Done it to you?" Stacia asked. "You, you, you! Why is it always about Damian?"

"That was wrong as hell, Stacia, and you know it!" Damian shouted.

Stacia placed her fingers on her temples and closed her eyes. "I'm sorry that I even told you. I don't know what the hell I was thinking."

"You're sorry that you told me?" Damian asked. "You're sorry that you just decided to reveal to me that I have four children?" Damian nodded.

"Oh, I'm sorry? I'm sorry?" Stacia jabbed Damian in his chest. "You're the one who's sorry! You're the one who's lived his life worried about what everyone else thinks! You're the one who was so worried about his reputation, that you weren't man enough to love who you wanted to love!"

"Stacia, I was a kid!" Damian shouted. "I was a kid, and so were you. And don't you try to change this conversation around. And don't you try to blame me for your moments of weakness!"

"Moments of weakness?" Stacia threw her hands into the air. "Oh my God, Damian! Are you really this stupid?"

"You destroyed the trust in our relationship, Stacia, not me!" Damian shouted. "You did it!"

"I didn't do anything, you stupid ass!" Stacia shouted. "I never slept with any of those assholes! I've been with two men my entire life, you, and my goddamned husband!"

Damian reeled. "What?"

"Surprise, surprise, surprise!" Stacia wailed. "Sorry to disappoint you, Damian, but I'm not the harlot that you made me out to be. I allowed you to use me, Damian. I allowed you to use me all of these years, out of love. I played the role of the naughty mistress, the cheating wife, the evil

244

vixen, because that's who you wanted me to be. That's who you believed that I was. And if that was the only way that I could fit into your world, then so be it."

Damian shook his head, pulled her close, and embraced her tightly.

"Do you know what it does to your heart, when you have to live a lie?" Stacia asked him, with tears streaming down her face.

"Stacia, I'm sorry," Damian whispered. "I'm sorry for everything. I'm sorry for not believing in you; I'm sorry for forcing you to live a lie all of these years. I'm sorry that I wasn't man enough to do what I should have done. I, I can't marry Illyassa, not now."

"Stacia pulled away from him and shook her head. "No, don't you even think it. This family needs her to survive, Damian. We all need her political connections."

"Things are getting better for us," Damian told her. "We can survive without her."

Stacia shook her head. "No, we can't. Damian, the landscape has changed considerably. Politicians are a dime a dozen now. Just having a few senators and representatives is not enough. Bio One places you on an entirely different level. It's a whole other playing field out there, Damian. You're an African-American male, with sole ownership of one of the largest biotechnological, scientific, pharmaceutical, and medical research firms in the world. You have research contracts and grants totaling billions of dollars from governments and research institutes all over the world. Local political protection is not enough anymore."

"Damian, now that you know, I'm sure that things are going to be different between us," Stacia said softly. "You know how much I love you, and you know that I've always been true to you, and most importantly, you now know that we have a family together."

Damian hugged her tightly. "We have a family together, Stacia, four kids."

Stacia leaned back and stared into his eyes. "No,

Damian, we have five."

Damian smiled. "C'mon, let's go in the kitchen so that I can introduce you to our youngest."

"I'd love that," Stacia whispered.

Damian took Stacia by her hand, and led her through the door into his kitchen.

Chapter Twenty Seven

Senator Sandra Fitzhugh detested flying. She had logged more than four million air miles during her sixteen years in the Senate, and ten years in the U.S. House of Representatives, but had a deeply routed fear of flying. Only birds and angels should fly, the senator often told others, in her deep Southern drawl. And since she wasn't feathered or dead, she preferred to keep her ass on the ground, she often quipped.

Her flight plans had already begun with an ominous sense of what was to come. Her initial departure had been delayed due to bad weather, and on top of that, she had to switch charters because of an engine malfunction on her original flight. Had she not been pressed for time, she would have taken a commercial flight to the speech she was scheduled to deliver in the Midwest. She swore that the gods were conspiring against her.

Senator Fitzhugh stormed aboard her alternate charter, where she was met by the pilot.

"Senator Fitzhugh, welcome aboard," the pilot told her, "My name's Captain Windcrest, and I'll be your pilot this afternoon."

"I hope the flight's more pleasant than the service your company has thus far provided," Senator Fitzhugh snapped. "And I trust that your aircraft's in better shape than that last disaster waiting to happen that they had previously assigned to me."

Captain Windcrest bowed slightly. "Please accept my apologies for the inconveniences that you've thus far experienced, Senator. My staff and I shall do all within our power to ensure that the remainder of your experience is first class."

"I should hope so," the senator snapped. She brushed past the pilot and seated herself next to a window in the center of the small Dassault Falcon passenger jet. The senator lifted her briefcase, opened it, and took out her reading glasses and a small manila folder. She placed the glasses on her nose, and then began thumbing through the file.

"We're going to be taking off immediately, Senator," Captain Windcrest informed her. "The tower has already been notified and they're simply waiting for me to request clearance for takeoff."

Senator Fitzhugh grumbled without looking up. Windcrest turned, and went back to his cockpit, closing the door behind him. The male flight attendant who had been standing behind the pilot, seated himself, and then fastened his safety belt for takeoff.

The small corporate jet taxied quickly to its runway, and paused until clearance for takeoff was given. The clearance came quickly from the tower, as the flight controllers were well aware of the flight's VIP passenger. A flight controller would not have the nerve to hold up the deputy chair of the Senate Transportation Committee. Not if he wanted to remain a flight controller. The small Dassault quickly taxied down the runway, and lifted off into the air.

The flight traveled east for a short while, before the attendant unbuckled his safety belt, rose from his seat, and walked down the narrow aisles. He reseated himself just across from the senator.

"I don't fraternize with the help," Senator Fitzhugh said dryly.

The attendant folded his legs and reclined back into

the comfortable lounge-like seat.

"May I help you?" the senator asked, peering over the top of her reading glasses.

"No, Senator, you've done quite enough," the attendant told her.

"And what's that supposed to mean?" Senator Fitzhugh snapped.

"You don't even recognize the man whose family you've been trying to destroy for the last four years," Dante told her. "Didn't you even bother to examine photos of us? At least a two by three of the men whose lives you've dedicated yourself to destroying?"

Senator Fitzhugh leaned back inside of her seat, exhaled, and closed her eyes. "Damian Reigns?"

Dante shook his head. "No, I'm Dante, the other brother."

Senator Fitzhugh nodded her head. "I should have known. Damian's the leader of your little cabal, while you're the operator. So, tell me, Dante Reigns, why are you here today, on my flight?"

"It's margin call, Senator, time to settle all debts."

"I owe you something?" the senator asked.

"You owe me everything, Senator," Dante told her. "You owe me a life. My sister-in-law's dead because of you. Many others are dead as well, because of your little personal vendetta against us. Did you really think that your little Vegas friends could protect you?"

"Mr. Reigns, I think you're sadly mistaken, if for one second you think that I'm in need of protection. I'm a U.S. senator; I'm protected by the resources of the most powerful nation this world has ever seen. And I owe you nothing, Mr. Reigns. Nothing! It's you who owe me!"

"Your god son?" Dante asked.

"You're god damned right!" the senator snapped. "He was my god son, and you murdered him. His family has yet to find his body, so that he can be given a decent burial! I raised that kid! I was there the night that he came into this world! He spent the weekends at my home, and he was my son's best friend. I've known his parents for more than fifty years. His mother and I have been best friends since elementary school. I was with that woman when the news of her son's disappearance came, and I saw a woman whose life was obliterated instantly. You're responsible for that."

"No one inside my family has ever been tried or convicted for the disappearance of your god son," Dante told her. "So why on earth would you just automatically assume that someone inside my family killed him?"

"He was investigating your organization at the time of his disappearance, Mr. Reigns," Senator Fitzhugh snapped. "We're educated people here; let's not belittle one another's intelligence!"

"What makes you think that he didn't just up and disappear from a career that he despised, Senator? From a life that he hated?"

"Do you have children, Mr. Reigns?" the Senator asked.

"I do," Dante told her. "One."

"Would you disappear and leave your child behind?" The senator asked. "His name was John, and his daughter's name is Hannah. She has the curliest blond hair that you could ever imagine. And her eyes, her eyes look like a beautiful crystal blue lagoon. You look at her, and you become lost in them. They remind you of the waters off a beautiful South Pacific island; you just want to dive into them."

Dante nodded. "My brother's wife, her name was Daisalla. She was of Ethiopian descent. She had skin like burnished copper and hair like thick black strands of silk. She was a university professor, with a mind sharper than a 1930s straight razor. She was beautiful, and brilliant. She had the glow, the walk, the regality of a queen. She left behind a daughter, Cheyenne, and a son, D.J. Her departure left a void in all of our hearts. She was the best and the brightest that ever wore the Reign's family name."

250

"So, we both suffered great losses," the senator told
him. "And now?"

"Now, it's time to settle our debts. "We lost Daisalla,
we almost lost Little Dajon, we almost lost Princess, Damian,
my Mother, and so many others. You arranged to have the
Justice Department hold up it's anti-trust approval of our
company's last three acquisitions, and you held up FDA
approval of a couple of our pharmaceutical discoveries.
Those things have to be accounted for."

"What do you mean accounted for?" the senator
asked.

"Damian Reigns controls something that no other
person on this planet controls. A privately owned
biotechnology corporation. A corporation that's so massive in
breadth and width and scope, as to defy description. A
company that's on the cusp of discovery. Senator, our last
great frontier is the human body. Cell mapping of the human
genome and the rapid expansion of nanotechnology is
reshaping our world. Biotechnology is to this century, what
computers and computer chips were to the last century.
Damian Reigns is the next Bill Gates, but the amount of
money that Bio One stands to make, will make Microsoft
look like a five-and-dime store. My brother's more than just a
captain of industry; he's Caesar. And you tried to destroy
this black Caesar."

The senator nodded her head.

"In ancient times, what happened to those who plotted
against Caesar?" Dante asked.

Senator Fitzhugh leaned back inside of her seat and
smiled. "Young man, these are not ancient times, and this is
not the Roman Empire. In case you haven't noticed, there's a
pilot and copilot in the next room, and we're thirty thousand
feet in the air."

"Well, Senator, you're half right," Dante told her.
"There's a pilot in there, but he's dead. The copilot works for
me, and he's not on any of the flight plans. As far as anyone
knows, it's just you and the pilot on this flight."

The senator peered out of the window and smiled.

"That still doesn't change the fact that we're in a tiny little airplane, high up in the air, and that your copilot must land in order for you to escape. What, are you going to shoot me on the runway, Mr. Reigns?"

Dante shook his head. "No, Senator, I'm not going to shoot you."

The copilot strode into the cabin holding two large backpacks.

"Senator, I want you to meet Niccolo Costa Mendez, formerly of the French Foreign Legion."

"Costa Mendez?" The senator sneered. "Don't you mean, Nicanor Moreno Mata, of the Honduran death squads? I know who he is. A name change means little to me. I sit on the Senate Intelligence Committee; remember?"

Dante nodded and smiled. "Yes, you do, don't you. I forgot. Well, anyway, Nicanor here, is an expert at high-altitude, high-speed parachute jumps. We're going to slow the jet down almost to stall speed, jump, and then have the autopilot resume a predetermined speed and course."

"And what course is that, Mr. Reigns?" the senator asked dryly.

"Why, into a mountain, of course." Dante smiled. "Look out your window, Senator. Those are the Rockies below us. We're going to jump into a valley between two of the mountains, where we have transportation waiting for us. I'll be at Denver's shiny new airport in time for dinner. You on the other hand, will be one with nature And, Senator, I mean that literally. You're going to become part of a mountain."

"I see that you've thought of everything, Mr. Reigns," the senator told him. "You're determined to have me die in a loud and fiery plane crash."

"Yes, that's how we kill senators," Dante told her. "Senators, congressmen, governors, and international Statesmen; you all get the honor of accidental plane crashes. We can't just put a bullet through a senator's head, you know."

"And why's that?"

"Because the president would vow to the nation that your killer would be brought to justice. So, ever since ancient times, senators have always been given the privilege of an honorable death. And by that, I mean, a tragic one. Your death will be lamented because you were taken in your prime; you'll be eulogized as a national hero, a woman of the people, a citizen dedicated to serving her nation. The president will attend your funeral, all the flags will fly at half-mast, and you'll receive your twenty-one-gun salute. More importantly, they'll be no investigations. The FAA will chalk it up as engine failure."

"And how can you be so sure?"

"Because the engine's going to fail," Dante told her. "That was the reason why we changed your plane. This ones all rigged up and ready to go. The black boxes have all been preprogrammed, the engines are preprogrammed to failed, and everything has already been taken care of, Senator."

Nicanor handed Dante a large parachute, and then assisted him with putting it on. The alarm on Dante's watch began to beep.

"That's my cue, Senator," Dante told her. "That tells me that the plane has slowed down, and that we have approximately two minutes to get off before the autopilot increases the plane's speed again. It also lets me know that we're nearing our drop zone. It's been a pleasure, Senator. I just want you to know something. I respect you. You've came the closest so far, to destroying my family. You were a worthy adversary, but like all the others, you just didn't have enough to get over that hump. But don't feel bad, because you're in good company. No one can fuck with us."

"I'm a senator, Mr. Reigns; I'm used to wheeling and dealing," Senator Fitzhugh told him. "So, let's make a deal."

Dante shook his head. "Sorry, Senator, you should have thought about that before. You're our enemy, you made a deal with our other enemies, and most importantly, you tried to kill Caesar."

"Do I get a drink of wine before I have to fall on my sword?" The senator asked.

Nicanor opened the fuselage door, and gave Dante a thumbs-up.

Dante turned toward the senator and shook his head. "No, wine was given to the enemies of Caesar so that the pain of their deaths would be less painful. I want you to feel every moment of this, Senator. I want you to have excellent clarity of mind, as you contemplate your fiery death. Good-bye."

Dante and Nicanor leaped from the tiny jet and into the brisk evening air, leaving the senator sitting in her seat. She had made war on the Reigns family, she had tried to avenge the death of her god son, and she had chosen to make the Las Vegas mafia dons her partners in her mission to destroy them. She had made many choices in her life, many of them difficult, but good ones. She sat at the pinnacle of power, in the most powerful nation that the world had ever seen. Her choices had won her a seat in the U.S. Senate, and seats on some of the most powerful committees in government. Her choices were the reason why she sat as deputy chair of the Senate Foreign Intelligence Committee, chair of the Senate Intelligence Committee, and chair of the powerful Senate Steerage Committee. Her choices had brought her great wealth, great prestige, and great power. Her choices her brought her face-to-face with some of the most powerful men to ever walk the earth, and they had allowed her to whisper into the ears of the rulers of the universe. She had chosen the right path. This time, she thought to herself as she looked out of the window and watched her plane began to wobble and began its terminal maneuvers, she had chosen wrong.

Chapter Twenty Eight

Damian watched from the sofa as Little Damian played quietly with his newly purchased mountain of toys. Damian's massive game room looked as if Christmas had come and gone three times within a matter of minutes. There were toys on top of toys, piled more than four feet high. The sight of his son playing so peacefully, so serenely, brought home a sharp sense of responsibility to him. He realized more so than ever, that he was ultimately responsible for his son's safety and happiness. He was responsible for keeping the monsters away.

Princess breezed into the room, and headed straight for her brother. "Oh, there you are."

Damian leaned back on the sofa and smiled. "Just watching Little Damian play."

"Hi, Auntie Princess," Little Damian waved.

"Hi, sweetie," Princess told him. "Where's my sugar?"

Little Damian puckered his lips, and Princess leaned forward and kissed him, making a loud smacking noise. She followed that kiss, with another to his forehead, and then headed for the couch where Damian was seated. She took the seat next to him.

"Message from Dante," Princess announced. "He's made it back safe, and he's lying low, relaxing, skiing, and snowboarding."

"And his assignment?"

"CNN says that there's breaking news," Princess told him. "Senator Fizthugh's charter's missing."

Damian nodded.

"You don't seem happy." Princess told him.

"I'm just thinking," Damian told her. "We made it through this one, and maybe the coalition against us will fall apart this time, but what about the next time? What about the next senator, or representative, or judge, or FBI agent with a bird up their ass? What if we're not so lucky the next time?"

"We're not lucky, Damian," Princess told him. "We're good."

"When does it all end?"

Princess shook her head and turned away. "Not this again. You're out, and I'm going to take over the family's business. You' going to run Bio One, and I get the seat on the Commission; that was our deal."

"Princess, as long as any one of us has anything to do with that Commission, we're all targets."

"Damian, don't be naive," Princess countered. "We can never leave this business. We're trapped. It's our muscle, our affiliations, and our ability and will to operate outside of the law that keeps us alive. Damian, we can never go back to being just nobody, and you know that."

Damian nodded hesitantly. He knew she was right. They couldn't just walk away from it all. They would be dead within a week. From now, until the rest of their lives, and possibly even for the rest of their children's lives, the Reigns family was trapped. Their history locked them into a future that they very much wished they could change, but knew that they couldn't. Their destinies had been decided a long time ago.

"I want to end this, Princess," Damian told her. No more one foot in, one foot out. If this is our family's destiny, then so be it. But let's do it right. Let's finish the game."

"I'm just waiting on the soldiers to take California, and

256

Dante's waiting on the necessary manpower to take Nevada," Princess told him.

Damian shook his head. "I know that we can take care of California and Nevada. I'm talking about the others. Those assholes in New York, and that son of a bitch in Columbia, are the ones that I'm talking about."

"You want to take on the entire New York and Vegas, as well as the Commission and El Jeffe?" Princess asked.

"I want to end it all, and I want to end it all now," Damian told her.

"Damian, you want to hit El Jeffe?" Princess asked incredulously. "Do you understand what you're saying?"

"Princess, I've sat here for the last two hours, watching my son play," Damian said softly. "We all have children."

"We have to end this. For the sake of our children, we have to end this."

"Damian, are you sure you want to go after El Jeffe?" Princess asked again. "What if we don't succeed?"

"Hell, we're already practically at war with the son of a bitch anyway," Damian told her.

"Have you thought of the consequences of success?" Princess asked. "What if we do get him? What happens to the situation in Colombia? Who takes over for El Jeffe? What if they want to discontinue their affiliation with us?"

"We control all access to this country," Damian told her. "They want to continue supplying this fifty-billion-dollar a year market then they have to come to us. They'll come begging, and we'll get to set the terms."

Princess nodded. "Damian, I hope you know what you're doing. It took us ten years to get our man on the inside and gain El Jeffe's trust. We have one shot at this, so don't waste it."

"Do you think I should send Dante or Niccolo down to assist with the operation?" Damian asked.

Princess shook her head. "No, El Jeffe would know of Dante's presence the moment he landed. He owns that country, remember. No, we'll just get the message to our man, and arrange for his transport out of that country once it's done."

Damian shifted his gaze toward his son, who peered up from his toys and waved. "Send Niccolo anyway. And get some new photos of our guy in some compromising positions, just in case he goes soft. Princess, make it happen."

"Yes, sir," Princess rose from off the couch, and headed out of the room.

Emil considered himself a man of the people. He loved to socialize. He patronized all of the hottest clubs in Atlanta, went to all of the hottest events, and had his own box at all of the local sports studio and arena. He was single, and mingling gave him the opportunity to meet people, especially women. It also gave him an opportunity to tune into the latest news on the streets. He thought it gave him an edge, and since he was the head of the entire state of in Georgia, he needed each and every advantage that fortune threw his way.

Today, Emil's latest outing took him to one of Atlanta's trendiest barbershops, 'Cuts over Atlanta'.

Cuts over Atlanta was actually located in Stone Mountain, an African-American neighborhood that was growing more affluent with each new suburb. It was considered the place to be, if you were a business that was trying to attract a young, urban, and upwardly mobile clientele. It was considered the new Buckhead.

Cuts, as it was called by those in the know, was located inside a three-story stone and glass building that was decorated with all of the most modern, and most trendy status symbols. It had mocha-colored Italian leather sectionals; massive seventy-two-foot wide fish tanks hanging from the ceilings; heat-n-glow cyclone fireplace tubes; KWC Murano chrome and glass faucets; eighty-four-inch flat screen monitors; scantily clad women serving refreshments;

a club-like stereo system; and its most impressive feature of all, was the gun metal gray and black Lotus Elise it had mounted on the main wall inside the shop area. Money had been spent making Cuts the premier barbershop in the nation, and people with money flocked to the establishment.

Emil had long ago stopped taking security with him to his barbershop appointments. The war with his troublesome Savannah faction had long been settled. The Reigns family had come in, waged war with the fury of Armageddon, and pacified his troublesome territory for him. It was for that reason, that he was forever grateful to them. The Savannah bosses had grown particularly strong, and much to his chagrin, he would not have been able to defeat them. Had it not been for Damian, someone else would be sitting in his seat on the Commission right now. Those times were over with, and those types of worries long gone with them.

Willie, Emil's barber, waved his hand for Emil to come over and take his seat in the barber's chair. Emil placed the USA Today that he had been reading, back onto the coffee table, and ventured over to the chair, where he seated himself.

"So, what's the word today, E?" Willie asked.

Emil shook his head. "Can't call it, Will. You tell me, what's the haps?"

"Same shit, different day," Willie announced.

Emil laughed. "I hear you."

"You catch the Falcons last night?"

Emil nodded. "Yeah, I saw that shit. The Saints, man? How could they lose to the god-damned Saints?"

"I think all that shit's rigged," Willie told him. "You know them white folks take turns at winning. They gonna just pass the money pot around to each other, let everybody get a chance to juice their home crowd for a year a two, and then pass it on to the next cracker."

Emil shook his head and laughed. "You and your conspiracy theories, Willie."

"Boy, haven't I told you to wash this stuff outta your

head before you come up here messing up my clippers?" Willie asked.

"Willie, I just flew into town this morning; I didn't have time to wash my hair."

"Bullshit!" Willie told him. "You seem to like clogging up my damn clippers for some reason."

"Willie, don't I tip you enough to buy you a new pair of clippers every time I visit?" Emil asked.

"Man, get on over there to the basin so I can wash this mess outta your hair," Willie told him.

Emil rubbed his hand across his thick wavy hair. "Don't be hatin' on my waves, Willie!"

"You got enough Murrays in your hair to grease a whole transmission, boy," Willie told him. "You don't need that much grease; I keep telling you. Just smooth a little bit on your hands, rub it on, and then use a hot towel."

Emil rose from the barber's chair, and walked to the sink, where Willie tied a plastic cape around his shoulders.

Then he rubbed some shampoo into his hands. Emil stuck his hand under the running water, to test the temperature.

"Just trying to make sure that you're not trying to burn the grease out," Emil laughed.

"Boy, come on and hurry up," Willie told him with a smile. "I ain't got all damn day."

Emil leaned his head beneath the running faucet, while Willie rubbed the shampoo in his hair, washing the pomade from his waves. After awhile, Emil felt the water turning hot.

"Hey!" Emil shouted. "Willie, what the hell are you doing?"

Emil's head was forcibly pulled up from the sink, and a thick cord was quickly wrapped around his neck.

"What the fuck." Emil grabbed at the cord, and struggled to break free of the stranglehold. He turned to see Willie being held in a stranglehold as well.

One of the attackers stepped in front of Emil, and

punched him in his stomach. Emil's legs buckled from underneath him, but he was held up by two large men. A second punch landed in the same vicinity as the first.

"Tell your bitch ass daddy Damian, that he can't have the entire world," one of the attackers told Emil. "Tell that punk ass motherfucker, that we're watching him, and if makes any more moves on anybody else's territory, that he's going to wake up dead. Dead, do you hear me?"

Emil nodded.

"Good, bitch," the attacker told him.

The cord wrapped around Emil's neck was attached to a pair of clippers on one end, and to a wall socket on the other. The clippers were tossed into the running water in the sink.

Electricity shot through the clippers, including the section of cord that was wrapped around Emil's neck. Sparks flew through the air, and Emil fell to the ground and began convulsing. The lights in the barbershop went out as everyone ran out into the street in a panic.

Willie dropped to his knees next to a still smoking Emil, and lifted his friend's head into his lap.

"Message to Damian," Emil said weakly.

"Who?" Willie asked.

"Got to get a message." Emil again said weakly. His head fell to one side, and he blacked out.

"Just rest your head and keep quiet," Willie told him. He turned and peered over his shoulder. "Can somebody call an ambulance?"

Chapter Twenty Nine

"To my new son!" Minister Malaika toasted, lifting his glass filled with Pinot Cuvee into the air.

The others gathered around the table, lifted their spirits in a toast to the betrothed couple, and joined in the good-natured cheers. Tonight gave those gathered at the dinner a reason to celebrate, and celebration was something many of them needed. There had been so much tragedy in their lives of late.

Tonight's gathering was being held at Le Reve, a French restaurant located on the city's famed River Walk. The heavy continental cuisine was a culinary treat rivaling the best of Paris. The minister had rented the entire restaurant for the evening, as well as the highly acclaimed chef and his impeccable staff. They had been ordered to keep the wine and champagne flowing.

"May the Almighty Father bless this union, and make it a long, happy, and fruitful one," Deborah Malaika toasted. She turned toward her daughter. "Illyassa, it seemed as if it were only yesterday, that I watched you skip and collect seashells on the beach. I can still see you building sand castles, with your doll by your side; even then, you were trying to build something great, something lasting, something monumental. Building that castle is much like building a marriage. Make it as strong as you possibly can, make it big, make it beautiful, build it with great care and lots of love, and like a castle, your marriage will endure. Like a great castle, your marriage will stand the test of time, and like a great castle, after a tragedy, you can always rebuild, as long as the foundation's there."

"To building castles!" Dante lifted his glass in toast.

"Here, here!" Several of the men around the table shouted.

Damian stood, holding his glass his hand. He turned and faced his bride-to-be. "Illyassa, when I first saw you in person, it was at a fashion show in Paris."

Illyassa nodded and laughed. "You told me that I should model."

Bursts of laughter permeated the room.

Damian looked down and blushed. "Okay, how was I to know that you were already an international supermodel? It's not as if I read Vogue or Elle."

"Damian, you would have had to have lived in a cave, to not have seen me on television or in any magazines," Illyassa laughed.

"Okay, so I don't watch television, and I don't read fashion magazines," Damian told them. "Now, would you please let me finish my toast?"

Laughter shot throughout the room.

"Illyassa, when I first laid eyes on you, my heart stopped," Damian continued. "It was as if time itself had stopped, and the world around us had ceased. I looked into your eyes, and at that moment, it was as if no one else existed. I love you, Illyassa. And I have loved you from the moment that I first laid eyes on you, and I will love you until the last breath leaves my body. I can truly say that I have found my soul mate."

Illyassa wiped the tears streaming down her cheek. "I love you too, Damian. I do; I really do."

Illyassa turned to her mother and the two of them embraced tightly.

"To soul mates!" Dante toasted.

"To soul mates!" the gathering toasted.

The meeting had initially been scheduled to take place in Bismarck, North Dakota. The Reigns family had vetoed that idea, based on the fact that too many ultra-expensive business jets landing at the same time would cause too much undesired attention. It was for this reason, that the meeting had been moved to Jackson Hole Wyoming International Airport. Several Gulfstream G-Vs on the tarmac at the same time would draw absolutely no attention in Jackson Hole, as the airport was used to having numerous high-dollar private jets whisking in and out on a regular basis.

This evening's meeting was between Princess, who was here to represent her family's interest; Don Graziella Biaggio, who was representing the New York and Las Vegas families; and Don Vincent Liviano, who was here representing the Chicago families. It was the Chicago families who had called the meeting, and it was the Chicago families who were guaranteeing everyone's safety. They wanted to end a war in which their men were dying, but that they stood to profit very little from.

The executive jets pulled up next to one another, and formed a semicircle on the tarmac. The meeting was to be held in the center of this circle, and no bodyguards or assistants of any kind were allowed to exit their respective jets. It was to be a meeting of only the principals.

Princess strutted down the ramp of her black and gold G-V, and headed toward the center of the meeting place, where the other representatives were already standing. She extended her hand, and Don Liviano clasped it firmly.

"Princess, so wonderful to see you," Don Liviano told her. "You look lovely as ever."

"Thank you, Vincent," Princess smiled. "You're not looking so bad yourself."

"Hello, Princess," Don Biaggio greeted her. He extended his hand, and Princess shook it firmly.

Princess released Don Biaggio's hand, and turned her attention back to Don Liviano. She rubbed her hand across the Don's chest, and then over his shoulders. "I see that you're still working out, Vincent."

Don Liviano blushed, and nodded. "A little bit. I do what I can."

Princess batted her eyes and twirled at the ponytail that was protruding from beneath her black Chanel fedora. It had been awhile since she and Vincent had their last romp in Chicago. Vincent was young for a Don, thirty-three by now, if she remembered correctly. He was an avid bodybuilder, before the untimely deaths of his father and older brother thrust him into his current position. He had muscles on top of muscles, strong squared cheekbones, dark chestnut-colored hair, and sparkling gray eyes that looked like two brushed aluminum disks. She had known Vincent since graduate school, and he had been a very willing and eager partner. Much to her pleasure, what they said about Italian men and their tongues was absolutely true. She found herself becoming moist at the thought of what tonight may bring.

"Dinner, for old time's sake, Vincent?" Princess asked.

"I haven't eaten a good meal in awhile," Don Liviano told her with a smile.

"I haven't had Italian since the last time I was in Chicago," Princess smiled.

"That's good to know," Don Liviano replied.

"We're here tonight to discuss a truce between our two organizations," Don Biaggio informed Princess. He knew what was going on between Princess and Don Liviano. And he thought their behavior was inappropriate since they were here to discuss something important. Flirting had no place when they were talking about a truce, which was a tremendous step.

"Yes," Don Liviano nodded, straightened his tie and cleared his throat. It was time for business. "I'm here on behalf of the Chicago families. We're interested in securing a truce. This war's becoming too costly for everyone involved."

"We're not suffering from this war at all, Vincent,"

Princess said nonchalantly. "I'm well, Dante's free, Damian's back in charge, and we're growing stronger with each passing day. It's only a matter of time before we decide to take Las Vegas."

"You're busy in California, Princess," Don Biaggio told her. "We're not fools. You'll have your hands full with that state for years. And once we start sending soldiers into the state to really mess things up, you'll be fighting for California until you turn old and gray."

"And bodies will continue to pile up, and people will begin clamoring more and more for the feds to do something," Don Liviano added. "And federal attention is something that we all desperately want to avoid."

"We'll take all of California by summer, whether your soldiers are there or not," Princess announced.

"Princess, the Chicago families are obligated to step in with both feet, if this thing keeps going," Don Liviano told her. "You cannot possibly win. This thing will become a long and drawn out bloody mess. At least hear our proposal."

Princess hesitated for several moments, and then nodded.

"You've taken half of Pennsylvania, you have for all intents and purposes taken Maryland and New Jersey, and you've taken something that we hold very dear to our hearts. You've taken Brooklyn."

"We want it back," Don Biaggio said flatly.

Princess smiled. "We spent lives and resources taking it, and now, you want us to just give it back to you?"

"We'll stay out of California, and we'll give up all of Pennsylvania," Don Biaggio proposed. "In exchange for all of New York, New Jersey, and everything north of the two states. We also keep Delaware."

"Which means that you get Boston, and that we have to give up New Jersey as well as Brooklyn," Princess said. "I don't know."

"We only want New York, New Jersey, Nevada, and the New England states," Don Biaggio told her. "You can have

266

the rest of the damn country!"

"And our interest in Las Vegas?" Princess asked. "We have interest in several casinos down there."

"Pull out," Don Biaggio told her. "Pull out of the casino business for good."

Princess laughed. "This deal sounds very one sided. If I would have known that I was going to get fucked, I would have worn my best underwear."

Don Liviano laughed.

"Your family will take over all of our interest in illegal narcotics," Don Biaggio told her. "We pull out of drugs, and turn over all of our action to you, and you pull out of the casinos, and turn over your stake to us."

"And you think that the Commission is going to allow you to just buy us out?" Princess asked.

"To our understanding, they don't have a choice," Don Biaggio told her. "You have the most powerful organization on the Commission and you're free to sell your percentages to anyone you chose. Some members of your Commission chose not to participate in your casino ventures, while some of your casino ventures have participants who aren't members of your Commission."

Princess smiled and nodded. "You've done your homework, Graziella. But the question is; what's the take on your illegal narcotics ventures?"

"A lot more than what your stake in those casinos are worth," Don Biaggio answered. "Hell, probably twenty times as much."

Princess lifted an eyebrow and nodded. "And what of the narcotics interest in the territories that you control? Who gets the New York and New Jersey markets?"

"You do," Don Liviano told her. "You get to operate and sell whatever the hell it is you want in those territories, as far as narcotics are concerned. All other action still belongs to the families."

Princess exhaled. "So, you get Nevada, New York, New Jersey, and the New England states, as well as our interest in the Vegas casinos."

"You get California free and clear, Pennsylvania, Maryland, and our interest in the illegal narcotics business," Don Biaggio told her. He smiled and shook his head. "Princess, California alone's worth it. You consolidate your hold on California and then take Arizona; the entire drug market is at your mercy. Your family will control over ninety percent of the entrance points in this country. You'll be a fucking monopoly! You can charge whatever you want to charge, and you'll be able to tell your suppliers what you want to pay."

"We understand the implications clearly, Graziella," Princess said coldly. "I just don't think we're getting much, in exchange for what we're giving up. We already own Pennsylvania, we already control Maryland, and we're in the process of taking California. We don't need a peace agreement. You'll have to give more."

Don Liviano and Don Biaggio exchanged glances for several moments, before Don Liviano nodded.

"Okay! Okay!" Don Biaggio exclaimed. "We want Brooklyn; we want all of New York; we want all of Nevada; what will it take?"

"We sold all of our other businesses in order to raise the capital to expand Bio One," Princess explained. "Some of those businesses, we really wanted to keep. We want them back."

"You want us to buy them back for you?" Don Biaggio asked.

"Precisely," Princess said with a smile. "We want our car dealerships back; we want our entertainment corporation back; we want Energia, our oil exploration and refining corporation back; we want our bank back; we want our food chain back; and we want our construction company back. We also want our Internet access company back, and we want a percentage of the new casino that you're building."

"You want a piece of the Coliseum?" Don Biaggio shouted. "Why don't you just ask us to kill off all of our

268

firstborn sons? And your old companies! What you're asking will cost tens of billions!"

"We also want California free and clear," Princess added. "We'll keep Maryland, we'll keep Pennsylvania, and we'll keep Delaware. You can keep your narcotics operations, but you'll buy from us. You can have all of Nevada, but we'll keep our current casino operations, and you can have all of New York, New Jersey, and all of the New England states. You get what you want, we get what we want, and we're all happy."

"Yeah, only you want too much!" Don Biaggio told her. "There's no way I can give you that. The states are okay; we can agree on that. Your current casinos in Vegas, we'd be willing to accept that. But the piece of the Coliseum, and the buying back of your old companies?" Don Biaggio shook his head. "I don't know about that."

"What's Brooklyn worth to you?" Princess asked. "What's New York worth to you? We're talking money, that's all, just money."

"Okay, even if we approve the money, the Coliseum request is out of the question!" Don Biaggio announced.

Don Liviano turned toward Princess. "He gave a little; now you give a little."

"I'll give you peace," Princess told Don Biaggio. "You'll get Brooklyn, and our guarantee that we won't expand into those territories again."

"How much of a percentage of the Coliseum are you asking for?" Don Biaggio asked.

"Just an equal stake," Princess told him. "Whatever percentage that the rest of the shareholders currently own. Of course, this must come with a guarantee of our safety."

"This is where the Chicago families come in," Don Liviano told her. "We're guaranteeing whatever agreement is made today, and we're guaranteeing the peace and the safety and security of everyone involved. Whatever side violates the agreement, will have to contend with the Chicago families as well as with the offended party. We're placing our honor on the stake of this peace agreement."

"If you don't have the authority to make such an agreement, then I understand fully," Princess chided the Don. "Ask whomever you must, and then get back to us."

"I have full authority to make a deal, and whatever deal I make is binding," Don Biaggio said angrily. "You can believe that, sweetie."

"You were sent here to stop the bloodshed, and to get Brooklyn back," Princess told him. "You were also sent here to save Vegas. All of those things are within your grasp. The proceeds from your illegal narcotics sales should be able to cover the expense of the acquisitions that I've named. Hell, I'll even sweeten the pot. You can have the narcotics at our price, until you've recouped your money."

Don Biaggio shook his head hesitantly.

"I'll throw in Rhode Island," Princess told him.

Don Liviano and Don Biaggio exchanged glances for several moments, before Don Biaggio nodded his head.

"You have a deal," Don Biaggio told her, extending his hand.

Princess clasped the Don's hand, and shook it firmly. "Deal."

"Peace, finally!" Don Liviano exclaimed. He wrapped his arms around Princess and Don Biaggio, and pulled them both close. "May this peace be eternal!"

"There's one other thing," Princess told them. "We're running an operation in Colombia, and we have to wrap up our war against our own Commission."

Don Biaggio shook his head. "Your war with your Commission is of no concern with us."

"Do what you have to do," Don Liviano told her. "You have our blessings."

Princess nodded. "That's good to hear."

"This peace is binding, and guaranteed by the families of Chicago," Don Liviano told them. "It must not be broken."

"On my honor, I swear we won't break this peace," Don Biaggio told him. He kissed Don Liviano on both his cheeks.

"I swear that the Reigns family will not be the first to strike," Princess told Don Liviano. "We will not break the peace."

Don Liviano nodded. "Then this meeting is adjourned."

Chapter Thirty

Basilica de Santa Maria was the largest cathedral in the Western Hemisphere, and it was also the second largest cathedral in the world. Its massive copper-covered dome rose 520 feet into the air, and some 12,000 parishioners were able to be seated within its confines. The cathedral boasted of more than 7,000 stained glass windows, and some 4,000,000 tons of imported Italian marble. Basilica de Santa Maria was one of the largest, most impressive structures ever constructed in Colombia, and it meant so much to so many people. For some it was a symbol of hope, for others it was a symbol of faith, while for a select few it was a symbol of their status. It was a basilica that had been built for the ages; it was a basilica whose construction costs ran into the hundreds of millions of dollars; it was a basilica that had been constructed with bags and bags of drug money.

Basilica de Santa Maria was the cathedral of choice for one Senor Jairo Crisologo Valfredo-Urbez, also known as, El Jeffe. El Jeffe built the basilica as a gift to his home town, and to the peasants who worked his poppy fields and chemical plants. It also prevented him from having to drive forty miles into the nearest town, to attend service at the tiny local chapel, which was normally overcrowded during Mass. In front of the Basilica was a private section near, just for El Jeffe, his family, and his VIP guests. This area was equipped with larger, more luxurious seating, and it was cordoned off with imported Italian marble columns and balustrades. El

Jeffe's special section was surrounded by a larger VIP section that was constructed for Colombia's ruling class, as well as for other dignitaries who were in attendance during services. They were protected by armed security.

It was with great reluctance that the Vatican finally accepted the basilica after intense debate among the Vatican's hierarchy. One could not refuse such a gift, despite the origins of the funds used in its construction. It was a building for Christ, constructed to administer the gospel, and to salvage the souls of the tested. That, and the fact that the basilica came with a $30,000,000 donation to the church, and a one hundred million dollar trust fund that had established for the building's upkeep, was very helpful in swaying the Church's decision. The heated debate lasted all of two minutes.

El Jeffe had been raised in a strict Catholic household, like most of the people in South America. He attended Mass faithfully, and went to confession regularly. Today was one such day. It was time for him to make his weekly confession.

The confessional was a large intricately carved mahogany booth that had been hand carved in Sicily, and shipped over on a special transport. Its sheer size, prevented it from being shipped on a standard cargo vessel. Lloyd's would not have insured it. El Jeffe could still smell the faint scent of turpentine each time he entered the booth. He also loved the faint smell of pine cleaner that wafted throughout the booth whenever he entered.

"Bless me Padre, for I've sinned," El Jeffe whispered, while making the sign of the cross on his body.

"Confess your sins and repent, my son," Padre Alejandro Landerico Balderama told him.

"Padre, I have had two men killed since my last confession one week ago," El Jeffe whispered. "I killed one man myself, on Tuesday. Please forgive me."

"It's not up to me to forgive, my son," Padre Balderama replied. "It's up to God. Your sins are terrible, my son. You must realize that, and you must repent. Show great acts of contrition to the Lord, so that your good deeds may outweigh your bad ones."

"Hail Mary, full of grace." El Jeffe began.

"What are you doing?" Padre Balderama asked.

"Saying my Hail Marys and Our Fathers."

"You come in here week after week and confess to me how many men you have killed, and you think that a few Hail Marys will suffice?" Padre Balderama asked.

"Padre, you always absolve my sins after I perform my Hail Marys," El Jeffe told him. "I thought."

"No, no, no, my son," Padre Balderama told him. "Things are different today, son. Way different."

"What's different, Padre?"

"Times are different, my son," Padre Balderama told him. "It's my time to go."

"Go?" EL Jeffe asked. "Go where? Padre, where are you going?"

"To my next assignment, my job here is nearing the end."

"Your job here, Padre?" EL Jeffe asked. "You were sent here by the Holy Father to administer to the poor, to help the diocese with the basilica. You can't leave, Padre! I need you here. You are the best Padre."

"Those words fill my heart with joy, my son," Padre Balderama said softly. "But unfortunately, life's much too complicated for things to be as they should."

"What can I do to help, Padre?" EL Jeffe asked. "I have powerful friends in the church who can help."

"No, my son," Padre Balderama told him. "Even more powerful people own my soul."

"Powerful people?" El Jeffe laughed. "Who could be more powerful than I, Padre? No one, Padre, no one is more powerful than El Jeffe!"

"I'm indebted to the Reigns family," Padre Balderama finally told him.

El Jeffe sat in silence for several moments, as he

contemplated the meaning of what the priest was saying. The Padre, to whom he had poured out his soul for the last eight years, was indebted to the Reigns family. How much had he told the Padre and how much had the Padre told them? He went for the door.

"Padre, why's this door locked?" El Jeffe asked nervously. "How is it possible that it's locked from the outside?"

"It was built to be able to be locked in such a way," Padre Balderama told him. "It was built specifically for this day, my son."

"Padre, you're making me nervous," El Jeffe told him. "What's the meaning of all of this?"

"It's a long story, my son," Padre Balderama said softly. He leaned back and lit a cigarette.

"Padre!" El Jeffe said excitedly. "You're smoking! Inside this holy place?"

"I was once a priest in Houston, Texas," Padre Balderama explained. He exhaled forcibly, blowing the smoke from his cigarette into the air. "Unfortunately, I made some mistakes during my tenure at one of the cathedrals there. You see, I have a fondness for young parishioners."

"Padre, what are you saying?"

"I'm saying, my son, that we're all human, and that we all suffer from various failings and weaknesses as a result. My weakness for altar boys resulted in me being caught in an extremely compromising position. And let's just say that the boy's family was very influential. Certain death was my lot, had it not been for the Reigns family stepping in. They cleaned things up, and used their connections inside the church to have me reassigned to this post. Everything was taken care of. And it was all done in exchange for my cooperation."

"Cooperation?" El Jeffe asked nervously.

"My mission was to get close to you."

"Get close to me? For what, Padre?"

"So that when the time came, I could have you killed,"

Padre Balderama explained.

El Jeffe laughed nervously. "Kill me, Padre? Oh, come now, surely you don't intend to exchange one small sin for a very large one?"

Padre Balderama laughed. "It was not just one boy, my son. The Reigns family traced my indiscretions all the way back to when I first entered the priesthood. I could have been prosecuted, had they turned the evidence over to the states, as they threatened to do."

El Jeffe loosened his collar, which was now covered in sweat. "Padre, I can protect you. You never have to go back to the United States. Look, I walk out of here, and I'll make you a very rich man."

"Unfortunately, I can't do that, my son," Padre Balderama told him. "I've allowed myself to become trapped once again. They have photos of me, compromising photos. Photos that they threatened to turn over to the Colombian authorities, and to the international media. Colombia would most certainly extradite me to stand charges in the United States and Italy."

"Dios mios, Padre!" El Jeffe shouted. "Can't you keep it in your pants?"

"As I said, we all have our shortcomings, my son. That is why I must leave."

"Leave?" El Jeffe shouted. He pulled at the door handle again. "Padre, open the door!"

Padre Balderama opened the door on his side of the confessional, and in walked Nicanor Moreno Mata, Damian's Cuban-born hit man.

Padre Balderama made the sign of the cross toward El Jeffe. "I have a plane to catch, my son. May God forgive you and absolve all of your sins."

"I'll see you in hell, Padre!" El Jeffe shouted. "I'll see you in hell!"

"Maybe, but you'll have a pretty long wait," Padre Balderama told him. "I'm going to Miami, while you go with God." Padre Balderama turned, and fled from the confessional.

"Hello, Jairo," Nicanor told him. "Damian wanted me to tell you that when he said that he wants to quit, he means that he wants to quit. No, means no; didn't your mother ever teach you that?"

El Jeffe spit toward Nicanor. "You tell that pinche hoto that I said to kiss my ass! He can fucking kiss my ass!"

"Go with God, Jairo," Nicanor told him. He lifted his silenced pistol and pointed it toward El Jeffe.

"Fucking mayates!" El Jeffe shouted. "You go to hell, you fucking niggers!"

The silenced rounds from Nicanor's 10-millimeter Beretta sliced through the wood screen dividing the booth, and struck El Jeffe several times in multiple locations. Nicanor emptied his 18-round magazine into the former cartel boss's body; leaving it a bullet-riddled bloody pulp. As always, for confirmation of his kill, Nicanor pulled out his camera, and took photos of the body from several angles. He would carry this film back to Damian personally. When finished, Nicanor put his camera away, and slipped through the same door from which the priest had escaped. He would be in the air and long out of Colombian airspace, before El Jeffe's bodyguards grew suspicious enough to break down the confessional door and find their boss's body. The mission was a success.

Dante hung up the telephone, and turned toward Damian and nodded. "It was a success."

Damian smiled and clapped. "And they said that it couldn't be done! Dante, you're a fucking genius! A fucking mad genius! Thank God that you're on my side!"

"So, what do you think's going to happen?" Dante asked.

"I believe that there'll be a short power struggle, and then Oso will take over. He's the most powerful of El Jeffe's underlings, and also the most cunning. He's a survivor, and I believe, the most logical horse to pick, if I were a gambling man."

Dante nodded. "I think so too. How long do you want to wait, before we send out feelers to him?"

Damian shook his head. "As soon as they find out that the son of a bitch is dead, send Oso a congratulatory message, on his ascension to power."

Dante nodded. "And the truce with La Cosa Nostra?"

"Strangely, they were a lot less unified than what I thought they would be," Damian observed. "I guess this is the modern Mafia. Profits, before anything else."

"Chicago really stood to gain little from this war," Dante observed. "It was natural for them to want to broker a peace deal."

"You think they'll enforce it?" Damian asked, with a lifted eyebrow.

"The word that I'm getting is that they're serious. Whoever violates this agreement, are going to throw their hats in the ring with the other side."

"And you think that if the Vegas families violated this agreement, that the Chicago families would actually go to war with Vegas?"

Dante frowned. "Hard to say. But the feelers that I have out there, are reporting that they're dead serious about this agreement. It brings them a lot of prestige. They put their names on the line for this one."

"Sounds like they cut a deal."

"A deal?" Dante asked.

"Same deal we cut," Damian explained. "The FBI probably begged them to help end the war, in exchange for looking the other way on something else."

Dante whistled. "The Feds are wheeling and dealing, aren't they?"

"Those dirty cutthroat son of bitches would cut a deal to sell their mothers, if they thought that it would give them an advantage," Damian told him. "The problem has never been with them cutting deals; the problem has always been their reneging on their deals. Those motherfuckers are so crooked they would fuck a snake if you could hold it straight long enough."

"We got a good deal from the Old Ones, and El Jeffe's dead. And now, with Senator Sandra Fitzhugh dead, our acquisitions are on the way to antitrust approval, and we're about to make a political move that'll guarantee Bio One's ability to play internationally. We won."

Damian shook his head. "Too early to say that."

"We wrap up our business in California, we take Arizona, and we're fucking untouchable, Damian. We've fucking won!"

"I wish I could share your enthusiasm," Damian exhaled.

"Wedding bell blues got you down?" Dante asked with a smile.

Damian shrugged.

"Aw, hell," Dante waved him off. "Use it for the family, big bro. Use it for the family. It's just another fucking weapon in our arsenal, remember?"

Damian smiled and nodded. "I guess you're right. Hey, get a message to Princess. Let her know everything that has transpired."

Dante nodded. "Will do." He slapped his brother across his back as he headed for the exit. "Calm down, bro. We're in charge now. We're two shakes of a lamb's tail from kicking everybody's ass."

Damian shook his head and stared off into space. "I sure hope you're right, bro."

Chapter Thirty One

Stacia pulled up to her home and climbed out of her crimson red Dodge Viper. Her husband, Michael, exited their home and approached her.

"Where have you been?" Michael asked.

Stacia lifted the bags she held in her hands, into the air. "Shopping."

"This long?" Michael asked. "You left this morning."

"Yes, I went shopping, and I had lunch at Biga's," Stacia told him. "What's this? The Spanish Inquisition?"

Stacia brushed past her husband and stormed into the house. He followed just behind.

"Who bought those things?" Michael asked. "Did he buy those things for you? Did he?"

Stacia stopped, turned, and faced her husband. "Michael, what's this all about?"

"You were with him again, weren't you?"

"With who?" Stacia shouted.

"With your fucking dope-dealing boyfriend, that's who!" Michael shouted. "You know who the hell I'm talking about! Don't play stupid with me, Stacia! You were with him again; weren't you?"

Stacia exhaled, shifted her weight to one side, and dropped her bags. "No, Michael, I wasn't with him. And he's not my boyfriend. I've known Damian since we were babies; we grew up together. I can't change that fact. We attended the same schools, we attended the same church, and we went to the same camps. If you have to blame someone, blame my parents for that, okay?"

"Your parents didn't tell you to fuck him!" Michael shouted.

"I'm not fucking him!" Stacia retorted. "What the hell's the matter with you?"

"What's the matter with me?" Michael huffed. "What's the matter with me? How about what's the matter with you? I don't make enough money for you, Stacia; is that it? I'm not exciting enough for you? What is it, Stacia? Tell me. Tell me why my wife is screwing the man who that I'm trying to bust. Why's my wife fucking the man who tried to kill her father? The man who her father spent the last eight years of his life trying to bring down. Tell me that, Stacia."

Stacia shook her head. "You're crazy."

"Am I?"

"Yes!" Stacia shouted. She tried to walk past him and go to the bedroom. Michael grabbed her arm and pulled her back.

"No, Stacia, I'm not crazy," Michael shouted. "I'm the laughing stock of the entire god damned Bureau; that's what I am! My wife's screwing Damian Reigns! The most notorious fucking drug dealer in the god damned country!"

"So if I were having an affair with someone who was a nobody, it would be okay?" Stacia shouted. "Michael, listen to yourself! I'm not having an affair with Damian Reigns or with anyone else for that matter."

"Liar! You're a god damned lying whore!" Michael shouted. "At least have the decency to admit it!"

Stacia could smell alcohol reeking from Michael's breath. "Sweetie, I understand that you're under a lot of pressure right now. You've been suspended from your job, and my father's hospitalization has been difficult for you."

"Your father's hospitalization?" Michael threw his head back in laughter. "You can't even say it, can you? You refuse to even admit that he had something to do with what

281

happened to your father. Damian Reigns had a bomb placed inside your father's mailbox, and he blew your father up! Say it! Say it! Damian tried to kill your father!"

"Where are my children?" Stacia asked. "I'm going to take them away from here, until you sober up!"

"You're not taking my children anywhere!" Michael shouted. "They don't want to go with you while you're whoring!"

"Fuck you, Michael!"

"No, fuck you!" Michael shouted.

Stacia jerked her arm away from him, and started to storm off, but Michael grabbed her arm and pulled her back.

"Don't you walk away from me!" Michael shouted.

"Stacia jerked her arm away even more forcefully this time. Michael reacted by slapping her across her cheek. Stacia stumbled back and fell onto the couch.

"You bastard!" Stacia shouted. She placed her hand over her reddened cheek. "You hit me! I can't believe that you actually hit me!" Stacia leaped up from the couch. "You get out of my house, you son of a bitch!"

"This is my house, and I'm not going anywhere!"

"You get out of here, you bastard!"

Michael swung again, this time striking Stacia across her left cheek, sending her soaring onto the couch a second time.

"You bitch!" Stacia screamed. She rose and ran at her husband, where she began to scratch his face and claw at his eyes.

"Get away from me, you crazy bitch!" Michael shouted. He grabbed Stacia's hands, and head butted her on the bridge of her nose.

"You motherfucker!" Stacia screamed and bit Michael on his nose. He screamed like a wild banshee.

"Mob whore!" Michael shouted. He punched her in the stomach, sending her to the ground. Michael leaned forward, lifted her by her hair, and punched her in her face. Blood from Stacia's lip shot onto his pants leg.

"You love him!" Michael shouted. "Well go and tell him that I did this! Go and tell your big tough boyfriend that I did this! Tell that motherfucker that we'll handle this thing one-on-one!"

Michael punched Stacia in her eye, and then punched her again in her mouth. The sound of her jaw cracking could be heard throughout the house.

"It's not so funny now, is it?" Michael shouted as he continued to punch her. "You want the pleasure; now take the pain!"

"Michael!" Stacia screamed. She tried to crawl away from her husband, who began to kick her.

"Senor Rogers!" the housekeeper shouted, as she ran into the room. "No, senor! Stop it! Stop it!"

The housekeeper wrapped her arms around Michael, and pulled him back onto the love seat. Stacia willed herself to rise, and then ran out of the house and into her next door neighbor's yard. Her neighbor, Warren Rutledge, a fellow FBI agent, was outside watering his lawn.

"Jesus Christ, Stacia!" Warren cried out. He dropped his hose and grabbed Stacia, who collapsed into his arms. "What the hell happened to you?"

"Telephone!" Stacia shouted, breathing heavily. "I need to use your telephone!"

"Sure!" Warren told her. He placed her arm around his shoulder, wrapped his arm around her tiny waist, and helped her inside.

"That son of a bitch is going to pay for this, Warren!"

Warren held up his hands. "Stacia, I'm an FBI agent. I don't want to hear this. Let's just keep that kind of talk hush-hush for the moment."

Stacia nodded. "I need your phone and some ice."

Warren nodded. "The phone's in the kitchen, and so is the ice. Come on, I'll fix you an ice pack."

"Thank you, Warren," Stacia told him.

"Hello?"

"Damian?"

"Yeah. Who's this? Stacia?"

"Yes," Stacia broke down into tears. "He beat me, Damian. Michael beat me!"

"Oh my God," Damian exclaimed. "I can't believe this shit."

"He accused me of sleeping with you, and he beat me," Stacia told him through her heavy sobbing. "He was drunk, Damian. I can't believe this; he's never behaved like this before."

"And he had no reason to now," Damian told her. "It's a trap, Stacia, a setup. He did this, knowing that you'd tell me, and now I'm supposed to race over there and confront him. Then he'll have every right to shoot me, and claim self-defense."

"What should I do, Damian?" Stacia asked nervously.

"Where are you now?"

Stacia nodded. "I'm at a neighbor's house."

"Are the children safe?"

"I don't know," Stacia said nervously. "I don't believe they were home."

"He sent the children away," Damian told her. "I want you to call the police, and make a full report. Call the paramedics, and let them check you out. I'm going to send a car over, just a regular car, with one of my female employees. If the paramedics decide not to take you to the hospital, then she'll drive you. Go with her, and afterward, she'll take you to Dante's penthouse. I'll be there as soon as I can get away. Illyassa and her family are here now."

"I just want to go to Dante's right now," Stacia told him, while wiping away her tears. "I just want to get away from here."

"Are you sure that the children are safe?" Damian asked.

"I don't know. I'll send someone over to make sure they're okay."

"Are you done with him, Stacia?"

284

"Yes, Damian!" Stacia told him. "I'm no one's punching bag! After what he did to me, I just want to kill that son of a bitch!"

"That's what he wants you to do, Stacia. But we're smarter than that. We're going to play this one the right way. Are you with me?"

"Yes, Damian," Stacia sniffled. "I'm with you."

"Good," Damian told her. "My assistant's on her way. She's armed and very dangerous. So once she gets there, you won't have to worry about anything."

"Okay, Damian."

"Just stay inside and you'll be safe, Stacia."

"I will."

"I love you."

"I love you too."

Damian placed the phone into its cradle, and turned toward Dante. That was Stacia. Michael beat her; he accused her of sleeping with me. I want to kill that son of a bitch!"

Dante lifted his hands, calming his brother. "You played it right, Damian. It was a trap. You know it, and I know it. It was so fucking obvious, as to be almost comical. Let Mina handle it."

"I want that son of a bitch dead, after all of this is over with," Damian told him.

"It's always been my intention to kill him, ever since he shot you," Dante told him.

Damian nodded. "We'll have to plan it just right."

"And the kids?" Dante asked. "The man who they think is their father after all these years, is suddenly blown to pieces could have a devastating effect, you think?"

"We'll make it appear as if it was a tragic accident," Damian explained. "And then, we'll break the news to them that I'm their real father."

Dante exhaled. "Anyone ever tell you that you have way too much shit going on?"

Dante slapped Damian across his back. "Get some rest, bro. You have a wedding to attend tomorrow."

"Don't remind me."

"It's for the family, bro," Dante told him as he was exiting the room. "It's for the family."

Chapter Thirty Two

Geshom had arrived at the Las Vegas International Airport only this morning. He slept very little on the airplane, for as with all of his previous missions, he found that sleep didn't come easy. He had a target list, a list that he had memorized very carefully in case he had to dispose of it in an emergency, and he was already in position to intercept his first mark.

Geshom had been neutralizer for the Ministry of Secret State Security for the last eight years. He had become quite good at what he did for a living, and had even recently gained a promotion within the ministry to the rank of major. He had been chosen for this particular mission because he had operated in America twice before, and because he had never missed a target. He was one of the ministry's best assassins.

Geshom found the case containing the high-powered Russian sniper rifle exactly where his contacts said that it would be. He opened the case, removed the rifle, and began to assemble it. It was almost show time.

Princess tugged at her brother's black bow tie, straightening it. "Nervous?" she asked.

Damian shrugged his shoulders. "I guess it's hard not to be."

"Don't think of this as just a political marriage,

Damian. That woman in there would kill or die for you. She worships the ground that you walk on. And on top of that, she's breathtakingly beautiful, she's independently wealthy, she comes from a good family, and she has brains to boot. She's all that a man could ask for."

"Then why do I feel guilty?" Damian asked.

Princess exhaled, and shifted her weight to one side. She gently caressed her brother's cheek. "Damian, don't feel guilty about Stacia. Stacia's one of us; she's tough and she's a survivor. What you and Stacia have is something special, and it'll always be there. What you and Stacia have began the moment that the two of you came into this world. You two have a love that's truly ordained by God. Nothing, no ceremony, no priest, no vows, nothing, can change that. Everyone knows the love you have for Stacia, just keep loving her with all your heart."

"And Illyassa?"

"Love her with all that you can give," Princess told him. "She's a good woman."

Damian sneered. "A man trapped between two women."

"Three."

"What?"

"You forgot Grace," Princess told him with a smile. "Who do you think you're fooling? You were in love with that little FBI tramp."

Damian's silence told her enough.

"Hey, we can't chose who our hearts fall in love with. We can't. We can control our emotions, we can control our actions, but we can't control our hearts, Damian." Princess brushed the shoulders of his black Hugo Boss tuxedo. "There, all finished. You look like a million bucks."

"I'm worth billions," Damian told her with a smile.

Princess shrugged. She turned, peered into the full-length mirror just behind them, and adjusted her hat. "We can't all look that good, Damian; it's unnatural. I got the beauty; you got the brains; let's just roll with that."

Damian laughed, wrapped his arms around his sister, and lifted her into the air. "What would I have done without you?"

"You would have survived," Princess told him. "Now, put me down before we both get all wrinkled up. You have a wedding to attend."

Damian put his sister down, and straightened his jacket. Princess headed for the door.

"Show starts in less than five minutes," Princess told him.

"Princess, one question," Damian asked. "Would you really have killed me, if you had gotten the chance?"

Princess paused, peered at the ground for several seconds, and then shifted her gaze back to her brother. "Yes, Damian. I would have."

Damian nodded. "I figured as much. Love you, sis."

Princess blew her brother a kiss. "Love you too." She turned and walked away.

Asnakech was the ministry's best assassin. She had trained most of the current generation of black operatives, despite the fact that she was only twenty-seven. She had worked for the ministry since she was fourteen. Her first hit was against the leader of a child sex slave organization in the Sudan. She had fucked him, and then slit his throat in the middle of the night.

Today's target would be a comparative cakewalk compared to most of her previous assignments. Americans were such easy targets. Their slovenly girth made them easy to hit, and their upright, loud, and boisterous natures made them fun targets. She despised Americans, and all their confidence, their pride, and their wastefulness. She could feed an entire village for a week, just from two day's worth of table scraps and leftovers from the average American family. She despised Americans for their interventionist ways, and for their global racism. They were worse than the British, and almost as bad as the French. It would be her pleasure to take away these American lives today. Asnakech locked and loaded her Barrett fifty-caliber rifle, and waited for her first target to make an appearance. He was currently gorging himself on some starch-filled seven-course meal.

"Hey, hey, hey!" Dante clapped his hands as he strode into the room. "Let's get this show on the road!"

Damian exhaled, and stared at himself in the mirror.

"Hey, you aren't thinking about hitting a window, are you?" Dante asked.

Damian shook his head. "I can do this."

"Yes you can," Dante told him. "Hell, with all of the damn security the minister has here, I don't think you have a choice. He's probably got men guarding all of the escape routes."

Damian laughed.

"See, there you go," Dante slapped his brother across his back. "A little bit of laughter, a drink, and we're halfway there. You'll be on your honeymoon before you know it."

"Let's do this," Damian nodded.

Don Patrizio Giovanneta exited the tailor's shop, surrounded by his bodyguards. He was glad that he was once again able to hit the streets and engage in his favorite pastime; shopping.

Because of the war with the Reigns family, he was ordered to remain indoors, away from the long tentacles of those black demons and their flunkies. He was relieved that it was now over. Relieved that he could now go out into the city and dine, and shop, and hit the casinos again. He planned on shopping and eating until nightfall, and then hitting every major casino on the strip. Today was a day for celebration!

Geshom adjusted the sights on his rifle, and aimed carefully. He now had his target within the crosshairs of his sights. He adjusted his breathing, placed his finger on the trigger, and began a controlled squeeze.

The silenced rifle jerked at the release of the muffled shot, causing Geshom to have to readjust quickly, in order to get off a second shot. He did so quickly.

Don Giovanneta never knew what hit him. He heard a slight whistle in his ear, and then felt the blow of a sledgehammer against his head as the bullet struck him. His head exploded and brain tissue and bone fragments covered the men standing around him. The second bullet sent his heart through his back, and onto his bodyguard just behind him. Don Giovanneta was dead long before his body hit the ground. In fact, he was dead before he even began to collapse.

His bodyguards dropped to their knees and pulled out their weapons. One of them ran back inside to call for the paramedics.

On the rooftop of a building several blocks away, Geshom quickly broke down his rifle and began to pack it away. He had other targets to get to, and they had to be taken out before word spread of Don Giovanneta's demise. Geshom laughed as he slung his rifle case over his shoulder. At the rate things were going, he could be back home by tomorrow morning.

The wedding was being held at San Fernando Cathedral in the city's historic downtown. The cathedral was just a stone's throw away from the banks of the famed River Walk, which added to its beauty. The majestic stone structure rose some four hundred feet into the air, and was one of the oldest Catholic structures in the Western Hemisphere. It had survived countless wars, numerous tornadoes, and many other disasters, both man made and natural. It had stood the test of time, and endured to serve dozens of generations within its massive confines.

The main chapel had been decorated in white, despite the fact that it was a winter wedding. White floral arrangements had been flown in from South America, and white doves had been imported from England. The globe had been scoured for just the right materials, so that Illyassa could have her dream wedding.

Don Nicostrato Cinzia emerged from Justin's Restaurant, yawned, and stretched his arms. Eating always made him sleepy. He could already picture himself falling into his super-king-size bed, and wrapping himself inside of his thick down-filled comforter and satin sheets. The Don waved for his limousine driver to hurry up.

Asnakech pulled back the bolt on her rifle, chambering a massive fifty-caliber round. She lifted her rifle and carefully took aim at her target. Don Cinzia yawned again, and Asnakech caught him with his mouth open.

The fifty-caliber bullet flew into the Don's mouth, exiting at the back of his neck. The round exploded upon striking the Don's vertebrae, causing his entire neck to explode, and his head to tumble onto the ground. All of his men took one look at his head rolling along the frozen New York sidewalks, and fled back inside the restaurant. Asnakech's laughter could be heard for blocks.

The service was being performed by the archbishop himself. Damian's enormous donations, had ensured the archbishop's participation, even though the archbishop knew it was drug money. The archbishop had even chosen to dust off his finest garments, ones that he usually reserved for papal visits. He stood resplendent in his purple and gold miter, his fine purple and gold alb, his matching purple and gold chasuble, his gold cincture, and golden pallium. Archbishop Farina looked as though he were ready to stand before the Holy Father himself.

Don Umberto Constantino swung at the tennis ball. His age and arthritis prevented him from being any semblance of the tennis player that he was in his youth; however, he loved the sport too much to give it up. Don

Constantino waited for the automatic server to fire off a soft pitch to him, so that he could return it. He readied himself for the serve.

Geshom hid inside the hills outside of the Don's neighborhood. He could see most of the Don's property clearly, including the tennis court. He lifted his rifle, and placed the Don inside of his crosshairs.

The automatic server shot the ball toward the Don, who readied his backhand. The tennis ball and the bullet arrived at the same time. The Don swung at the tennis ball, which, along with the bullet, flew through his tennis racket and struck him in his chest. Shocked, the Don examined his tennis racket. A hole six inches in diameter had been burned through it. The Don followed the path of the hole through the racket, and into his stomach. His white tennis outfit was crimson red.

"My God!" the Don exclaimed.

Geshom's second bullet removed the Don's heart from his chest.

Damian took his place before the altar, with his brother standing by his side. Dante had always been more than just his brother; he had been his best friend, his backbone, the yin to his yang, and he now took his place of honor as Damian's best man.

The organist began the traditional wedding march, and soon Illyassa turned the corner and began her march down the aisle. Her white Christian Dior beaded wedding gown, and its ten-foot long flowing train, gave her the appearance of an angel floating just above the ground. She looked as though she were a goddess blessing those around her with a vision of her beauty.

Illyassa arrived at the altar, where her father handed her to Damian. Together, they turned and faced the archbishop.

"You look beautiful," Damian whispered.

She allowed herself a girlish giggle. "You're not

chopped liver yourself, Mr. Reigns."

"Dearly beloved, we are gathered here today to witness the union of these two, into holy matrimony," the archbishop began.

Cooking was something Don Gianpaulo Cipriano loved to do. It was his favorite pastime. He loved to cook everything, especially Italian food. Pasta was his favorite.

The Don's kitchen would make Chef Emeril green with envy. He had two sixty-inch Wolf dual fuel ranges, one with six burners, a double oven, a grill, and a griddle. The other had six burners, a double oven, and a French top. Two forty-eight-inch sub-zero refrigerators occupied one corner of the kitchen, while two microwave ovens, four dishwasher's, and a stainless steel sink occupied the other. The Don's kitchen was for serious chefs only.

Today the Don was preparing Hawaiian chicken and rice for his guest. He had just finished preparing a succulent, sweet and tangy sauce consisting of pineapple and coconut juices, mixed with papaya sauce and various tropical nuts. He had lobsters boiling, along with some caramelized chocolate for his after diner treat of chocolate covered-strawberries. He was pulling out all the stops today.

Asnakech steadied her breath as she tightened her grip on her rifle. She knew that she had him, and that she could take him. The idiot loved to cook in front of his window.

Don Cipriano stirred his pot of chocolate, as he carried it with him to his sink. He lifted a wooden spoon to his mouth for a taste. The fifty-caliber bullet shattered the wooden spoon, sending splintered wood as well as hot lead into the Don's mouth. Don Cipriano fell dead into his sink.

Damian sat in the center of his reception, accepting gifts from family and friends, wishing him a happy marriage. His father-in-law leaned over and whispered into his ear.

"I have another gift for you," Minister Malaika told

him.

"You don't have to give me anything. Your daughter's hand in marriage is all that my heart desires." Damian told him.

Minister Malaika smiled, patted Damian's hand, and then handed him a small box.

"Minister, this really isn't necessary," Damian insisted.

"Open it," the minister insisted.

Damian opened the small felt box to find several small white pills inside. He turned to the minister with a look of confusion.

"It's aspirin," the minister told him. "For your headaches. We're family now, and we take care of one another's problems."

Damian stared into space for several moments, confused at what the minister was saying. And then it hit him.

"Oh my God!" Damian exclaimed. He shifted his gaze back to the minister. "Tell me that you didn't!"

"It had to be done," the minister said proudly.

Damian rose. "Oh my God! What have you done? Do you know what you've done, you fool!"

Minister Malaika rose. "I avenged the death of my daughter, and I'm assuring the life of my other daughter!"

"We had a truce, you fool! Do you realize what you've done?" Damian exclaimed. "You've just started a war! A war with the entire Mafia! You've just thrust us into a war with La Costa Nostra!"

Don Pancrazio's head exploded like a watermelon that had been tossed out of a second-story window. Superglue would not have been able to glue all of the pieces back together again. The Don's men sought cover.

Asnakech broke down her fifty-caliber assault rifle, and readied it for the drop sight. Her contacts wanted their rifle back, so that it could be rethreaded, and utilized for future missions.

Asnakech yawned and stretched, as her thoughts turned toward home. She had a long flight ahead of her, and it had been a full day. She had taken out four targets in a matter of hours, all while avoiding police blockades and nosy onlookers. Her mission had been a complete success, and she could count on the minister personally rewarding her with another medal, and probably with a promotion.

Asnakech slung her rifle case over her shoulder and headed for the main street. She would take the subway to the airport, and then board a plane for home. Why, what for, and whom she had killed was not for her to ask. She thought little of her targets, and even less about the consequences of their deaths. Asnakech hailed a cab so that she could get out of the area quickly, and head for one of the main street subway boarding stations. She peered out of the dirty cab windows at the blaring sirens rushing past them to her latest victim's location. She yawned again, and leaned her head back against the comfortable headrest of the cab, hoping to catch a five-minute nap before arriving at the rifle drop-off point. Her eyes closed and she rested peacefully, unaware that her actions had just sparked the largest Mafia war the world has ever seen.

The war with the Old Ones had now begun.

THE END

IN STORES NOW

True to the Game
B-More Careful
The Adventures of Ghetto Sam
Dutch I
Triangle of Sins
Tell Me Your Name and
Dutch II
Deadly Reigns I
Double Dose

COMING
SOON

ANGEL

PREDATORS

DEADLY REIGNS III

DUTCH III

FOR GANGSTERS ONLY

TRUE TO THE GAME
PART 2

TERI WOODS
PRESENTS

ANGEL

TERI WOODS

COMING SOON

PROLOGUE

The Present - As the music drifted throughout the house, I silently sang along.

Don't want to make a scene, but I really don't care when people stare at us / sometimes I think I'm dreaming I pinch myself just to see if I'm awake and I...

That Jagged Edge CD be cranking like shit, I thought to myself as I sang the rest of the song. *Plus, those twins in the group are fine as hell, talk about doubling your pleasure.*

I put a little more seasoning on the steaks and flipped them over. Tony likes his steaks medium well and I make one of the best steaks in the metro area, if I must say. At least, that's what I've been told.

I always cook my baby something special when I have good news. And I have very good news for Tony. I can't wait to tell him and I know he's going to be anxious to hear what I have to say.

I tossed the fresh greens of salad and sat them in the fridge to marinate. A good salad always brings out a meal.

1

I cooked the broccoli a little too much, but the cheese sauce I made should set it off very nicely.

I bet none of those hood-rat chicks in Liberty Park cook for Tony the way I do. I bet his baby momma don't do half the shit I do for him. If she did, the nigga wouldn't be here with me.

It's been two years since Tony and I met at the HOBO Shop fashion show. I remember that day like it was yesterday.

CHAPTER ONE

The HOBO Shop Fashion Show was held at the Ramada Inn on Annapolis Road, off Route 450 in New Carrolton.

HOBO stands for Helping Our Brothers Out. I personally knew Jason, who owned the shop. He made some hitting fly shit the whole family could wear.

I was a regular customer, so when the tickets for the fashion show went on sale, I bought them out the store from my friend Shawnie.

The motel ballroom was packed with people, cameras, local celebrities, and the whole nine. I kicked it with a few of my friends; Sharmba, Keith, Jermaine and Madd Flow, an upcoming local rapper, before I took my seat in the back of the ballroom. *I can't believe Shawnie sold me these fucked up seats. Shit, I'm all the way in the back of this motherfucker.* I looked up and saw Paul staring at me. Paul was Jason's father. He waved at me to come to him. *I hope he got a better seat for me than this,* I prayed to myself.

"How you doing, Paul? Where's Jason so I can cuss him out for sitting me all the way in the back of this chumpie."

"Don't worry I got a seat for you. Jason done went to

3

California. He's getting ready to open the HOBO Shops in LA, Philly, and Atlanta.

Jason's father, Paul, was the one who ran things in his absence, and since Jason took his whole entourage with him to California, all the seats in the front reserved for the VIP, were empty. That's how I ended up in the VIP section.

I took a seat next to Paul, who introduced me to a man sitting next to him. His name was Tony Bills. If he hadn't been bling-bling-ing, I would have thought he was a bamma. At first glance, I didn't like Tony that much. He was fine; don't get me wrong, but something about him screamed out playa, liar and a cheat. I still checked him out though, and I liked what I saw. He was pretty flyyy with three Y's. Boyfriend was hurtin' them. He had on brand new Prada loafers, black linen shorts, a Prada contour tee-shirt, and a Prada hat flipped up in the front. His jewels consisted of a three carat diamond earring in his left ear, an iced out Frank Muller, and a diamond platinum chain. I couldn't see the pendant hid under his shirt. But, I knew it was iced out as well.

His Aviator sunglasses complemented the whole outfit. He flashed an award-winning smile at me with the whitest teeth I had ever seen in my life.

We exchanged numbers after the show; and I really went home anxious to see him again. So anxious that I literally sat by the phone waiting for him to call. But, he never did. Two days went by, so I decided to be bold and called him instead. I believe in going after what I want. I called his cell phone. He answered on the third ring.

"Hello, is this Tony?"

"Yeah, who's this?"

"This is Angel. Do you remember me?"

"How can I forget you? We met at the fashion show a few days ago. I was going to call you, it's just been hectic as hell. What's up?"

"Nothing much, I just wanted to call and say hello," I

lied, wishing he was on his way over to see me.

"Okay, well now that you've said hello, would you mind calling me back in ten minutes?"

Is he trying to get rid of me? Maybe he's busy. What if he's with another chick?

"I'm sorry; I forgot to ask you if you were busy. Sure, I'll call you back." I felt kinda dumb. *What if he don't want to talk to me. Maybe I shouldn't have called him.*

"I'm on the other line with my daughter's teacher at school. So, make sure you call me back and we'll talk, alright?"

Daughter's teacher, thank God.

I gave him fifteen minutes instead of ten. We talked all day on the phone. He told me everything about his self. That is why I like him so much. He never lied to me, not even once. He told me all about his baby momma, how they still fucking around, how he got her a house in Kettering, Maryland and how he takes care of his kids. And I guess because he kept it so real with me, I didn't mind. It wasn't no need in tripping because he was with his baby's momma. Shit, actually it was better, that way, when I got tired of his ass, I could send him right on home. From the beginning, I accepted the fact that I could only have a piece of Tony, but that piece would be the only piece I would need.

Tony was a known street hustler, but he didn't serve shit hand to hand on the street corner. He was a major supplier to all the other dudes in his hood and beyond. Tony had his eyes and ears in tune with the streets and the people roaming around in them, so much that he preferred to hang on the curb with everybody else.

I really started to dig Tony. He took me everywhere there was to go. From the movies to concerts, we hung out everyday, even if it was just going out to eat.

His physical appearance was awesome. He was 6'3 and weighed 235 pounds, all muscle. Tony had a Range Rover, a S600 Mercedes Benz, and a Continental Flying

Spur. He said he got his baby momma in a BMW X5 and his momma was pushing an E Class Benz.

He was always dressed in some fly expensive designer shit like Armani and Versace and the nigga had so much money his shit was the Federal Reserve, that's why I decided to give him the kittykat. From the first time I saw Tony at the fashion show, I knew we was going to get busy. I knew that he wanted to do me just as bad as I wanted to do him. I seen the nigga watching my ass all night long and I mean literally watching my ass, staring at my print, and licking his lips. He was sweatin' me and I loved every minute of watching him lose control.

Tony hung out on 14th Street in Liberty Park, which was a small section of Congress Heights. I would hang out with him on the curb sometime. All the dudes he fucked with gave me the utmost respect. They knew I was fucking with Tony, so they had no choice. However, every now and then I would catch them undressing me with their eyes when Tony wasn't around. Honestly, I couldn't blame them if I tried. I was fine as old wine, honey; if I say so myself.

Truth is I practically live in the gym trying to keep my figure in blast as my old boyfriend, Buck, use to say.

"Bitch, keep that ass in blast."

I can still hear him to this day. I'm 5'3 and weigh 135 pounds, all hips and ass. So it's a lot to keep in blast. My caramel complexion accents my hazel eyes. I keep my fingernails and toenails done up real proper, with some help from pedicures and manicures every Saturday from Ms. Kay's Nail Salon. My curly hair is cut short. It has often gotten me mistaken for some sort of exotic mixed breed. I have really nice skin, glowing and blemish free. For me, my ass and thighs are too big for my taste, that's why I stay in the gym eventhough niggas can't get enough. But my breasts are just right, a real trademark stamped with perfection.

When I started seeing Tony, I decided to cut off all my other male friends and other sexual partners; after fucking

Tony, who needed them. I would go around to Liberty Park and literally sit on a bench for hours and eye hustle as Tony conducted his business. At first, he didn't like me hanging around so much, but in time I guess I just grew on him.

It seems to me that Tony knew half of the people in DC. People would drive up and get out of their cars just to speak to Tony or shake his hand. I knew that he was ghetto-fabulously rich, but I didn't know that he was famous as well. Fourteenth Street in Liberty Park was like an office to Tony and everyday including Sunday, he ruled the streets like a powerful CEO.

I would always roll out by midnight. Eventhough I was fucking the nigga, I still had to get up early to go to work; I'm a secretary. Every night though before I would leave; I would sit on Tony's lap. I would straddle him fully clothed and kiss his juicy lips for what seemed like hours.

Everyday, I'd call Tony to see if he was hanging out on 14th Street and then I'd drive over there as soon as I got off work. It was bad enough I had to be at my job for eight hours of the day, not to mention his baby momma; I didn't need the potential piranhas lurking in the pond to get their teeth in my man. I had my hands full.

One night when I was sitting in the truck with Tony, listening to a CD he started kissing me and using his hands to hike up my skirt. Like magic, it was up to my waist and he had my thong to the side with the skill of a pick-pocketer. In one fluid motion he had his face between my legs, awakening the inner demons in me until they roared their approval. Child, it was broad daylight and I had only known the nigga for two weeks. It was way too soon for me to be giving him my goodies. Like R. Kelly said, "My mind is telling me no, but my body is telling me yeah." I tried to stop him, but he licked my clit and that was all she wrote in the middle of daylight, with a damn stranger. *Oh, shit, I know them niggas ain't lookin'.* My legs were wide open with my knees holding themselves up on the dash board. Honey, we didn't have to go no further. Tony was the man, his tongue was a dangerous weapon and he had me open, in broad day light in front of everybody. *What was I suppose to do?* Of course you would say wait till we was in the house, right? But, if Tony was licking and sucking on your pussy, you'd be just like me getting fucked in a truck. Tony's tongue danced around my womanhood like an explorer in search of the new world. He was the bomb. I tried not to let him know that, but my moans betrayed me. *What was I suppose to do with three inches of tongue hitting my spot?* Like an expert Tony stayed inside my kat, until I responded by orgasming all over his freshly trimmed mustache.

We hopped in the back seat like the Rover was a hotel room.

"I want some of him."

"Who, this big guy right here," Tony said pointing to his dick.

"You got some condoms?"

He played coy for a minute. Then he pulled out a pack of condoms and unzipped his pants. I watched as he pulled out his perfect brown dick that looked to be about nine inches with a curve in it.

As he slid on the condom, I became conscious of where we were and what was about to happen. I glanced at the windows of the truck and was relieved to see that the truck was equipped with factory dark tints, so that no one could see us in the back seat.

But the truck was shaking and the noise I made gave us away anyway.

Tony hit every tender spot inside my body as we put in work, both of us coming as Tony laid on top of me and shivered violently. From that day on we were inseparable. Tony continued to live at his house in Kettering with his baby momma and their daughter, but he also lives with me in an apartment on Martin Luther King Jr. Highway in Seat Pleasant.

Chapter Two

The rice is a little sticky, but Tony won't mind, other than that the meal is perfect.

I set two places at the table, then went and got Tony from in front of the TV. *All he does is play them damn video games like a big ass kid.*

"Baby, this steak is good as shit and this cheese sauce is the bomb. Boo, you did it. I'm gonna have to hit the gym for a whole week straight to work this off."

"You should have been up Run and Shoot trying to work out. You're getting love handles on your six pack. When you go to the gym I'm going with you. My butt's getting too big." I stood up and showed Tony my butt.

"Your butt looks fine to me, boo," he said as he got up, grabbed my butt and kissed me.

We talked some more during the rest of the meal as I carefully thought out my plan.

Tony's a good man and a helluva provider.

Our apartment in Glen Willow was laid out. Tony had me living ghetto fabulously with a sixty inch big screen plasma TV, high-tech stereo systems with surround sound, theater vision, and the finest Italian leather furniture that money could buy.

I always was fly and I always had money, but with Tony, I was spending his and he didn't mind. I took a trip to New York and shopped in Barney's and Saks on 5th Avenue and complemented my closet with all the latest fashions. From shoes to handbags, I had it going on. There wasn't a chick in the Metro area who could out do me. Tony even went so far as to cop me a SL55 AMG. So, I'm rolling with my top down screamed 'money ain't a thing', especially since the money was Tony's. For the past two years that I have been with him, nothing has changed since the first time we met.

After dinner, I ran a bath for the two of us. The bathroom was equipped with an oversized Jacuzzi. I lit some candles and played an old Isley Brothers CD in the background. Of course, our naked bodies in the tub couldn't resist one another. He lathered me with soap and I returned the favor, rubbing his rock hard body with soap made me want him so bad. I gently lathered his balls and took my time washing his dick as it poked straight up at me. Forget the bath. We rinsed each other off in the shower, before Tony gently forced me on my knees. I dropped down and put half of him in my mouth. I let his head tickle the back of my throat as I tried to engulf his whole dick. Tony couldn't help but to grab the back of my head as he started to make love to my face. I loved the way he forced his self on me, holding and guiding my head to do as he pleased.

Giving Tony head actually turned me on and I felt myself climax as Tony grabbed my curly locks and drove his dick deep into my throat. I couldn't help but to gag as Tony let go in my mouth. His juices went straight down my throat and I swallowed it all, loving every drop. What can I say, real bitches do real things.

And just when I thought it was over, it was actually just getting ready to begin. Tony must have snuck one of those Viagras in on me, because his dick never got soft. He went down on me causing me to cum, from his slightest touch.

Then he did the unexpected. He turned me around so

that I was facing the wall, rubbed some soap into the crack of my ass and stuck his finger in my back-door. Before I could turn around or protest, he replaced his finger with his dick. I rose up on my tip-toes to ease the pain and I tried to close my eyes as I bit down on my lip, but I couldn't relax. I knew this is what he wanted and I knew that I had to give it to him. I wanted to scream out in pain, but I didn't. I let him have his way, pushing in and out of me. It felt like I was being ripped in two, but once he got it in real good, I relaxed and to my surprise, the pain turned to pleasure and as he began to thrust in and out of me, I actually felt myself about to cum. My legs got weak and I came harder than I ever had in my life. Seconds later, Tony came too, inside me, as we both collapsed.

"I love you," he whispered.

"I love you too."

We made our way into the bedroom and both of us collapsed on the bed. Now, it was time for my plan to be put into action. I could tell Tony was still up for a little more bumping and grinding so I started to kiss his neck a little.

"Daddy, I want to try something I seen in one of those nasty videos."

"You ain't stickin' me with nothin' or putting nothin' crazy on my body."

I laughed and tried to lighten the mood.

"No silly, you can do all the stickin'. I want to tie you up and then I want you to tie me up. In the video, the guy was all tied up and the girl was sucking his dick like crazy and all he could do was lay there and enjoy it. And after I do you, then you can tie me up and do things to me. I even want you to fuck me in my ass, again."

His brain started working in overtime and I could see the curiosity building in Tony's eyes mixed with the thought of much pleasure. I went to the closet and got the cord that I had placed there earlier. Tony looked a little nervous at the cord.

"What? Relax, I got you," I said smiling from ear to ear

11

as I stretched the cord out in my hands.

I tied both of Tony's feet together and then his wrists.

"Girl, this better be good or I swear I'm going to kick your ass later. Don't be pinching my nipples, be gentle with the nuts, and don't go anywhere near my ass. I'm not playing."

Promises, promises, I thought to myself and licked all over his neck as I licked him from head to toe, I even sucked on his toes. I turned Tony to the side and laid down to give him a little head.

"Damn, baby, you got the best head this side of the Mason Dixon Line."

"I know, that's what you tell me," I responded with my mouth full of him.

I stopped and got behind him and licked his back. I stood up and jerked his dick as I reached under the bed with my other hand. I felt the handle of a .40 caliber I had placed there earlier. I pulled the gun from under the bed, turned Tony onto his stomach, and whispered sweet nothings in his ear. Then, I put the barrel of the gun near his head and quickly pulled the trigger.

The music inside the apartment was on as it always was. All the neighbors heard was a loud pop. Tony's body jerked once as blood splattered on my face. His body went still as the Federal Hydrashock bullet penetrated the back of his skull, turning his brain into a bloody pulp.

I knew Tony was dead, but I checked his pulse anyway. I quickly went to the bathroom to wash off. I looked into the mirror and the face that stared back at me was the same face that stared at me in Charlotte, North Carolina so long ago.

Pull yourself together. Stop acting like this is the first time you've killed someone. A little bit of blood won't hurt you.

I went back in the bedroom and retrieved the gun. I carefully wiped it off, leaving no fingerprints on it and put it in the trash can. I slipped on my slippers and took the trash outside to the dumpster. Then, I took a flat head screwdriver out of my robe pocket and jimmied the locking mechanism on the balcony door. That would help support my story of a break-in. *Relax, you've got everything covered.* I kept telling myself.

I put on latex gloves and opened Tony's safe. My pussy felt fire at the sight of all his money. *Damn, this nigga had mad loot in this motherfucker.* It was way more than I expected. It was so much money, I felt like playing with myself right there as I fondled the cash. I stuffed all the money into two Louis Vuitton carrying bags. I put two kilos of coke in there too that were in the safe.

I took the bags outside to my truck which was parked conveniently by the dumpster. *No one will see me, no one will remember, it's too late.*

I cut the latex gloves up into tiny pieces and flushed them down the toilet. The trash people came promptly at 3:30 a.m. and they would unknowingly dispose of the gun. I checked the balcony door. My work looked good, real good. I left the door ajar and then went back in the bedroom to check on Tony. His naked body was laying silently still on the bed with the bullet hole in the back of his head. I had carefully planned this night for the past thirteen months and so far, everything was going as planned

Looking at Tony made me think of Andre. He was the first man I ever killed that I had ever truly loved. *Stop crying. What's wrong with you, finish what you started.* I had to stay focused. It was time to call the police and play the grieving girlfriend. The acting class I took in high school had certainly come in handy in my older years.

I picked up the phone and dialed 911.

"Someone just killed my boyfriend," I screamed hysterically.

The police arrived in minutes and were all over the place. Both the plain clothes detectives and the uniformed cops were all over the apartment like roaches. A detective had me in the living room asking me all kinds of questions. How many dudes did I see? What did they look like? Height and weight? What were they wearing? Then what happened? Did you hear the gunshot from the bathroom?

For the twentieth time I told the same story. I had it memorized. In between sobs and plenty of tears I told my story over and over.

"Tony and I ate dinner in the living room. After dinner we got into the tub. We made love in the tub for about an hour. Then we dried off and rubbed lotion on each other. We got in bed and called it a night. I was awakened by two hands snatching me out of bed. Two gloved hands picked me up as if I weighed nothing. One of those hands quickly covered my mouth. The lights were dim but I could see two other dudes standing over Tony. They carried me into the bathroom and told me not to scream or they would kill me. They said I would be safe as long as I stayed calm and followed their instructions. The big dude held me for what seemed like an eternity. Then I heard a single loud pop. The dude holding me said that he would keep his promise and wouldn't hurt me. He told me to stay in the bathroom, count to one thousand, and then come out. He said if I came out of the bathroom before I finished counting, he would kill me. I was so scared, I just did what he told me to do. When I walked out of the bathroom the dudes were gone; that's when I saw Tony. He was lying there on the bed tied up. I saw the hole in his head. I felt for a pulse; there was none. I saw that the safe was open and that's when I called 911."

I watched the coroners carry Tony's body out in a black bag and that's when I really performed. I cried and screamed and even convinced myself that intruders had really been there. The detectives had to hold me down and even offered me tissue and a glass of water.

"Calm down, ma'am. It's going to be okay. We're here now."

They let me get dressed and pack my things that I had in his apartment, then the area was officially sealed off as a crime scene.

I drove straight to Fatima's house, my best friend who

lived in Silver Springs. Fatima woke up and let me in. I showed her the bags and their contents.

"What have you done?" she asked a little nervous.

"Sit down and let me tell you."